ONLY THE WICKED

THE SINFUL STATE SERIES

ISABEL JOLIE

ISABEL JOLIE

*To Emma—spread your wings and fly, my baby girl. May you
have delightful and wicked adventures, but not too wicked.
There's time yet for that.*

Pride is more than the first of the seven deadly sins;
it is itself the essence of all sin.
– John Stott

There is a method in man's wickedness; it grows up
by degrees.
–Francis Beaumont

PROLOGUE

The message jolted me at 3:47 a.m., cutting through the silence of my San Francisco penthouse like a serrated blade. I'd been awake anyway, staring at financial projections that made less sense with each passing hour, more determined than ever that we needed a new CFO.

This is Brandy Sussman from Congressman Mitchell's office. The Congressman would like to schedule a meeting with you regarding ARGUS and an upcoming Senate Intelligence Committee hearing on surveillance technologies. ARGUS has been identified as a priority review target. Please respond with your availability.

My blood chilled. Miles, my partner, told me he'd shut this down. *Priority review target.* In Washington-speak, they're coming for us.

I set the phone down with hands that weren't quite steady and walked to the floor-to-ceiling windows overlooking the bay. In the reflection, I caught sight of myself: rumpled hair, two days of stubble, dark circles under eyes that had seen too much in forty-one years. I looked like what I was—a man whose creation was about to be dissected by politicians who didn't understand the first thing about technology or privacy.

This was exactly what I'd feared when I built ARGUS. The moment when government decided that private innovation was too dangerous to remain private.

My phone buzzed again with a text—this time from Alex, my CFO. Given the time, I could only assume that he, like this early bird congressional assistant, was on the East Coast. Another in his latest series of increasingly urgent messages about taking the company public.

> Rhodes, Jonathan from Capital Partners met with Lehman yesterday. They're talking about forcing an IPO whether you agree or not. We need that capital for infrastructure, and they want their return. Call me.

I deleted Alex's message without responding. Going public now, with Congress circling like vultures, would be corporate suicide. But staying private meant fighting both political pressure and investor revolt simultaneously.

Dictating a message to Miles, my co-founder, it was all I could do not to call him and wake his ass.

> You told me the congressional investigation was handled. It's not. Combined with the investor pressure...this isn't good, Miles.

I checked it and hit send.

Seconds later, the phone rang, the subtle electronic pulse ring tone amplified in the early morning silence.

"Why are you awake?" He sounded half-asleep.

"It's happening—"

"No, it's not. I told you, it's handled, and it is."

I rubbed my palm over my face, over my burning eyes. I could have fought Miles, but he'd only tell me the congressman should be ignored and reiterate it was handled.

"We need to discuss the CFO situation. It's time we bring in someone with more experience."

"Wait. What? I'm getting whiplash here."

"It's called running a business." Miles frustrated the hell out of me. The laid-back, friendly bullshit worked for investors and clients, and back in college it was mildly fun, but I needed him to keep up. "You told me the hearing is handled, I'm moving on. Let's talk about Alex."

"At three in the morning? Jesus. You need to get some sleep."

"Alex needs to be controlled. He's not aligned with us.

He's pushing the investors to push us. Going behind our backs."

"Wait a minute. Rhodes. Come on. The paranoia is beating you, man. He's not going behind our backs. This is Alex. Our friend. Get some sleep."

"I'm not paranoid. We brought Alex on back in the garage days. He doesn't have the skill set. He's relying on old plays that he learned in B-school. We need someone with a different approach. Someone who gets our game plan."

"He just had his third kid and you want to shitcan him?"

"You want to keep him on? Fine. But we need to bring someone on with more experience. Someone who can monitor his dealings with our investors and package clever financing deals."

"Can we just…" I could hear his frustration, but it was nothing compared to the alarm coursing through my veins. "Will you take a break? Christ, when was the last time you slept through the night? Lack of sleep breeds paranoia."

"For the last time, I'm not paranoid."

"Remember when you were convinced that tech journalist was investigating us? Turned out she was writing about facial recognition in retail stores. You're seeing threats everywhere."

He had a point about the journalist. Maybe I was seeing shadows where there were none. "Maybe you're right."

"I know I'm right. You need to get away. Clear your head. Sleep. Remember what it's like to think about something other than risks and assessments. Maybe take Sara."

"Seriously?" He'd stayed close to my ex, but I hadn't.

"Forget I mentioned her, even though she probably could get away right now and she'd be good for you. She knows you. It's been ages. You're still friends, right?"

"Miles." If I pinched the bridge of my nose any harder, it would have bruised.

"Fine. But take a break. I refuse to make any major personnel decisions when you're running on fumes."

When was the last time I slept for more than a few hours? I was way overdue for a break.

"I am overdue for a visit back home." Nana couldn't easily travel anymore.

"Perfect. Book it today. And Rhodes? Don't bring your laptop. Don't check emails. Don't even think about D.C. —which I promise is taken care of. Just...exist for a few days."

His concern was genuine, and despite my frustration, I found myself considering a break. Maybe some distance would give me perspective on both the congressional threat and the CFO situation.

"And Sara..." Miles could push me on many scores, but my ex wasn't one of them.

"I prefer solo. I need space."

"Good. You'll come back with a clearer head. Trust me on this. Whatever's happening in Washington can wait a week. The world won't end if you're offline for a few days."

Miles was right about one thing—I did need space to think. But as I tapped out travel instructions for my assistant, I couldn't shake the feeling that this congressional hearing was just the beginning. Someone wanted to control ARGUS, whether through political pressure, investor revolt, or outright acquisition.

In the mountains, away from Silicon Valley's pressure and Washington's threats, maybe I'd find the clarity I needed. Maybe I'd figure out how to keep ARGUS independent while navigating the political minefield that was about to explode around us.

From consumer groups to privacy advocates to investors, risks to ARGUS—my creation—darkened the horizon, but I refused to surrender. Not to Congress, not to profit-hungry investors, not to anyone who wanted to turn my technology into a weapon.

First, I needed to get away, escape to a place where the only oversight would be my own conscience and the only pressure would be deciding which trail to take. Maybe then, I could sleep. Recharge.

Miles was convinced I was being paranoid, seeing threats that weren't there. I hoped he was right. But my gut told me that in Washington, in Silicon Valley, paranoia was just another word for preparation.

CHAPTER
ONE

ONE MONTH LATER

RHODES

It's Tuesday morning and there's not a soul around. Clouds in the distance, winds from the southwest, a slight chill in the shade, and enough heat to break a sweat in the open sun. I lean on the railing, taking in the famed three-hundred-and-sixty-degree Blue Ridge views. A need for solitude brought me to these mountains from my youth, bum elbow and all. Miles was right—I needed distance from more than just the boardroom pressures. It took weeks to get away, but I'm finally here.

I close my eyes and inhale, breathing in the fresh, crisp air. High-pitched chirps punctuate the quiet. A vision of my office and the white board with red and black scrawls infiltrates my inner sanctum, and I open my eyes, choosing the real-life view before me. The canopy of leaves provides shade from the sun and a sense of wilderness, the feeling that undeveloped lands exist and flourish. It's a perfect, languid summer day. Back in San Francisco, summer lost meaning. But here, I feel the season in my bones, or at least, I remember what it used to mean, before...

Miles was right to shove me out the door and insist I take time to recharge. Besides, if one of us didn't step away—give some space to our disagreements—we might have resorted to blows.

A falcon flies overhead, flapping its wings until it hits an air stream and coasts high above. Fast, fierce, and powerful, falcons are a symbol for Horus—an Egyptian god who represented the sun, the sky, healing, and protection.

If I had my phone, I'd refresh my memory of the falcon-headed god. Protection and healing—exactly what I came here seeking. But my phone connects me to the world and with that connection I am inundated with messages and emails. No phone is good. This is what I need. An electronic detox. Space to decompress.

I close my eyes once again, resting my thighs against the banister. The breeze cools my skin. Behind me, the unmistakable sound of footsteps on wood breaches the quiet. My muscles tense.

The Yellow Mountain fire tower is on almost every North Carolina hiking map. A beautiful summer day like this, others were bound to come. And you don't hike the trail without taking the time to take in the view.

With one last glance across the Smokies, I turn to

cede the tower to the recent arrival. A dark-haired woman, hair pulled into a ponytail that swings slightly with her movements, climbs the ladder, her back to me.

"Ow. Fuck." Her progress stops, and as if sensing she's not alone, the woman turns her head, giving me a view of cheeks flushed with exertion. She's not sweating, but it's not that hot—yet.

Did she take the steep shortcut like me?

Two paths to the top. One easy six-mile trek, or a steep mile-and-a-half climb.

The way she's frozen in place, stuck in a trance, reminds me of a deer in the forest, evaluating the need for flight.

"Hi there," I say, stepping back from the hold, giving her more space, letting her know I'm not some sicko.

Which, come to think of it, is she alone? I only heard one person approach.

"Hi."

She resumes her task of climbing the ladder. It's a wooden ladder, the kind a person might attach to a tree house, only this one ascends into the tower through a cut-out on the deck platform.

I watch closely as a lithe, fit body rises. With each push from her right leg, she mutters to herself, lower this time, presumably to prevent me from hearing her cuss. Her legs are lean, the muscles flexing beneath smooth, lightly tanned skin. Either she spends her days outdoors or she's naturally tan. She could be a park ranger.

But no. A park ranger wouldn't wear those sporty short shorts. Lots of the girls in my high school wore shorts just like those, loose at the leg openings, designed for running, and while parents frowned, I did not. That was a long time ago. Maybe the styles have changed. Or maybe I stopped noticing.

She reaches for the banister, her feet on the second rung, and my southern upbringing kicks in, prompting me to step forward and offer my hand.

"Thank you." Her voice is light, the words automatic.

More weight than I expected presses down, but I easily take it, offering balance as she climbs out of the hold. A bloody spot on her right knee catches my attention. A thin stream of dried blood forms a line from her knee to the base of a thick hiking sock.

"You okay?" I ask, although, it's not like I have a first aid kit. I don't even have my phone.

"Oh. I'm fine." Her right knee bends, and only the right toe of her hiking boot touches the deck.

Her gaze travels over the perimeter, captivated by the view.

For her to turn her back on me, I must come across as trustworthy.

As she studies the horizon, I examine the woman's profile. Smooth skin, tiny silver studs for earrings, no visible tattoos above the neckline. Her chocolate brown hair shimmers with healthy shine. She's younger, but I'd guess she's late twenties, maybe.

It's a Tuesday and she's not working. Unless... Internal alarms ring and I take a second look over her frame, hunting for what? A camera?

You're full of it, Rhodes. No one here knows who the fuck you are. And that right there is why you're here.

Still, the paranoia Miles accuses me of having makes

me scan the tree line once more. No one. Just mountains and sky.

The woman steps forward to the railing, still entranced.

I'm halfway down the ladder when a board creaks from her one-legged hop. She's injured and alone.

Rhodes—

I stop my grandmother's lecture before the replay.

Fine, Nana. How exactly am I going to help her? Walk with her down the six-mile return trail?

What else are you going to do? You have the time. Unplugged. Remember?

What am I supposed to say? She said she's okay. If I insist on staying to help her, I'll come off as a misogynist ass.

You're really going to leave an injured woman to manage a six-mile trail to the parking lot on her own?

She's the one who went hiking by herself.

So did you.

The woman twists around, one hand on the railing, her right leg bent. At this angle from the floorboards, I'm offered a clear view up the back curve of her thigh. The hem of her shorts juts out from her ass, shading the path higher, revealing a mere glimpse of white cotton panties.

"Are you okay?"

Of course she'd wonder given I'm hanging on a ladder and gawking like a teenage perv.

"Yes. Ah, I'm just wondering… Did you park in the lot? Cloud Catcher Lane?"

"Yes."

Of course she did. Where else would she park?

"Ah." I bend my head, a gesture that sometimes

disarms. "How are you planning on getting back with an injured leg?"

She looks down at her bloody knee and shrugs. "I'll be fine. I'll find a stick in the woods."

"And you're going six miles," I say, more to myself, wondering about the stats for the likelihood of being attacked if injured. Without my phone, I can't check them, but logically a woman would be at greater risk.

"Six miles?" Now it's her tilting her head, only she's doing it to imply I'm wrong. "It's a mile and a half, tops."

"You're taking the shortcut with an injured leg?"

"I'm not walking six miles on it."

She'll break her neck if she attempts the steep decline without help.

She smiles, amused by my question, not offended, I think. Her brown eyes are warm, a deep hue with golden flecks, her pupils small from the abundant sun. She comes across as a good person, like maybe a school-teacher or a nurse. A nursing schedule could explain her freedom on a Tuesday.

"I'll be fine," she insists, brushing me off and returning her attention to the view.

Rather than disagree, I give a quick nod, descend the ladder, and wait on the ground below the tower. It's not a big deal. I'm unplugged and have all the time in the world. When she's had her fill of the view, I'll help her down the decline. We'll be slower, but I'm not in a hurry. If anything, slow is good. Once I'm back, I'll check my phone.

Although, I really shouldn't. If the boss can't take a break, then he chooses employees poorly. And I hire the best—I've built a system that runs perfectly, even without me. Or at least, I'm about to discover if that's true.

This break is overdue. Fuck the naysayers. The board. The investors. The constant inquisition surrounding projections and growth and purpose.

About five minutes later, she descends the ladder.

"Are you waiting for me?" She sounds incredulous—not scared. I suppose that's a good thing.

"Figured you could use some help."

"I told you I'm fine. I'm an expert hiker." She pats her backpack strap like it's got all the world's answers.

I give her an agreeable nod. "And I'm sure you are. But all the same, we're headed back to the same place. I'm better than a stick."

She sizes me up, a hint of a smile playing on her lips.

I hold my hands up in the air, the defensive gesture to convey I'm not a threat. "You can trust me. Eagle Scout here."

"You've got to do the right thing." Her smile spreads wide, revealing a set of straight white teeth and natural, sun-kissed lips, and I'm reminded of how much I like the small-town girl vibe. It's not the clothes or even the smile; it's the warmth and unguarded friendliness that's rare in a big city like San Francisco.

"I can do it alone, you know?" Her question is a singsong tease, laced with independence.

"Oh, I know."

She smiles in response, and I return the stubborn woman's smile.

She'd go down that mountain without me if I didn't insist on helping—an unwise move, but she's fearless. Is a sense of immortality a small-town or big-city characteristic? Perhaps it's not so much a sense of invincibility, but overconfidence. Could be both, I suppose.

Doesn't matter. I'll get her down safely. And I can rest easy, knowing for once, Nana would be proud. Maybe doing the right thing isn't always about business decisions and board meetings.

RHODES

Given she's hobbling, I offer my arm. She presses down on my forearm, using me like a crutch.

And she thought she could get down without help?

"You from around here?" I ask as we approach the trailhead.

As down-to-earth as she appears, I haven't picked up on a southern accent, and given I'm a North Carolina native, I'm good at picking up any range of southern dialect.

"I'm from Chicago. Originally."

"What're you doing here? Visiting?" That could explain why she's on her own. She's not familiar with these trails. Or she's assuming it's safer here than Chicago.

"In between jobs."

It's conceivable I'm projecting, but I swear her chin

tilts higher, defiant, almost daring me to say something negative.

Or projection colors my perception. If I found myself unemployed, booted from the company I founded, I'd be defensive.

"Where all do you plan to travel?" I ask, skirting the unemployment topic.

"Taking it day by day. What about you?"

"I'll be here through the end of the week."

"Are you from here?"

"Charlotte."

"Oh, so is this a day trip for you?"

"No. Charlotte's not that close, and while I was born in Charlotte, I live in San Francisco. I spent a few days with my grandmother and now I'm just..." I let the words trail as I've said too much to this stranger.

"That's sweet."

Yes, I've said too much. She's looking at me with interest. It's the grandmother reference. "I don't make it back here that often."

"How do you like San Francisco?"

Not my favorite. "It's fine."

"That's not a resounding endorsement."

I bite back a chuckle at her observation. She's right. San Francisco shall not receive a Rhodes MacMillan endorsement.

We reach a particularly steep spot, which is more of a four-foot drop. On the way up, I climbed this piece one-handed, preserving my injured elbow. Red dust puffs beneath my running shoes when I hop down. I hold out both arms.

"Jump. I'll catch you."

"I'll knock you down. I'm too big. Move."

Her face screws up like me catching her is the worst idea in the world, and I bark out a laugh. No...I'm actually laughing. I almost forgot what it feels like to laugh.

"You're not big. What else are you going to do?"

I'm now closer to eye level with her bent leg and inspect the injury. Compared to her other knee, there's no noticeable swelling, but the boots and thick socks hide her ankle. The bloody knee does nothing to diminish the appeal of her spectacular legs. A runner's legs that would probably look phenomenal in heels and a short skirt. Hell, they're eye-catching now in Umbro shorts and hiking boots.

"I don't want to hurt you."

She's being ridiculous. I'm at least a foot taller than her, and I lift three times a week and have maintained my workout regime for decades.

"Jump," I insist.

She bends closer to me with outstretched arms. The dirt below her boots crumbles and tiny rocks cascade down the trail.

"Come on, I've got you," I encourage.

She leaps forward, and I catch her, flat against my torso. Her arms are over my shoulders, and her brown eyes are inches from mine, the brown a lighter shade, the flecks of color closer to topaz than gold this close up. My gaze falls to her lips, full and pale pink, glossy as if she just licked them.

My dick hardens, and my hands grip her sides, putting distance between us. I just met this woman. She doesn't need to feel that. I shift, looking down, willing my body to calm down while double-checking my khaki shorts conceal that unexpected response.

"You okay?" she asks from behind me.

"Can't believe you thought you'd take this path on your own." Feeling like I'm in the clear, I turn slightly, offering her my arm, and take the lead, stepping slightly in front just in case she slides.

"While I appreciate your help, with the right stick, I could've made it down."

I bite back a derogatory response. "Do you go hiking by yourself often?"

"Yes."

"Is that wise?"

"Probably smarter than going rock climbing by myself."

"Do you climb?"

"When I can. I was planning on hitting Linville Gorge tomorrow, but I don't think I'll be doing that now with this leg. I'll see how it is tomorrow."

"What's injured? The knee or the ankle?"

"Both." Her lips twist.

"You slipped?"

"Slammed down hard on my knee. Ankles a little sore, but it's probably fine."

"Rock climbing's inadvisable." I'm stating the obvious, but she might benefit. "I planned to climb today. My elbow." I lift my right elbow for emphasis. "Giving it a rest."

"What's wrong? Tennis elbow?"

"Something like that. Tendonitis. Extends into the forearm."

"Do you play tennis? Golf?"

"Not enough to get injured. I climb." I have a rock wall in my penthouse. Memberships at multiple climbing gyms. But the reason I climb is for the chance to push myself outdoors, in the elements. I love the challenge.

"I love to climb, too." My gaze falls to her hands.

Short, unpainted nails. I reach for the hand that's not clutching my arm and run a finger along the underside, confirming callouses.

"Didn't believe me?" She grins. "That's a reason I climb."

"What is?"

"The look on men's faces when I outclimb them."

There are plenty of women who climb, but I understand what she means. I get why she'd be proud of excelling in an area dominated by men.

"So you're a badass," I say with all due respect. "Too bad we can't go climbing together on this trip."

"We can find other things to do."

Is that innuendo? *No. It's just the way you want to read it, Rhodes.*

And why not? She's attractive. For once, she's not someone I work with. And we're far from San Francisco and Silicon Valley. She has no idea who I am. She's not a journalist or a photographer.

"What's your name?"

"Sydney." Her left leg slides on loose gravel and I grip her arm, bending my legs to help her until she regains her balance. "What's your name?"

"Rhodes."

She didn't give her last name, so I won't give mine. Excellent. She can't Google me.

"Nice to meet you, Rhodes. I do appreciate your help."

I grunt, instead of stating the obvious that she needed my help. "Where are you staying?"

"Old Edwards Inn."

"You don't say. Me too."

She shrugs her shoulders. "It's got the best ratings in the area. It's cute, right? I love it. Wish I was staying longer than a week."

It's my favorite place in the Highlands. I love the history and the connection to a small, enduring mountain town. But it's not cheap.

What does this woman do that she can afford to stay there while between jobs?

Does it matter? All that really says is she's done well, or maybe she's got a trust fund. *If you ask, you risk falling into a line of questions you don't want to answer.*

"And you said you return home at the end of the week?"

"I didn't say that." Her coy smile confuses me, something she must pick up on, because she adds, "You said you're going back at the end of the week."

"Oh. Then what are your plans?"

"I haven't decided. I'm taking it day by day, remember?"

That's right. What must it be like to have an empty calendar? No investors tracking your every move. Or board members questioning every decision.

A comfortable silence falls between us, until she breaks it, saying, "I said I'm from Chicago, meaning I was born there. My old job was in D.C. I haven't decided where I'll live. Checking this place out. Considering here. Is that crazy?"

"No. I love this state. It's a great place to live." As the keynote speaker to the Stanford class of 2023, I spoke of the importance of loving where you live. I'd been thinking of my home state, of growing up here, of simpler times. "Are you ready to settle down? Is that why you're considering a small town?"

She laughs. The sound is light and carefree and rings across the wind like a chime.

"Is that a no?"

"To settling down?"

I lift a shoulder, gesturing affirmatively. It's not a crazy question. Or maybe it doesn't feel crazy to me because at forty-one there are those in my life who lob the question at me all the time and have for years.

"There might be a job opportunity here. But it'll involve a lot of travel, so no, not settling down."

Her gaze drifts through the trees, and I sense a change in topic is advisable.

What does one talk about other than work? Politics? Absolutely not. The economy? The value of the dollar?

"What was growing up in Charlotte like?"

Her question has me smiling. She saved me.

"No complaints. It's a good place to grow up. Was." My eyebrows lift as the weight of how much time has passed sinks in. "Twenty years ago."

I'm not sure where to go with that, so I step quietly, wading through a sense of nostalgia.

"Did you learn to climb out here? In the North Carolina mountains?"

Once again, she saves me with her conversational direction.

"Not really. More out West. But I'll come back one day. Hit places like Linville Gorge." I pause, wondering if I should throw it out there. The angle women love. And, what the hell. It's a means to an end and a benign tactic. "One day we'll come back together. When we're all healed, we'll see who's the better climber." She flushes. Referencing a joint future is always an easy win. "What skill level are you?"

"Expert."

A lift of the eyebrow, a jut of the chin. Proud of her abilities. I chuckle. Yeah, she's a lot like me.

We share climbing stories the rest of the way down. It takes us about twice as long with her bum leg, but it's all good. To Sydney without a last name, I'm a random guy who helped her down a mountain.

We reach our cars; two of four cars parked in the gravel lot. We didn't cross any other hikers, which means they chose the long way.

Her car's parked further away than mine, but there's a gravitational pull I can't control pulling me to my rental.

I'm a fucking idiot. I should help her to her car, then grab the phone. It's a fucking addiction.

I sling the door open and snatch the phone from the charger.

Fifty-five missed messages.

"Everything okay?"

I click the screen and skim the notifications. Nothing requiring immediate action, but the pattern of messages from investors, board members, and our CFO gnaws at me. The message from Daisy is the only one I care to see.

. . .

DAISY JONAS

Got what u need

Excellent. I toss the phone onto the seat and head to Sydney, arm out for her. My car door's open, but that's fine. No one is going to hop out of the bushes and nab my phone.

When we arrive at her vehicle, a small-sized SUV, I tuck a strand of hair that escaped from her ponytail. The move is instinctive, but my breath catches, waiting for her reaction. A breeze picks up and I inhale a light floral scent. I'm so close her perfume mingles with the outdoors.

Her dark eyes flicker to mine, and she pushes higher, brushing her soft lips over mine. The unexpected touch rushes through me, from my mouth, down my spine, to my groin.

Her cheeks flush and I grasp her wrist, stopping her before she can pull away. I didn't expect a kiss, but I'm not averse. No, she and I are on the same page.

"Go to dinner with me."

The words come out before I fully process them. Maybe it's the mountain air, or maybe it's been too long since I met someone who doesn't know my net worth before my name. Either way, I want to see her again.

CHAPTER
THREE

SYDNEY

"I'm in."

The winding road climbs higher up the peak through the trees, passing homes and mailboxes jutting out an arm's length from the asphalt.

"Good work." The deep male voice on the other end of the line belongs to the man who recruited me from the CIA. He introduced himself as Hudson, and I still don't know for certain if that's his first or last name.

Given recent events, I'd been an easy recruit. Four of my assets: dead. Top brass determined in all likelihood I had been exposed, and my career as an overseas operative ended. The fact a friend asked me to take a call from Hudson, the director of her newly formed entity, served as the linchpin.

KOAN, which stands for Kaleidoscope Observation Analysis Network, is officially an investigative entity. The kind of work the FBI should be doing but can't—or won't

—when powerful people are involved. KOAN references a paradoxical question with no clear answer, the purpose to transcend logical reasoning and encourage intuitive insight. Caroline pitched it to me as "asking the questions that have no right answers but need to be asked anyway." After watching my assets die because someone higher up the food chain decided their lives were expendable, that philosophy resonated.

"What's your plan?" Hudson asks, his question confirming I'm taking lead.

"We're going to dinner. I'm going to head back to the rental to meet with Quinn." She's the team's tech and equipment resource. "Then to the hotel."

When we acquired Rhodes MacMillan's itinerary two days ago, I checked into his hotel. If the hiking interlude didn't pan out, I would've tried again with an impromptu run in at the hotel.

"What's your read? Do you need backup?"

"My read after initial contact is that the initial profile assessment is accurate. He doesn't strike me as overtly dangerous. He had no security. Drove himself. Classic white collar." It's the deals he may be striking that are dangerous. But he's too connected for any government agency to investigate. Rumors abound, and investigations were started, but halted by the DOJ. This is why my friend founded KOAN, an organization that conducts under the radar investigations—work that might be halted the moment they cross the desk of a vested influential power player.

"Touch base after you meet with Quinn." The line goes dead.

Yes, sir.

In my rear, I clock an SUV two back. I make a quick right.

The two cars behind me pass.

Wait for it.

I whip back out onto the road.

The higher I go in altitude, automotive traffic declines.

I pass an older white male watering flowers with a water hose and wave. He doesn't appear to notice.

Near the peak, I pull into a concrete parking area with a drive that loops down to the garage. From the street, the house appears to be a one-story wood and stone structure. But it's deceptive. Built into the side of the cliff, the living areas are below street level, and the back of the house offers stunning views across a panoramic mountain scape.

I shift my Jeep into park and hop out onto a cracked paver, wincing when pain shoots up my right knee into my thigh. The injury, while minor, is real. Hudson, on this first assignment, is proving he trusts his recruits— and it's a refreshing change from the micromanager I landed in the behavior and analysis division in the CIA.

After venting to Caroline, who also hated serving under the same prick and first fled the CIA to a privately held group on the West Coast, she shared her latest venture. With the encouragement of her husband, a billionaire with more than he can spend in his lifetime, she founded KOAN, because tackling corruption is something she's passionate about.

During her pitch on why I should join the team, Caroline asked me the age-old question, "What do you have to lose?" She probably expected me to list off the usual things—career stability, pension, health insurance. Instead, I thought about Dimitri's last message, sent just hours before they found his body in that Parisian alley. Perhaps she meant for the question to be rhetorical, and for me, it absolutely was—and the answer: Nothing. The CIA had already taken everything that mattered.

If this team doesn't work out, Caroline says she can find something for me within the West Coast outfit she initially joined—not as an analyst, which I hate, but doing something in the field. I probably could've pushed her right then for an introduction, but no project coming out of the Arrow Tactical team will help me uncover the leaks that led to the death of the assets I recruited. Maria, a mother of two young daughters, who'd been doing nothing more than feeding us itineraries—her death hit me the hardest, but I'll never forget any of their names.

As a member of the intelligence community, it's natural to distrust. Those I mistrust the most? Those who believe themselves to be above the law and reproach. Like whoever sold out my assets. Like whoever decided stolen secrets were worth more than lives. If Rhodes MacMillan is part of that network, I'll make sure justice is served.

Our target, Rhodes Macmillan, created ARGUS, reputed to be the best AI surveillance product on the market. Rumors abound about what he can access, and more than that, what he can derive from those databases and which countries he's serving. If there's a secret society of the powerful, he's undoubtedly a man such a society would recruit.

The government won't ever investigate MacMillan or ARGUS as he's got ties on every floor of the Department of Justice, and it's fair to assume he owns most senators and a chunk of Congress.

ARGUS isn't his first company. His first was a boring financial payment system that made him billions, and he and those original partners are now some of the most influential people in the world.

Of course, with success and influence comes attention.

That fact is why my plan held a high probability of failure. Rhodes MacMillan is a wary creature. He has to be. Anyone around him might be tempted to make a quick buck selling a story to the highest bidder. He bought stock in a company? Sold stock? Prefers a specific hotel chain? Ate lunch with a CEO? Any little detail of his life can be sold. His most benign conversation will be of interest to the right people.

Yes, the plan was risky, but I played it to perfection, and he doesn't suspect anything. My approach had to feel like more time together was his idea, and I nailed the approach.

"Is that art or real?" Quinn stands in the front door of the rental, watching me as I pick and choose what I want to carry inside from the duffel bags stowed in the back. "That looks like a busted knee."

Quinn has her long, curly, blonde hair pulled back so it's half up, half down, and she's wearing a long, loose skirt that skims the tops of her bare feet. In her light brown cardigan and white tank, if I met her on the street I'd expect her to be an English teacher or a grad student, but that's where looks can be deceiving.

"Blood's real. Limp isn't." I flex my knee, testing the scrape. "Though it stings more than I expected."

"Wait a second. You purposefully fell?"

I shrug. "Do what you gotta to do."

"What would you've done if you'd really hurt yourself?"

She's appalled, but makeup to fake an injury would've been a poor choice. I step past her through the wide front entrance. Inside, there's a small foyer, a step down to a living area with a bedroom off to the side, and a spiral staircase to the second floor below.

The second floor opens up to the main floor, which is also accessible by a lower garage level. Six bedroom suites are on the lowest floor. It's a beautiful home but the furniture is dinged and faded, and from what I understand, came with the property. Or maybe it's rented. Either way, someone clearly believed brown shag carpet was a design choice rather than a cry for help.

I had no role in selecting this place. No, while Hudson and Quinn coordinated this effort, I studied Rhodes. I scraped every article, social post, and even yearbooks from high school, Stanford, as well as the one from the one year at Harvard Business School before he dropped out. I learned he likes solo sports and loves rock climbing, so much so he has a twenty-foot wall in his penthouse that was featured in an interior design magazine. While Rhodes doesn't post any images, and his Bluesky posts and Threads read like an employee from his PR department wrote them, he had a girlfriend who tagged him daily. And from what I could gather, they broke up two years ago, and given his ex wasn't one to delete history, it appears they parted ways directly after an engagement party he chose not to attend. Ouch.

People reveal more in what they don't post than what

they do. Rhodes' digital silence speaks volumes—either extreme privacy or something to hide. His ex-girlfriend's posts, however, painted a picture of a man who prioritized work over relationships. Useful intelligence. I also learned his private plane scheduled a flight plan to Franklin with no return trip. I read an interview with him for *Climbing* magazine where he mentioned he'd climbed most of the notable places in California and Washington State, and when asked what's next for him, he answered visiting places he read about in his home state, back when he was a kid and not yet into climbing.

Quinn found his hotel reservation, proving her skills. Yesterday I discreetly followed him through town wearing a floppy hat and a gray, long-haired wig and heard him ask the guy at the hardware store if there were any pharmacies within walking distance. That's when I learned his elbow is bothering him, and I figured if he's not up for climbing, he'd go for the most challenging hike. While I'd had my gear in my car, I'd been pretty certain it wouldn't be a climbing day, and I'd been correct.

"What if your knee shattered?"

That's extreme.

"What if you couldn't walk?" Quinn's not going to drop it.

"I wasn't that far away from you. And it's a beautiful summer day. Someone would've come by and helped me." Like Rhodes did. He could've moved on, minded his own business. Instead, he stayed, made sure I was okay.

She shakes her head in disapproval. "I'm telling Hudson you need backup."

"I do not need backup. It's overkill and it increases

operation risks. He might catch on. We're in a small town." My voice rises and I can't stand that I have transitioned from victorious to beseeching. "It's harder in a small town to remain unnoticed."

She glares at me and I'm taken aback by her eyes. I swear, they're almost purple. I'd ask her what shade but her stern expression tells me now is not the time.

"Fine. I promise. Fake blood from here on out."

She exhales and heads to the spiral staircase.

"Come on down."

I follow behind her, noting that her paisley skirt is so long she picks up the hem to prevent herself from tripping over it. The painted white spiral staircase leads to more shaggy brown carpet. Yes, architecturally the house is beautiful, but the design sensibility is questionable.

"It doesn't impact you, but we might have another operator on the inside. In San Francisco."

Attempting multiple angles is understandable, but it still feels like a slap, like they didn't fully trust I'd connect.

"On the inside how?"

"She has an interview at a consulting company ARGUS hired for a human resource project."

"That's a slow take." It'll take a long time for someone working for a tangential organization to learn what's really going on inside ARGUS, if they ever gain that level of access.

"True." Quinn pulls out a chair in front of her desk. The three monitors on her desk face the wall, so all she has to do is look to the side and take in the mountain view. "But really, what do you think he's going to reveal during a dinner conversation? If we can get a full understanding of ARGUS's resource needs, we can get a much better handle on what they're doing. What kind of deals they're making."

She pulls out a file drawer with stacked boxes in the back and wires neatly bound in the front.

"I'm not saying you won't get anything valuable. I'm always in awe at the CIA's methods, questionable as they may be."

"Wait a minute. It's not like I dressed in a slinky dress or brought him back to my hotel room and drugged him."

She stares at me like I'm irrational.

I throw up my hands. "We're going on a date. He's here by himself. It's a prime opportunity to get to know him."

"My point is, how close are you going to have to get to him to get anything valuable? And what's involved in getting close?"

She's not wrong. The chances of placing a bug on a guy like Rhodes MacMillan and it going undiscovered for over forty-eight hours is slim. But it's a contact. Men like Rhodes don't meet the low-level consultants working on human resource issues. Now, maybe if a coding phenomenon made it onto their payroll... My gaze falls on Quinn's waist-length twisty Rapunzel strands. Maybe we should've sent her to ARGUS. With her skills and those stunning violet eyes...she might be the best option.

"I'm not saying your plan is a bad idea, I'm simply urging you to be realistic with your expectations." She sounds like a mother.

"I resent the implication that my plan, that Hudson approved, is anything but aboveboard. I'm not doing anything they didn't teach at Langley." With a pointed pause to let my words sink in, I add, "The human connection—"

"Is unreliable," Quinn interrupts. "And may not be needed if you can hack into the right systems."

She's a hacker. It's her perspective. It's not personal.

"All I'm asking is that you trust me to maintain professionalism. Trust me to do my best for this team."

I want this op to succeed. It's a long shot, but if ARGUS is cutting the rumored deals, then the company is a national security risk. If he's truly selling classified information to the highest bidders, and my assets were on some high-valued CIA asset list, then this is personal.

A bedroom door opens and Hudson steps out. He's in a button down and khakis, and behind him there's a desk with a single monitor. He removes an earbud and his gaze shifts between Quinn and me.

"You're trusted," Hudson says.

My eyes drop to his forearms with the sleeves rolled up, past his clunky silver watch, down his khakis to his bare feet, the tops barely visible in the thick brown carpet. "We have no reason to believe you will be anything but professional. We're a team with a common goal: to learn if ARGUS is selling secrets to the highest bidder. Our resource on the West Coast has the same goal. Even if nothing pans out from the human resource angle, she may overhear internal work discussions or find a disgruntled employee willing to share project details. And you may not get more than dinner."

Unfortunately, the boss is right.

"We can't expect a home run on every attempt. Investigations of this nature take time. We're in on two fronts but neither are sure wins. We keep trying until we succeed. And we support each other. Copy?"

I nod, shoving my hands in my pockets. Quinn spins right and left in her desk chair, twisting the long skirt.

"In an abundance of caution, I'm bringing in backup."

I open my mouth to argue with him, but he ignores me.

"I want backup nearby. This effort is not resource constrained, so there's no reason to take unnecessary risks. That doesn't mean I disagree with your assessment that he's not dangerous, but we'll be ready if his security shows up or if the parameters change."

I'm skilled and trained, and the argument is on my lips, but I swallow it down because Hudson's argument is reasonable.

"I'm going to head to the hotel. Plan to sit outside by the pool with a book on the off chance I might run into him before our dinner."

"Rough life," Quinn says, grinning.

I return her grin, letting her know I'm not pissed.

She bends down and passes me a zippered bag with two of the charging cords. "Throwaway phones, surveillance devices, the usual." She shrugs. "I assume you don't need a weapon?"

I don't miss that her question is directed at our boss, not to me. Still, I answer. "I have a personal handgun secured at the hotel. I'm good." I pause, unable to resist. "Though if you think Rhodes MacMillan is the type to require heavy artillery for dinner conversation, maybe we should reassess our intel."

I'm halfway up the spiral stairway when Hudson calls,

"Sydney, keep a tracker on you at all times. And call me in the morning."

My brain immediately goes to the gutter - something about his commanding tone and that particular phrase combo strikes me as oddly sexual, deserving of at the very least a snarky "Depends on your performance," response.

"Depends on—" I clear my throat, catching myself two words too late. "Copy that."

Tonight, I might not immediately get valuable intel, but I'll get a good sense of Rhodes' character, and if he's capable of selling out our country.

CHAPTER
FOUR

SYDNEY

Ten minutes before six, I'm in a cozy room in front of an unlit fireplace, steps away from the check-in desk. My time by the pool proved a waste, if one counts time half-reading, half-people watching a waste. Rhodes never appeared.

In the heart of the Blue Ridge Mountains, the world-renowned spa attracts many of the visitors to the inn, and if I were to guess, that's why I had the pool to myself. If I'd known I wouldn't run into Rhodes, I might have scheduled a massage. But, given there was no chance of running into him in the women's area of the spa, I stretched out in a lounge chair and, in a solitary moment, broke down and called Caroline.

"Hey, how's it going?" Her voice sounded bright and cheery, but in the background I heard a click that I assumed was a door closing.

"Fine. Am I catching you at the office?"

"Home office, today, but Dorian's working from home today too. He can be loud."

I smiled at the way she drew out the word *loud*. It's been a long time since I lived with someone, and I've never lived with someone I was romantically involved with, but I fully expect there would be challenges.

"How's Dorian?"

Although I've been friends with Caroline for years, I've never met her husband. For one, when she and I first met, they'd split. They only recently reunited. She came to visit me not long ago in D.C., but he had meetings or something. But I don't need to know him to approve of their reunion. She seemed happier, livelier.

"He's fine. How are you? You're at the new job, right? Do you like it? How's the boss?"

"Well, obviously the boss is an improvement over asshat."

She snorted. "Obviously."

"But no, I like him. He's levelheaded. Fair. Trusting. I'm thrilled to be back, doing my old thing." There was no one around me, but Caroline understood my purposeful vagueness.

"That's good. I'm happy for you."

"Thanks."

"Is something wrong?"

"Ah, you know. No guarantees." Quinn laying it out there and then my poolside nothing served as a cautious reminder. In this situation, failure is a realistic scenario, but failure isn't acceptable. I'll find a way.

"If anyone can crack the guy, it's you," Caroline said, as if she could read my mind. "Remember the test?" My mind flashed to the evening in a ballroom with classical music and champagne flutes. "You scored higher than anyone. You pulled one over on an instructor."

Yeah, rumors spread that I slept with him because how else could a woman pull one off on a target aware of the assignment?

The reality? I distracted him and successfully retrieved his phone and returned it. Yes, he was aware of my objective, but diversion is a skill. The others needed more practice. Years have passed since The Farm and our hyped banquet test.

"What's it like being in the field again?" Caroline joined the CIA knowing she'd never enter the field, as she'd been in the press too often thanks to her marriage to an influential, highly visible man.

"Honestly, there's no adrenaline rush quite like it."

"You love it." I could hear the smile in her words.

"I do," I admitted. "Thank you."

She scoffed. "No need to thank me. We wouldn't have recruited you if you weren't the best for the job."

That one comment of hers was something I needed to hear. And, I suppose, Caroline sensing that, is what makes her good at her job too.

After ending the call with Caroline, I showered and dressed for my date and now I wait.

From my perch in the armchair, I have a clear view of the lobby doors, although it's likely my target will approach from behind, entering the lobby from the labyrinth of hallways that connect the inn.

The Smithsonian article on my phone covers nine mythological sites that archeologists believe are real. Rhodes' ex-girlfriend once posted a pic of him reading a Percy Jackson novel with the caption, "My man loves his mythology." And his mother responded with, "That's my boy" and a heart emoji.

It's not a lot to go on, but if he approaches from behind and sees my phone, it's a conversation starter. And maybe reading the Smithsonian magazine will boost my perceived intelligence quotient. With Mr. Stanford, it's a reasonable assumption he's judgey over reading habits.

In six minutes, he'll be late. In a Harvard Business Review article on leading management practices, Rhodes stated he expects timeliness from all employees. "A late arrival to a meeting wastes the time of the participants and costs the company hundreds, if not thousands, of dollars."

On the hike, he didn't come across as the stiff I expected, but put a suit on him and he's probably a different man. Of course, as one of the Silicon Valley self-made T-shirt and blazer crew, he's infamous for eschewing ties.

Another minute ticks by. If he's late, then either he holds a distinct set of standards to his private life, he handles himself differently on vacation, or that entire article was bullshit.

The bell over the door rings, and he enters. Is he coming in from the parking lot? Where did he spend the afternoon?

I check the time. Five fifty-nine.

His dark, hooded eyes scan the lobby. Earbuds protrude from both ears. There's an iPhone in his hand, and his dark gray trench coat falls mid-thigh. He's changed into jeans, a heathered gray tee, and hiking boots. He wore running shoes when he went hiking.

What's he been doing this afternoon?

He nods and says something to someone. Where I'm sitting, I can't see the check-in desk, but based on the angle of his body, presumably, he's chatting with the person behind the desk.

Static lifts several of his dark brown strands. Cut short on the sides, and longer on the top, he's got one of those hairstyles that say *I'm a businessman, but I'm not one of the zero-nonsense types. If you want me to model, I can do that too.*

The idea of this man doing something as plebeian as modeling is laughable, and I grin at the thought—though honestly, with that face and those shoulders, he'd probably be damn good at it—and then his gaze falls on me.

The lobby chatter fades to white noise, the scent of dinner from the restaurant sharpens, and the space between us seems to contract.

My skin thrums, and I catalog the reaction: elevated heart rate, dilated pupils, the kind of physiological response I've been trained to recognize and control. Except I'm not controlling it.

Lost in his focus, my mind momentarily blanks.

His gaze drops and the oxygen whooshes back into my lungs. Sounds clink around us, louder than before, and the scent of melted butter, fresh thyme, and something sweet baking in the distance reminds me I'm genuinely hungry.

With a swift movement born of habitual habit, his earbuds are gone and deposited in a pocket.

I push up from my chair, the mythology article forgotten. Wasted effort.

He smiles, softening his expression. The crinkling

around his eyes highlights the inner warmth of his brown eyes that shift to moss green in the light. "You ready?"

"Yeah." I double-check the chair I occupied.

Phone? Check. Handbag? Check.

"Do you have a coat?"

"It's summer," I say, blinking.

"Can get chilly at night."

His business trench belongs in the city, not out here in a small mountain town. I doubt it provides much warmth, but it adds to his business vibe. And maybe date vibe?

I glance down at the outfit I chose. A short capped-sleeve Prana dress that hugs my curves loosely and falls to my calves with gold-buckle Birkenstocks that balance outdoorsy and feminine. These clothes are from my wardrobe, but I selected them for our date as they fit the part of a young woman on vacation in the Highlands.

"The temperature will drop into the sixties. Do you want to get a cardigan? I mean, you can take my coat, but it will swallow you."

At six-two, he's tall, but at five-seven, I'm no shorty.

"And frankly, I'm enjoying the view too much to cover it up."

Did he actually just say that? I blink, processing what is, in all fairness, a slightly cheesy comment. Completely uncalled for, heat rises along my neck and cheeks, while a visual of the jean jacket I didn't pack that would've gone so well with this dress flashes.

"I'll grab my fleece," I say.

"Come on." He steps to the door, leaving me to follow. "I've got a solution in mind."

I follow him through the cozy lobby with dark wood

and small windows that make you wish it was winter and outside a snowstorm raged. But when we step outside, we're greeted with a touch of humidity and a golden evening sun. A profusion of red, blue, and white flowers bloom in window boxes and baskets in storefronts all along idyllic Church Street.

There's a subtle chill in the air, but it's still undeniably warm, possibly exacerbated by the undercurrent running through my veins. A challenge, that's what's contributing to the heat. It's the excitement and intense awareness of a mission.

He stretches an arm out, exposing a Garmin. "There's a shop we can catch before it closes."

He holds out a hand, and I dutifully take it. My legs stretch to match his long strides as we slow for a passing car, but the Subaru stops, waiting for us to cross.

Warmth circles my fingers, but it's more than warmth. Tingles glide along the underside of my arm.

It's a compromising reaction.

This is a job. Yet my gaze falls to our connection, to his capable hands and long fingers with trimmed nails and confident hold.

Two silent minutes later he releases my hand and swings open the door to Lulu Bleu and holds it for me.

"I'm fine," I insist, attempting to cover my frustration at his insistence I need a sweater with a soft smile.

He rolls his eyes, grins, and steps inside, leaving me on the sidewalk.

What is he doing?

I scan the street and the handful of pedestrians. Sun shines on the windshields of the cars parked along the street, blocking any view inside, but there's an SUV I recognize at the far end.

The back up is unnecessary.

He's not dangerous. He's not that kind of criminal.

With an internal huff, I swing the door open to join my date. He holds up a cropped camel-colored cardigan that's several shades lighter than my chestnut sundress.

"Will this work?"

It's cute. I check the brand. I'm not familiar with it, but it doesn't strike me as crazy expensive. It's soft, not itchy. I reach for the price tag, but he lifts it out of my reach and passes it to the young woman at the register.

"We'll take this."

He flashes his phone at a reader, and hits confirm. The woman at the register blushes, smiling at him like he's bought it for her, as she undoes a small gold clip that holds the price tag.

"Would you like a bag?" she purrs.

"No, she'll wear it out."

"Would you like your receipt? Texted?" Her addendum rings several octaves higher.

It takes effort to control the eye roll. Yes, he's got charisma in spades. He's attractive. But really? She's probably almost twenty years younger than him and she's hoping to score a date when he walked into the store with another woman and bought said woman a sweater. *Have some dignity.*

"No, thank you. Have a nice evening," he says with all the grace of a southern gentleman.

I hold the door for him and he steps through it, bracing his arm against the door for me. Out on the sidewalk, he gestures.

"This way. We have reservations."

"That wasn't really necessary," I say, glancing at the sweater he's holding in his far hand.

"Well, after dinner, I figured we might walk around. There's a fire pit on the hotel property."

"Near one of the outdoor bars."

"Exactly." He smiles. "If dinner goes well."

My stomach flutters, and I'm cognitively aware it's the physical reaction of a real date, which this is not.

"What'd you do this afternoon?" The question comes out cocked and poorly timed.

"Oh, I went on another hike. Drove around. Checked out a few properties for sale."

"Are you considering moving?"

He shrugs. "I like it here. Plus I tend to look at real estate everywhere I go."

"What did you say you do?"

He pauses outside the door to On the Veranda, a cute restaurant with a black awning.

"I didn't." He's smiling, like he's fully entertained, even happy.

"Realtor?" I ask, playing it up.

"Programmer."

"Ah. I didn't peg you as a nerd." He throws his head back, barking out a laugh. "Although, the business over-coat…" I lightly touch the fabric.

"I have meetings in D.C. Had to pack clothes that worked for this jaunt and…" He angles his head to the back of the restaurant, and I presume he thinks he's nodding in a northern direction, indicating D.C.

"Carry-on suitcase only?"

He side-eyes me.

What am I saying? He flew a private plane.

But I don't know that.

"If I could get by with only a duffel, that's what I'd carry." He stops, hands in his pockets, watching me. "I have a favor to ask."

I tilt my head, curious. "Okay?"

"It might come off as strange, but...can we steer clear of work conversation? I need a break from it."

The request surprises me—most successful men I've encountered love talking about their achievements. "That's not strange at all. What would you rather talk about?"

"Anything else." His gaze rises skyward and his eyelashes flutter closed. For a man, he has noticeably long, thick eyelashes. When he opens his eyes, there's an earnestness I didn't pick up on before. "I haven't taken a vacation in years. Real vacation, where I'm not checking emails or thinking about quarterly projections or..." He trails off, then refocuses on me with renewed intensity.

"That sounds exhausting."

"It is." He steps closer, and I catch a hint of his cologne—something woody and expensive. "I need this. A night out with an adventurous, stubborn—" He looks at me with a pointed grin. "—kindred spirit."

"Kindred?" I raise an eyebrow. "We just met."

"Did we?" His voice drops lower, more intimate. "Can we just...for tonight, pretend we're going to spend forever right here? No past, no future obligations. Just this."

CHAPTER
FIVE

SYDNEY

I'm still processing Rhodes' words—*pretend we're going to spend forever right here*—when the hostess leads us through the warm glow of On the Veranda. His request lingers between us, creating an intimacy that makes even this simple walk to our table feel charged.

"Right this way," the hostess says, leading us to a table in the center of the restaurant.

Booths line the walls, offering more privacy, and Rhodes points to an empty spot at the back of the restaurant.

"Can we take one of those?"

"Those are reserved," the hostess answers with distracted ambivalence. The young girl in a flowered romper and clogs can't be over seventeen.

"Can you check? Or may I speak to your manager?"

The romantic spell broken, I give the hostess an understanding smile, grateful for the distraction. His flirty request caught me off guard, but now I'm grounded again, focused.

If this were an actual date, I'd intervene and insist the table is fine. Given I'm uncertain how a CEO like Rhodes would react to someone questioning his viewpoint, even on something as mundane as table selection, I clasp my hands together, politely observing.

"He's over there," the hostess says, pointing at a middle-aged man with a plaid shirt, dark jeans, and pointed dress shoes. There's something about him, maybe the high waist of his jeans or the tapered hem, or those pointy, shiny leather shoes, that makes me suspect he's European.

H-1 Visas are popular with hotels throughout the Highlands, according to the bartender at the pool this afternoon, a college-aged guy from Australia, but while the Aussie works in the Highlands, he lives in Georgia in a more affordable area that's commuting distance.

Rhodes heads in the manager's direction. There's something deliberate about the way Rhodes approaches this—not entitled, exactly, but confident he'll get what he wants.

It's chilly in the restaurant, so I put the gifted cardigan on and mouth, "I'm sorry," to the girl.

She shrugs and responds loud enough that the man and woman sitting at a nearby table hear her say, "I only have two more weeks here. I don't care."

Rhodes and her boss shake hands, chat, and a minute later, Rhodes follows the restaurant manager to the booth he requested. He hangs his jacket on a hook on the booth's post, and I slide onto the bench closest to his coat.

He bends, and says in my ear, "I'll be right back."

I watch him as he retreats to the restroom, and only then do I allow myself to breathe. His request outside—to pretend we could spend forever here—is exactly the kind of thing that makes this job challenging. Objectivity is a requirement.

My gaze falls to his overcoat hanging on the booth's post, the slim phone visible in the gaping pocket. This is why I'm here. Not for romantic fantasies, but for this—the intelligence that will either clear him or gather enough evidence to ensure that no one can halt an official investigation. I scan the room methodically. The gray-haired woman entering the restroom hallway. The group approaching the hostess stand. The hunched man exiting the restrooms. No direct eyes on me.

I retrieve the phone with practiced efficiency, my hands steady despite the adrenaline.

This is almost too easy.

He uses an iPhone, which is difficult to hack. I set my iPhone next to it, exchange contact information, which he'll see, but that's easily explainable. Pushy and bad date etiquette, but my goal isn't marriage. Then I pull out a custom device Quinn provided. I set it over the phone and wait for the small button to flash green. Part of me hopes we'll find nothing incriminating.

The woman with gray hair and a long, swishy skirt exits the restroom hallway. At the front of the restaurant, a group of four middle-aged women enter and approach the hostess stand. An older man in a plaid short-sleeve shirt on the opposite side of the restaurant walks toward the restroom.

Quinn said this thing works fast.

I should've tested it.

Our server approaches. "Good evening. Welcome to On the Veranda."

"Would you mind coming back? My date's—"

"Oh. Sure thing, sugar. Have you had a chance to look over our cocktails?"

"I'll wait for my date. He may prefer wine."

The green light flashes in my lap and my gaze darts to the restroom hallway.

Rhodes exits, gaze locked on me.

Fuck.

"Take your time," she says, stepping away with half her focus on the order pad.

The device drops into my pocketbook and my thigh shifts over Rhode's phone, so I'm basically sitting on it, just as Rhodes slides into the opposite bench.

My heart hammers against my ribs. One wrong move and everything unravels.

"Did you order?" he asks.

"No, I said I'd wait for you."

I keep my breathing calm in spite of the adrenaline coursing through my veins like liquid fire.

He lifts the menu. "I should've told you what to order for me." His brow crinkles as he takes in the menu.

I edge forward, placing one finger on the cocktail section as distraction while my other hand delivers his phone to his coat pocket.

"You want a cocktail?" he asks.

"I thought some of them looked interesting." I scan the menu, hoping the cocktails are indeed interesting and not standard fare.

"Do you like sweet drinks?"

I crinkle my nose. "No. Can't stand them."

"Same," he says.

"Wine's fine," I'm quick to say, as the custom cocktails listed all include simple syrup.

"Can you hand me my coat?"

Oh, shit.

"Don't laugh, but I need my glasses. Or maybe I need light." He scans the ceiling as if the lighting might be to blame for his inability to decipher the menu.

Relieved, I laugh, and feel in his pockets, first the pocket with the phone, before locating a glasses case in his other pocket.

I pass him his glasses and watch as he transforms from frat boy handsome to geeky sexy with black, boxy frames.

My college self sighs wistfully. With one set of glasses, he transformed into every crush I had from the ages of seventeen to twenty-one.

"Hazards of a life spent staring at screens," he says as much to himself as to me.

"I thought we weren't talking about any of that."

He grins. "Quite right." He points a finger at the frames. "These are new. Haven't gotten used to them yet."

"Are you one of those people with enormous font on their phones?"

"Can we broaden the untouchable topic list?"

I shrug, grinning. "Why are glasses embarrassing?"

"They're not, except I never needed them until I turned forty."

"Ah. You're on the downhill spiral."

He looks up from the menu. "As if you know anything about that. How old are you?"

"Thirty-one," I answer easily, as age isn't one of my hang-ups.

"Give it ten years," he says. "Then ask me about my font size."

He's forty-one. Five years ago, he made the forty under forty list. I'd ask him what his goals are now that he's past forty, but I'm not supposed to know about his prior accomplishments and work life is banned conversational material.

"So did you see any houses you liked?"

"Actually, yes. You should've joined me. They had chocolate chip cookies and freshly squeezed lemonade set out for the open house."

"That's a nice touch."

"I'd say so. Kept me chatting with the agent for two glasses of lemonade. All of which hit about the second we walked into this restaurant."

"Is that another side effect of forty?"

He lowers the menu and shoots me a how-dare-you pseudo glower. I smirk and he grins.

"So tell me, Sydney…"

I wait, wondering where he'll take the conversation. By his own accord, the easy first date work convo is off the table.

"When on vacation, what are your favorite things to do?"

I lift the glass of water and sip to buy time. The upped attraction quota frazzled my focus. He's beyond handsome, which makes the job easier, but I still have to keep my wits.

Be real. Be yourself.

But I know everything to do with the man across from me, so in the words of the great Bono, I can be exactly what he's looking for—based on everything that's been published or shared on social media by his ex and his late mother who passed away four years ago. His father lives in Florida, and from what I could find, never opened a social media account.

"I don't take many vacations."

It's an honest answer, and one I know he will grasp.

His gaze lifts from the menu. "You good with a cabernet?"

I nod, and he sets the menu down.

"That's not an answer." He rests his back firmly against the booth and a slight smile plays across his lips. "What do you like to do? Or let's play it this way. On your Pinterest board of idyllic vacations, what's on it?"

"I don't have a Pinterest board." His ex did. She never deleted her wedding board, but she had so much on there I couldn't derive what she planned. "But if I did, it would probably be a wish list of locations, not activities." There's no way my wish list will match an unknown list, and if he has a Pinterest board, it's unknown to me because I never found it. "I do have a private bookmark folder filled with links to activities. Workouts. Weight routines. Hiking trails. Yoga studios."

"You're a yogi?" His grin widens.

My nose crinkles reflexively. "Not like that," I say.

He barks out a laugh. "What's *that*?"

"Granola. That's what you're thinking, right? No, I mean, I force myself to do yoga at least once a week for stretching. To avoid injury." It's an approach my lacrosse coach drilled into me—the healthy way to remain fit.

"Smart," he says, lifting his water and taking a sip.

I scratch an itch on my collarbone and add another point I suspect he'll relate to. "I have a hard time relaxing on vacation."

"I get that," he says, nodding.

"When I first got out of college, I hated weekends. Still went into the office." I hold up a hand. "I know, we said no work talk, but..."

"And now here you are on vacation."

"Listening to music and hanging out by the pool."

"What kind of music?"

"Depends on my mood. Today was alternative rock. Foo Fighters, actually." His eyes light up.

"Seriously?"

"You're a fan?"

"Dave Grohl's a legend," he says with genuine enthusiasm, and once again, I'm grateful I prepped.

His ex shared a photo of them at a concert in Washington state, shaking hands with Dave Grohl himself and the caption, "The Greatest Day of Rhodes' Life."

"What about you?"

The server stops by, interrupting us, and Rhodes orders a bottle of wine, and we end up ordering appetizers and entrees all at once, while a sommelier returns with the wine. As Rhodes tastes and approves it, I study his profile. The confident way he handles every interaction, from the hostess to the sommelier. The slight smile that never quite leaves his lips when he looks at me.

When we're alone again, I lean forward. "Okay, seriously. Favorite vacation activities?"

"Oh, now that's a loaded question." His smirk carries a promise that makes my pulse quicken. "You sure you want me to be honest?"

I'd be lying if I didn't say his confident, at-ease persona didn't ooze sex appeal. Hell, with those black frames, he's hot as fuck.

I open my mouth, prepped to probe.

"Sex," he answers, and the way his dark eyes cut straight, head-on, strikes a match on my starved libido. "Hands down, my favorite activity."

"Ah." I lift my glass of water, momentarily speechless, but wise or not, the real Syd slips out. "Sex. Most powerful word in the English language. Makes the world go round."

His lips purse, and his eyes gleam with amusement, and maybe something else. Anticipation.

I set the glass down. My skin burns. His gaze doesn't break. With this tiny bit of innuendo, I find myself squeezing my thighs and taking deeper breaths. I swallow.

Focus.

If anyone can crack him, you can.

"I hope I'm not being too forward. Honesty is the best policy, right?"

I swear, the way he's looking at me, my heart stops beating for a split-second.

Be real. What am I thinking? Work this.

"Not too forward at all. It seems we have something in common."

CHAPTER
SIX

RHODES

The blush on her cheeks deepens ten shades. Her trimmed, unpainted nails glide along her slender neck beneath a subtle red burst.

With her shoulders back and her chin at a defiant angle, she's the picture of a headstrong woman with a modest streak she'd rather hide, but her traitorous body gives her away.

We're both on vacation. There's no need to dance around a series of dates or pretend there's relationship potential.

Perhaps I should give her a reprieve. Shift to mundane conversation. Ask if she's been scuba diving.

Fuck that.

I lean forward, pushing the place setting back to make room for my folded arms. "Tell me exactly what you believe we have in common."

Her luscious milk chocolate eyes widen and a silky

dark veil of wavy hair swings forward, partially hiding her face, but her gaze never breaks. I half expect her to retreat to the restroom, and that's the only reason I don't give in to the itch to reach across the table and touch those glossy strands. I wish I was sitting closer, that this table wasn't between us.

All in good time.

Her shoulders rise and she braces against the bench, pushing up on the vinyl cushion. Using the physical to gather her strength. Fuck, maybe even pressing her thighs together, wanting this as much as I do.

"Orgasms," she says, the strength of her defiance going straight to my cock.

Holy fuck. Outstanding.

"Plural," she adds, and with that addition, I'm forced to shift to readjust my pants because my dick is now hard as stone. "I'm a fan of pretty much any path to get there. Slow. Fast." She tucks the veil behind her ear and licks her lower lip. "Dirty."

Alright. That does it. Where the fuck is our food? Can I just ask for the check?

As if hearing me, the singsong server appears with our appetizers. The talkative woman makes a production of detailing what we ordered, while the space between Sydney and I smolders.

Orgasms. Plural.

Challenge accepted Ms. Sydney.

Syd.

All we have to do is make it through dinner.

After the server leaves us, I ask, "What's your last name?"

Her head tilts to the side. "We're doing last names now?"

A cautionary voice whispers through my conscience. Once she has my last name, she'll Google me. But what does that matter? I'm not ashamed of who I am. We're on vacation. I'll likely never see her again, but I hope to see a lot of her tonight.

"Given what I'm mentally doing to you sitting here right now, sharing last names strikes me as appropriate."

She lifts her glass. "To last names and wishful dreams."

Our glasses clink, and our gazes remain locked over the rims as we sip.

Wishful dreams?

A warning sounds in my head. Is she mocking me? Telling me to dream on? Or is she a romantic? Dreaming of a vacation fling lasting into eternity? Neither scenario ranks as good.

"Parker," she says quietly over the rim of her glass. "Sydney Parker."

"Does anyone ever call you Syd?"

Syd and sex. Yes, both my heads are going there.

"My parents. Close friends." She smooths a finger over the crisp white tablecloth. "And your last name?"

"MacMillan. Rhodes MacMillan."

"Anyone ever call you Mac?"

I stifle a laugh. "Never. Do I look like a Mac?"

She shrugs. "It's a sports thing. And MacMillan is a mouthful."

"Well, I tell you what, when it's just the two of us, if you need to shorten my name to Mac, I'll allow it."

I feel her inhale in my tightening chest. Feel her

swallow in my groin. I'm damn fucking positive cum leaks from my tip.

She pats the table the way one would pat a dog and slides out of the booth.

"I need the restroom," she whispers with a demureness that contradicts her earlier *dirty* innuendo.

She grabs her purse, hips swaying all the way to the restroom. The sundress she's wearing falls loosely over her ass cheeks, the fabric flirting with her curves. The cropped cardigan I purchased ends just above the small of her back, highlighting the seductive motion of her hips.

Yes, I want her.

CHAPTER
SEVEN

RHODES

Subtle shifts in the restaurant crowd reflect the late evening hour. A crowd of five or six gathers before the hostess stand. Staff hurry to bus tables. My glass is half empty. Syd's still in the restroom. I check my wrist. Five minutes.

Is there a line? No, no one else has come or gone from the hallway.

Did she escape through a back door?

Calm yourself down.

She's into this. Undeniable chemistry buzzed between us through dinner. She prompted sexual innuendo.

I pull out my phone.

I shouldn't. It's an addiction.

Although, with Sydney sitting across from me, the urge to check it didn't strike. Highly unusual.

Not really, though. I want sex.

She's been gone for five minutes and I'm still hard. Not painfully so, but there's no doubt I'm aroused by her, by the thought of getting her out of that dress, teasing her nipples, discovering exactly where she craves touch.

I hold the phone to my mouth while keeping a watchful eye on the hallway entrance Sydney entered.

"Find out everything you can on Sydney Parker, born in Chicago. Current Washington D.C. resident."

I squint to see if voice diction got it right and hit send.

She'll probably get back to me with a need for her middle name. Place of employment. Physical address. Email address. Phone number.

"Hey dipshit? What the hell? You think there's only one Sydney Parker?" I can hear Daisy's screech.

I'll ask for her phone number. That'll play well. And it'll be good to have. I'm here until Friday.

What the hell is Sydney doing in the restroom?

I scan through notifications.

I'm on vacation. I should flip the phone over. Put it in my pocket.

In my periphery, I see her slender silhouette exit, and I openly ogle her as she approaches.

The bright flush from earlier has faded. Her dark waves brush her shoulders, and her lips bear a faint pink gloss. For the briefest of seconds, I imagine the pink stain on my cock.

The connection between us thrums, and the rest of the world fades.

It's been a long time since I wanted someone this badly.

As she slides into the booth, I wiggle my phone.

"Before I forget, can I get your number?"

Her cheeks flush a deeper crimson and the splotch on the crest of her collarbone returns. She runs her fingers through her strands, ruffling the smooth curtain.

"Sure." She digs her phone out of her brown leather handbag, directs her phone to mine, presses, and I glance down to see a notification light my screen. "I just texted you."

I forget sometimes how easy Apple makes it to exchange information. For that matter, how much information we can collect on an individual. It's just as well. My company wouldn't exist without the wealth of data to mine.

I slip on my glasses, open her information, select create new contact, and under company name, type in "Highlands Hottie." Memory cues. The older I get, the more necessary they become.

She exudes confidence, but when she batted her eyelashes and reminded me she's between jobs, I picked up on her underlying insecurities. We all have them. If I was unemployed, I'd be insecure. Hell, when I dropped out of business school, I became deeply insecure. Ultimately, I proved the doubters wrong and hit an untapped market with perfect timing. All I really needed was the Stanford degree for doors to open. One day I expect Harvard will give me an honorary degree, at least, if I get around to donating the funds for an AI research and training center.

For the most part, over dinner we successfully skirt all work-life conversation. She's an only child, like me. Her close friends live in either Southern California, Chicago, or the D.C. area. She doesn't care for San Francisco, which, truth be told, neither do I. Like me, she prefers the Seattle vibe. And like me, she's a novice vacationer.

My holiday find possesses a healthy appreciation for alternative rock. Linkin Park, Green Day, Foo Fighters, Evanescence, The Strokes, Blink-182, Red Hot Chili Peppers—she likes them all. I'm not familiar with Chappell Roan, but I promised to check her out. With Billie Eilish, we agreed to disagree. She said she's always wanted to listen to Dave Grohl's *Storyteller* memoir, and I shared that it's worth her time, and that I listened to it on a business trip to Saudi Arabia last year. Business…it always leaks in.

As we wait for the check, I ask, "What's your favorite film?"

"*Almost Famous*. Yours?"

"*A Complete Unknown*."

"That's a new one," she says, sounding surprised.

"Yeah it is. And next year I'll probably have a new favorite."

"Interesting. I wouldn't have expected that."

Her comment strikes me as odd. What did I do that made her expect I'd have the same favorite movie into eternity? The server arrives, and the question of what she meant slips away.

Uncertainty strikes as we exit the restaurant. It's barely nine as we walk down Church Street. The faint scent of honeysuckle floats on the breeze, and laughter and conversation converge into a low hum on the sidewalks as tourists mill about. A line extends from the one ice cream shop in town, and a blue haze descends over the mountains in the distance as the setting sun lingers, casting an ethereal, otherworldly glow.

With the idyllic small-town thoroughfare to our back, I hold the lobby door to the inn for her. A young woman with freckles behind the reception desk smiles a greeting.

"Thank you for dinner," Sydney says when we're out of earshot of the reception desk and at the juncture leading to the suites.

I slow my steps, placing a hand on her lower back, closing the distance between us. "Do you mind if I see you to your room?"

"That's not necessary. The inn is safe and I can take care of myself." She smiles, but I can't help feeling that she's teasing.

I make a show of leaning back to eye her scraped knee, which I can't see as it's covered by her dress, but she gets my point. "Are you sure about that?" Her grin widens. "I'd feel so much better if I saw you safely to your door."

Her eyes narrow into slits. It's the wide smile and the coquettish tilt of her head that lets me know I'm headed upstairs.

"Eagle Scout, remember? Southern gentleman."

"Is Charlotte really part of the south?"

What did she read about the Queen City? "It borders South Carolina. I'd say that's southern by any definition."

She releases a dramatic sigh and says, "Okay southern boy, see me home."

We don't travel far before she stops at her door. We're the only two in the hall.

"This is me."

"You're not inviting me in?"

"Trust me, you don't want to come in."

I open my mouth to argue. "Oh, I—"

"It's my time of the month."

Oh. Disappointment strikes like a rogue wave. That's why she spent so long in the bathroom. It clicks.

Damn.

My gaze falls to her lips. There's nothing more awkward than asking for a kiss, but... "A goodnight kiss?" I raise both eyebrows, playfully hopeful.

She twists her body and steps closer, bending her head to look up at me, offering her lips. Her fingers fall to my chest and I swear her touch singes my skin. My hand finds its way to the curve of her lower back. Her eyelids flicker closed and her lips open slightly. My heart thuds unusually hard, the reverberations noticeable.

It's just a kiss, Rhodes.

My lips press to hers and a warm buzzing sensation spreads over my extremities as our lips brush lightly, once. Twice. My fingers rise to her nape, tangling with her silky strands, and I gently angle her head.

She opens and I deepen the kiss, consuming sweet hints of our lemony dessert that fuel a desire for more. Her body presses against mine and my hand on her lower back glides lower, over her bottom, pressing her into me.

Fuck. I want her.

This woman can kiss. I love how her tongue flirts with mine, how her breasts feel pressed against my chest, the pressure of her against my now very hard erection.

Voices mingle and footsteps sound.

She breaks the kiss, breathless, lips over her mouth, eyeing me through her lashes with a timid smile.

An older couple pass us in the hall.

"You two make a lovely couple," the elderly woman says. I cut my gaze to them as they pass in time to see her husband pat her on her butt, likely telling her to keep walking.

Sydney sinks her teeth into her lower, glistening lip.

We share a confessional grin.

"I mean, I guess you could come inside. We could have a drink."

I'm not interested in alcohol. "There are other things we could do."

She tilts her head, questioning, reminding me of the current predicament.

"You don't actually believe that story about Thor, do you?"

I bark out a laugh that echoes down the quiet corridor. She's referring to the myth that Thor gained immortality by swimming in a river of menstrual blood.

"You like mythology?"

She shrugs like, of course she does. "Who doesn't?"

This woman. She's too good to be true.

"You've got great taste in music and you like mythology. I definitely want to see you again."

"I'd like to see you again, too."

My hand remains stubbornly on her hip. I don't want to let her go. I'm not ready to say goodnight. It's still early. And there *are* things we can do.

"Did you pack your vibrator?" The look she gives me will be seared into my brain for eons. It's the deep brown eyes, her slight intake of air through her rose-pink lips, the slope of her neck.

"Excuse me?" Those swollen lips spread into an incredulous half-smile.

"Vacation. Lots of women do."

"And I'm like lots of women?"

"Are you?" My fingers caress her bottom, up and down, shifting the summery fabric over her curve.

"I guess I am."

Fuck, yes. "Excellent. Then there are definitely things we can do."

CHAPTER
EIGHT

RHODES

She opens the door, uncertainty painting her features. Perhaps I should heed her hesitation and ignore the electric charge reverberating through my extremities. It's been so long since I've experienced a physical reaction like this to a woman I just met… Hell, I can't remember the last time I met a woman outside of the corporate world. The random hook-ups don't count.

Would I be pursuing her if she lived nearby? If I might run into her again? No, the intensity of my desire would have me backing up, taking time and space to ensure I maintain control.

Perhaps that's what I'm sensing from her. As far as dinner dates go, we had a good one. Take the win, regroup… It would be the reasonable thing to do.

"Come on in," she says, the curve of her lips eliminating any sign of unease. "We're two adults, right?"

"On vacation."

With my pointed statement, I step past her, briefly taking in her room. There's a gas fireplace with two chairs in front of it and a four-poster bed against the wall, directly behind the chairs. A door opens into what I presume is the bathroom. French glass doors open onto a small balcony with an iron rail and blooming flower boxes.

The door clicks closed.

"Where's your vibrator?"

"You're serious?"

I raise an eyebrow.

"That's… Let's get a drink." She approaches a cabinet next to the fireplace with two wine glasses and a bottle of wine with a price tag dangling from the neck. I have the same set up in my villa.

She rests her hands against the cabinet, twisting to face me. Her posture pulls the sundress tight against her chest.

"What's your longest relationship?"

"Seven years." I move closer. "Yours?"

Her gaze travels to the far ceiling corner.

"Syd?"

"Closer to seven months." Her lips purse, possibly amused. "I'm not one to keep track. But is that why you're so comfortable with this…" Her hand sweeps her middle as if she can't say the words.

"For the record, period sex can be hot."

Her nose crinkles.

"I agree that for our first time, it's not ideal. And to be clear, I'm not proposing sex."

No, I'm apparently an extremely horny fucker. I reach around her for the unopened bottle, but I hesitate, unsure about opening it, as we don't need more alcohol.

"What exactly are you proposing?"

I set the bottle back down. "Let me make you feel good." I reach for her hand and lift it from the cabinet. "Are you game?"

"Is that an attempt to appeal to my competitive side?"

I've no chance of hiding the smirk that breaks out with her accusation. People say I'm good at reading people. I suppose I am. Her insistence on hiking while injured tipped me off to a few proclivities.

I should probably back out, beg off, but I want to kiss her again. So I do.

When I lower my lips to hers, her body melds into mine, eliminating any distance. Any trace of timidity evaporates. The urge to lift her onto the cabinet, period be damned, intensifies, so I break the kiss.

Months from now, I want her to remember the man she met on her between-jobs getaway. But there's no need for self-torture.

I lead her to her bed and pat the mattress.

Her eyes narrow. "You said—"

I stop her with a finger over her plush, no longer glossy, lips.

"I said I'm going to make you feel good. Turn around."

Her fingers sink into the comforter.

"Trust me?"

The color of her eyes deepens as her pupils expand. Nerves? Desire?

Obediently, she turns, baring her back to me. I brush her hair over one shoulder and press my lips to her nape.

Tiny goosebumps rise along her arms. With a gentle tug, I lower the zipper and slide the thin straps of fabric over her shoulders, letting the dress fall unceremoniously to the floor.

My gaze roves down her spine, over the curve of her lower back, to the black lace thong covering her smooth, shapely bottom. My throat tightens and the heart symbol on my watch lights with what I am certain is a significant pulse rate increase.

She looks over her shoulder at me, eyes dark, a shade of uncertainty mixed with want.

Me too, Syd.

I spread my fingers over the comforter, brushing the silky fabric back and forth.

"Lie down, face down."

She climbs onto the bed, back to me, sheltering her braless breasts from my view.

Once she's settled, I toe off my shoes and climb behind her, straddling her thighs. I slap my palms together and rub vigorously.

She rises a few inches, looking over her shoulder at me.

"Warming my hands. Head down now. Arms above your head."

I press my palms to her lower back, and pause, letting the heat seep into her skin.

"Do you have cramps?"

"No," she says, sounding small.

Embarrassed?

"Do you not get bad periods?"

"This is very strange first date conversation."

I lift my palms, rub them vigorously again, and place

them once again on her lower back. Her head visibly sinks deeper into the pillow, and the muscles in her lower back soften. Knowing she's giving in, relaxing into this, I knead along her spine, up to her shoulders. I'm not a trained masseuse, but I've had my share of massages, and I work her muscles in the pattern I've grown accustomed to with Swedish massages.

"Oh, my god that feels amazing."

"I told you I'd make you feel good."

She lets out a not-so-subtle groan as my hands spread across her rib cage, climbing higher until I reach the underside of her breasts.

"This is heaven. Did you do this for all of your girlfriends?"

I half-chuckle but then realize an answer is expected.

"Girlfriend. Singular, really."

"I take it you left her, because no woman in her right mind would leave this."

The goofy smile on my face stretches my facial muscles.

"She left me, actually."

"Really?" She rises and I pat her spine.

"Lie flat."

"Moron," she says.

"Eh, she had her reasons."

"Did you cheat?" There's enough humor in her tone that I take it she doesn't believe I would. And she's right.

"I didn't cheat. At least not with a human."

"Do you have a blow-up doll fetish?"

"You're a regular comedian."

"Now that's a job I haven't considered." She shifts

and her rib cage expands beneath my fingers. "What'd you do? The not with a human bit is a touch creepy."

"I didn't mean…" Well, fuck, might as well tell her. "I skipped our engagement party."

"Skipped?"

"Got caught up at work. She was understandably distressed. To apply politically correct terminology."

"Have to say I commiserate with her. Can't say I'd be too pleased."

"In my defense—"

"Oh yes, I want to hear this."

"I proposed under duress. She gave me an ultimatum."

"That didn't work out well for her."

"My grandmother says that my forgetting the party was my subconscious telling me I didn't want to go through with it."

"Your grandmother? Are you close to her?"

"Nana Libby. The only person who made any attempt whatsoever to take my side when Sara and I split."

"That's what grandparents are for, right? To love you unconditionally."

I resume kneading her back, although my touch isn't as intense.

"How long ago was that?"

"That Sara and I split? Two years ago, give or take a few months."

"You're like me. Don't really keep count."

"I suppose so. In retrospect, our relationship ended years earlier. We were just going through the motions. And it was totally my fault."

"It's never entirely one person's fault."

"Says the woman who has never had an anniversary?"

"Hey now."

I lean over her and sink my teeth into her shoulder playfully.

Her lips spread into a grin, and I press my lips to the corner of her mouth.

"Now where's that vibrator?"

SYDNEY

The cool air teasing my sensitized nipples as I saunter through the hotel room to dig out my vibrator wars with my conflicted brain.

During training, of course we covered sexual attraction as a tool. But it's not a requirement. Official policy doesn't condone its use. But I'm no longer working for the CIA.

Still, when Hudson recruited me and we jointly developed a plan, he made it clear the goal is to breach Rhodes' electronics. Which, after tonight, I hope I accomplished on his phone. His laptop is bound to be in his hotel room.

You're not a freaking red sparrow. The Russians stooped to seduction to gain access. You don't need to resort to their honey trap tactics. You're smarter. Better.

At the same time, a male officer might engage when it

suits. Why can't a woman do the same? Why can't I have fun?

Alena's soft smile comes to mind. A Russian living in Paris, she had dreams. She might have been a member of the embassy cleaning crew, but she'd been a valuable asset. She reported on schedules, meeting attendees, and the kind of inner politics one can only glean from tone of voice and respect. She'd been found on a street, an apparent OD. But no one believed that, not really.

Rhodes MacMillan didn't take part in her death. He might not have even sold the asset list that ended lives and terminated my CIA career. But intelligence suggests someone in his company did.

I unzip my cosmetics bag and catch his heated gaze, glued to my naked form.

He's fully dressed. I wiggle a finger at him.

"Take that shirt off. I don't like being the only one barely dressed."

He grins as he unbuttons his shirt, but it's the way he's looking at me like he's a wolf and I'm a lamb he's about to devour that's almost enough to make me call off the charade and locate a condom. The need to take control is a strong one. And in this situation, if I give in to my desire, it only puts me closer to finding answers.

There's nothing wrong with wanting sex. Enjoying sex. We're both consenting adults. It's not like I have to share intimate details with my new boss or the team. We're looking to understand who he's cutting deals with. Which countries or individuals are benefitting from his AI surveillance system.

The man undressing is a brilliant engineer. An

unscrupulous truth finder. Wildly successful, brilliant, and possibly morally gray.

And far too gorgeous for his own good.

This man could have anyone, but right now, he's in my hotel room, staring at me like I'm a worthy centerfold. Of all the women in the world, at this moment, he wants me. I have the power.

My thumb presses on the flat end of the lavender device, checking the charge. Vibrations emanate through my thumb to my wrist, and as the pressure continues, the low hum increases in decibels exponentially.

He tweaks his finger in a slow, come-hither command.

The gravitational pull to those molten eyes is so intense my knees weaken, yet my legs deliver me to him.

He holds his palm out, asking for the vibrator.

Obediently, I place it on his palm. The pads of my finger brush his skin, and in return, every inch of my skin awakens—a live wire.

"This is what you use?"

He holds it up and inspects the simple design. The circumference is about that of a lipstick case, the length slightly longer.

"It's good for travel." Feeling braver, I add, "Minimal embarrassment through TSA."

He smirks.

"Lie down."

My gaze tracks his broad shoulders, down to his pectoral muscles, and lower to his firm abdomen. I itch to run my fingers over every divot and curve, to press against the firm muscle beneath his unblemished skin, to tease the smattering of black hair over his chest and the thickening trail that leads lower.

I crawl back on the bed to assume my prior position, stomach down.

"On your back. If you like, place your head on a pillow."

As if in a trance, I do exactly as he says. I shouldn't. No, I should feign cramps, ask to see him in the morning, tease him along. He's not going to share anything with me tonight.

I captured his phone information and sent it on to Quinn earlier tonight when I went to the ladies' room. They could have everything they need. My mission might be accomplished. Done. Over.

Yet here I am. If my mission is completed, if I'm doing this solely because it's what I want to do, does that make what I'm doing less reproachable? Less wicked?

"Gorgeous." Rhodes' appreciation, in his guttural, deep breath, pools between my legs and I literally feel my clit pulse.

Just touch me.

The mattress dips with his weight, sinking as each balled fist and knee crawls closer. He hovers over me, biceps straining, the hum of the vibrator intense thanks to the proximity to my ear and the physical tremor through the rumpled comforter.

He lowers, consuming the oxygen between us and slowing time. His lips are soft, his tongue's exploration slow, and his thigh, the one between my legs, presses down, hard and firm over my core. My hips instinctually roll against him, seeking pressure my body craves.

His finger softly traces my lips.

"Fuck, you make me want you."

His lips find my neck, my throat, my breast bone, and

finally, my peaked, needy nipple. His tongue swirls and my back arches.

His is a slow seduction, one that makes it clear my ploy worked against me, because he's made this entire episode all about me. Perhaps of the two of us, he's the red sparrow, the seducer, the one using physical prowess to break down walls and infiltrate crevices.

His lips trail lower, to my belly button, and with his hooded eyes, he watches. The press of the vibrator flat against my seam has me rolling my eyes up to the ceiling. The scrap of lace does nothing to blot the cool metal or the tremors.

"Do you like that?"

I force myself to swallow, to nod.

His teeth graze my thigh, and he nips.

"I think you do," he says, altering the position, placing the blunt end right over my center. My knees rise and my thighs squeeze.

"On your side."

I lift my head, uncertain.

He slides his body beside mine.

"Roll against me, gorgeous. Back to me."

I do as he says, and his body wraps around mine, spooning me.

My ass presses to his groin, the motion smooth until he ratchets up the vibrations, playing with the speeds. My thighs clamp together, but with his placement of the vibrator and the heat of his body on my back and over my mound, it's not long before my body trembles with an orgasm, arching into him.

His hot breath on my shoulder, along my neck, in my ear relaxes me into his body.

"Fuck, that was hot."

I agree, but I'm too spent to utter a word, and maybe, just maybe, too embarrassed.

"Only thing better…" His words trail.

He releases the vibrator, which he turned off at some point and cups my breast, thumbing over my nipple in an intimate gesture.

"Is if you had been inside me," I say, finishing his sentence, rolling onto my back and looking up at him.

This close, under the room's golden light, I spot the variations in his irises. A subtle striation of earthy shades, comforting, grounding, and intense. I suspect always intense.

My fingers roam the coarse skin along his jaw, down his throat, and across his firm chest, and along the divots of his abdomen.

He lifts my fingers and presses his lips to the backside, then to my knuckles, and pushes up off the bed.

"What're you doing?" I ask, puzzled. "Don't you want—"

"Tonight is about you." He taps my nose. "Only you, gorgeous."

The door closes to the bathroom and I sit up. Shell-shocked.

A bolt of thunder draws my attention to the balcony. The night sky lights up, eerily illuminating a path across the roofline through the courtyard and silhouetting the flowers swaying in the wind.

Pat. Pat. Pat.

Streaks of rain ping against the glass in a torrent.

The bathroom door opens as a flash of light brightens

the room for a tenth of a second and a loud boom sounds.

"Looks like I'm about to get drenched," Rhodes says with a grin as he reaches for his shirt.

"Where's your room?"

"I'm in a villa. Back of the property."

"Stay." The word slips out thoughtlessly, without strategy or design. "You don't need to run off."

"I won't melt. Trust me." His sexy smirk is only topped by the way his eyes glide over my breasts.

"I've always read that southern thunderstorms are no joke. Don't people die in Florida?"

His smirk breaks into a high wattage grin.

"You want me to stay. To sleep?" His teeth bite down on the corner of his lip and his eyebrows lift.

The rain patters against the glass, blowing sideways onto the panes.

"It can be done. Up to you."

I'm honestly uncertain what I want him to do. Part of me wants him to leave so I can clear my head and process. But a warring faction wants him safe in bed with me...and not to sleep.

RHODES

Getting soaked running to an empty villa holds little appeal. Still, if I were back home in San Francisco, I'd be out the door. Nothing quite says relationship like staying the night and not having sex. But I'm not in San Francisco, I'm on vacation.

She hasn't yet Googled me. It's not possible. She hasn't had time. And we hit it off before she learned my last name. It's rare to meet someone who has zero knowledge of my accomplishments or net worth. It's the reason my circle is suffocatingly small. Sex or not, I could use a friend outside of Silicon Valley.

"Tell you what. I'll stay and keep you safe from the storm, on the condition that tomorrow we hike together."

"Where do you want to hike?"

"The beauty picks."

"Deal."

"I'm going to brush my teeth and..." The domesticity of my statement pummels the confidence in this decision and renders me incapable of completing the sentence. The words ring of my seven years with Sara and I've no desire to repeat mistakes.

I grab my phone, a purely instinctual move, and step into the bathroom.

Behind the closed door, I break open the plastic wrap on the hotel-provided spare toothbrush, and with my other hand, swipe my finger down the glass phone panel to scan the notifications.

DAISY JONAS

Need a little more to go on. 206 Sydney Parkers in the US

Figured. I'll get her more info tomorrow.

EVIE THOMPSON

Heard you're coming to town. Time for drinks?

Interesting.

What does a newly minted assistant attorney in the US Attorney General's office want with me? I've met her a few times. Her father's a client. A good guy. She's in the criminal division if I recall correctly.

I hold the phone up to my mouth and dictate: "I get in Friday. I'm open after four."

I double-check the message and hit send.

One annoying email from Alex about a meeting I declined.

Nothing from Miles. Seems he's still forcing the holiday on me. It's just as well. I'm enjoying my break.

When I finish up in the bathroom, I exit and find Sydney is beneath the comforter. A crack of thunder shakes the room. The rain lashes the glass, but the storm might be lessening. It's been years since I experienced the wrath of a southern quencher. As a kid, I'd sit by the window and watch mesmerized as bolts of lightning lit the darkened sky, and I'd imagine Zeus high above, furious at the wicked minions below who failed to meet his expectations.

"Do you think there's flooding?"

"Probably not here," I answer with authority, although the truth is I'm not an expert on this section of North Carolina. But I did read about the catastrophic flood that happened after Hurricane Helene, and while all of western North Carolina felt the impact, Asheville took a much more significant hit than the Highlands.

"Do you have an extra charger?" I wiggle my phone. If she doesn't, then it's the fates intervening and I'll brave the storm.

"Yeah." The sheet pulls tight over her breasts as she rises to point to her luggage. She's still clad in only her lace thong and that knowledge has far more appeal than it should. "There's a small, zippered bag beside my cosmetics bag. Should have extra chargers."

Open on the luggage rack, zippered bags fill both sides of the open suitcase. Impressive organization.

After plugging my phone into a wall outlet and leaving it silent but charging, I flick off the lamp and head over to the far side of the bed.

"What?" she asks as I pull back the covers, let my slacks fall to the floor, and climb into the plush bed.

"This seems remarkably domestic," I admit.

It's one thing to hook up and crash. It's another to climb into bed beside a gorgeous woman one barely knows and *talk*.

She settles into her pillow, rolling on her side to face me, her expression a mix of knowing and amused.

The cool sheets surround my legs and torso and as my body relaxes into the cocoon, I mimic her position, facing her. With the rain pattering outside and the wind howling, lying here like this with a stranger strikes me as eerily similar to summer camp. Only then, we were in bunks separated by a narrow galley, and I talked to dudes. Now, I'm across from an insanely attractive woman who I'm apparently not going to fuck tonight. Or possibly this week.

"Domestic? Is sleeping over in my bed giving you flashbacks of past relationships?"

She's perceptive.

"And summer camp," I add defensively.

"What?" She laughs and I grin.

Beneath the covers, my leg strays seeking heat. Our legs tangle, removing any similarity to camp.

"Are you scared of storms?"

Minutes have passed since lightning struck, but I can't help but wonder. She invited me to stay, after all.

"No. I moved around a lot, saw all kinds of weather. I've never been scared."

"No fear?"

"Hmm." A low vibration emanates from her throat as she considers. "I'll admit this one is unnerving. I'm not scared, but the way the lightning lights the shadows is eerie. But again, I'm not scared. Tornados frighten me. But not much else."

"Earthquakes?"

"No. But I haven't lived through a big one."

"Why'd you move around a lot?"

"My dad was in the military."

"Is he still?"

"Yes. Coast Guard. Based in Alaska."

The drum of rain becomes the only sound. In the darkness, I can make out her silhouette and sense her gaze.

"Just think…" she says, almost dreamily, "There was a time when a storm like this would inspire theories about what angered Zeus."

"Or Thor, or Indra." Everyone thinks of Zeus and lightning, me included, but there's so much more to the old religions.

"Indra? I've never heard of her."

"Him," I correct. "In the Hindu religion, god of heaven, lightning, rain, storms and thunder."

"Huh. I didn't know that." Her words are soft, and I reach between us to caress her cheek. The muscles in my injured elbow tense, and I lower my arm, resting it against my side. It's the oddest injury, mostly fine, but the wrong movement causes pain.

"As a kid, I studied mythology." It's not something I'm embarrassed about, but at the same time, it feels like a geeky admission, on par with admitting I aced a test that the rest of the class bombed.

"Inspired by Marvel? Thor?"

"Inspired by my grandmother."

"Really? Was she a teacher?"

"Middle school math and science. But she didn't have a lot of children's books, so when I stayed over, she'd tell me stories from mythology."

"Any favorites?"

"Oh, several. Cupid, for one. Mainly because everyone has the Hallmark version in their head, but the story is far more complex."

"Tell me."

"Well, let's see. The way my grandmother tells it, it begins with three daughters, one named Psyche. She was beautiful. Stunning. So beautiful she was deemed a goddess among mortals. But yet her sisters married first and married well. She prayed for a husband, as you know, all women did."

"Of course."

I chuckle at her attitude. Something tells me the woman in bed with me would never pray for a husband. Thinking of her on the hike, she's got what Nana would call an independent streak.

"Anyway, Venus became quite jealous. Her temples were falling into disrepair because the mortals were so taken with Psyche."

"But yet no one married her?"

"No. These stories don't always make sense. Men came from far and wide, but they would fall for other women. Now Cupid was a winged youth who did Venus' bidding. Jealous, Venus instructed Cupid to make the hussy—that's my Nana's word, we can assume Venus chose another—fall in love with the vilest mortal. And he might've done her bidding, except Cupid had fallen under Psyche's spell. All this time, no one proposed to Psyche, which distressed her father."

"Naturally."

"Her father traveled to an oracle of Apollo. The oracle told her father to take her to a distant hill, and leave her, where a god would descend and take her."

"Let me guess. Cupid told the oracle to tell him this."

"Yes. The wind lifted her to a home with servants and riches beyond imagination. She felt her husband but never saw him. And she was happy. Until her sisters came to visit. They were jealous and convinced her that this husband of hers remained hidden because he was a serpent. Afraid they were correct and doubting her love, she brought a lantern at night. When she saw him sleeping, he awoke and said that without trust, there could be no love."

"That's the story of Cupid? That's tragic."

"You didn't let me finish."

A flash of lightning lights the room and for a brief second, I'm entranced by the amusement playing out on her face, the upturn of her full lips, her dark hair tousled over the pillow.

"So what? Does he strike himself with an arrow?"

"There's no need. He's already in love. He's just devastated she didn't trust him."

"So what happens?"

"She goes through a series of trials and tribulations, proving her love and her trust."

"I'm getting the abbreviated version?"

"Her journey involves fleeces of gold and the River Styx. Venus sent Psyche on a quest to find a box—"

"Oh no, not Pandora's box?"

"Not Pandora's, but one she should not open. But she's prideful and believes she deserves to open it, and when she does, she falls into a deep sleep. Venus had locked Cupid away, but while the door was locked, a window was open, which Nana said shows it's impossible to restrain love. Cupid flew out to rescue his wife with a tip of his arrow and by wiping away her sleep."

"That's sweet."

"It gets better. Cupid took Psyche before Jupiter and an assembly of the gods, and Jupiter declared them officially married and he made Psyche immortal. Cupid represents love and Psyche the soul."

"I like that story. After their trials and tribulations, the gods declared love and the soul are forever joined."

"Exactly."

"My favorite mythology tale had been Icarus."

"Flying too close to the sun?"

"Overly confident. Proud." She fingers my chest and I close my eyes, loving the feel, the touch, the intimacy.

"Cupid dethroned Icarus?"

"Yeah, I think so." Her lips press to my shoulder, then against my throat.

And fuck if I don't want her.

I'm the brilliant one agreeing to lie in bed with a woman I can't fuck.

Her palm flattens on my shoulder, pressuring me onto my back. Her lips trail down, the hard edges of nails lightly scraping as they explore, going ever lower. She palms my erection through my briefs.

Jesus.

"You don't have to do this," I grit, wanting her to do exactly *that*. Yes, I spent the time giving her a sensual massage and I did so without expectations. But now...I'm only human.

Her grip tightens and my head tilts back in ecstasy.

I hiss, groan, and hell, all resolve to make tonight all about her dissolves when she pushes my boxers down, releasing me. She takes me with her hand and finally her mouth. She's not tentative. She's observant, watching with rapt attention, learning what I like, and well, I'm a man. I like it all. And she's an expert. As she works me over, taking me deep, I relax into the pillow. Absolute bliss. Her grip. Tongue. Mouth. And to top it all off, when I warn her, my hips surging upwards of their own volition, because I'm that close, she doubles down and my tip hits the back of her throat. She wants my release, and I give it to her in thick, heavy spurts. Fuck.

If this is what solo vacations are like, Miles was right —I'm way overdue.

CHAPTER
ELEVEN

SYDNEY

Harsh sunlight streams through the windows, cutting through the room like an interrogation lamp—merciless and exposing. A deserved intrusion given I failed to close the drapes last night. Failed to maintain the barriers that keep things professional. And the man sleeping in the bed beside me?

Don't think about it.

One tweak of the watch charging on my bedside table and the time glows in bright green numbers. Barely seven in the morning and I'm up. There's no going back to sleep for me. I've trained my psyche to wake with dawn, to push myself hard.

And how's that working out for you?

In bed with the enemy. But is he really the enemy?

If he cut deals to sell lists of assets, then yes, he's the enemy.

But my gut says he wouldn't. He comes across as

genuine and from what I've gleaned from studying him, his heart's in product development—the actual mechanics and coding. It's widely known his system can parse through reams of data and produce useful calculations. But that, in and of itself, is not illegal. The US government is one of his clients. He's vocal in defense of the system he's built and of its varied uses.

When Hudson approached me about joining the team, about leaving the CIA, he shared a closed case file he acquired from an undisclosed source. I read the redacted file. The death rate of US assets across the world increased 45 percent. Any number of theories existed, including the normal leaks and sloppy spycraft. But a source claimed ARGUS had completed closed-door deals with sanctioned countries. Also, ARGUS was listed as a potential source for highly confidential asset and personnel lists. An investigation into ARGUS had been opened and summarily closed. It had all the markings of high-powered connections.

In and of itself, nothing in the redacted file included evidence. However, for the investigation to close so quickly was suspicious. I would've left the CIA to investigate the breach regardless, but Caroline's pitch that KOAN will specialize in investigating those deemed too connected, too powerful to be investigated—well, I couldn't accept the contract offer fast enough.

I need to confirm with Quinn that she gained access to his phone. If I can get to his laptop, that could be gold. If there's a way for Quinn to breach his network through his laptop...we might confirm leading deals or if there are questionable sources of income.

I slip out of bed, careful to let the sleeping genius rest.

As far as male specimens go, he's beautiful. Curled on his side, facing away from the intrusive light, he's a vision. Chocolate-brown strands twist every which way, and a rough scruff emphasizes his masculine jaw.

Rhodes MacMillan is a person of interest. In more ways than one.

I turn on the tap and lift my toothbrush from the water glass. The hotel-provided toothbrush and mini toothpaste lie on the counter, a reminder the man in question stayed the night.

If he weren't on the other side of the door, I'd call Caroline. She's the one friend I can count on to justify anything. Working in the field had never been an option for her as she'd been in the news too much for marrying and divorcing President Moore's nephew. What started as me sharing tells of dreary, boring days slowly building relationships with possible assets, evolved into mini-therapy sessions, with her justifying my lies. Every friendship I slowly built for clandestine purposes, she reminded me the friendship was real, even if it had a purpose.

When I told her I was leaving the CIA, she flew into D.C. to take me out to celebrate. What would she say about this? I could use one of her therapy-like sessions to help me hash through what I'm doing, what I've done.

The reality is, male officers wouldn't think twice. Hell, in some countries, seduction is expected of intelligence officers. When I ran my hiking interception idea by Hudson, he expected I'd flirt. He didn't expect I'd make headway by becoming a platonic friend.

I spit in the sink and splash some water on my face.

What we did last night? It was fun.

A tremor climbs my spine as I relive his groan, the weight of his hand on the back of my head, the pulsing in my mouth. His hazed expression. The glorious knowledge that I left him dazed.

I didn't have to do what I did. But I wanted to. I let myself enjoy the moment and we both had fun.

When I open the bathroom door, he's still in bed, the shades partially drawn, and he's reading his phone. He's been up and about.

What's he reading?

Has he requested a background report on me yet? It's only a matter of time now that I've shared my name.

I've shared as much of the truth as possible with him. His surveillance capabilities are second to none. A fake identity was never an option when approaching Rhodes. The chances of his system identifying red flags are too great.

He lowers his phone, and his countenance darkens. The energy between us? Last night served to intensify the reaction. His wolf-like hunger reminds me I'm in only a thong. Theoretically, there should be a tampon string tucked in the scrap of cotton, but of course, there's not.

My nipples harden, either from his heated gaze or from the cool breeze wafting from the overhead fan he must've turned on.

"You're getting back in bed, right?"

I grin. "I can't fall back asleep."

"Did I say anything about sleep?"

I stride for my suitcase and unzip the compartment holding tops.

"I thought we were going hiking today?"

"Do you have any idea how gorgeous you are?"

My hair slides over my shoulder as I glance back at him, smiling. "I need a shower."

"I can join you."

I narrow my eyes, tempted but...

He groans, shaking his head. "Fine. If I stay here, I'll beg and that's not attractive."

With an audible groan, he moves off the mattress, scoots by me with a slight caress of my ass, and the bathroom door shuts.

I pull on a T-shirt that hits at my hips and stare at the closed door.

Should I confess to my lie and haul him into bed? Say, screw the hike and screw him?

No. Go on the hike. Get to know him. Get the job done.

You're a professional. Score access. Allow the team to breach his systems. Withdraw.

The door swings open and in four long strides he reaches me, tilts my head back, and places his lips over mine. A profusion of mint fills my mouth. Strong hands grip my bottom and haul me against him.

My arms lift over his shoulders and I rock against his hard, lean body, loving the pressure against my core and the heat rolling off his hard chest.

He breaks the kiss, brushes his thumb over my lips, slaps my ass, and says, "I'm going to shower. Meet in thirty? We'll grab breakfast and head out?"

The beats of my heart reverberate through my breastbone. It's like I've run a marathon, but I've only kissed the man. The novel reaction to a kiss is one I've got to wrap my head around, because the strength of the physical reaction goes beyond lust. Adrenaline? The thrill of an op?

He's at the door when it occurs to him I haven't responded.

"Syd? Is that okay?"

I nod, and he's gone.

Syd? How is he already shortening my name?

The silence that follows his departure feels heavy, loaded with everything I'm not letting myself think about.

I sink onto the bed, stunned by my reaction to his kiss. This isn't good.

I should call Quinn. Check in. Do my job.

But my hands shake slightly as I reach for the work phone Hudson gave me. When was the last time a target affected me like this? I've cared for targets before, but intimacy? Never.

The phone feels foreign in my hands, heavier than it should. I stare at Quinn's contact information, thumb hovering over the call button. Once I make this call, I'm back in mission mode. Back to thinking of Rhodes as a target instead of...whatever he's becoming. Dozens of assets died last year in addition to mine. Professional distance is a luxury I can't afford. I dial Quinn's number and set the phone to speaker, busying myself with digging through my suitcase to pick an outfit for the day. Multitasking maintains the illusion that this is just another check-in call.

"Sydney?"

"Hey Quinn. Checking in."

"How'd last night go?"

"Good."

A male voice says, "How good?"

"Am I on speaker?" *What the fuck?* "Can you take me off?"

"Ignore him." Static crosses the line, along with footfalls and a loud click that I assume is a door closing.

"Who was that?"

"A juvenile jerk. Backup Hudson called in should you need it. Are you stopping by the house today?"

"No. And I've got to jump. I'm meeting him for breakfast in thirty."

"Awesome. I won fifty bucks."

"What?"

"Oh. When I was bringing Jake–your backup–up to speed, he bet me you'd spend last night with him. I bet you wouldn't. I win."

"Noooo," a muffled deep voice groans.

Grand. Quinn bet I wouldn't do what I did. Whatever. Juvenile is a good word for any bet.

"It doesn't matter. Look, I need you to do me a favor. Tell Hudson to hold my paycheck."

My first payment should hit my account on Friday.

"What?"

"I told Rhodes I'm between jobs. It's too likely he'll see a deposit to my account or payroll tax or something will be picked up on his systems."

"Yeah, I guess," Quinn says. "It's not hard to verify employment and salary. Are you not going with the cover I created?"

"It's not that I don't believe you're good, but his systems—"

"You told him the truth? Right down the line?"

"Yep."

"These are things we should all be in agreement on. To back you up, this is need-to-know." There's clear annoyance in her tone, and she's right to be annoyed.

"I know, I know. I adapted on the fly."

"I'll run a check to see if anyone's pulled a background check. Will be good to know if he's curious about you."

"If he's using his system, he likely won't need to resort—"

"Yep. What else you got?"

"He's leaving for D.C. Friday. Any news from San Francisco?" I pointedly don't mention the KOAN operative's name. If there's no reason to mention a name, then it shouldn't be mentioned.

"She's scheduled for HR orientation on Friday."

"Orientation for consultants?"

"Yep. It's a process. Welcome to corporate America."

"Did you access the phone?"

"Yes, but as you'd expect, it's clean. His history is wiped. My bet is he runs a program that uploads anything of value to a cloud and clears the hard drive on his phone daily. There are some things we should be able to get from his phone number, but he's savvy."

"Well, he would be. He built a surveillance system based on access to all the information you were hoping to scrape."

"I'll keep at it, but you do the same. This guy has his backside covered from all tech angles. You might be right."

"How's that?"

"The best way to infiltrate him is the old-fashioned way."

Inside, I grimace and will away the shame. People died. We need to find the leak.

"Are we good here?" I really do need to hop.

"What's your game plan? Do you need backup today?"

"He's not dangerous." I don't need muscle sitting in a parking lot. "I'll spend the day with him. See what that gets me. He believes I'm unemployed. Maybe I'll angle to get brought along to D.C."

"You could say you were planning on going. I saw his itinerary on his calendar app. He has a couple of events he might need a date for."

"He rarely brings dates. Or at least, he's not photographed with dates. Did you find something else?"

"No. If he has a date already planned, he didn't notate it in his calendar."

"Or his assistant didn't. Okay. I gotta jump. I'll be in touch."

"And to repeat, no backup?"

"Clear it with Hudson, but in my opinion it's an unnecessary risk. What if Rhodes spots someone watching?"

"I'll cover with Hudson. Do you know where you're going?"

"Nope."

"If you can, message me plans. Either way, I'll track you."

"Thanks Quinn."

"And Sydney?"

"Yeah?"

"Trust your instincts."

Taking her advice to heart, I call Caroline. She

answers on the second ring, instantly alert despite the early hour. "Syd? What's wrong?"

No grogginess, no confusion even though she's in an earlier time zone.

"I'm—how did you know something was wrong?"

"Because you only call me at dawn when you're spiraling. Remember Jakarta? Paris?" A door clicks in the background. "Give me a second. Go back to sleep." I hear muffled conversation, then her clear voice returns. "Okay, talk to me. Is this about Rhodes?"

"How do you—"

"Because I've seen this pattern before. You get an assignment, you execute flawlessly, then you call me in a panic because you're unnerved. Second-guessing yourself."

I don't panic.

"What happened, Syd?"

With her softer tone, I sink onto the edge of the bed, the words catching in my throat. "I think I'm making the same mistake I made in Paris. Getting too invested."

"Paris was different. You were blindsided. This is about—what? You like him?"

"It's not that simple."

I stand and pace past the window. "The intelligence says one thing...but when I'm with him..."

"You don't believe he's capable of it."

"Exactly. And that scares me, Caroline. What if we're wrong?"

Silence stretches across the line.

"Do you remember what I told you about Dorian?" Dorian—President Moore's nephew. Caroline reunited with him after years apart. Their split splashed across every tabloid.

"You said powerful men are expert manipulators."

"I said some of them are. But I also said the truly dangerous ones are the ones who make you forget they're powerful at all." Her voice drops. "Dorian's father never let me forget his connections, his family name. He wielded it like a weapon. But Dorian, he wasn't always like that. He'd talk to me for hours about books and travel, never once mentioning his degrees or pedigree. He made me feel like the only person in the room."

"Yet you left him."

"And eventually we reunited. Dorian is a good person, but he almost followed in his father's path. If I'm honest with myself, both sides still exist in him, we're just better at working through our differences. And he's more like the man I first met." She pauses. "The point is, Sydney, your instincts about people have kept you alive. If something feels off about the intelligence, maybe it is. But it's also possible there's more to him than he's let you see so far."

My chest tightens. "What if my desire for him to be innocent—"

"Then you're human. And empathetic intelligence officers are the ones who build the most fruitful connections." Another pause. "Syd, you've always cared about a target's well-being. That's what makes you good at your job."

The truth resonates and I knead the discomfort beneath my breastbone.

"I think I'm in trouble, Caroline."

"Good trouble or bad trouble?" I catch sight of the

hotel toothbrush on the bathroom counter, evidence of a night with more intimacy than I've experienced in years.

"I honestly don't know."

"Then figure it out. Explore. But don't you dare apologize for feeling something genuine. For caring. And Syd?"

"Yeah?"

"If your gut says he's innocent, maybe start asking who benefits from him looking guilty."

CHAPTER
TWELVE

SYDNEY

What's your room number?

The winding path weaves between a manicured lawn and beautifully landscaped flower beds juxtaposed against stone and wood villas. He planned for us to meet in the lobby, but I'd like to get a look inside his space. I expect I'll only see his suitcase, but there could be something useful. Notes left out on a table, a name jotted down on a notepad, anything.

A door up ahead cracks and Rhodes steps out, a backpack strap slung over one shoulder. He's in hiking boots that rise above his ankles, navy twill shorts and a Foo Fighters T-shirt. The sleeves from a plaid flannel shirt wrap around his waist, turning him into a replica of almost any frat boy from my college years.

"I'm hearing after last night's rain it's going to be muddy. How's your ankle?"

"It's fine. I hit my knee hard, but it's good today."

The door locks behind him, and I keep my face neutral to mask any disappointment.

"You sure?"

I hop on my toes, letting him see I'm good to go.

Yesterday's scraped knee was the real deal, but the limping qualified as an acting job. I could've kept it up through the evening, but then I'd risk not being invited along for whatever activity he planned.

"Great. There's a place down the street where we can get breakfast to go. I hope you don't mind, but I'm told we'll have the best chance of avoiding crowds if we hit the trail early, so I figure we can eat on the way."

"Works for me."

In the car, conversation covers the trail options, the waterfalls in the area, and how if it wasn't for his elbow injury, he'd be climbing mountains.

"Did your father teach you to climb?"

"No. He's a golfer. Taught me the sport that could help me succeed in business."

"Are you close?"

"No."

The straight line of his lips and the flex of his jaw tell me I've stumbled on a sore subject that won't get me anywhere anyway, but before I can redirect, he asks, "What about you? Where are your parents?"

"Alaska." The lie slips out, as it's one I've told often through the years.

"Get to see them often?"

"No." At least that answer is the truth. "Do you still golf?"

"Rarely. If I'm away from the office, I prefer something more challenging."

"Challenging like what?"

"Climbing. A full body workout. Hell, I'd take racketball over golf."

"You must hate that we have to go hiking."

He grins. "You'd think. But truth is, I'm perfectly happy spending the day with you. Hiking. It might be because I haven't slept as well as I did last night...well, not in a long time." He pointedly looks away from the road and at me. "I think I have you to thank for that."

My face warms and I place my attention on the window and the passing forest.

His hand falls to my knee and he squeezes gently.

"I hope this trail's good. It got good reviews." And just like that, he transitions the conversation back to trails. For the short drive to our destination, we alternate between listening to music and commenting on houses tucked away down gravel roads along the winding road.

Glen Falls Trail, the one Rhodes picked, is a popular one, and although it's still early in the morning, the gravel parking lot at the base holds quite a few vehicles.

"Let's hope the trail isn't crowded," Rhodes mumbles as he locks his SUV.

I check my phone and slip it into the small backpack I'm carrying that also holds a bottle of water, sunscreen, all-natural bug spray, and Neosporin. He's got a full-sized backpack that's stretched with contents, and I'm curious what he felt he'd need on a five-mile hike, but I'll ask later, when we're on the hike and I'm struggling for conversation.

Although, the awkward silences I typically experience

on dates have been absent with Rhodes. Conversation flows easily, but maybe that's because I'm not trying to second-guess myself at every turn or questioning if I'm wasting my time.

That's the therapist you hired way back when speaking. There's no place for her here.

"There are a couple of less traveled offshoots I found. We can explore those if you're game."

"Lead the way." That's what I say, but as we approach the mouth of the trail, it's clear we can walk side by side.

He slaps at his neck.

"Did you use bug spray?"

He presses his lips together and shakes his head. "It'll be fine."

"I thought you're from here." I sling my bag around and whip out my spray. "Arms out."

He grins. "Nana would like you."

"Why? Because I'm preventing you from getting some mosquito-borne disease?"

"Yeah. Something like that."

I spray Rhodes down, attempting to not fixate on the pull of his T-shirt across his muscular chest or his rounded buttocks and thick quads when he turns, allowing me to spray his back.

My skin tingles—an annoying reaction. The attraction refuses to dim, simmering at all times, thanks to us opening Pandora's box last night. Instead of lifting the top off, we peeked inside without unveiling the full mystery.

At the mouth, the trail is wide enough for a car, but up ahead through the trees, the trail narrows. The tree limbs, heavy with last night's rain, create a dripping canopy of green overhead. The boulders shoved haphazardly to the side, damp with moisture, evoke the feeling of entering nature's freshly washed kingdom. The air smells of wet earth and pine needles. A chorus of birds chattering reminds me of something I read about how the health of a forest can be determined by the noise level. The notion of a quiet forest, conjured in horror stories, actually portends a dystopian future where we've killed off the birds and owls.

"You know, I know we agreed to not mention work…"

I side-eye him. His hands grip his backpack straps and he's removed his sunglasses. The Johnny Fly frames dangle from his tee. We're both wearing baseball caps at my insistence, because from what I've read the ticks are no joke in this area of the country.

"Your rule. Not mine. I'd love to hear what you do when you're not on vacation."

"Does that mean you didn't Google me?"

"When would I have? You were with me all last night."

I play into the deception with a casual smile, keeping pace with his long strides. But, truly, I'd lie about Googling any guy I was out with. And I shouldn't have to lie. This day and age, online sleuthing should be assumed.

"True."

His gaze remains locked up ahead, never looking my way, and it clicks.

"You Googled me."

"Something like that," he admits, a touch sheepish.

I know damn well he didn't Google me. He probably used his vast AI surveillance network. He might know my credit card balances and my net worth, an unimpressive number to someone like him, I'm sure.

"What'd you learn?"

"The internet isn't without flaws. I could've been learning about a different Sydney Parker."

"Penn?" I ask, studying him for his reaction. "Fencing?"

The slight nod says it all.

"So you got the right one."

"Why'd you leave the CIA?"

Yes, he did a deep dive.

"Asshole boss," I blurt. *Honesty for the win.*

"You couldn't get transferred to a different group?"

"The easy answer is not easily. If I shared with you the details, I'd have to kill you."

He chuckles, and I grin.

The trail narrows and at his insistence I take the lead.

"A southern gentleman," I quip.

"I like the view," he says, his gravelly tone increasing the lust quotient a notch. "I was asking because I know what it's like to have uncertainty about your future. You said you're between jobs. If you send me your resume, with my connections, I might be able to, you know... I mean, no guarantee. But half of job hunting is connections, right?"

Is he thinking he might hire me? Does ARGUS hire ex-CIA?

The incline increases the deeper into the trail we go, and rocks protrude through the earth, requiring a focus on foot placement. Our boots squelch through patches of red clay mud, and I have to grip exposed tree roots for balance on the steeper sections. Fallen leaves, darkened and slick from the storm, create a treacherous carpet that shifts underfoot. One wrong step and I risk stumbling backwards into Rhodes.

Somewhere below us, I can hear the rush of swollen streams rushing toward the falls. The storm has turned every trickle into a torrent, and the sound of moving water grows louder as we climb higher. Puddles mirror the sky through breaks in the canopy, and everything feels alive with the energy of the night's deluge.

Up ahead, past the twist, it opens, and a woman comes into view. There's a boulder to the side, and she's leaning against it, probably waiting for us so she can continue down.

When we reach the landing, we see she's not alone.

Her companion says, "It's a nice hike. The falls are gorgeous."

"Thought they'd be worth the visit after last night's storm," Rhodes answers. "Are a lot of hikers out?"

"We didn't come across many, but we struck out early. Today's going to be a hot one. At least until the thunderstorms this afternoon."

"Right," Rhodes says.

These women are maybe fifteen years older than him and completely unaware of who he is, yet they're drawn to him. It's like I don't exist and he leads the conversation with ease.

The landing area is tight for four, and the two women continue down the trail, ending their rest and ceding us the space with gracious goodbyes.

"Want water?" Rhodes asks.

He's already unzipping that full pack of his and pulling out a water bottle.

I lean against the boulder, stretching out my legs. "I'm good."

He chugs his water and swipes his mouth with the back of his hand.

"When you said that half of job hunting is connections, is that how your company hires? Mainly from connections?" I ask, wanting to get back to opening his company into approved conversational topics.

"I'm not heavily involved in hiring." He glances sideways at me. "But yeah, some of that. My partners went to business school with me."

"Business school? Which one?"

"Harvard." He shrugs. "Don't get too impressed. I dropped out."

He lowers his chin, avoiding my gaze. He's actually embarrassed.

"I mean, it all worked out for me. But it was a huge gamble. One my father will never forgive me for. You don't walk away from Harvard. At least, that's what dear old dad said."

"How many years' tuition did he pay?"

"Oh, it wasn't about the money. And I paid him back. It was his friends. Having to tell his friends his son dropped out, after he'd bragged... He's old school conservative."

"Ah," I say. "He lit into you?" I haven't picked up on any of this in my research, but I noticed there was essentially no mention of his parents in any article, and his maternal grandmother is the only family member I picked up on who followed his ex-girlfriend's socials. But all that could mean is that Nana was the only family member who got along with his ex. Or the only one who uses social media.

"It was the most classic conservative male bashing imaginable." He crosses his arms over his chest and rears back, exaggerating his mouth movements. "You drop out, you are on your own. Don't come here groveling if you need something. No, sir. A Harvard MBA is gold. You leave that young man...it's a colossal mistake. We will have no part in digging your grave. I don't care if you find yourself homeless. I won't give you a dollar."

"Wow." *I bet his father ate crow.* "And now?"

"He's still an asshole."

I laugh and he sort of grins.

"He can't still be upset? How many years ago was that?"

"Is that an age jab?"

He gestures for us to continue on our hike, and I step forward, leaving the open area and leading us onto the narrow path.

I'm not supposed to know that he's hailed as a wunderkind, or that he went to Harvard straight out of undergrad. But I do know all of that and it's impossible to conceive a parent taking issue with his choices.

"You're taking a long time to respond. Are you mocking my age?"

He pinches my ass, and I squeal, swiping his hand away. "No, it's just, college feels like a long time ago."

"Well, almost ten years for you. A decade is a long time ago."

Wait, did I tell him my age? Yes, I did. At dinner, we shared ages.

"It was a long time ago for me too," Rhodes concedes.

"For any other father, the disagreement would be settled history. But my actions injured Dad's pride." I sense there's more to be said, but he's swallowing it down. "But yeah, those were some tough years. Lots of self-doubt. And I leaned on connections. Not for a handout, but for investments. I mean, truthfully, the connections helped. But...I didn't need the diploma."

"So, what do you do now?"

"I own a company."

That's an understatement. "And how's it doing?"

"Let's just say I'll never be homeless and Dad will never get the great pleasure of denying me a place to stay and sending me to the streets."

"I'd think saying he's proud would be a bigger pleasure."

"You'd think that." He clears his throat but maintains his pace. "Anyway, I don't normally share any of that. But the point I was trying to make is that I understand what it's like to be uncertain about the future. And I also understand the value of connections. If I can help, let me know."

"You never said what your company is, what it does."

"It's a software company that deploys data integration and analysis platforms. In a nutshell, it processes information into useful formats."

That's a highly simplified take on ARGUS.

"You started that company straight out of Harvard?"

"No. I started a boring backend systems company. Sold it. Took that money, started another one."

"Must be nice to start a company without any financial pressures. I mean, I'm assuming you did well when you sold your first company."

"We did well. But there are always financial pressures."

"Oh?"

"Yeah. Just ask my CFO. And, by the way, I'm not saying that you'd be a fit for my company, but I am connected. If you have a target list, I might know someone."

"Six degrees and all that?"

"Exactly."

We reach a steep incline, one that will require me to haul myself up a boulder or take a longer loop around the protrusion. When I stop, taking in the options, he's right there, and we're inches apart. He looks down at me, and there's that pull, drawing me in.

"You know, for what it's worth, your father was wrong. He should've supported you. Believed in you."

"Yeah?"

"Yeah. I mean, you didn't make a mistake, but even if you had, if you love someone, you rally behind them, you don't…"

I don't have the words, I'm so frustrated that his father would do anything other than support his incredibly gifted son.

He cups my chin, tilting my head, and his thumb strokes my cheek. His eyes in this light are shades darker than the foliage, his gaze intense.

And then we're kissing. Heat seeps down my spine and pools in the cradle of my hips. His skin is hot to the touch. My palm glides along rippling muscle, smooth and toned. His breath coats my neck, simultaneously cooling and heating my skin, and it feels like he's holding me close, but straining to control himself. And I feel the same. I want him.

It's a problematic reaction. Because everything I'm feeling, all the desire, none of it's manufactured. Everything I'm feeling is 100 percent real. In training, we learned about the Mata Hari complex that occurs when sexual relations mix with undercover roles, and I didn't think I'd be susceptible. But I recognize what's happening, and that's the first step in preventing emotional entanglements, so I'm ahead of the game. I didn't think of the Mata Hari complex when I was on the phone with Caroline this morning, but I should've.

He breaks the kiss and brushes his thumb over my bottom lip. Then lifts my hand and presses his lips to the back of it, entangles our fingers, and leads the way.

I like sex. Hell, I love great sex, as elusive as it is. That's why I'm doing this. We're having fun. As long as I remember my training, I'll be fine. I can do this. And when the week comes to an end, he'll go his way, I'll go mine, and I'll be a woman he met on vacation, and he'll be a man I got to know on a personal level, for professional reasons.

The most successful operatives are as true to themselves as possible. That's what Caroline meant. This week, I'll be true to myself, and Rhodes and I will both enjoy this vacation. I'll go down as a memory, and he'll never know I'm part of the team infiltrating his private company.

Infiltrating his company. I can't think like that. So I brush that thought away, and instead focus on his hand holding mine, the swoony sensation when he kissed the back of my hand, and the mix of leaves, grass, and dirt beneath my feet.

CHAPTER
THIRTEEN

RHODES

The hiking guide rated the Glen Falls Hike a medium difficulty level, but it's a joke. It's the sort of frustration that under normal circumstances would have festered into a foul mood, given I prefer rock climbing. I like to push myself, sweat, and strain, not go for a leisurely stroll.

But yet, my mood's fantastic. I don't remember the last time I felt this light, just fucking happy. Maybe the last time I chewed some of Miles' gummies.

The air smells green—that mix of fresh leaves, soil, and the slight tang of pine sap that gets sharper in the heat. "It's around here," I say, directing Syd to the real reason I chose Glen Falls. I hope it pans out. It's been over twenty years since I've been here, and we didn't take this route.

"Why isn't this on the trail map?"

"Well, we've crossed onto private land."

"What?" She squeaks the question in a higher octave, clearly not okay with trespassing.

"Based on the aerial footage, we should now be on private land."

"You saw this trail from a satellite image?" She stops, mouth slightly agape, quizzical.

"I zoomed in." It's actually… Anyone can do that. "And I checked with a buddy."

"That's right. You're from here."

"Well, Charlotte. But an old classmate grew up nearby."

"Does he still live here?"

"Nope. But he has family in the area."

"So they know we're out here today?"

"Eh, no. Probably not. He told me no one ever comes out here. This piece eventually butts up to a pasture, but he said no one ever really goes in the woods."

"Have you ever been here before?"

"Long time ago."

The place we're headed is about a mile off the public trail. The sounds shift as we move deeper into the woods —distant chattering voices from the main trail fade away, replaced by the persistent chirp of cicadas and the soft crunch of leaves underfoot. It's the kind of quiet that makes your ears search for sound. Still an easy grade hike, not as well maintained, but something has kept the center of the trail downtrodden—probably goats.

This could be a colossal waste of time, but it's fun to take the less traveled trail. I've needed to use the compass on my watch and when the fuck do I get a chance to do that?

The trail loosely follows a gurgling stream, almost a ditch. Up ahead, the trees break open and the blue sky glimmers. My pulse quickens.

"Is that..." She slows her steps and I almost slam into her back. "A swimming pool?"

"Well, in the south, we call it a swimming hole. All natural. I came in high school. That old classmate? His grandparents owned the land. Now it's like an uncle or a cousin or some other family member who owns it."

The stream feeds into what's basically a dug out deep quarry. If memory serves, maybe twenty feet deep. Boulders surround the perimeter. The acoustics change in the clearing—the water hits the rocks with hollow plunks that echo slightly against the surrounding stone walls. Birds call to each other overhead, their songs weaving through the trees.

There used to be a rope from a tree. We swung across like Tarzan, cannonballing into the water. I scan the trees but don't see a rope. Even if it was here, I wouldn't trust it to hold. That was a long damn time ago.

I reach out and tug on her ponytail, give her a quick kiss because I can't seem to stop kissing her, and wiggle my eyebrows.

"Up for a swim?"

Given it's her time of the month, I doubt it. Besides, while the water should be clean, it's not chlorinated. No one's checking the levels or clearing the tall grass that surrounds the embankment.

Sydney traipses right up to the edge, hands on her hips, looking into the depths.

While she explores, I'm assailed with memories of my friends and I sailing into the freezing water and yelling like maniacs. Those were simpler times. I mean, there were pressures. We attended a challenging Charlotte private school and the adults in our lives placed heavy expectations on us. We also expected great things from ourselves. My friends and I, we were the twenty-first century version of great expectations.

"How deep is it?"

Sydney's question draws my attention to the present, and I rapidly blink, processing.

She's naked. Breasts bare.

Saliva pools in my mouth.

The only thing she's wearing is a thong. Or no, is she wearing anything?

She's standing on the boulder in the spot where we used to snatch the rope from a nearby tree limb.

"Can I jump?"

"Feet first." It's an automated response, drilled into me in my youth.

And she jumps.

Toes pointed, lean legs straight, arms held out like she's reaching for the sun, an uninhibited, free spirit. I've never seen anything sexier in my life.

The whoosh of her body cutting through air followed by the crisp splash echoes around the quarry walls. For a moment after she disappears, there's perfect silence before the displaced water settles back with gentle lapping sounds against the rocks.

I charge forward, dropping my backpack to the ground.

How the fuck did I not see her getting undressed?

She bobs up, squealing, her youthful grin so wide her teeth gleam.

"Fuck, it's cold!" she screeches.

"Not as bad as California," I challenge. Hell, I wear a wetsuit in the Pacific.

She splashes the water with her palm. "Are you coming?"

I'm hopping on one leg, struggling with the laces. I can't strip fast enough.

"Stay in!" I shout.

I don't want to miss this.

I finally get everything off, leaving the clothes in a pile and charge forward, leap into the air, knees high, and cannonball into the water, splashing water from the center to the edge.

The chill burns and I tilt my head up, propelling upwards. When I reach the surface, I swipe at my face, clearing water from my eyes in time to see her bare bum scrambling up the rock.

Holy fuck. I'm going to fall in love with this one.

The thought comes out of nowhere, but it buries itself in my bones, in my core, in my soul.

She stands on the boulder. Her toned body is sensational and judging from the way she stands there proudly, high above, she knows it.

I wish I had my waterproof camera because I want these photographs forever. But there's no need. Sydney beaming at the top of the boulder, naked, and radiant, imprints in my mind.

And then she jumps with a yell that sends a few birds flapping through the branches.

Once again, the water claims her as ripples speed to the edge. I search the water, seeing her dark shape, my legs kick, churning the water, keeping me upright.

Where is she?

And she's up, right in front of me, grinning, as free and happy as I felt decades ago.

Our laughter floats around us, shaving years, placing me back in time, or no, it's nothing that sci-fi. I'm still a forty-one-year-old workaholic without a life. But at this moment, my younger self has emerged. He didn't die. I just buried him during my quest.

My arms loop around her and I pull her to me. The contrast of her warm body against my chest and the cold water swirling around our lower halves creates a disorienting sensation. Her skin is silky smooth against mine but covered in goosebumps that I can feel under my fingertips. The water creates a buoyancy that makes her feel almost weightless in my arms. She extends one arm, sending a spray of water as I spin her around.

"You do it," she says, breathless.

"What?" Her perky nipples press into me and, yes, there are things I would definitely like to do.

"Jump," she urges.

I laugh, stretching towards the edge. I scramble up the boulder, slightly aware of my semi-stiff dick flapping about, but if she can be free with her body, so can I.

I reach the top and mimic her, arms to the sun, and leap.

This time when I kick up for air, she swims into my arms.

"Wasn't that fun?"

"Yeah," I agree, shaking the water from my hair like a dog.

"This is awesome!"

I love her enthusiasm.

"So, there are no snakes in North Carolina?"

I laugh.

"Wait." I hear the caution in that single word. "There aren't snakes—"

"Any snakes in here skedaddled after we jumped in."

She stills and curls into my body. I'll admit her clinging to me is nice, but her smile is gone.

"What kind of snakes?" She scans the edge like she expects to see one sunbathing on a rock.

"All kinds."

"Venomous?"

"Some. Water moccasins. Copperheads, but I don't know that they swim. I didn't really—"

She pushes out of my arms, leaping through the water like there's flames over an oil slick.

"It's safe," I call after her.

Her head is shaking and I follow; a grin plastered on my face.

The earthy smell of the bank intensifies as we climb out—damp soil and crushed grass under our feet. I catch her on a grassy spot and I sink my teeth playfully into her shoulder. She squirms against me, wet and smooth.

"I've got towels," I say, refusing to let her go as I pull her writhing, naked body to my backpack.

"You planned for this," she says, eyes wide, figuring it out. "And you didn't tell me to bring a suit."

"In my defense, I didn't expect you'd actually swim. I thought I'd lay these out so we could rest by the water."

Sara would've refused to sit on the grass without a towel below us, but I bite that reflection back. I'm not always smooth, but I'm never a total dumbass.

The sun beats down on the patch of weeds before the

water, and I spread one oversized towel out on the area, then take the other and wrap it around Sydney. Heat radiates from the ground, warming my feet through to my ankles. The rough texture of the towel against my water-softened skin feels almost abrasive at first. Small pebbles press into the soles of my feet, grounding me in the moment. Droplets pool on my shoulder and she smooths her thumb over one, then sucks the water off her thumb. A guttural groan releases as my blood gushes to my groin.

The transition from water to air makes every nerve ending heightened. The warm breeze raises goosebumps as it dries the water on my skin, creating a delicious contrast between the lingering chill from the swim and the heat of the sun above us.

"I have a confession." She peeks up at me through dark lashes, her dark hair dripping water into the towel.

Jesus fuck, she's a wet dream.

My gaze focuses on her full, pale pink lips.

"What's that?" A low thrum pulses in my ears. My mouth dries. The tips of my fingers tingle with the need to touch her, to take her.

There are so many things I want to do to this woman.

"I'm not really..." She tilts her head, bashful. "It's not my time of the month."

My throat tightens.

"I lied to prevent doing something I'd regret."

Which is why she jumped bare naked. I didn't even think to look for a tampon string. I actually didn't think at all.

Perhaps that's a warning.

She wiggles in my hold, and the towel drops to her ankles.

"And now?" I choke out.

I swear I can barely fucking breathe.

"I regret lying."

CHAPTER
FOURTEEN

RHODES

"I regret lying."

The contradiction between the meaning of the words and her lust-filled gaze short-circuits my thought processes, but the smaller brain overrides, computing the most important fact.

"Now you want to have sex?"

She steps forward, one arm over my shoulder, her fingers on my nape, pulling me to her. For one brief second, I question if this is what I want, if it's the right time, if this will be another slippery slope with me falling hard and fast into a tar pit of boredom, but I push the uncertainty aside. I want her.

I wanted her last night at dinner. Last night in bed. And I especially want her now.

Her naked body presses against my cool, damp skin. Sensations overwhelm my senses. The roll of her tongue. Minty taste. Soft curves. Slick hair.

A sharp thorn pierces the side of my foot, and on instinct I lift her as I stumble, hopping to the stretched towel. Her chin presses into my shoulder.

When I'm on safe footing, I slow, lost in the dark pools of her eyes, the pupil somehow overtaking the iris. Her feet slowly drop to the ground, her thighs gliding down mine, but my hands remain on the globes of her ass, holding her close.

"You okay?' she asks.

There's a tease in the question, like she's stifling laughter.

My foot stings, but that's immaterial.

I tilt her head and resume our kiss. My erection, incredibly firm given where I just swam, presses into her abdomen.

Does she mind? Should I adjust?

"What was that?" Sydney presses against me, her body completely aligned to mine, and scans the woods.

"I heard nothing."

"It sounded like…I don't know…a limb falling."

"Might've been. Or a deer. You don't need to worry. No one's going to stumble on us out here."

She raises her gaze skyward. Blue sky intertwines with leafy limbs.

"Or see us on satellite?"

Her paranoid question shows she has no detailed understanding of satellites' capabilities, and I could enlighten her, but I settle for a simple, "No." Her soft breasts press against my chest and I create space between us, cupping her breast, tweaking her nipple. "You're perfect, you know that?"

I don't give her time to answer, instead lowering to

take her nipple in my mouth, to twirl my tongue over her sweet peak.

Her knees bend and I follow until we're both sprawled on the towel. I continue my exploration, feeling more free than I did last night, as I don't need to hold back. She wants this.

"I've never…" I slow, my mouth over her navel, my fingers caressing the smooth curve of her hip, and my gaze raises, waiting for her to finish, wondering where she's going with that. "Outside."

"A first for everything." My fingers reach her apex and her thighs spread open, ever so slightly. She's bare, completely void of hair, smooth to the touch. "You wax."

"Started on the swim team. Never stopped."

My finger glides slowly over her center. Hot. Wet.

Her knees rise with my touch.

"I've tried to let it grow out, but it bothers me and I end up waxing again. I might get it lasered, so I never have to deal with it. It's been on my to-do list. I just haven't done it."

I register the increasing frequency of her words, but my focus and intent aren't on what she's saying. I lower my head and lick slowly up her center.

She gasps.

"A friend used to say every woman needs a landing strip. I don't—"

My mouth lowers over her as I press a finger into her heat. As a second finger plunders, I lift and utter a, "Shh".

Her eyelids flutter closed. She's lifted on her elbows, and as her head tilts back, she transforms into a summer goddess, and I resume worshipping her. I love her taste, her silky touch, her little noises and the tightening and loosening of her muscles, and when her fingers press into my scalp, directing me, it's fucking perfection. Her thighs press to my ears as her body tightens, culminating in a rewarding orgasm.

She relaxes back onto the towel and I press kisses to her thighs and dry my fingers on the edge of the towel.

She's fucking gorgeous spread out in the speckled sunlight. There are no sun lines, yet her skin glows with a slight tan, her natural skin tone. She has the body of an athlete, limbs lean and toned.

I trail kisses up her body and she lifts her head, a slight smile playing across those luscious lips. When I reach those lips, I press mine to them. But the kiss I claim is quick. She presses on my shoulder, pushing me back.

"Your turn," she says.

My gaze lifts skyward, and I swear it's like I'm flying or spinning. The sky, the sun… How long has it been since I laid down in the grass and stared up at the sky? Taken in nature from the lowest point…on a weekday, no less. All the world scurries like ants between offices and home, and I'm sprawled like a king luxuriating in the riches of the world.

She grips my cock with commanding strength, eliciting a guttural groan, and I watch transfixed as she flattens her tongue and licks my shaft. Teasing, she circles my tip, lapping at the precum. When her mouth finally takes me, I swear my eyes roll into the back of my head.

Best fucking vacation.

What she's doing feels so good. I relax into her

ministrations, loving the feel until a familiar tightening in my balls and my lower back has me popping my head up.

"That's…" I reach for her arm, warning her. "Too close," I bark out.

She smiles and straddles me, positioning herself over me, but fuck.

"Condom," I grit out, gently gripping her hips while scanning the ground to locate my backpack.

I twist beneath her and crawl across the towel until I snatch my backpack and rummage inside.

"Boy Scout," she says, almost to herself. "Always prepared."

"Eagle Scout," I correct, holding up a condom. And not as prepared as I like. I examine the square, checking the date. "This is my only one. We'll need to head back to the hotel after this."

I offer her a wicked grin.

"We're on vacation," I can't help but add, then rip the foil with my teeth.

She takes the condom from me and presses me down onto my back.

Interesting. I'm not sure Sara ever offered to put the condom on. There's something scintillating about watching her roll it down my shaft, but it's nothing compared to watching her position herself over me. She moves my tip between her folds.

All things holy.

And then she lowers, stretching, taking me into her tight heat.

"Jesus fuck, you feel good."

I grip her hips, and piston into her, pressing against

the hard earth for leverage. She leans forward, rolling her hips against me, our gazes locked.

"That's it. Use me."

Her lips spread into a wide smile. "I intend to."

She leans back, and her nipples, a tawny rose, pebble in the light. I twist one and her hips grind. My thumb presses against her clit, and she mewls. She's so fucking wet, so turned on—and so am I.

Shivers climb my spine as her muscles seize and I grip her hips, holding her tight against me as she rides through a second orgasm, head back, eyes closed, sunlight drenching her in gold.

"You are so fucking gorgeous." I don't actually intend for her to hear me, but her eyelids flutter open, and she falls forward, claiming my mouth.

I twist her to her side, then slap her ass.

"On your knees."

I grimace as I pull out and am careful to check the condom while holding the base.

"You don't want to lie on your back. The ground's not that smooth."

"Oh. Did that hurt you?"

A couple of rocks dug into my back but…"Worth it."

She complies, palms flat, back slightly curved, ass out, in position. She looks over her shoulder, smiling, ready.

I position myself at her entrance and thrust. She's fucking heaven. Tight. Hot. With each surge, she rocks against me and bright specks of light dance across my vision. I cup her breasts, tweaking those aroused nipples, and she moans.

With one roaming hand, I find her clit, palming her, rubbing, thumbing to the time of my thrusts.

Our grunts and moans mix with the gurgling stream, rustling leaves and the chatter of birds, and I'm hit all over with a sense of flying, of freedom.

I'm so fucking close. I sit back on my legs, bringing her with me, so her back is to my front, and I rock into her, teeth on her neck, holding her to me, fingers digging into hips, as she arches and I lose my rhythm, spilling everything into her.

The back of her head lulls against my shoulder, and I rain kisses on her temple, the side of her face, and then when she turns her head, I give her a sloppy, awkward kiss and grin.

"That was fantastic."

I'm still inside her, but I'm softening. And I don't want to move. I want to hold her, just like this, indefinitely.

She caresses my jaw.

I nip at her thumb, and reluctantly help her up, grimacing as I slide out of her warmth.

"I'm glad you came clean."

I walk to the edge of the towel, my back to her as I remove the condom and check it for tears, a habit I started before Sara.

I kneel, searching my backpack for something to dispose of the condom in. It wouldn't be good for the environment to leave a used condom behind. Some animal might choke on it.

"I really like this spot. It's fantastic."

I look over my shoulder, and she's splayed out on the towel, sunbathing.

"Yeah, it is." An idea forms, and I spit it out without

weighing consequences. "Any interest in heading to Asheville?"

"Didn't they get hit hard by a hurricane?"

"They're welcoming tourists back. I haven't been in decades. I'd like to check it out. See what's changed. Maybe for the night? Friday I have to leave for D.C."

She rolls onto her side, and good god I thought she was gorgeous, but looking at the seductive sway of her breasts and the curving line from her abdomen over her hip and the slope of her thighs… "Come with me to D.C., too. If you want. We can leave from Asheville."

Hope flickers in her eyes and I'm quick to add, "You live near D.C., right?"

"Maryland," she says. "But close."

"Why are you so tan?" I reach for my boxers and shorts.

"My grandmother is Hawaiian."

"That explains it." I breathe deeply, gathering my thoughts as I dress.

Am I jumping the gun? She knows you live on the West Coast.

"Dude, lighten up." Miles' voice rings loudly in my head.

Yeah, why the fuck am I second-guessing now?

A thread of an unsettling notion surfaces, but I can't grasp the elusive thought. I locate my socks and shirt, searching my brain. What was it?

The satellite comment. She said she didn't search your name online, yet she asked about satellites. Because you discussed finding this location. Right. That's all it is.

"Is it time to go?"

Jesus, I need to take a photograph of her.

"We've got a five-mile hike back to the car. It's getting

hotter by the second." A hunger pang throbs. "We can grab lunch. Then check out of the hotel."

"Fine," she grumbles, but she's smiling. She strides to her clothes, and yes, I watch her every step.

"We don't have to go to Asheville." The place we're staying is highly rated. She might not want to leave. Might even have spa appointments scheduled. "We can play it by ear," I offer.

"It's past check out time now," she says.

I mean, she's right, but I don't care about paying for an extra night. It's only money. Can't be buried with it.

"Whatever you want," I say, because it is up to her. She may not join me in D.C., but until Friday, I'm staying with Sydney.

As I load the backpack and she rolls on her socks and hiking boots, I check my phone. I shouldn't—vacation and all—but habits die hard.

MILES

Bids being placed for Forbes' database.
Let's bid.

ME

Need to evaluate. Let's discuss next week.

DAISY JONAS

CM

Call me. Hmm. What does Daisy need?

. . .

ME

TXT

NANA LIBBY

Does 1 still work?

Shit. I check the time.

ME

The cell service isn't horrible here, but it's not San Francisco. And I'm not sure where Sydney and I will be at one. We'll be finished with lunch. Possibly headed to Asheville? Might have to go old school, sans video.

Sydney's legs are bent, tying her hiking boots. At that angle, with her cargo shorts scrunched low, her legs look fucking amazing.

Does it matter if she's around when I speak to my grandmother? Probably not. What am I thinking? Sydney isn't the issue. If Nana gets wind of Sydney, that's when the issue will arise.

I grin, thinking about my visit with my grandmother this past weekend. At eighty-eight, she's a firecracker. But she's slowing down. Prefers to stay close to home and not travel so much. Her house backs up to Dilworth Park, which allows her to get out and walk. She's an active member of a gardening club and actively supports the arts. Last weekend she finally agreed to me hiring a home aide. Which reminds me...

I open my contacts, select message, and hold up my phone to my mouth to dictate a message.

> Hi. This is Rhodes MacMillan. When we met on Monday, you said you would send over prospects. Status?

I skim Siri's work and hit send. It's Wednesday. Sometimes I wonder how people keep their businesses running.

"Everything okay?"

Sydney's beside me, peering over my arm. I pick up my pack and unzip the front pocket.

"Yeah. Fine," I grumble. "You ready?"

The phone vibrates in my hand. I flip it over and read: *Evie Thompson.*

Hmm.

Sydney's eyeing me, probably wondering who Evie is and why she's calling. *Let her wonder.* I'm not going down that path of explaining every female interaction. No way, no how.

I step away from Sydney and speak to the speaker, dictating the response, but in a low, private voice.

> Can't right now. What's up?

CHAPTER
FIFTEEN

SYDNEY

I make a mental note to have Quinn look into Evie Thompson. If I'm reading Rhodes correctly, my questions are unsettling. Something about his reaction doesn't fit the profile I was given. A man selling state secrets wouldn't react with genuine discomfort about a past relationship—he'd deflect or charm his way around it. Unless jealousy was an issue in a past relationship.

The man runs a company with hundreds of employees. He's headed to D.C. in forty-eight hours and has meetings set up through next week. If he's expecting jealousy from me, he's off. He'll learn I'm far too rational. Besides, out of necessity, this is a vacation thing.

If all goes well, I'll gain some insight and drift into the recesses of his past, a woman he had fun with for a few days. He'll never learn I had ulterior motives.

But his reaction sparks suspicion that perhaps his long-term girlfriend from the past trained him to be wary.

Perhaps his long hours at the office were met with mistrust, perhaps her questions led to fights. That could also just be me reading into him. If this thing between us was real, I might prod. Pick at the thread to learn more. But it's not and any insight on that score wouldn't meet the objective. If anything, touching a sensitive subject might drive him to throw up a wall.

No, I thought the way to get to know Rhodes would be to flatter him, to play into what I assumed was a robust ego. So I asked about his climbing adventures, Eagle Scouts, even high school since he grew up in this state. I poked and prodded, but he never copped to being valedictorian or the men's lacrosse MVP. He's not boastful, and that's surprising. Perhaps a lifetime of being hailed brilliant has left him without a need to brag. But there's something else. Most people with dark secrets have tells—a need to overcompensate, to project an image that distracts from their corruption. Rhodes doesn't have that energy. If anything, he seems...solid.

When Caroline approached me about this assignment, I expected questionable deal practices, or possibly questionable ties. The briefing made it sound straightforward: tech company prioritizes profit over patriotism, sells sensitive data to the highest bidder. Case closed.

But the more I learn about Rhodes, the harder it becomes to square the man I'm getting to know with the profile. A suspected corrosion of integrity doesn't seem to fit. Rhodes fought for ARGUS to be a nonprofit. The fight is documented in interviews and posts. That's not the action of someone chasing money at any cost.

What if we got this wrong?

It's the same question I asked Caroline. But there are

questions I haven't asked of her. Did anyone hire us to investigate ARGUS? Could there be ulterior motives? I know why I signed on. Given my experience, I was the ideal recruit for this project.

KOAN investigates those deemed potentially above the law due to connections. But someone is setting priorities. Did a private party hire KOAN to secretly investigate ARGUS? Is there someone out there who benefits if an investigation is opened into ARGUS?

ARGUS parses volumes of surveillance data. Five years ago the management team had a semi-public debate over whether or not the firm should be nonprofit. Rhodes MacMillan weighed in at an AI conference stating all AI firms should be nonprofit, and then he got mocked in the trades when ARGUS registered as a for-profit company. The company is private, so their financials aren't public, but I found threads ruminating on a potential upcoming funding round.

The questions that have been nagging at me all day crystallize: Did a venture capital firm hire KOAN for due diligence on ARGUS? Does someone out there see them as a competitor? Or a potential acquisition target? I've been assuming we're the good guys investigating the bad guy. My friend hired me after all. But what if we're just corporate spies in patriotic clothing?

Back at the hotel, Rhodes and I face each other awkwardly near the valet stand. Conversation on the return hike flowed freely, punctuated with relaxed lulls, especially as we sped down the decline with me sometimes several feet in front of him. In the car, his rental, he shared his Spotify playlist and before long, zipping through the curvy roads lined with trees, I relaxed into holiday mode, thinking about nothing but the music. He beat the steering wheel like a drum, his demeanor aloof, the sky blue, the day perfect.

We went from sex to casual conversation to listening to music, lost in our own thoughts. He never reached for my hand to hold it.

Outside the vehicle, I concede that *going for it* back at the swimming hole may have been a strategic error. I acted impulsively, doing what I wanted, and now, I'm not sure what he's thinking. But even as I worry about the implications, part of me realizes I acted impulsively because...I wanted to. Not because it served any operational purpose. Is that so bad? When was the last time I did something just because I wanted to?

And now, what will the repercussions be? Is he going to say, "Thank you for a great time and see ya"? I've done it to men in my past when I didn't see a reason to invest time.

"I've been thinking about Asheville."

Here it comes.

"Why don't we stay here? It's a gorgeous day, and I don't really want to be cooped up in the car. We can hang by the pool. Tomorrow it's supposed to be rainy, so it won't be a great day to explore Asheville. I'll book us some spa appointments. Maybe a couple's massage? Or separate. Whatever you prefer."

I blink, processing his words. I didn't screw things up. We're still a go.

"I'll never turn down a massage," I hear myself saying as I register the balled-up anxiety dissipating as relief courses through my sore limbs.

"We can come back to Asheville another time." Then,

as if he's realizing what he's saying, moves one shoulder forward in a weird shrug. "Or meet up there next time."

"Sounds good to me." I bounce on my heels, aiming to reassure him I like his plan, but the move is too energetic and cocked. "I mean, you know…"

What the fuck am I saying?

"Cool. Ah, I need to check in with the office. Want to meet up later…maybe you can swing by my villa. If the thunderstorms hit, we can Netflix and chill. They have Netflix… I can connect to my account. We can watch pretty much anything."

Does he know what Netflix and chill is a euphemism for? I doubt it. He doesn't come across as a pop culture kind of guy. His playlist was straight from the nineties and early two thousands.

"Sounds good. I'm gonna make some calls too, then."

I spin past him into the lobby and he heads off to the side of the inn and the path that leads to the back of the property with the villas.

In my room, I unzip my backpack and pull out my phone, immediately smiling upon seeing his text.

RHODES FROM THE HIGHLANDS

Give me an hour, then swing by whenever you can.

Perfect.

Although, no, perfect would be an invitation to hang in his villa while he conducted business. But, if I go with him to D.C., that's going to happen, right? Quinn trashed the idea of installing a program on his laptop or attempting to catch him with a phishing attempt—said his system would catch it. She's probably right. He's an elite programmer.

She's doing what she can with access to his phone. Hopefully she's been able to monitor his texts and calls remotely. The CIA has programs that can do that with only a number, but we're not the CIA. With luck, thanks to her gizmo, she can monitor him undetected.

RHODES FROM THE HIGHLANDS

Chance of thunderstorms rises after three. Avoid the deluge. Get here before then.

After giving his text a thumbs up, I stare at the phone for a moment. Should I be questioning the project? I've discovered nothing about Rhodes that fits the profile of a man comfortable with betraying his country.

But not fitting a profile doesn't mean he's innocent.

I dial Quinn, press speaker, and set the phone down. I take a seat on the chair and begin working on my hiking boot laces.

"When do you leave for Asheville?"

"Whoa, no hello? What's—wait, is shit going down?"

A door clicks in the background.

"No. You're just catching me in the middle of something."

"Should I call back?"

"The boys are packed. Ready to follow your tail."

"Wait—boys? Plural? How many—" My hiking boot hits the ground with a thud. "Never mind that. We're staying put."

"What? Why?"

"Tomorrow's supposed to rain, so he figured the spa here would be better than exploring a rainy city. He mentioned D.C. Loosely. I'm likely in but no guarantee."

"Really?"

"Yes." *Pause.* "And don't say it like that."

"Like what?"

"Like you think I'm making bad choices. I can hear it in your voice, Quinn." I pause, ensuring she notes my conversation change. "Anyway, did you access his phone?"

Technically, once she accesses his phone, my job's obsolete. They'll get more from monitoring his email and texts than I could from being in the same room with him. Phone access is a goldmine. Of course, it's doubtful he's going to freely talk about illicit deals. But he might talk about an upcoming meeting.

Scratch that. He's a smart guy. He won't talk about illegal activities around me. The only way he would is to couch the discussion in terms that a bystander wouldn't pick up on. It's possible Hudson will pull me; tell me it's time to wrap it up.

Wrapping up means telling Rhodes I have a job interview and I'll see him the next time we're in the same city. Easy to do, but the idea of that plan delivers a sinking sensation.

The sound of knocking, no pounding, on a door comes through the speaker.

"What do you want?" Quinn barks.

"What's the ETA? Do we have time for another round of Call to Action or are we hopping soon?" I recognize the voice as the one who placed a bet, and from the clearness of the audio, I assume he entered Quinn's room.

"Cleared for another round," she says.

The door clicks again.

"Who is that?"

"Jake."

"Are they seriously gaming right now?"

"Yes, ma'am."

"How many guys are on the team now?"

"For your backup? It's just Jake and Noah. By the way, they swept Rhodes' villa while you were hiking."

"Did they find anything?"

"Nope. Not even a laptop, but they didn't open the safe. Cleaning service came by and they had to jet."

"Surveillance in place?"

"No. Interrupted by cleaning service. And a wedding party with an outdoor celebration took over the courtyard."

The villas open into a courtyard but you'd think they could find a way inside.

"What do you think of them? Jake and Noah?"

"Impressive backgrounds. Hudson's recruits. Based on their records, they're skills extend beyond a joystick. But they are used to working on bigger teams." She clears her throat. "So, Rhodes' phone—as expected, it's secure. I'm not getting anything. And to be honest, if I did, it'd be too easy. There are way too many interested in ARGUS right now. Our West Coast operative is having trouble on her end, too. She hasn't called it quits yet, but the network she's on as a consultant isn't connected to the mainframe. Servers aren't in the building."

"Where are they?"

"Multiple countries. I'm working on mapping their data flow patterns between server locations. If I can figure out which clients access which servers, that might tell us who they're really working with. Plus, I'm prepping surveillance tech for your D.C. trip. What's your next step?"

"Rhodes said he needs a little time to catch up on work and then I'm going over to his villa for the afternoon."

"Nice."

I glare at the phone. "Why do I feel like you loaded that word with judgement?"

"Maybe because you're busy judging yourself?"

My mouth is open and the words "fuck off" are on my tongue.

"Check your messages."

Unknown Number: #whoremembers

"What the hell—Quinn, are you calling me a whore?" I'm getting louder, but I don't care. "Because if this is some kind of—"

Laughter peels through the speaker.

"Oh, you think this is funny?"

I'd like to see her computer geek ass enter the field. Although, truth be told, Quinn's pretty fucking hot in a PhD candidate, grad student kind of way with her thick blonde curly hair pulled back and giant blue eyes. She'd probably be better at this than me because she's got trustworthy down and she's brilliant.

"I had to see if we could be friends. If you'd read it as

who remembers, I wouldn't say anything." A snort sounds through the phone. Did she just blow her nose?

I lean over the screen and reread her text. Ah, I see what she did.

"So now that we can be friends...I'm going to tell you a secret."

"Okay."

"I can't believe I'm going to tell you this. But I need to tell someone, and also, you need to get the chip off your shoulder if we're going to work through this together. Especially if I'm talking you through a trip to D.C."

"There's no chip."

"Right."

I open my mouth to argue.

"I slept with Hudson."

Silence.

"Sydney? You there?"

"I'm sorry, what? You—with Hudson? Our Hudson? Boss Hudson?"

"Yeah, that Hudson."

"Jesus, Quinn. When?"

"Before I knew who he was. I got into town a night earlier than everyone. So did Hudson."

"And you stayed at the same hotel?" I ask, putting the pieces together.

"Met at the airport bar before our flight. I missed my connection—"

"Wait, back up. You met Hudson at an airport bar?"

"Yeah and ended up getting booked on his flight when mine got delayed."

"And so, like now, what... Are you two?"

"Absolutely not. When I discovered he's my boss, we had all the appropriate conversations and agreed, you know, I mean, it was never supposed to be anything. It's just—"

Now it's my turn to laugh. "You didn't think a guy headed to the Highlands might be on the same project you're on? Given we hadn't met any team members?"

"Hey, we both lied about why we were going there."

"Of course you did."

"So, now that you know my dirty little secret, you can stop thinking I'm judging you at every turn. If you fall for him—"

"Whoa, hold up. I'm not falling for anyone. This is work, Quinn."

"I didn't say you were. I said *if*."

I release a long, pointed sigh.

"You don't need to feel guilty. If it was Jake or Noah, you think they'd be feeling guilty? It wouldn't even be mentioned."

"You're right about that." If there's any field that's filled with sexist BS, it's intelligence work.

"Do you like him? I mean, you're not repulsed by him, right?"

"I genuinely like him." That's what I told Caroline earlier and now here I am telling Quinn, a colleague I barely know.

"If you didn't, he'd pick up on that and you wouldn't have done more than dinner last night. It's spycraft basics. It's the secret of every undercover agent. The good news here is you won't need to lead him away in handcuffs. Even if we discover he's breaking ten thousand laws, we aren't the law. We'll hand evidence over and a different crew will take charge. He'll never suspect you played a role in his getting caught."

"I don't think he's breaking any laws."

"Really?"

I narrow my eyes at the speaker, not that she can see me, but her response was way too high pitched.

"Just keep us in the loop," she says. "We're nearby if needed. Send me deets on D.C."

"Quinn?"

"Yeah?"

"That thing with Hudson? Mum's the word. And don't worry about it. This little group of ours—KOAN— it's not like we follow a corporate structure—"

"I don't date colleagues. Especially bosses."

"Got it."

"And Hudson doesn't date people who work for him. He's got that military background. And honestly, our personalities don't mesh. He's closed off. Arrogant."

"Well, all I'm saying—"

"Be careful out there. Touch base."

"How are things with Hudson now? Is it weird?"

"Not at all."

There's a loud rap on my door.

"Hang on, someone's—"

The rap returns, more insistent.

"Syd? What's going on?"

"I don't know, but I gotta go. Talk later."

"Wait—"

I hit the red button and end the call.

The weight of uncertainty hampers my movement. Three days ago, I was certain of my mission, my target, and my purpose. Now I'm questioning everything—

except my attraction to a man who might be completely innocent and undeserving of an investigation.

With slow steps, I approach the door. I'm barefoot and indentations from the tight socks over damp skin post-skinny-dipping mar my calves. I'm still in my shorts and tee.

"Hello?" I say to the door.

"Syd?" Adrenaline-inducing endorphins whoosh through me, all from the deep voice resonating through the door.

"Couldn't wait?" I ask, swinging the door open, somewhat incredulous he's here.

He's in a fresh T-shirt that clings to his biceps and shoulders. My gaze falls to the flip-flops on bright white feet and I can't stop smiling because right now I'm getting a Rhodes that few see. He grins, and it's boyish and endearing.

"I've got an addiction." He leans against the doorframe and the way he's smiling, his tease is obvious.

Me?

"Work," he clarifies quickly, but his smile falters slightly. "And apparently, I'm worse at this vacation thing than I thought."

I deflate slightly, but...

"Seriously. My partner bet me I couldn't go a week without working." He runs a hand through his hair, looking slightly sheepish. "Miles has been on my case for months about never taking time off. Says I'm going to burn out before I'm forty-five."

"Didn't you go back to your villa to check in?"

"Well, yeah. I had a call scheduled with my grandmother. She wanted to make sure I was still on vacation."

His boyish grin has me grinning. "And I called my partner. But he's a friend. So, not just work." He pauses, looking almost embarrassed. "And he reminded me of our bet. Also mentioned that if I was really serious about this vacation thing, I'd stop making excuses and just...be present. With you."

"And you don't lose bets?"

His lips purse, and he shakes his head. "I don't lose. Period." He shifts against the doorframe, his grin shifting into a devious smirk. "Though Miles pointed out that coming here instead of working might actually be me losing the bet in a different way. Said I'm substituting one obsession for another." His eyes meet mine. "Not sure he's wrong."

The arrogance playing across those refined lips should not turn me on, and yet...

"Kept thinking about what I could do to distract myself—answer emails, catch up on reading. But the thing is..." He steps closer, and I catch something almost uncertain in his expression. "There's only one thing I actually want to do. And it has nothing to do with work or any of the shit that usually consumes my brain."

He steps into the room and kicks the door closed. His dark eyes shift from humor to downright predatory as his gaze rakes over me, but there's something almost...surprised in his expression. Like he's caught off guard by his own reaction.

For a moment, he just looks at me, and I see something flicker across his face—like he's processing something unexpected. "You know what's weird?"

"What?"

"I haven't thought about work—really thought about

it—since this morning. That hasn't happened in..." He trails off, shaking his head. "Years. Maybe ever."

He steps closer, and my breath quickens.

"You haven't showered."

"Nope."

"What were you doing?"

"Called a friend."

"Huh." He scratches his jaw, but the smirk is softer now, almost self-deprecating. "Well, since I'm apparently terrible at both working and not working..." His voice drops lower. "Care for assistance in the shower? Might be the one thing I can actually focus on properly today."

CHAPTER
SIXTEEN

RHODES

I didn't come here planning to maul her, but now that I'm here…

My fingers itch to tug that shirt over her head and to unclip the bra I watched her put on an hour ago.

Her eyes widen and a smile plays on her lips.

With each step backwards, expectations rise that she's going to turn this into a game.

She's going to run.

My skin tingles. I actually feel the tips of my fingers, my toes curl, prepped to kick off my flip-flops and leap. The mountain air tastes different—sharper, cleaner—like it did when I was twelve and spent summers here with my grandparents.

Why am I feeling like this?

Maybe because she stripped and stood on Hangman's Rock and torpedoed down.

My pulse thrums. I haven't felt this energized since my first successful funding raise.

It's Sydney. She's spunky. Feisty. A live wire whose spark lights a fire I forgot I possessed.

When our eyes meet, something shifts. The playfulness remains, but underneath it, something deeper. Something that makes my chest tight.

She squeals.

Twists.

Yes!

Game on.

I'm on her.

We're laughing.

When the fuck do I laugh?

Somehow, through flailing limbs and tickles, the clothes get tossed in our rush to the shower.

"I'm surprised you didn't shower first thing."

Her breasts are bare and Christ, she has really great tits.

"Why's that? Is there something about that watering hole I need to know?"

I shake my head because my verbal abilities falter in the presence of a naked woman.

My shorts drop to the ground and her gaze falls. Yes, I'm rock hard.

But I'm also close to her warm, smooth skin, and when our lips connect, all pretense vanishes.

The need to taste her, to worship her, overwhelms every rational thought. I trail kisses down her throat, between her breasts, following the path of water droplets until I'm on my knees. The tile digs into my knee cap when I kneel before her, but it's pretty fucking hot with her leg over my shoulder and steaming water pounding my muscles. She squirms, moans, and it's not long before she's directing me, fisting my hair. Her legs quiver with her climax, and I press my forehead against her as her fingers tease my hair. She lowers her leg and I trace kisses along her skin as I rise. Her fingers wrap around my length and I meet her gaze, then bend to take her mouth. Her strokes are divine, but I ache for more.

"Let me get a condom."

"I have an IUD. I'm clean. I don't do this often…it's been years."

I see the truth in the depths of her eyes and I willfully shut off my thought processes, instead choosing to feel. To let loose. I lift her, placing her back against the tile, and plunge into her hot heat. *Fuck. Nothing's ever felt like this.*

The sensation is overwhelming—her slick heat, no barrier between us, the trust implicit in her words. Having her ride my cock, thighs gripping my hips, my hands cupping her ass, holding her in place while trying my best to avoid slipping and injuring us both? *This beats every power move ever made.*

When I come, it's with an intensity that leaves me shaking. I press my face into her neck, breathing hard, trying to process what just happened. We're skin to skin, nothing between us, and it feels like crossing a line I didn't even know existed.

Once the aftershocks fade, my considerate side comes out and I wrap her in a towel, examining her back for any sign I was too rough.

"You okay?"

And there's that grin.

"Think we'll ever make it to the bed?"

Have we not? No, we have. "Our first night...and morning."

I tweak her nose.

"Does that count? We didn't." She wiggles her eyebrows and I squeeze her toweled ass.

"Hmm. So it only counts if we *hmm?*"

She giggles at the muted vibrations coming out of my throat.

"Anyway, believe it or not, I didn't come over here for that."

"No?"

I step away from her and wrap my lower half in a towel. Steam fogs the mirrors and rivulets rain down in streaks. And that happened with the bathroom door open. Maybe there was a fan we should've turned on.

"Didn't you come in saying you needed to win a bet and there was only one thing you wanted to do?"

"Well, what I meant was I wanted to spend time with you."

Good save, MacMillan. Miles mocking me forever present in my head.

She stands in front of her open suitcase, back to me.

"And you know those storms are coming in this after-noon." I step up behind her, caressing her bare arms, running my fingers along her dewy skin as a vision of her sweaty, muscles flexed, scaling a rock wall flits, and I blink it away, looking instead to the open window and the red gardenias filling the window boxes.

Clouds mask this morning's bright blue skies. I haven't checked the radar recently, but earlier today they were forecasting a tornado-inducing system to roll across from the Midwest.

"Netflix and chill," she says, smiling over her shoulder at me.

"Precisely." I press my lips to her bare shoulder and playfully drag my teeth over her freshly washed skin. "I came here to help you with your bags. Figured you could stay with me for the night."

"A sleepover?"

"Well, a second sleepover. I stayed here last night. You stay with me tonight."

I can't see her face because she's sorting her zippered bags.

"But if you prefer we stay here, I'm game for that too. But my place has a wood burning fireplace."

Do I sound like a schmuck? My room's better than yours?

"Reading between the lines, I'm your distraction to ensure you win your bet."

Is that annoyance? Have I offended her? "I wouldn't say distraction."

"What would you call it?" She spins around with one hand on her towel and the other clutching clothes against her chest.

"Secret weapon?" I suggest, giving her my best puppy dog eyes. Haven't used those since forever, but they used to work, so...

She rolls her eyes, but she's grinning, so I win.

"Give me a sec to change and pack my toiletries."

I scramble to gather my clothes from the floor, and once I've accomplished the task, she closes the bathroom door.

Huh.

Doesn't matter. We're leaving this room together. When I pull on my shorts, my phone slaps against my thigh. Out of habit, I check it.

DAISY JONAS

Miles says you're still with this one. We're placing bets.

I should let it go, but can't. Daisy's been like a little sister to me since she started at the company, all sharp edges and brilliant code.

ME

And?

I set the phone down on the mattress and slip on my tee.

DAISY JONAS

Want me to look into her?

ME

U already did.

How'd she forget? Did Miles give her some of his gummies? What're they doing while I'm out of the office?

DAISY JONAS

For realz

Oh. She means use ARGUS.

ME

No

Go pester Miles

The bathroom door opens. Sydney's in a sundress. Her wet, raven hair has been brushed smooth, and the thin straps on the dress are drenched.

I drop my phone in my shorts pocket.

"Is this little bet of yours an honor system arrangement? Did I just catch you cheating?"

"My word is good," I tell her in my deep, what I hope is an I-am-a-sexy-male voice. "You ready?"

She's holding several zipped bags, presumably from the bathroom.

"You are one organized packer."

She shrugs.

"A woman after my own heart," I mutter.

"What was that?"

She busies herself arranging her suitcase, and I shove my hands in pockets.

Should I ask?

She never really confirmed.

"You're coming with me this weekend, right? To D.C.?"

I step up to help with her suitcase as she tugs on the zipper.

"Isn't that for work?"

"Meh. I have some mandatory meetups." The truth is, I can't picture getting on that jet without her. The thought of ending this—whatever this is—on Sunday feels wrong. "But I'd rather not go alone."

"Is meetup your word for meeting?"

"It's not really a meeting." I shrug.

"Aren't you supposed to be on vacation?"

She's looking like she's caught me in a trap, but really, she hasn't. Miles isn't counting this weekend as vacation. It's just two days that butt up to my vacation. If I actually stay away from the computer until Monday, that would be an exceptional performance. One Miles would approve of, but Alex probably wouldn't, given he's in a tizzy about an upcoming investor meeting. Me avoiding work over the weekend won't happen anyway, of course, but if she joins me, I'll do less work.

"Technically, I'm on vacation through Friday. I'll have some things to take care of this weekend, but I'd still like for you to join me."

"I'd need to adjust my flight. I'm not sure—"

"You'd fly with me."

Her eyes narrow, and yes, I'm giving away more than I planned about me, but hell, I'm staying in a suite by myself. She didn't think I was broke.

"Company plane. Small one." I add the last part because it is one of our smaller jets.

When I told her I didn't want to spend the afternoon in the car, the reality was I didn't feel like calling my assistant and having her run down a pilot. And really, a jet is overkill to get from the Highlands to Asheville. A helicopter would be the better choice and that's just another annoyance to deal with because then we'd still need to move the jet to Asheville for my trip to D.C. Or we could drive like I mentioned. But then I'd still need to deal with the jet. My AI assistant can do a lot, but I'd need to double-check her work as she wouldn't be pulling from my standard vendor list. Yeah, staying is the easy plan.

"What do you say?"

She shrugs her shoulder. "Sure. I'd love to hang with you in D.C."

And that's another reason I like this girl. She's chill. She doesn't need explanations or justifications. She just...goes with it. When's the last time anyone in my life just went with it?

SYDNEY

"Well, look who it is."

"Checking in," I respond to Quinn in a hushed voice.

"Why are you whispering? Is he near?"

"I'm in the women's changing room at the spa. It's a cell phone free zone." The scent of eucalyptus drifts from the steam rooms, and soft instrumental music plays overhead.

"Ah. Well, I've been tracking you, so I knew you were on the property. Or at least your phone is. You know, we pulled on-site surveillance at your recommendation—and I agreed with you. But it doesn't work if you don't check in. I'm tracking a device. Not you. It's not foolproof. There's no video or audio on you."

"I hear you. But I couldn't get away to message."

"If he checks your call history, who you are going to tell him this call is to?"

"My friend." She can't see me, but I shrug. What else

would I say? "What information will he find if he researches this number?"

"He'll learn it was activated a week ago. This is a KOAN-issued line."

"Can't you adjust the history?" I exhale frustration. "You should've thought of that."

"Hey." Her tone is sharp. "I did. But we're a new team on our first rendezvous. And you're straying off plan by using your personal cell. If he digs into your call history, bail. Even if I were to alter your history, there's a good chance my alteration wouldn't match what ARGUS has already downloaded."

"Fully aware."

My personal cell was a last-minute decision, made at the same time I jumped script and used my real identity. I stand by my decision. It's one thing to fake an identity for a foreign government pulling from known data sources. It's quite another to fake it for the owner of an AI surveillance firm with unknown capabilities. And the reality is, if it comes down to him doing background on each number I call, then it's time to exit.

"If he asks, tell him I'm a friend from the CIA and my number changes regularly."

A woman in a plush robe pads past in spa slippers, the soft slap of her footsteps on heated stone floors barely audible over the gentle hum of ventilation systems.

"That should throw him enough to get you time to get out of there. Because if he's asking—"

"It means I'm blown. I understand."

"I take it since you've been with him constantly, then D.C. is on?"

"Yes."

"Deets?"

"We're leaving tomorrow on his private plane. Wheels up at 12:30."

"As expected. Staying where?"

"InterContinental."

"I'll see if I can locate his reservation. I'm gonna guess you'll be in one of the suites. Maybe Thomas Jefferson? We'll see what surveillance we can put in place."

"He has drinks scheduled with an Evie Thompson on Friday. She texted him."

"Texted? Or does he use a messaging app?"

"Text. On the number I gave you."

Clicking sounds come across the line. She's looking her up.

"Huh."

"What?"

"If I've got the right one, she's an Assistant DA. Will you join them?"

"He hasn't said. He said he has some things to take care of and some meetups. He said it like he'll need to do them on his own."

"I could see how Evie Thompson would find ARGUS's information beneficial. She works in the Violence Reduction and Trafficking Offenses Section in D.C. Human trafficking. I'm going to look into her further. Anything else?"

Over the last twenty-four hours, I've learned we are highly compatible in bed, on the sofa, the shower, and on the kitchen counter, and he has a mild obsession with Dave Grohl—not celebrity worship, but the kind of deep musical connection that reveals something vulnerable about him. It's the only time I've seen him completely unselfconscious, air-drumming to "Everlong" like he's seventeen again instead of a tech billionaire who usually controls every detail of his image.

"He hasn't been working. He's on vacation."

"How are you holding up?" This time, I don't pick up a judgmental tone. For a techie, she's a good handler.

"I'm good."

"What's your plan?"

"I'm hopeful this weekend will provide some insight. If it doesn't, I'll likely bail at the end of the week. He's offered to help me find a job—"

"Another person on the inside." She sounds impressed. "That would be a huge score."

"He's not talking about a job at his company. But would you mind looking at my resume? Spruce it up, so when I share it with him, it's impressive. Who knows? He said he wouldn't hire me in his company, but if my qualifications appear desirable enough..."

"I'll see what I can find on who they're hiring. Why wouldn't he hire you? Is he pulling the I-don't-date-employees card?"

"You mean like someone else we know?"

"Syd."

I stifle an amused snort. "We didn't really talk about it, but I think that's what he was implying."

"It's a good policy. Anyhoo, our West Coast peep stole a colleague's ID card. She might use it tonight—if the employee doesn't notify HR it's missing. If she does, I'm betting today is her last day in the office. There's no way video surveillance won't ID her."

"Why the push?"

"She's confirmed her consulting firm's access is limited. It'll be six months minimum before the project's completed, and that's a lengthy engagement for the chance that she'd be offered a permanent job."

"Go big or go home."

"Right now, you're our one in. If they catch her tonight, they'll be on edge."

"Come on, now. As a company? They've got to live on edge. We're not the only ones attempting a breach. A blocked attempt is just another day in Candy Land for those guys."

"Good point. Okay. So, how do you want to make contact?"

"I'll call you?"

"Negative. Your call history is too easy to check. We're sending two guys to D.C. They'll have eyes on you when you're out and about, but they'll likely lose visuals over the course of the weekend. The real purpose is having backup nearby if needed."

"They're staying at the same hotel?"

"Yes, ma'am."

"I can leave written messages at the front desk for them."

"But they can't reach you that way. You're a runner, right?"

"Yes."

"Let me check area maps and come up with a contact plan. You've still got your rental car, right?"

"Yep."

"Tell him you have to return the car. If that buys you solo time, swing by here and we'll review the D.C. plan."

"Sounds good."

"How are you for clothes?"

"He's seen my suitcase. He knows what I packed."

"He also knows you live in Maryland, right? He has your home address?"

"I haven't given it to him, but yes, it's easy enough to find."

"Has he mentioned stopping by your place? Are you concerned?"

"I understand we're proceeding with caution, but my operational assessment is that Rhodes poses minimal direct physical threat. He's not the type to personally get violent—white collar all the way, no background with weapons or physical confrontation."

"Wealthy, powerful men like him are dangerous in a different way. They don't need to be personally violent when they can afford to delegate problems. You can't underestimate what someone would do to protect their company. Their net worth. Their reputation."

She's correct. My training taught me to distinguish between personal capability and institutional power. Rhodes might never lay a hand on anyone, but that doesn't mean he's harmless—it just means he'd handle threats the way he handles everything else, with money and influence. The real risk isn't Rhodes losing his temper and attacking me. It's Rhodes calmly making a phone call to people who specialize in making problems disappear.

A flash of last night, his expression as he pulsed inside me, the way he clung to me as he gasped for air— the physical attraction is real. His guard was down. He trusts me. He's not suspicious.

He won't find out. He can't. I won't dwell on the

possibility, not out of fear of a violent reaction, but because my duplicitous activity would hurt him, and that's a result I plan to avoid.

The call ends and I deposit my phone in my assigned spa locker, the soft click echoing in the cedar-lined space that smells of lavender and expensive skincare products. Quinn's little don't-underestimate-him speech rubs me the wrong way.

I roll my shoulders back and consciously relax my jaw, forcing my body language to shift from receiving intel to woman enjoying a spa day. I'd like to call Caroline for a friendly chat to clear my head, but I won't. The fewer calls I make, the better.

I pour myself some cucumber water from the glass dispenser and sink into a heated lounge chair by the fireplace. The plush blanket is impossibly soft against my skin, and I close my eyes, letting the gentle crackle of flames and distant sound of a water feature wash over me. There's a lot going on here, but I know exactly what I'm doing.

I'm not some rookie operator stumbling through her first honey trap. I was CIA, trained at The Farm where half the candidates wash out. I survived what broke others. Quinn might run tech, but she hasn't been in the field, hasn't made the hard calls I've had to make. She doesn't understand that sometimes you need to get close —really close—to extract the truth.

If Rhodes is using ARGUS to expose operatives—or if someone else within the company is—they need to be stopped. My methods might blur lines, but I'll get results. I've always been the best at what I do, and that's why Caroline recruited me and Hudson selected me for this investigation. When I commit, I deliver. Always have.

But Quinn's points were solid. As a professional, I must remember that while I don't believe Rhodes would physically harm me, that doesn't mean he's innocent. Men like Rhodes believe that their wealth insulates them from consequences. His confidence, nay, his arrogance, is critical to his success. I can't lose sight of the reason I signed on to this op.

The mission justifies the means. It always has. And if I happen to enjoy certain aspects of this particular operation more than usual? Well, that's just a bonus—a bonus with an end date.

When I step outside of the women's spa area, leaving behind the sanctuary of heated floors and whispered conversations, two powerful hands grip my white terry cloth robe and pull me into a hard chest. The sudden shift from the spa's hushed atmosphere to Rhodes' immediate presence makes my pulse spike.

"What've you been doing in there?" The question is more of a growl.

"Resting. What about you?" I raise an eyebrow. "Did you get bored?"

"You could say that."

"Is it that pesky addiction?"

"You?" He grins. "You are my new addiction. Are you ready to go back to the villa?"

A woman perusing beauty products on the far wall peers in our direction. The scent of expensive moisturizers and the soft lighting designed to make everyone look younger doesn't disguise the curiosity in her eyes.

I whisper, "I'll change and meet you."

"There's a steam room on your side, right?"

"Yes," I answer slowly, sensing where he's going with this.

"Want me to join you?"

"You can't," I say with a wide grin.

"Hmm. There are things we can do in a steam room."

I back away from him, shaking my head disapprovingly. "Go change."

He places his palm over his heart. "Two days in and you're already wanting me to change. Ow."

"I'd never ask you to change." I look straight into his dark, mossy, amused eyes, and it hits me that I'm speaking the absolute truth. Whatever he's doing with his company is completely separate from who he is as a person. And he's pretty fantastic. That is, if he's not selling state secrets that get people killed. "You're perfect."

"If that's the way you see me, then it's best we're parting ways on Sunday. Wouldn't want you to learn the truth."

Right back at you, MacMillan.

He blows me a kiss, walking backwards, and nearly plows over an older woman. I can't stifle the giggles as I walk away, listening to his profuse apologies. It's not until I'm away from him, back in the eucalyptus-scented solitude of the changing room where the soft music fails to lighten the weight of my deception, that my heart grows heavy.

CHAPTER
EIGHTEEN

RHODES

The flight to D.C. takes less than an hour—barely enough time to process what I'm leaving behind in the Highlands. As the plane climbs above the mountains, I catch myself already missing the simplicity of the last few days.

If I find the time to get my pilot's license, I could fly a short leg like this one. As it is, we're in a small six-seater. ARGUS owns a more luxurious jet, but I let our executive team take it for a meeting in Europe this week.

The seats on each side of the aisle are comparable to a first-class seat, wide with plenty of legroom. The attendant, an accessory I added last minute when I realized I'd have company, is already seated up front with the pilot. Sydney fell asleep in her reclined seat within ten minutes of departure.

I can't really blame Syd given I woke her in the middle of the night. There's something about her that makes me feel fifteen years younger. Or maybe it's the vacation.

When Miles forced me out the door after my request to fire our long-time friend, sleep deprivation led me to agree. But, as usual, Miles has proven himself correct. I needed a change in scenery.

I thought I'd be itchy to jump back into things, but instead I'm resentful of the handful of meetings I have planned later on today during my vacation. Am I still annoyed with Alex's pressure campaign? Absolutely. He'll either get on board with our mission or he'll exit. Even if he gets on board, we still need someone with more experience.

The temptation to check email is there, but I brush it aside. I'm not quite ready to dive back into it. Miles is right on this front. We hire the best. I need to trust the people we've placed in charge—everyone except Alex. We haven't built a sustainable company if I can't step away.

But before I check messages, I check in with Nana. I'd normally video call, but I'm in the air.

ME

On the way to D.C. Glad I got to see you.

Three dots instantly flicker. She's always quick to respond.

NANA LIBBY

So good to see you sweetheart. Did you have a good vacation?

ME

I did

NANA LIBBY

I wish you didn't spend it alone

I hesitate. It's tempting to tell her, but there's no need to open Pandora's Box. Not yet. Though I find myself typing and deleting "Actually, Nana…" three times before settling on my response. Perhaps I'll introduce Nana to Syd on my next video call.

NANA LIBBY

One day you're going to find someone who gives you a reason to exist outside the office. You might believe this old lady is foolish but trust me on this one.

My finger hovers over the phone, torn between sending her a photo of a sleeping Sydney and wishing Nana a peaceful evening so I can read through my messages.

NANA LIBBY

The Mahjong game is about to start. Let me know when you land. Love you dear.

ME

Love you too.

. . .

After ending the text exchange, I settle back in my seat, watching Sydney sleep. Her face is peaceful, completely relaxed. The contrast between her serenity and the email overload awaiting isn't lost on me. I flip over to my messaging app. As expected, there are tons of unread messages. I scroll through, purposefully skipping any that can be dealt with Monday morning.

DAISY JONAS

Question 4 U

ME

Y?

DAISY JONAS

Where r u?

ME

OTW 2 DC

DAISY JONAS

Alone?

ME

Why?

DAISY JONAS

Color me suspicious

ME

Of?

DAISY JONAS

The one who claims she didn't know you

Can she read this exchange?

ME

No.

I glance over at Sydney. Her mouth is slightly open, and she's curled to her side, peacefully sleeping.

ME

What's up?

DAISY JONAS

Sydney was in the same CIA class as Caroline Moore.

ME

Dorian Moore's wife?

DAISY JONAS

Bingo

ME

So?

DAISY JONAS

You don't find that suspicious?

ME

I've never met Moore.

. . .

I swear, it's like Daisy thinks everyone in our industry knows each other. None of Moore's companies are in the AI space. It's been ages since I attended industry events to mingle.

What's her logic?

DAISY JONAS

Still gonna dig

ME

I appreciate your concern but put that big brain of yours to a better use.

She's protective, but I can't fault her. When she dates, I'm just as protective. The small crew of us that built ARGUS are family, and Daisy's like my sister. A brilliant little sister who can almost code as well as me.

I'm still processing Daisy's paranoia about Sydney when another message pops up.

MILES

You're bringing her with you to D.C.?

Damn, Daisy.

ME

Still on holiday. I win our bet.

MILES

When do I get to meet the lady friend?

ME

She lives in the D.C. area.

I start to type that I won't see her after Sunday but delete that part of the message. I want to see her again.

MILES

Denial?

ME

Holiday

MILES

Please. The last time you went on three dates with the same woman you dated her for seven years. You, my friend, are a serial monogamist.

ME

I've had 2 relationships

MILES

Point made. You don't do casual.

That's bullshit. I just hate dating. If I find someone I enjoy spending time with, why keep circulating?

ME
That you're aware of

Unlike that fucker, I don't brag about my hook-ups.

MILES
One night hook-ups OR relationship. Those are your two circuit pathways my binary friend.

ME
Compared to...you? Mr. Poly?

MILES
I'm open-minded. You should try it.

At this point, I wouldn't be surprised to learn that Miles hosts full-blown orgies. I don't ask, I don't care. It's his life.

MILES
Is the lady friend moving in?

ME

East Coast

Of course, I'm going to help her find a job and San Francisco has a fantastic job market.

MILES

Want to bet?

I exhale a degree of frustration.

ME

Stop

MILES

Sara moved in in under four weeks.
Should I put a timer on it?

ME:

Fuck off

MILES

Speaking of…I had drinks with Sara last night

ME

Good for you.

I'm being an ass, but he's put me in a bad mood.

MILES

She still pines for you. But she'd neuter me for saying that.

I'm glad that he's still friends with her, but...

ME

We weren't right together. You know that, right?

I cared for Sara, I did. But, we had nothing in common. If I'm honest with myself, we lasted as long as we did because my intense work life allowed me to avoid confrontation at home.

MILES

In all seriousness, I agree. Plus, at the risk of obliterating your ego, IMO she loves the chase—not you. The moment a guy is into her, she's over it. If you ever really fell for her, she would've dropped you too.

ME

That's deep Johnson.

MILES

That's what he said.

I roll my eyes. I'm sure there's a story there. He's set her up on dates or met guys she's dating. I don't want to know, so I drop it. Our friendship with Sara is one of our few commonalities these days, which I assume is why he keeps bringing her up.

The plane begins its descent, causing my ears to pop. Sydney blinks and stretches.

I glance out the window. The pristine blues and greens of the Highlands have given way to the geometrical grid of the capital region. Concrete and glass replace the mountains and trees. Where the air in North Carolina carried the scent of pine and wildflowers, even through the plane's filtered cabin, the approaching cityscape promises exhaust fumes and the metallic tang of ambition. It's a transition I've made countless times, but today it feels particularly jarring—like stepping from a dream back into reality.

I delete the text exchanges, erasing the evidence of my friends' theories about my love life. The last thing I need is Sydney accidentally seeing Miles' commentary. I offer the attendant a smile when she enters the cabin.

After she retrieves our drinks, I shift to face Sydney.

"Do you always sleep on planes?"

With a bashful yawn, she says, "No. But this is a

smaller plane than I'm usually in. And a much more comfortable seat."

Her gaze drops to the phone in my hand.

"Checking in on things?"

"No." I grin, damn proud I'm telling her the truth. "Miles and Daisy don't count." She raises a questioning eyebrow, and it's as if she's experienced enough with me to call me on my BS. Of course, she doesn't know *that* side of me. "My laptop remains secure in its case."

"Are Miles and Daisy your partners?"

"Miles Johnson is a co-founder. We dropped out of B-school at the same time, founded a start-up at the right moment, sold it, and when I had the idea for another venture, he handled all the aspects I hated. Daisy is a programmer—an engineer. She's been with us for years. And yes, they're colleagues, but close friends."

"Only one partner?"

"Well, there's me. CTO."

"The programming nerd?" She smiles.

"The creator," I correct. The company wouldn't exist without me. "Miles is CEO. And then we have a CFO."

"Do you not like him?" If she picked up on that from my tone, then I need to watch how I say things.

"It's not that. We go way back. Harvard, actually. When Miles and I dropped out, he stayed on. Got his degree. Worked for a VC firm. We snagged him when we started up ARGUS." I pause, searching for any flicker of recognition. We're not a household brand. But she's silent, listening, so I continue. "He took a chance on us, and I don't have an issue with him as a person. But I worry we're at a stage now where we need someone with more experience.

We have capital needs." I run my hand through my hair, as I consider how to simplify the problem. "He's pushing for standard solutions, and we need someone who has a more creative approach and long-term strategy."

"That's got to be tough. Given you're friends."

The insightful comment reminds me why I like her. She's intuitive. Miles has never considered my position on Alex isn't without internal conflict.

"It is. But bringing someone in with more experience, in the long run, is best for Alex too."

The flight attendant enters the cabin and lets us know we'll be landing momentarily and returns to the cockpit.

Sydney adjusts her seat, allowing the seat to return to the upright position, and the shift underscores the end of vacation and the inevitable consideration of next steps.

"So about that resume..."

Her eyes widen slightly with guarded surprise, but I'm not scolding her for not having sent it yet.

"Like I told you, I know recruiters. But if you're not in a hurry..." I lift a shoulder, letting her know I have no intention of pressuring her.

"I'd appreciate that. Any connections you think might be a good fit would be great."

Her response is a bit too professional for my taste. There's a distance in her tone that wasn't there in the Highlands, as if she's already shifting back into job-search mode. I don't like it.

"Are you wanting to stay in D.C.?"

Back in the Highlands, our conversation never drifted to the future. But as we close in on D.C., my inner gears automatically shift to reality.

"I'm not sure," she says, and I get it. I'd never let a

location drive a career decision. "What about you? Did coming home to North Carolina make you rethink where you're living?"

Nana would love it if I moved closer. But she's never complained about our scheduled video calls.

Would I like to move? Sure. I'm tired of San Francisco. There's too much traffic and the weather sucks. But I spend so much time in the office, either at home or at our headquarters, my home base doesn't factor.

But maybe that's about to change.

"Have you been to San Francisco?"

She tilts her head and emits a slight sigh before answering, "Yes."

If I'm reading her correctly, she believes that's a silly question. The unstated *obviously I've been* hangs in the air.

"When you come visit, I'll take you somewhere you haven't been."

"Where's that?"

"I don't know. Give me a list of where you've been."

She half-laughs and leans to look out the window as we descend.

The private airport we're landing in is outside of D.C. proper, but the area is so developed buildings fill the landscape. There's not much to see.

She didn't say no to visiting, but she didn't say yes, either.

I'd like to win her over before she learns who I am. Before she's bored in front of her laptop and queries my name.

Am I looking for a serious relationship? No. The obligations? The fights? The guilt? Definitely not.

But do I want to keep seeing this breath of fresh air? Yes.

Would I prefer she not learn my net worth for quite some time? Also, yes. But preferences are not always feasible.

The plane lands, and as we taxi, she removes her phone and checks it for incoming messages.

I check the time. I have a meeting at the Russian embassy at three and then drinks with Evie at four.

Sydney's sundress worked perfectly in the Highlands, but she's going to need an appropriate wardrobe if she's my plus one over the weekend.

"You live close, right?"

"I don't know exactly where we are," she answers, looking up from her screen.

"Just outside of D.C." I don't know exactly where we are either, but I know from looking on the map she doesn't live too far from the D.C. metro area. "Do you want to swing by your place to swap out clothes?"

She hesitates, like she can't decide how to answer.

She could easily decide she'd rather go home than join me at a nearby hotel for the weekend.

"Tell you what. Forget I asked."

I tap a message to Elena, a personal shopper in the D.C. area who's saved me from numerous wardrobe emergencies when business trips ran long.

"I've got it handled."

"What exactly do you have handled?"

Her head tilts to the side, and I smile, excited for what's in store. "The weekend."

CHAPTER
NINETEEN

SYDNEY

The Willard InterContinental is known as "the residence of presidents," and I suppose I should have expected the tech titan Rhodes MacMillan would choose to stay at such a prestigious location, yet it's not what I would have predicted from the outdoorsy, laidback guy I've spent the last several days with in the mountains. The lobby's high ceilings and marble columns command respect, and the traditional furnishings speak of times of grandeur. The air feels different here—cooler, crisper, with the subtle scent of lemon polish and old money. My footsteps echo against the marble, a stark contrast to the soft crunch of mountain trails. Even the light is different, filtered through crystal chandeliers rather than forest canopy, casting everything in a formal glow.

Every single president since Franklin Pierce has either slept in the hotel or attended an event on site. Martin

Luther King Jr. wrote his "I have a dream" speech from his hotel room in this hotel in 1963.

I've visited the hotel before, driven by it countless times, but I've never stayed overnight.

Hotel guests dressed in a mix of business casual and expensive-looking suits meander through the lobby.

"Yes sir, it appears," the woman behind the check-in desk squints, leaning closer to the monitor, "you have a delivery awaiting in your suite. Suite 7." She beams as if she's announced we've been given access to Shangri-La. "How many room keys would you like?"

"Two, please."

"Excellent. Simply hold the card up to the pad. You'll need your card in the elevator as well to gain access to your suite. Is there anything else I can assist you with?"

"No, we're good."

"Thank you, sir. I hope you enjoy your stay. Jonas will escort you to your suite."

The valet whisked away our luggage, leaving us clutching our computer bags, the last remnants of our separate lives before this weekend together. Of course, my bag is a tote bag with a laptop tucked inside, whereas Rhodes carries a charcoal gray backpack.

Rhodes takes my hand and we follow Jonas, a middle-aged man with a thick moustache and a rounded middle. Based on his jolly demeanor, he doesn't mind wearing a polyester uniform and stiff, shiny black dress shoes all day.

When we arrive at the elevator, the attendant shows us how to press the card to the pad before hitting our floor, as if the technology is new and he expects we need the explanation.

In the reflection of the brass-plated elevator doors, I catch sight of Rhodes and me, holding hands. The clothes we're wearing feel far more casual than the guests in the lobby. We're still dressed for a vacation in the mountains. Of course, Rhodes' black T-shirt probably cost several hundred dollars, the same for the faded jeans he's wearing and the sneakers. There's not a logo on him, but his outfit feels expensive. And of course, there's his watch—a brushed steel Rolex submariner, with a chunky body and pedigree that compliments his stealth wealth.

Growing up, my parents took me to hotels like this on vacation, hotels listed on the Forbes recommended list, so I'm not in awe. Knowing what I know about Rhodes, I wonder, should I act like I'm impressed?

Our gazes meet in the reflection, and a warmth spreads through me that settles the second-guesses. Above all else, we're having fun. Our reflection is that of a couple on a weekend getaway, and I suppose, that's what we are.

If I wasn't here for KOAN, would I be acting any differently? Without a doubt, yes, I would. For one, I definitely wouldn't get in a plane and go away with a random guy. On my own, when not on a job, I would've taken his phone number and suggested we meet up again at some unnamed time in the future, and scoffed at cutting my vacation early, no matter how much I wanted to spend time with the guy. I don't lose my head or let fluctuating hormones alter my direction.

Yet here I am. Fortunately, I want to spend time with Rhodes. He joked I'm like a drug to him, but it's a contagious sensation. An unsettling one, but I don't need to stress. True to my disciplined nature, I'll stay on task.

I'll enjoy my time with him, and as planned, say goodbye on Sunday. And what about that resume? Am I going to push for a job with ARGUS? If Brie, our West Coast operative, gets discovered, is that what Hudson will want? I should regroup with the team.

I scanned the lobby and didn't see anyone I recognized. But that doesn't mean a KOAN operative wasn't there.

The elevator doors open, and I'm reminded that Quinn aimed to plant listening devices in the suite. Did they succeed?

Let's hope not. I don't particularly treasure the idea of facing colleagues after they've overheard me having sex.

Jonas opens the suite with a flourish, revealing a circular entry with a crystal chandelier in the center and a wooded mural scene painted on the wall behind a sofa curved to align perfectly with the rotunda.

A brass rack of clothes and stacked Neiman Marcus boxes greet us. The scent of new fabric and tissue paper mingles with a distinct fragrance—something floral with hints of sandalwood. My fingers brush against silk, satin, and other luxurious textures as I circle the rack. My parents took me to nice hotels, but they never brought a retail store to us. The gentle rustling of protective garment bags sounds almost obscenely loud in the hushed opulence of the suite.

"Your delivery, sir." Jonas announces. "Your luggage is in the bedroom. May I give you a tour?"

Rhodes passes him something, I presume cash. "We're good, thank you. I've stayed here before. I'm familiar with the layout."

"Excellent, sir. Please let us know if we can be of assistance."

And with that, Jonas exits.

"What is all this?" I ask, circling the rack, noticing some garments have protective liners while others don't, but everything looks expensive..

"I said I'd take care of everything." Pride oozes from his smile. "There's a formal event tomorrow night and I was hoping you'd be my plus one, and..." he shrugs, like it's no big deal, "some of the restaurants in town have dress codes. There should be shoes and whatever else. My instructions were to send anything you might need for a weekend in D.C. and to provide options."

Even knowing he's wealthy, this level of casual extravagance catches me off guard. "That's why you said not to worry about going back to my place."

"Yep." He has his phone in his hand and has already stepped past what must be tens of thousands of dollars of clothes, shoes, and whatever else he had sent up. "We'll send back what you don't like."

"How did you know my size?"

He has the wisdom to appear abashed. My brain kicks into gear. He used ARGUS to check my purchasing habits. *Is that possible?*

I wait...patiently watching him squirm.

He rubs the back of his neck. He's uncomfortable.

"Don't read anything into this."

My arms cross over my middle. It's a defensive position, but my instinct tells me to shift, to appear more open, less like I'm appalled. I lower my arms and that feels unnatural, so I sit, knees slightly apart. This position might not be best either.

"My ex was your size." He rubs the back of his neck. "You're completely different people, but she was about your size."

Am I his ex's size? It's hard to tell in photographs. *Maybe.*

But no. There are shoe boxes in that stack. He totally used ARGUS. But copping to a similarity to an ex is preferable to sharing that he owns the world's best detective, and that he might be using it in ways that shred privacy laws.

"How much did all this cost?" I tilt my head thoughtfully while gesturing to the extravagant display. I may be without a long-term relationship in my past, but I've dated enough to know that what he's done here is not normal. Even with my Ivy League connections, I've never seen anything quite like this.

With one last brush of his hand over the back of his head, he assumes the seat beside me but leaves enough space between us that our thighs don't touch. This way, when he leans over, he can comfortably talk without being in my space. The velvet sofa sighs beneath his weight. His cologne—subtle notes of cedar and something uniquely him—drifts toward me, familiar now after days in his company. The temperature between us seems to rise despite the precisely controlled climate of the suite, a reminder of the chemistry that's complicated everything from the start.

"My company. I mentioned it?"

"Yes, you did," I answer, aiming for both curious and skeptical with my features. "You said your company does well. How well?" I dramatically widen my eyes, pretending to be dismayed and suitably surprised.

"I've done well. This is technically my third company. The first was something small and a hobby when in undergrad. But the others, my second company especially, they've done well. When I contacted the professional shopper, she understood the task should be completed without allowing costs to impede decisions."

"Wow."

"Don't look at me differently, okay?"

A sharp pang of guilt cuts through my chest. He's being vulnerable with me, worried that his wealth will change how I see him, and here I am—the perfect example of someone who knew exactly who he was before we even met. But I'm doing my job. I can give him what he's looking for—genuine assurances that his success won't change how I treat him. Because it won't. The man sitting beside me, nervous about my reaction, is the same person I loved getting to know in the mountains.

"That's one of the things..." he pauses, rubbing his thumb over his index finger, gaze downward, "when we met, you didn't know who I was. Believe it or not, that's a rare thing."

He can never learn about KOAN.

I never planned on telling him, of course, but the potential damage of my deception suddenly feels overly personal—making this assignment increasingly complicated.

He lifts my hand and tangles his fingers with mine.

"You're so different from anyone I've met."

I have been myself with him, my real self. I so much want to deserve the compliment.

But you haven't been honest with him.

This is the part of the job that sucks—the moment when someone's trust in you becomes a weapon you're wielding against them. But I force myself to remember why I'm here. The man who just bought me tens of thousands of dollars' worth of clothes has access to surveillance capabilities that could topple governments. Finding my dress size is harmless—charming, even. But if those same capabilities are being used to sell classified information to the highest bidder; if he's providing kill lists to foreign governments who want to eliminate assets and whistleblowers; then the man I'm falling for is responsible for the deaths of people like me. People who put their lives on the line for a better world.

The thought sits like a stone in my stomach, but I can't ignore it. Not when the stakes are this high.

"I love that you're so open, so real. You probably don't even care about any of this stuff, and it makes me like you even more. But my ex would've flipped out with worry over how she presented herself and...I really want you to go with me to the event tomorrow night. Will you?"

The chandelier light catches the slight movement of his throat as he swallows, waiting for my answer. Outside the window, a distant siren wails—a reminder of the bustling city that surrounds us, so different from the quiet mountain retreat where we met. The plush carpet beneath my feet feels too soft, too manufactured after days of natural terrain.

"Go with you to the event?"

He nods.

"I already figured we'd be together this weekend," I force out, hoping for a natural sound.

"Good." He checks his watch. "Shit. I've got to go. I'm late."

"Oh. Want me to join you? What should I wear?"

"This one's a meeting. Boring. Stay here and relax." He hops up, selects a sports jacket to wear over his T-shirt, and rubs the back of his neck again. The movement is definitely his discomfort tell. "Are we okay?"

I nod, and he gives me a thumbs up. An actual thumbs up in the air.

I call out to him as he's approaching the door.

"You do realize I'm going to Google you the moment you leave this room, right?"

He stops, frowning.

Our eyes connect and he senses I'm teasing, because a smile slowly overtakes his frown. The air between us vibrates with unspoken things—my secrets, his wealth, the growing complexity of whatever is happening between us.

Really, I only threw Google out there to open the door for more questions. And with us going to an event tomorrow night, I have a green light to be as knowledgeable as possible in preparation for the people we're meeting. He knows I'm CIA-trained.

"As long as you promise not to look at me differently, Google away," he says, his voice softer now, almost vulnerable. His hand on the polished brass doorknob, the slight creak as it turns—these small sounds echo in the room as loudly as my own heartbeat in my ears.

The question, "What does that mean?" dies on my lips. There's no need to push that hard into the lie.

CHAPTER
TWENTY

SYDNEY

The door closes behind Rhodes and I do a sweep of the suite, my fingers tracing along the underside of table edges where adhesive might still be tacky, checking light fixtures where a lens might catch a reflection, behind framed art with the practiced touch of someone who's found surveillance this way before. My movements are automatic, a dance I've performed across four continents.

The suite appears clean—it doesn't seem like our team, or anyone else, set up surveillance. But just in case, I step in the bathroom, turn on the shower, and dial Quinn.

"Syd?"

"Yeah. It's me. He left the suite five minutes ago."

"We're on him."

An uncomfortable sensation settles into my stomach. "Had a feeling. Who's here?"

"Jake and Noah. Staying in a room four floors below yours. Closest we could get."

"It's fine. I've told you he's not dangerous."

"Did you know he's got security?"

"No." I've seen no one.

"He's with them in the lobby now. If the facial recognition is accurate, one is former secret service. He's not playing around."

Really? He seems so aloof. Clueless even. Is that all a game? Or… "Could security be standard for him?"

"Perhaps in cities. Insurance might require it."

She's right. Depending on what insurance his company has, given he's the founder and his brain is partly what investors invested in, it's not inconceivable.

"When he left just now, he greenlit my researching him. Since he's opened the gateway, my plan is to pepper him with questions over the weekend."

"Nice work."

It is good work. I'm right where I need to be. The nausea roiling through is a side effect of having a conscience.

"How's San Fran doing? Did she get the boot?"

"Not yet. She used the key card. Explored the offices. She didn't find anything of substance. No file storage room."

"You didn't actually think there would be, did you?"

"Me? No. But Brie thought there would be files of contracts. Legal documents."

"Rhodes has a save-the-trees reputation. There was a *Business Week* article about how if he had his way, his business wouldn't own a printer."

"I don't remember that…"

I close my eyes and visualize the byline. "April 2021."

"Look at that," Quinn says under her breath. "So, what are your plans?"

"I'm going to change and head down to the bar. Scope the area. I think that's where he's meeting this Evie Thompson. If he sees me, maybe he'll feel obligated to invite me to join them."

"Jake will be close."

"Not too close. Remember, you just told me he has two security guards. There could be others. And did you guys access this room before us?"

"No. Prior occupants had a late checkout, then housekeeping, then his security followed. Stayed until shortly before your arrival."

"Warn Jake. Rhodes may be aloof, but he hired the best and they won't be. They'll pick up on a tail. You know, it's interesting that he didn't greet his security with me present. Maybe he doesn't want me to know he travels with security."

"Possibly. You have a device you can plant, right?" Quinn asks.

"Yes, but why would I? I'm here with him. He's not planning on taking any meetings in our room. It's an unnecessary risk. And if his team is professional, whenever we leave, they'll sweep."

"True enough."

"He invited me to a gala tomorrow night. I'm assuming it's associated with the Bastille Day celebration."

"Look at you. Did you pack for this? I accessed the security cam in the lobby. Swanky."

"Funny story. I've got an entire wardrobe from Neiman Marcus in the entry."

"Seriously?"

"Yep."

"Score."

The icky feeling swirling in my gut climbs my throat. I'm not in this for the clothes. I'm not aiming to use Rhodes. My objective is to learn about the deals ARGUS is making. Not what the official, public information states, but to verify the rumors circulating through the intelligence community.

Yet there's something else tangled in this discomfort —the realization that the man who quoted mythology and shared childhood stories feels real in ways that threaten my objectivity. That hasn't happened on an assignment before. Usually, my cover feels like a separate skin I can shed when needed. This time, the line between Sydney-the-operative and Sydney-the-woman is blurring in ways that make my training feel suddenly insufficient.

"Interesting." Quinn says. "Rhodes car service stopped in front of the Russian embassy."

The ickiness diminishes. A cold wave washes over me, numbing the conflicted notions. This single piece of information transforms everything—my objective, my conflicted feelings, even the luxurious suite. Rhodes visiting the Russian embassy isn't just confirmation that KOAN's suspicions were valid; it's validation that the version of Rhodes I've been connecting with is one facet of a multi-faceted identity. He's presenting the face he wants me to see, similar to me presenting him with my cover identity.

"Alright." Quinn's tone shifts to professional, triggering a similar shift in my mentality.

I've been having fun with one version of Rhodes. A version of him that by his own admittance hasn't seen the light of day in decades. I bonded with that version of him. But the man who built a billion-dollar empire has an entirely different persona, and Caroline was correct when she pitched me on KOAN. As an active mega donor, the government won't investigate rumors about Rhodes or his company. Politicians won't bite the hand that feeds them. We need to find out exactly what kind of deals ARGUS is structuring, and if Russia is one of its clients, our mission is critical.

"From here on out, only contact me through the portal. Keep one tracker on your person at all times. I checked the charge on your tags and you're good. You said he gave you permission to research him?"

"Yeah."

"Be wary."

"Why?"

"Classic projection. He might be doing a deep dive on you. Even if he didn't request it, by showing up in D.C. with him, his security team will be doing one."

"Right." Maybe I should've used an alias. But no. I can't second guess myself. If the rumored capabilities of ARGUS are correct, there's too high of a chance they'd smoke out an alias. "I'll take my laptop down to the bar. Get him used to seeing me working. I'll claim I'm job hunting."

"Good plan. And, Sydney?"

I pause, waiting for the "be careful" warning. "It might be tempting to accept a job he offers, if it goes there, but think twice. You'll be getting in deep, and no one asked you to sign up for a long-term undercover gig. Deep UC with someone who can track every detail of your life...that's a lot."

She's right. My employee agreement is for remote work with travel.

"If you decide to go for it, there's a resume on the portal that will likely land you a job."

I'm getting ahead of myself. He hasn't suggested I move to San Francisco. Yes, he asked for my resume, but he made it clear it wasn't for a position at his company.

No, I need to stay focused. This weekend I'll get a clearer picture of ARGUS capabilities and any black-market client roster, and when he boards a plane on Sunday, I'll regroup with the team.

One project leg at a time.

I step into the living area of the suite and peruse the clothes he's purchased, flipping over price tags that scream Rhodes got ripped off.

The black V-neck dress with pin-thin straps and a low, semi-fitted waist that drapes away from the bodice and skims my ankles is pure femininity, and tempting, but instead I select a straight, cream skirt; white, fitted tank; and a plush, cream cardigan, deciding that the cream color sets off my olive skin and dark hair. The gold Prada sandals lend a luxurious, casual touch.

I don't have a briefcase or tote that will blend with my laptop, so I unwrap the light gray Chloe handbag and gather my laptop, and head down to the hotel bar.

A man in a tan business suit with no tie meets my gaze from across the room. The absence of a tie has me thinking he's a power player. It's the men who don't feel obligated to tie a noose around their neck that are the ones with the real power and influence. The others who conform to uncomfortable apparel are struggling to fit in and make a name for themselves. That's a piece of education my pricey Penn diploma awarded me.

I order a sparkling water with lime and crack open my laptop. The bar's polished mahogany gleams under amber lighting, casting everyone in a flattering glow while making it harder to discern subtle details. The gentle clink of ice against glass and the murmured conversations create an acoustic blanket that would make most surveillance difficult. I've strategically chosen a spot at the bar that allows me to see anyone entering the establishment. Restrooms are to the back. There's only one access point.

At this time of day, the tables are mostly empty. Given the suits, I'd expect the table of two women to my left and the table of one man and two women one table over from them are here on business and they have time to kill either before flights home or before a work dinner.

I don't see anyone who strikes me as security. Rhodes' security detail is likely in his proximity.

The man with a tan suit approaches.

"Mind if I join you?"

"Actually..." I nudge the laptop, "planning on getting some work done."

"Oh, what company are you with?"

I narrow my eyes, studying this man and his thin rope necklace. He's not D.C. That's not the look of a lobbyist. Why is he approaching me?

"Don't want to say?" With one dose of his smug smile, I feel unclean. "Or a beautiful woman like you..."

He makes a show of looking at my ringless left hand, "You can't be single."

Ugh. What a blowhard.

I catalog the details: fake Rolex that doesn't quite sit right on his wrist, a tan that's too orange to be natural, suit that's expensive but poorly tailored, brand logos on his leather loafers. He's trying too hard to project success while missing the subtle markers that would make it convincing. A wannabe player who likely exaggerates his Pentagon connections—dangerous only in his desperation to seem important.

"I'm not single. If you wouldn't mind." I push my laptop screen further back for visibility, but purposefully don't wake the screen, as I don't want this sleazy specimen seeing my name or any other identifier.

To my dismay, the tan suit slides a bar stool back and sits one stool over.

"My name's Daniel. Let me buy you a drink." He holds up a hand. "I hear you, you're not on the market, but—"

On the market?

"Sir, there's a lot of room at the bar. The lady is here to get work done." Tan suit and I both direct our attention to a man in a navy suit with a pink and navy striped tie. I estimate he's in his mid-forties, with trimmed, dark hair combed to the side. It's conceivable he works for the hotel, although there's no name tag.

"Fine. Fine. I can take a hint." He nods his head like he's soothing us both and moves to the opposite end of the bar.

"Sorry about that, ma'am. Daniel can be…" He cocks his head to the side. He doesn't need to say more.

"Is he your friend?"

"No. He's a salesman. Does a lot of work with the Pentagon."

"Say no more." He's probably a lowlife who seals the deal with drunken nights out, and if friendly doesn't work, gathers compromising photographs of his client's escapades.

"I'm Ian Gregory. Iowa State congressional representative."

I shake his hand, assessing. His title fits. He's wearing a professional suit, but it's not too nice. There's no noticeable accent, which fits for the Midwest. And he naturally assumed the position of protecting the little lady sitting by herself at the bar. One glance at the gold band on his finger, and I sense his wife would be proud.

"Nice to meet you, Ian. I'm Sydney. I'm here for the weekend with a friend."

"Oh. Nice. Hitting the tourist spots?"

"If work allows." I smile, softening my comment aimed at getting him to move on, and then, to be cordial, I ask, "Which spots do you recommend?"

He hits the D.C. top five, and opens his phone, swiping up to show me where to go to get the best hand-made ice cream.

He's relaxed, and I almost miss it, but I catch the black device fall from his palm as he moves closer to my stool. The movement is smooth, practiced—a drop technique I recognize because I've used it myself. Time seems to slow as I track the device's trajectory toward my handbag.

Who the fuck is this guy? He's attempting to plant a bug on me?

It's not me he's after. Obviously, it's Rhodes.

My instincts kick in before conscious thought can interfere. I snatch the device mid-fall, the motion so fluid it could be mistaken for adjusting my position on the stool. Our eyes meet, and in that fraction of a second, I see his recognition that his game is blown.

Rhodes knows I'm former CIA. I don't have to play this off.

I lift the slim rectangular device and tilt my head, raising one pointed eyebrow.

"Ian Gregory. Who are you really?"

His Adam's apple bobs, and he glances over his shoulder.

Is he here with someone? The gross tan suit?

He reaches into his jacket pocket. I tense, calculating the distance to the exit, mentally mapping the positions of everyone in the room who might be part of his team. We're in a public spot, but that doesn't mean this couldn't go sideways fast.

He removes a black leather badge holder, and opens it, displaying an FBI badge.

My mind races through the implications. Whatever Rhodes is involved in has attracted attention from the very agencies we believed wouldn't touch ARGUS due to political donations. My fingers hover near my phone, ready to send an alert to Quinn if needed. The game just changed completely.

CHAPTER
TWENTY-ONE

RHODES

The driver stops to let me out at Boris Nemtsov Plaza. It's a beautiful summer day in D.C. and a group of tourists, led by a woman with silver spectacles and a European accent, stop along the wall of the Russian Embassy. A car horn honks farther down the street, and I nod at the automobile with a lit Lyft sign perched in the window before jaywalking in front of his stopped car.

I scan the sidewalk, aware that surveillance cameras are capturing every passerby. When Ms. Victoria Romanovich suggested meeting outside the Russian Embassy, I considered declining. But, the reality is, a meeting with a Russian diplomat will be widely observed and noted. Some might argue it's publicity for ARGUS. Now, if we met inside the embassy, rumors would spread about who I met with and questions might be asked regarding the secrecy. This way, it's out in the open. There are no laws against meetings.

A woman in a light gray suit with shoulder length black hair approaches. Her gaze travels from me, along the street, to the sedan I climbed out of that is now driving away.

"Mr. MacMillan," she says, her smile formal, eyes hidden behind a pair of black framed sunglasses.

"Ms. Romanovich," I answer, returning her firm grip as we shake hands.

"It's such a nice day. Thank you for agreeing to meet outside. Are you up for a walk?"

"How's my hair? Has the wind ruffled it too much?" I point in the general direction of my head, waiting for her to get the joke.

She stills, and I zero in on her thickly applied red lipstick and matching nails.

There's no reaction. She doesn't get it.

"You have a photographer somewhere out here, right? I want to be certain I look my best."

With that, she smiles, revealing a touch of red lipstick on her front tooth.

"Shall we?" she says, gesturing for us to walk away from the embassy.

I let my hands fall to my side and fall in line beside her.

"We might be photographed, but not by our photographers. That's not why I asked you to meet outdoors."

"No?" It doesn't matter what she says. I'll never trust the Russians. Doesn't mean I won't do business with them—with eyes wide open.

"The Forbes Intelligence System."

Her heels rap a steady stream of clicks on the concrete

sidewalk. I expect her to expand, but we arrive at the intersection in silence.

"Is there more to that? Did I miss something?"

"There are interested parties."

Yes, there are. She's right. It's been on and off the metaphorical auction block for years.

"And?"

"Are you bidding?"

Miles wishes to explore an acquisition. It might be something we need to buy through a separate entity to avoid congressional interest.

The pedestrian light flicks white and the two of us proceed.

"I think you should," she says.

"Why?"

"Would you prefer for it to go to Moscow or Beijing?"

"Excuse me, Ms. Romanovich, but are you not Moscow?"

"We would buy before we allowed adversaries to purchase, but you are our partner."

Technically, they are a client. But if a client prefers the word partner, I don't get lost in semantics.

"I'm looking into it," I say on an inhale.

"We want you to do more than look into it."

We stop on a section of sidewalk situated between a busy street and shrubbery.

"Let me explain," she answers in crisp, textbook English with a distinct Russian accent. "If we were to purchase, there would be opposition."

That's an accurate assessment. It would be easier to list the countries that would support the purchase than to list those that would oppose.

I can't see her eyes behind those oversized sunglasses, but I sense she's staring at me, waiting for a response.

"I've been looking into it. It's not clear cut. We do not wish to invite an investigation."

More than that, I haven't determined we need to acquire the database. We have a wealth of data. The beauty of our system is the ability to cull massive amounts of data into useful information. While acquiring the Forbes Intelligence System is tempting, I get nervous at the responsibilities that would result in strengthening ARGUS capabilities with such an acquisition.

"We want you to find a way."

"Thank you for sharing your position."

We're approaching Embassy Row, and up ahead I spot my security detail. Brandon, my head of security, insisted his on-call staff, men who work as needed for those visiting D.C., cover my visit.

It's overkill, but I trust Brandon. Plus, what's the point of hiring an expert if you're not going to heed their recommendations?

"I'm afraid you might not understand," she says.

"What's that?" I check my watch. I've got about twenty minutes before I'm due to meet Evie.

"If you don't buy it, there are parties that will be forced to expose an unsanctioned deal."

Saudi Arabia.

Goddamn it.

Those greedy fuckers probably hand-delivered evidence to Russia.

"We trust you will choose wisely. It would not be wise to lose the trust you've built with your clients."

And look at that. Now she's chosen the correct term.

Click. Click. Click.

The rapid fire of her heels proceeds down the sidewalk in the direction of her embassy. Walk and meeting concluded.

Fuck. This is all Miles' fault. He wanted the Saudi deal to help fund our expansion. Growth. Profit. I told him it was a bad idea. He argued sanctions would be lifted, and they have been, but it doesn't change the fact they were in place when the deal closed.

The security detail approaches at a fast pace. I glance behind me, halfway expecting to find someone charging.

The detail reaches me and says, "Mr. MacMillan, your car will be here in two."

"Thank you."

"Sir, I have an update."

Excellent. "Let me have it."

"The FBI approached Ms. Sydney Parker at the hotel."

"What?"

I spin so I can see his lips when he speaks.

"Yes, sir. We don't have audio. But she's with him now."

"In our suite?"

"No, sir. In the bar."

"Did it look like they know each other?" She is former CIA and lives in the D.C. area. It's possible this is nothing. They could be acquaintances.

"He flashed his badge, so I don't believe so, sir."

Has an investigation been authorized? Would the FBI approach her simply because she showed up at a hotel with me?

"You've got eyes on her?"

"Yes, sir."

Fuck.

"At the Round Robin bar?" The hotel bar at the Willard, nicknamed the Oval Office of Bars by Condé Nast, is an iconic Washington location. It's not surprising Sydney would check it out, but one isn't generally approached by the FBI when enjoying an afternoon mint julep.

"Yes, sir."

"I'll move my meeting." Evie might not want a run-in with the FBI. "Tell your guys not to let Sydney out of their sight. If you can overhear anything…"

"Yes, sir."

CHAPTER
TWENTY-TWO

SYDNEY

The blue field represents justice, as does the miniature shield with an eagle crest holding a sword and scales, and yet, I don't trust the badge. There's something about this pasty white man in a cheap suit that doesn't sit well with me. Yes, he just came to my defense, but it all feels a little too convenient in this sparsely populated bar.

He withdraws his ID, a smug yes-I'm-a-badass expression on his freshly shaven face.

"Keep it out," I say, pulling out my phone.

I snap a photo and smile.

"Later on I'll call your field office."

His eyes widen, his head jerks, and his fingers shift, all signs he's surprised. But he's not shocked, and there's no worry.

No, his thin lips spread into a semblance of a smile.

"Why would you call my field office?"

"That's the only way to verify you're sporting a real badge, right?"

In reality, I will not waste time calling a field office. I'll be sending this photo straight to Quinn so she can verify and, if true, determine who else within the government is investigating ARGUS. Because Caroline believes Rhodes MacMillan and his AI surveillance company are above the law.

Although, if I'm honest, our intel always felt shaky. It seemed to me that, at a minimum, the NSA would be all over ARGUS, possibly even serving as an invisible partner.

Ian Gregory's gaze travels around the bar, over my shoulder and up along the ceiling and the inset lighting. He must've clocked the small security camera tucked away near a carbon monoxide detector.

"May I put it away?" he asks.

"Be my guest."

"And may I sit?"

If you must is on the tip of my tongue, but confrontation isn't the best approach when I need information.

"Please."

He sits down and I search the area for the earlier jerk, wanting to see how he reacts to my welcoming a different man to sit.

He's nowhere to be found within these olive-green walls.

"What do you want from me?"

The FBI agent's lips press together in such a way that he hides the muted beige-pink lip color and puffs his pale skin. It's not a flattering look. He rests an elbow on the edge of the bar, and leans, exposing his dress shirt and a sweat ring below his armpit.

With one elbow on the bar, he clasps his hands together at chest level and crosses one leg over the other. A defensive posture—an odd one—but also one that minimizes any threat I might feel from a stranger. He relaxes his lips and waves the bartender away, declining to order. "Rhodes MacMillan is a person of interest. You're his guest. Yes?" He doesn't wait for confirmation. "Now, Sydney Parker, you no longer work for the CIA."

There's something about his off-kilter smile that makes my jaw clench.

"Ms. Parker, are you working for anyone right now?"

"At the moment, I'm unemployed." I look him directly in the eye. I'm not breaking cover for this guy. Not to mention, for all I know, this guy may not be investigating Rhodes, he could be doing Rhodes a favor and verifying me in an off-the-books quid pro quo.

The thought has me straightening, running through what I've said, hoping I didn't slip and expose our operation.

"But you're..." He pauses and the fingers on my left hand roll into a small fist, *"friends* with Rhodes MacMillan."

"I'm not a hired escort if that's what you're implying."

He coughs, covering his mouth with a balled-up fist.

"I did not mean to imply that," he says, blinking back his apparent surprise at my directness. "Look, I think we got off to a bad start. Since you're a former CIA analyst, I'm going to be frank with you. We've been monitoring

MacMillan for months, and when you checked in with him, it piqued our interest. That's all."

I sense he's telling the truth, but I still don't trust him.

"We met a few days ago. I'm unemployed. You can check that," I respond.

"After your dismissal, did you file for unemployment?"

"I wasn't fired." *Asshole.* "And no, I haven't filed for unemployment." As I say the words, the ramifications play out in my mind. If I follow Rhodes to San Francisco, I'll need to find employment somewhat quickly or I'll look suspect. But why does the FBI care? Is this an open investigation?

"I see. If we were to check, we would confirm you have no salary income but have not yet filed for unemployment. And you're staying for the weekend?"

This guy's questions are out of line. "Is being friends with Rhodes MacMillan against the law?"

"No." He emphasizes his answer with a quick shake of his head. He reaches inside his jacket and pulls out a business card. "Ms. Parker, you clearly know that Rhodes MacMillan isn't average. As a former CIA officer, you also understand the work we civil servants do to protect our country. If you find yourself in danger," I raise an eyebrow at his statement, "or you uncover information that puts our citizens in danger, please call."

"Is the FBI in the business of cultivating assets now?"

"We're in the business of protecting United States citizens and upholding the law."

"I see." I take his card, read it, and slip it into my bag. "Well thank you for all you do."

He pushes off the stool.

"I'm a friend, Ms. Parker. An ally."

I give him a short, cordial nod with a curt smile. My expression should convey that he should leave now, and he does.

I watch him walk away, noting a deep crease in his suit coat that lies over his rear. He's been sitting for a long time today. In an office? Doubtful. In a car parked on the street? Also doubtful given there's no parking on the streets near here. Perhaps an inconspicuous armchair in the lobby?

The urge to message Quinn is strong, but there are cameras. I can't send this via message from my phone. I need to access our portal.

I check my watch, questioning if I have time to do so before Rhodes meets with Evie Thompson. I need to be here when he walks in. She's not here yet.

Twenty minutes. That's plenty of time. I'll head to the room, reach out to Quinn, and be back down before the meeting.

I catch the bartender's eye and finger my napkin and drink.

"I'll be back. Don't remove my drink, okay?"

What the hell is going on? Rhodes went to the Russian Embassy this afternoon, and he's piqued the interest of the FBI. It appears all those rumors are true, and our intel that he's above reproach and investigation is cocked.

CHAPTER
TWENTY-THREE

RHODES

Evie Thompson stands on the sidewalk outside of The Hamilton, holding her phone, glued to the screen. She doesn't look up once.

Her dark hair with grown-out highlights is split down the middle, tucked tightly behind her ears. The charcoal suit she's wearing is no nonsense, as are her short, natural nails.

Her father is a secretive hedge fund manager, born in Egypt, and he maintains ties throughout the Middle East. As one of my first investors, I owe his daughter this meeting. I would've met with her anyway.

Evie could've gone the route of spoiled, entitled rich kid, but she didn't. She's worked her ass off. Top of her class at Harvard Law, and she chose the public servant route. Probably an easy choice for someone with what has to be a sizeable trust fund, but she could be spending her days traveling the world and chasing hard-to-get handbags, and she's not. Therefore, she intrigues me.

I stand in front of her as she types away on her screen. She continues typing, fingers flying, clueless that if I wanted, I could read the email response she's tapping out.

I clear my throat and large brown eyes flash.

"Just a minute," she snips.

Alright then.

"I'll go inside and get our table."

By the time the hostess has gathered two menus, Evie's at my side.

"I'm not going to eat," she rushes. "Why'd you change the location?"

"A precaution," I admit.

I should probably warn her to be more cautious. She's climbing in the ranks and there are those who might be interested in her work.

"What're you doing these days?" I ask as we slide into a window booth.

Before she can answer, I say to the hostess, "We're only having drinks. Do you have a cocktail menu?"

"On the back," she says with a smile. "Our smoked salmon appetizer is the best, if you decide you want something to snack on."

"Thank you," I say.

The restaurant is basically void of people this time of day but before long the after-five crowd will hit. However, at this time of day on a summer Friday, the patrons may be tourists. The D.C. power players are likely long gone for the summer weekend.

Evie taps on her phone and then with a sigh, sets it

down on the table and flips it over so she can't see the screen.

"Done?" I can't help but ask. I'm not certain if she's Gen Z, but she's definitely self-absorbed.

"Sorry." She picks up a glass of water and sips. Those eyes of hers are so large her portrait could be mistaken for AI. They make her look young, probably younger than she is.

"You wanted to meet?" I prompt.

"If I gave you a list of names, could you get me information on them?"

I sit back, amused. "What've you heard? That I sell information to the highest bidder?"

I've heard the rumors. There's a vestige of truth to them, but it's not as simple as the rumors insinuate. Nothing ever is.

She sits back and places her hands demurely in her lap. "Let me start over. I'm sorry, my mind is all over the place this afternoon."

I can see that. While her hair is pulled back tightly behind her ears, the strands around her shoulders fall uncontrollably around her in an unkempt, wind-blown fashion.

"I'm working a human trafficking case."

Ah. Okay.

"The case officially targets the Los Zetas cartel. We located twenty-two women in D.C. nail spas that were trafficked here by them."

I haven't read anything about that, but my news focus leans toward finance and international.

"Here's the issue. The more I learn about their process, it becomes clear they aren't doing it alone."

"You have suspects?" That's her list. People with leverage who could have customs officials or DEA look the other way. She's probably right. The volume of drugs alone coming into the country each year is evidence in and of itself of crime on the inside.

"Some senators, congressmen."

Hmm. She's going up the chain.

"Where's the list?"

She scans the restaurant.

Of course, now she's concerned about someone watching.

She hands me a rumpled list torn from a cutesy notepad with a rainbow on the top corner.

"Does your boss know you're looking into these people?" I scan the list of names. While some of the names are familiar, they don't mean anything to me. I live in California and these individuals aren't my representatives. None of them are on the Senate Intelligence Committee and they aren't Pentagon players.

Her pupils are dilated. *Fear.*

"You think your boss is in on it?"

"I don't know anything yet. But I know my searches are being monitored."

Her father's face flashes. He must hate that his daughter has been assigned to go after the lowest of the low.

About half of organized crime business these days is legit, but still, she's hunting groups willing to traffic humans. You can't sink much lower in the criminal food chain.

"Do you have a security detail?"

I didn't see one outside, but it's quite possible she'd insist a detail not follow her while she's working.

"No, that's not for the underlings," she says with a smile. Although, an assistant DA in D.C. isn't an underling. But I hear they work like dogs so maybe that's how she feels.

"What about your father?"

"No. If you're going to ask if he's going to pay the bills," she presses her lips together and shakes her head slightly, "he won't be. We're not really talking these days. I'm coming to you because my gut says you're a good guy and that you aren't obsessed with cutting deals for the sake of money."

She flips her phone over and taps it, flicking over photos of women with dark hair and haunted eyes posed in mug shot style.

"The cartel trafficked these women in?"

"It's a robust operation. It never stops. A bust here, there. It's not working. They just regroup."

"Does your father know what you're working on?" If she were my daughter, I'd insist she move to a different division.

"That's why we're not talking."

She's defiant. Did he also cut her off? I'm not a fashion savvy guy, but I can tell she's wearing an off-the-rack suit by the way the sleeves are slightly too short and the shoulder pads scrunch with extra material.

I fold the list and slip it into my trouser pocket. "I'll look into it. But, you know, if these men are involved, it's likely my systems aren't going to come up with anything that will help you."

"Could I possibly talk to someone who works for you? Brainstorm the kind of information that could be useful?"

I think of Daisy. She'd love to use our baby, ARGUS, for a project of this nature.

"Sure. I'll put you in touch with a person on my team. Do you have a secure laptop? Phone?"

The brown leather briefcase sitting on the floor isn't closed, and I'm guessing that's because it's loaded with files. *Paper files.*

"No. I have a personal phone, but I'm sure it's being monitored."

"I'll have Daisy send you a package. Follow her instructions."

"Thank you. We're underfunded, but I feel like…" her words trail and her head shakes slightly, as if she can't believe she's thinking the words she's about to say.

"You feel like someone is purposefully averting funds to limit the pursuit of this case."

She opens her mouth and releases a slow breath.

"You don't need to say more. Daisy will be in touch."

"It could just be that everyone at my level is overloaded and the budget is too constrained."

"Absolutely." Human trafficking isn't the highest of priorities for the United States government. In theory, drugs are a higher priority, and the fight against them has gone nowhere for decades. Possibilities abound.

We stand and a harried waitress appears.

"I'm so sorry. I was on break and they didn't come to tell me you'd been seated."

"No worries," I say.

I need to get back to Sydney. And I'm itching to call Daisy, both to tell her about Evie but also to ask her to proceed with that deep dive on Sydney. Her meeting with the FBI is likely innocent, but there's no harm in confirming she's been truthful about her identity.

Evie and I exit the air-conditioned restaurant and step back out into the heat. She sets her briefcase on the sidewalk and removes the suit jacket, revealing a wrinkled white silk blouse.

"Hey," I say as she situates herself for what I presume is a walk back to her office. "Do you have any contacts in the FBI?"

"Some," she answers, straightening but leaving her briefcase on the ground leaning against her calf. Her suit jacket hangs over her bag and trails the concrete sidewalk. "Mostly those who work human trafficking. You can't possibly need a contact."

I grin. "I have sources. But I'm curious. Would an FBI agent work on an unofficial investigation?"

"I mean, sure. We all have our pet projects. Why?" Her head tilts and awareness dawns. "Are they investigating you?"

"Not to my knowledge," I answer with a professional and curt smile.

But if a wise person were to investigate me, they wouldn't put it on the books, would they? Especially after Miles pushed to kill one. I'm considered a major donor. ARGUS works closely with the Pentagon and NSA.

She's looking up at me with an inquisitive expression. *And that's how rumors get started.*

"Forget I said anything. Daisy will be in touch," I tell Evie. "Are you good to get back to your office? Should I hail you a cab? I have a car if you—"

"That's okay. The walk back is the only exercise I'll

get in today." She bends and lifts the shoulder strap onto her shoulder and tucks the bag against her hip. "Rhodes, thank you. I know you don't have to do this, but it's for a good cause."

"Happy to do it."

She smiles. "I had a feeling you'd say that. That's one thing I learned from my father."

"What's that?"

"Highly successful people are still regular people. It doesn't hurt to ask."

Inside, I cringe. I'm inundated with people *just asking*. But she's not asking for an investment.

"You look out for yourself. And can I give you some advice?"

"Sure."

"If you find yourself in a precarious position, reach out to your dad. Whatever disagreement you've had, he loves you. You will be his priority. Always."

At least, that's the way it should be. With a demure smile and a nod, she turns to weave her way through the sidewalk pedestrians.

Ten minutes later, I've dictated a number of messages, conferred with Daisy, and I'm pushing the revolving door into the Willard InterContinental. As the air-conditioning blasts my skin, it occurs to me I should've also encouraged Evie to dictate her emails. Typing them out is inefficient.

The cool lobby air is a relief after the D.C. heat, but it does nothing to settle the unease that's been building since my conversation with the Russians. Blackmail attempts, FBI agents approaching Sydney, and now Evie's theory of corruption reaching the highest levels of government. Too much is happening at once for my comfort, and my instincts are screaming that something's off.

My gaze sweeps the round bar until I locate a transformed Sydney in a creamy outfit that sets off her silky shoulder-length hair. Hell, the creamy white stands out against the mahogany bar like a ray of light. The rest of the room blurs as she comes into focus. Laptop open, she's intent on the screen, and it allows me a moment to take her in. The healthy tan and energetic glow are more at home in the woods, on a trail, than in a stuffy bar, but I'm glad she's here, with me.

Four days in, and I am so fucked.

And if she's working with the FBI, I might be fucked in more ways than one.

CHAPTER
TWENTY-FOUR

RHODES

Syd's dark eyes flash with recognition. The connection between us strengthens to the point I half-expect to see a ray of light binding us across the oval bar.

A cocktail glass with ice and lime sit beside her laptop. Seats at the bar are filling up, with only a couple empty barstools. It's too early for dinner, given it's not even five, yet for the twenty- and thirty-something D.C. crowd, we're entering prime-time happy hour. Scanning the room, I'd bet most of the suits are out-of-towners, likely lobbyists, toasting the weekend. Perhaps some are in town for this weekend's Bastille Day festivities.

She closes her laptop as I approach, and I'm reminded once again the FBI approached her. But this is Sydney. The woman who met me on a hike and jumped naked into a swimming hole with a rebel yell.

As Miles claimed, I'm growing paranoid. But with

reason. Blackmail from the Russian embassy intensifies the suspicion that I've become a target.

Or perhaps it's this version of Sydney Parker, the sophisticated woman in a cream white V-neck silk top that manages to be both refined and sensuous, that intensifies the paranoia. With the addition of eyeliner, her deep brown eyes appear rounder, her gaze calculating. Her natural beauty shines through, but this is no longer a twenty-something on vacation. Seated at the oval bar, I'm reminded she's a career professional, which means she wants something. For some, it's a simple want. A successful company. Security. For others, it's a need to feed ambition, to rise in ranks. Pride.

Through pride, the devil became the devil. Pride leads to every vice. C.S. Lewis didn't mince words.

"That's a serious face," Sydney says.

I give myself the time to study her. Lips glossed, makeup tastefully done, shiny hair smoothed. She's wearing the clothes the personal shopper selected, so I can't read into those. The concern etched in her brown eyes reads as genuine. Her angled body and openness support the intimacy we've built over the last few days. Yet I can't shake the gut instinct clawing through my insides, preaching caution.

"Rhodes?"

With a slight shake of my head, an attempt to rid myself of this unease, I pull out the bar stool and keep it light.

"It's been a day."

The phrase slips out, and it's not until after it floats between us I realize how ridiculous a statement that is. I've been working for less than two hours. But that's the statement I uttered on repeat with Sara at the end of a workday.

"Are you done now?"

I lift her mostly empty glass to my nose, inhaling. There's no scent. I tilt the glass, clinking the ice.

"What is this?"

"Tonic and lime."

"No alcohol?"

She lifts a shoulder and smiles. Why is she sitting at a bar if she didn't want to drink alcohol? Why not relax in our suite? And why does someone who claims to be unemployed have what looked like a government-grade secure connection on her laptop?

"You said you live close by?" I know exactly where she resides, but I need a segue to ask the necessary question.

"Commuting distance," she says. "Do you want a drink? Or did you drink at your meeting?"

I did tell her I was meeting someone for drinks. Is that why she's down here?

"Location changed. And, no, we didn't get around to ordering drinks." The bartender approaches, but I wave him away. "Unless, do you want something?" I ask, catching myself, as I should always ask the lady if she cares for more.

"Rhodes MacMillan." A firm hand on my shoulder presses down. "I thought that was you."

"Senator Crawford," I say, racking my memory for his first name, but coming up blank.

He's on the Senate Intelligence Committee, and I've met with him on several occasions. Nice enough, midwestern, centrist. Served in the military—National

Guard. Always willing to listen on tech-related bills, but highly opinionated on all matters of defense. The kind of man who makes it his business to know everyone worth knowing in D.C.'s intelligence circles.

"What brings you to—" His words cut off mid-sentence, and his entire demeanor shifts. The practiced politician's smile falters as his gaze locks on Sydney. There's recognition there, immediate and unmistakable, but something else too. Satisfaction? Surprise?

The flush on Sydney that I'd assumed was makeup drains from her face entirely. She's frozen, staring directly at Crawford with the kind of deer-in-headlights look that no amount of training can completely hide. Her fingers tighten around her laptop case. Then, as if waking from a dream, she blinks, smiles a polite, fake smile, and gathers her laptop.

"Senator Crawford, Sydney Parker," but the way he's looking at her, and the way she reacted to him, I'd bet money these two know each other.

"I didn't recognize you, Sydney," Crawford says, adjusting the lapel on his suit coat.

"I'll see you back…," Sydney's voice drops to such a low decibel I can't hear the rest of her words, but I read her lips. She'll see me back in the room.

And then she's gone with Senator Crawford and I both following her with our gaze. Crawford's expression morphs into one of appreciation for her backside and I clear my throat, noting his gold wedding band.

I hate politicians.

"Is she still with the CIA?" he asks.

No is on the tip of my lips, but after her run-in with

the FBI today, and her sitting out here at a bar, I'm uncertain of anything.

"Why?"

"Are you with her?"

Once again, I find myself uncertain how to answer. If he's looking for me to say she's a friend so he can pursue her, then fuck that.

"Why?"

"Oh. It's nothing. I have nothing but admiration for her," he says.

The words themselves are unoffensive, but there's an unmistakable gleam in his eye that puts me on edge. The expression is akin to gloating, but I could be misreading what's nothing more than yet another pompous asshole.

What connection would the senator have to a CIA office? Did she leave because she was uncomfortable? It shouldn't take long to uncover the answer if it's a documented connection.

"I'm glad I ran into you," he says.

"Is that right?"

"I heard ARGUS is looking at expanding its footprint. Have you considered Kentucky?"

If I were in a jovial mood, I'd outright laugh.

"Tornado-prone, high heat." The answer is obvious. Weather risks can't be ignored.

"Thought you might say that, and I understand the appeal of Iceland. But we've got a couple of congressmen that would love the opportunity to make a pitch. We've got low taxes and a commerce group willing to make an offer you can't refuse."

Oh, but I can. Instead of stating the obvious, I choose the diplomatic path.

"I'll be happy to make introductions to the executive team scouting locations."

"Excellent. I'm sure you see the wisdom of leaving a state with high taxes and an affinity for—"

"If you'll excuse me." I don't want to hear him bash California. Our location was chosen for the talent pool, and while San Francisco might not be my favorite, I'm not moving our headquarters to Kentucky. Ever. This is the part of the job I hate, and the reason I pay others to deal with the salesmen.

"Will I see you tomorrow night at the ball?"

"I'll be there."

He casts a glance across the space and jerks his head, acknowledging another suit. "I'm meeting someone. We'll speak—"

"How do you know Sydney?" The question is left field, but I'm not seeking the answer as much as the reaction.

"We'll speak tomorrow night," he says, stepping away, then stopping. "Are you, is she…" he closes his eyes and tilts his head, apparently struggling to formulate his question. "Will she be in attendance tomorrow night?"

"Yes," I answer, although her being disinvited is no longer a zero-sum possibility.

"She's a good girl," he says, almost to himself.

He nods and heads to his awaiting friend.

A good girl.

In what way? A CIA way? An assistant way? Did they date?

What the hell is going on?

I ask the bartender if Sydney owes anything, and he says no, that she's already paid.

I open a billfold and drop a ten, then head out of the hotel bar to the elevator bank.

On my way, I pull my phone and message Daisy.

ME

Do the deep dive on Sydney Parker.

Within seconds, a response comes through. I pause outside the elevator bank, gesturing for a female hotel guest to enter, and I step away.

DAISY JONAS

Completed yesterday. Penn and CIA personnel file checks. No social media presence, but that's expected.

She means because of her employment with the CIA.

ME

See if you can find a connection to Senator Crawford. Also, any FBI connections.

DAISY JONAS

> Any connection between a CIA officer and the FBI?

> Is this your version of ruining a good thing?

I roll my eyes.

I don't run from relationships. As Miles pointed out, I fall into them the way one falls into an unclimbable well. But something is off here.

Crawford doesn't come off as sleazy. He's more the confident, arrogant, southern frat boy type.

Could it be I'm reading into things? Looking for an issue where there is none? Cold feet because my last relationship exploded spectacularly?

An elevator opens and I enter.

On the way up, out of habit, I open the Bloomberg app and skim through the headlines.

When I open the door to the suite, Sydney rises from a sofa, touching her fingers in front of her waist. She's barefoot and is a mix of the woman I met on vacation and the woman at the bar.

"I can explain," she says.

The soles of my shoes click against the tile floor, beating out a slow, steady rhythm.

My instincts didn't fail me. Something is up.

When I'm within striking distance, I say, "Okay."

"I had an affair with Senator Crawford. About a year ago. I didn't know he was married."

Whoa.

The unexpected answer sinks in. Unexpected, but it's not a personal insult. She volunteered the information. An affair...

"You didn't know a US Senator was married?" Does she expect me to believe a woman with CIA training wouldn't pick up on his marital status? How naive does she believe I am?

"My specialty is Europe. Not the United States," she says in a tone that's not particularly apologetic.

I narrow my eyes, attempting to control a surge of anger that I'm fairly certain is unjustified, but I'm not absolutely certain.

"At first, I didn't know he was a senator."

I raise an eyebrow, calling bullshit.

"He's young," she says. "Most of the senators are geriatric."

She has a point there. In his forties, Crawford is decades younger than the average.

"Much like you and I, neither of us shared where we worked. I didn't see him often. We weren't serious. He was someone I saw occasionally. I wasn't aiming for a serious relationship and when I learned he was married, I should've stopped it earlier than I did."

I hear the honesty in her words and the self-reproach.

"But you didn't?"

If she wasn't into him, why keep seeing him?

"Did he say anything?"

I scratch my jaw to distract from the annoyance that she almost sounds hopeful.

"Said you were a good girl."

I let the words sit there between us.

The tension proves too much. I need space. I step away, taking a seat on the sofa across from her.

"Why tell me? Did you believe he'd tell me?"

"It was awkward. I thought you might have picked up on something. If I didn't say anything and then later you found out, it might make it a bigger deal than it is. And it's not a big deal. It happened long before I met you."

Logical. I rub the back of my neck, kneading the tight shoulder muscle, considering. She likely made the wise choice, telling me immediately. If I'd pushed Crawford, one never knows. While he probably wouldn't have copped to it directly, a prick like that is more than happy to insinuate.

She also spoke with an FBI agent. Did she date him too?

"Did you run into anyone you know downstairs?"

With a tilt of her head, she avoids my gaze. "No."

I pinch the bridge of my nose and close my eyes.

Is Daisy right? Is this me sabotaging a good thing? Or is the former CIA officer up to something and she sat down at the bar to meet with an FBI agent?

If that's the case, why? What exactly am I suspecting?

I'll need to see the tapes. See how long they talked. Check her facial expression. Check his.

"What's going on?" Unease rings through her tone and I open my eyes, taking in the kindred spirit I met on a hike, the carefree woman who, what? We had fun together.

"Nothing," I answer. "Work stuff."

Another frequently used line that will buy me time.

I pat the cushion beside me.

"We haven't talked about our exes," she responds, not

taking the seat. Her chin's held high and her arms cross her middle, a defensive posture I recognize from years of meetings. "I wasn't hiding my past from you. I didn't do anything wrong. He deceived me."

I've known her for less than a week. I can't be angry that I didn't know about a past affair. She could've come up here and lied, and she didn't.

"Nevertheless, it's a part of my past that I prefer to remain private. It's a shameful action I regret and I hate that you know."

I've done things I'm not proud of, too. But this conversation isn't about my mistakes. I pat the cushion again and say, "It's over, right?"

"Long ago," she confirms, her tone lighter.

"Then get over here. Take off those clothes. Let me see the lingerie I bought you."

CHAPTER
TWENTY-FIVE

SYDNEY

I still. Uncertain.

Where's the guy from the trail? The smiling, laughing, down-to-earth guy? Because this guy is one I halfway expect to dangle handcuffs and a blindfold.

Is this his way of acquiring control? Is he testing me?

Did Crawford say something to him that set off insecurities? David is such an insecure prick I wouldn't put it past him to brag about his sexual conquest.

And if that's what happened, has Rhodes dismissed my value? Determined he can treat me however he wants because I'm no longer his perceived equal?

Fuck that.

But remember, none of this is real. You're playing a role Syd. Red Sparrow 101.

Still, you have to be believable, and the best way to be believable is to wrap the lie in honesty.

"I don't think I like your tone."

He leans back on the sofa, thighs spread, as he palms his crotch. I follow the movement, the outline of the bulge, mesmerized by the subtle movement over his length.

My skin prickles and heat pools between my legs.

My mind reels, spinning. We've gone from my sharing something deeply private to sex.

Whiplash.

"Clothes." His low, gravelly tone churns through any remote restraint.

If this were real, I might tell him to fuck off and I'd block his number on the way to the lobby.

But it's not real.

You've shared so much of the real you. How would he expect you to behave right now?

"What's going on? Is this how you think you can treat me?" There's a rawness to my tone, a vulnerability that I both hate for its existence and applaud for the authenticity.

He blinks. His fingers stretch wide, the space between them allowing air, stretching corded muscles.

"Dammit, Sydney." His jaw flexes, but otherwise, he's impassive, cold. "I had a shit afternoon. And that was before I walked into the lobby and had it thrown in my face I don't know you well."

The raw truth grates.

I swallow, my gaze locked with his, my heart racing so fast there's an ache beneath my breast bone.

"I hate the idea of you with a putz like Crawford. That's pretty cave man of me, huh?"

"Obviously."

The new Prada heels I tried on earlier come into view, and in two strides, I'm slipping into them.

"You're leaving?"

He spits out the words but his expression tells me he's too arrogant to believe I'd actually do it.

And he's right, but for the wrong reasons.

"If I'm going to strip for you, I might as well wear these sexy as fuck heels you overpaid for, don't you agree? I mean, these shoes cost what? A thousand dollars?"

If he wants to play power games, I'll give him exactly what he thinks he wants. Control the narrative, Syd. Make him think he's winning while you figure out your next move.

With the swiftness of the Santa Ana winds, his glower transitions from cold to heated.

"Whatever those shoes cost, they're worth it."

I undo the first button on my blouse.

"Easy for a guy who can afford this suite to say."

With the third button, the silky blouse falls open.

He swallows; gaze locked on my chest. "You haven't asked me much about that."

"Your business does well. What is there to ask?"

The blouse flutters to the floor.

Cool air dances through the mesh lace. His gaze rakes over the exposed skin.

"What about you? Unemployed and vacationing at one of the most expensive inns in North Carolina."

I wondered if he'd thought about that.

"A gift to myself."

My fingers work the zipper on the back of my skirt.

"I work hard. I can afford it."

It's true. All those years abroad on the CIA's dime, I stashed almost everything I earned. Until everything went to shit. All thanks to a yet-discovered someone.

The smooth silk liner glides over my butt cheeks, the outer curves of my thighs, and whooshes to the floor, raising goosebumps in its wake.

"Jesus, look at you." His voice is thick with appreciation.

My shoulders lift, my back arches, and I stand before him, chin raised, proud.

On autopilot, I enter his vicinity, standing between his spread legs, looking down on him.

His dark gaze meets mine, and I kneel.

The stretch in my calves burns. My knees flatten on the rug, and my palms flatten on each of his muscular thighs.

His hands fall to his sides and his knees spread, making room.

"Who are you Sydney Parker?"

I lick my lower lip and reach for his belt buckle.

As my fingers press into the soft, buttery leather, he unbuttons his shirt and removes it, tossing it on the far end of the sofa.

When I unbutton his pants, he leans forward and cups my breast inside the lace. My nipple swells with his rough touch.

"On my lap."

I follow his command, gaze locked on his lips, my mouth watering, my sex needy.

With my legs on each side of his thighs and the sharp points of my heels aimed behind me, I grind my hips over his groin, earning a guttural groan.

"Who are you, Rhodes MacMillan?"

His fingers tangle with my hair and he directs me down until our mouths meet.

Our kiss is hungry. Nothing is soft as we press into each other. If anything, a battle wages for dominance. For control. A competition.

It's no wonder. We're two alpha souls.

Heat encompasses my core, over my panties. The silk seam tugs tight, digging into my hip, and the tip of his finger dips inside.

Sensations swirl and my hips undulate.

His finger withdraws. There's a tight pull, a sharp pain, and the panties fall loose.

I break the frantic kiss, needing to see.

"You ripped my panties," I say, taking in my naked bottom half draped over his trousers, and the black lace looped around his fingers.

"Who was the guy from the FBI?"

TWENTY-SIX

SYDNEY

I snap back as if slapped. The temperature in the room plunges.

My breath catches. Not from surprise—I knew this was coming—but from the realization that part of me wants to tell him everything. The mission, KOAN, Caroline, all of it. That impulse is dangerous.

"Who are you, Sydney?"

I'm whoever you want me to be.

That thought, unbidden, stays within the confines of my mind, ricocheting with deceit.

Slowly, I recover from the ambush and shift back on his thighs to meet the inquisition.

I don't have to play dumb. He knows I worked for the CIA.

"I have his business card if you want it."

His thumb flicks over my nipple, and I swear the light

flick shoots fire to my clit, the lace so thin his touch brokers the feel of skin on skin.

"You didn't mention him."

The accusation cuts.

"How did you know?"

Our eyes lock, and my chest seizes.

"I know everything, Syd."

He believes his guttural confession, but he's wrong.

Or at least, he is wrong, right? He can't possibly know everything. But the way he's looking at me—like he's already solved me—makes my chest tighten.

He fists my hair, rough, controlling.

"Talk later."

His eyes are pure ice. The pull on my scalp sharp.

"Now. We fuck."

His grip on my hair tightens, and he jerks my head back.

"You okay with that?"

"Very."

"You want my cock inside you?"

He wants a little dirty talk. Fine.

"Yes. I want to choke on your cock. I want you to thrust inside me so hard it feels like you're going to split me in two. I want you to fuck me so hard sweat drips from your temple and you lose all control."

"Fuck."

The one word comes out with a growl. He flips me and I strain to see over my shoulder. With one hand, he releases his thick, hard cock. He positions his crown at my entrance and pushes inside. I'm turned on, wet even, but I'm not ready, and there's a burn with the intrusion.

My cry sets us off. It's not love making. It's fucking. Dirty. Hard. Cruel.

And it's what every single cell in my body craves.

Depraved punishment.

I deserve it. But there's also desperate need, the same craving I feel—to connect with someone who sees through all the pretense. Even as he takes what he wants, I'm taking something too. Something I shouldn't want.

By the time he shudders over me, a film of perspiration coats our skin. We're halfway off the sofa and one heel dangles from the corner of a credenza across the room. He threw it when I pierced his skin.

He pushes up and swipes his forehead as his chest heaves.

With a shake of his head, he hitches his pants up to his waist. They never made it below his knees.

I wrap my arms around me, warming my middle, and pull my knees up. The skin between my thighs is sticky.

His cum.

"I'm going to use the shower."

The absence of an invitation to join him chills the room.

I'm in over my head.

The bathroom door clicks closed.

I push up and pad barefoot into the bedroom. I step up to the closed bathroom door and put my ear next to the wood panel. The distinct sound of pouring water reverberates through the door and kicks me into gear.

I find an oversized T-shirt and panties in my bag and dig out my secure phone.

I shouldn't call. It's stupid and dangerous.

But I need to hear a friendly voice. Someone who knows who I really am.

Quinn answers on the first ring. I pull the bedroom door closed but sit outside on the floor where I can see a shadow below the door rim and will hear if the shower cuts off.

"Syd? Is that you?"

"Yes. I don't have long. Is the team here?"

"Yes."

"Are you listening?"

Shame heats my neck and my cheeks, a sharp contrast to the chill that wrapped around me after the sofa.

She snorts. "Only source is from your bag."

She's referring to a small device I packed that appears to be an old school recorder, one that if someone discovered, I could play it off as triggered in my bag and pull out a cassette to throw away.

"He's onto me." My eyelids close, hating the admittance.

"Pack your bags. Go."

"I don't think I'm in danger."

"Syd...we're flying free here. You're in the lead. You make the calls. But as a reminder, your life isn't worth intel. We're not building a criminal case."

"I know."

I pinch the bridge of my nose. Like a nicked scab, the pain of the past bleeds.

Four assets dead.

You're out.

To this day, I don't believe I was in danger when they pulled me. No one else agreed.

"Did you get anything on the FBI guy?"

"He checks out. We could be looking at an off the books op."

Off the books for the very reason KOAN is watching. The fear he has too much on the government for them to open a formal investigation. If he can access information on any one in the world, who's going to openly look into him?

I could ask if we've still got someone in San Francisco, but it doesn't matter. My focus should be on my role.

"Who are you Syd?"

My eyes sting and I blink away the emotion. Teary eyes are not a good sign. I need to nip it.

"Who'd he meet with?" Quinn brings me back to the call with a reminder.

"I don't know. The meet moved. Did anyone tail him?"

"No. He met with a Russian diplomat before his meeting. Outside the embassy. Then he got in a car. We lost him in traffic. If you're compromised, get out."

Standard, fair advice.

Quiet replaces the low shower hum.

"Gotta go."

I push up from the ground and cum smears my thighs.

That's a touch of reality I'd rather not dwell on, and as luck would have it, I don't have the time to spare. I'm back in the bedroom, tucking my phone away in the side pocket with tampons and maxi pads when the bathroom door opens and steam billows out.

"My turn?" I ask, stepping past him without waiting for an answer.

He grips my arm, and ever so slowly, I raise my gaze to meet his.

"That was...." He's impassive, but he wouldn't mention it if he didn't have questions and possibly regrets.

"It's okay," I say. "I enjoyed it." The truth in those words burns worse than any lie I've told him.

I step forward, but his hold on my arm tightens.

"We need to talk."

He's got questions and I don't have a clear head yet.

"Your cum is leaking down my thigh. Do you mind?"

As if stung, he snaps his hand back.

"Let me shower. Then we'll talk."

CHAPTER
TWENTY-SEVEN

RHODES

My skin itches and my fingers twitch. I'm jittery. Irritated.

I pace the suite. Perhaps I need music. The only sound in the suite is the low steady thrum of a rainfall shower.

I grab my phone, intent on locating my Spotify account, and see a message notification. That works too.

I click to read.

ALEX

> Met with Avent Capital. They want us. BAD.

Two clicks. No need for voice dictation on this one.

ME

No

Better off private

Of course those blood suckers want us to go public. It's the best way to fleece us. And we don't need them. Aside from that, we have no business letting profit and growth drive business decisions. Private is the only ethical option. If I get my way, we'll transition back to nonprofit.

Why is Alex still circling a public offering? We don't require a capital infusion.

I hit the microphone and say, "Ethics, Alex. Come on. The power of AI isn't something to underestimate. Profit cannot guide decisions. If we went public, growth would become the driving criteria. It's too dangerous. Irresponsible. You know this. Absolutely not."

I skim to ensure nothing's too outrageously misinterpreted and hit send.

I'm not sure I've ever felt so much empathy toward weapons designers. I'm not in the defense industry, but I feel for those engineers. I haven't sacrificed and dedicated everything to ARGUS for it to become a worldwide menace. I'm better than that.

The shower stream ends.

I click over to my chain with Daisy.

Me: Anything?

My gaze cuts to the bathroom door, which will likely open any minute. I don't know what I'm expecting—or why I'm still on edge. The sex should have burned through the worst of it, but my pulse is still elevated.

Syd's fantastic. That's the problem.

She has a history. Made a questionable choice. But the way she responded when I pressed her—no defensiveness, offered the FBI agent's business card without hesitation. She's not hiding anything. Right?

Christ. Maybe Daisy's right. Maybe I just took my suspicions out on her because I'm terrified of what I'm feeling. Freaking out because in my gut I know I'm going to ask her to fly back with me to San Francisco, and then I'll ask her to move in with me, and then seven years will pass and I'll be planning another engagement party.

The thought should scare me. Instead, it makes me want to lock the bathroom door and keep her here.

Why hasn't Daisy responded?

DAISY JONAS

Details incoming. Busted cover. Brought back stateside for her safety. Operative career over. Just like that.

ME

Source?

ARGUS can't access case files.

ME

What did you hack?

The fucking Pentagon?

DAISY JONAS

Friend of a friend

Of course. You can have the most secure site in the world, but there's always the human risk factor.

The bathroom door opens, and I slip my phone into my back pocket.

I'm standing a few feet away from the threshold, probably looking like I've been pacing, waiting for her, which I have.

"Are you ready to talk?"

"Yes."

She's changed from the outfit I purchased into loose jeans and a green crochet sweater tank. Droplets drip from her hair. Flush from the steaming-hot water, her skin is opulent.

We stand there, staring at each other as if in a stand-off. Tension exists, yes, but there's more going on between us than lust or irritation. Questions lurk.

We're compatible. There's no question. But can we trust each other?

She breaks the tension with a miniscule huff, tucks her chin, and steps past me to the sofa.

"Are you having me watched?"

She puts the question out there with the weight of a judge's gavel. Then she sits—on the same sofa where we just fucked. Her skirt and blouse remain on the floor.

Well, let's do this.

"I wasn't," I answer honestly. "My security team saw you."

"You have security in the hotel? Now?"

"Prudent." It's the word Daniel, my head of security, repeats, so I throw the word back at her.

She didn't ask me why.

"You Googled me."

She doesn't confirm nor deny.

What do I really fear? It's not a long-term relationship. It's that I'm being used. Deep down, I always suspected Sara stayed with me for the financial benefits. Why did Sydney come with me to D.C.?

"Did you know who I was when we met on the trail?"

I lift an eyebrow, meant as a warning to her not to lie to me.

She closes her eyes.

Holy shit.

I sink into the cushion near her, shift to pull out my phone, scan my messages, locate the photo security sent, and set it on the sofa between us.

She opens those doe eyes and I point at the evidence between us.

"Agent Gregory," I say. "What did he want?"

Her gaze falls to her hands cradled in her lap.

"Are you with the FBI?"

That gets her attention.

"No." She looks directly at me, hands still.

She's telling the truth.

But she didn't deny knowing me before we met. Was she playing me, wanting to get close to a wealthy guy? Or did someone else put her up to it? Did someone hire a former CIA…

"Are you working for someone?"

I'll uncover the truth, one way or another. But there's no way to verbalize that reality without it coming across as threatening.

"Why did you meet with Russia today?" Her question hits hard with a force straight to the solar plexus.

"*You* were watching *me*?"

How? She was here at the hotel. I have photographic evidence. Unless…she's not working alone. That's it. Someone hired her.

Fuck me.

"As part of my job I meet with representatives from

different countries. Who are you working for that that information is relevant?"

"What are you selling them?"

Yes. Definitely working for someone.

"The rumors are unfounded," I answer, looking her directly in the eye so she can see the truth.

She's working with one of the intelligence agencies. It's the only answer. If it's not the FBI, the NSA? Those guys are slippery.

"Is that why you're here? Investigating unfounded rumors?"

"What rumors?"

"This is going to be a painful conversation if you keep playing this game." She has to see the gig is up. She might as well play it straight.

"You're not exactly being forthcoming," she responds, chin lifted, fucking defiant.

Look at that audacity. Unbelievable.

"Rumors are I'm selling information to the highest bidder. Any information that can be used for blackmail. It's an unfounded rumor and it is false. ARGUS is an AI surveillance tool. It takes existing data and derives information from it. Any information ARGUS provides, a client already owns. I don't do under-the-table side deals. Never have. Never will."

She doesn't look away. Perhaps she believes me.

"Who are you working for? NSA?"

If it's NSA, I'm going to have words with my contact. I didn't sit through endless meetings only to be monitored.

"Why did you meet with Russia?"

"How can you expect me to answer your questions without knowing who I'm talking to?"

She sucks in her lower lip, contemplating before answering.

"Let me ask you this, which is perhaps the most important question. Was anything between us real? Or is the US government now readily employing Russian tactics and sending honeypots to targets?"

Her mouth opens into an O and her cheeks flush a brighter red. That got her attention.

"I genuinely like you."

Lovely. I push up off the sofa and scrub my fingers through the short hair on the back of my head, pacing the floor.

"You're a fucking honeypot? You fucked me to get information?"

"No." She jumps up and grabs my hands. "No! Not true. If you remember, I said I had my period. It was never supposed to—"

I throw her hands off mine. "You weren't supposed to, but then you said what the hell?"

"It's not like that."

Her eyes go glassy and my restraint snaps. "Oh, hell no. You sleep with me for what...what exactly were you hoping to get?" One lone tear spills over. "And now you're going to cry? And I'm supposed to say, 'Oh, it's all okay'? Are you out of your goddamn mind?"

"No!" She stomps her right foot and folds her arms below her breasts. "It wasn't... I'm not with the NSA. I work for a private group. Everything I told you is true. Everything. I've kept it as real with you as possible."

"Except the real reason I met you on that trail. You weren't on holiday. You were working. And I was your target." I tilt my head. "Since you obviously know everything about me, you also know I'm familiar with intelligence agencies. I'm familiar with their tactics. Who's behind this? Who sent you…" I pace the room, back and forth. I'm so fucking livid I can't speak. I glare at the lamp, stifling the desire to rip it out of the socket and hurl it against the wall.

"Jesus, I'm such an idiot. I actually thought I lucked into meeting someone pretty amazing." Every kiss was a lie. Every vulnerable moment, a calculated move in her wicked game. And I fell for it completely.

"Stop it!" A vein bulges in her forehead and her hands ball into fists at her sides. "I'll tell you everything! Just listen, okay?"

There's no way I can sit, so I pace.

"I work for a newly formed group called KOAN. The goal is to watch those with significant power and influence. Those who might be tempted to believe they're above the law."

"And because of the rumors, it was deemed I fit the bill?"

"You're a billionaire—"

"On paper, I'm a billionaire. Unless I cash out, it's mostly paper, you get that right?"

She tilts her head, calling my bluff.

"Yes, I'm wealthy. I sold a business. But I'm not one of the big-time billionaires." Even as I say it, the qualification sounds ridiculous, but that doesn't matter at all. My wealth doesn't give anyone the right to target me. *What the actual living fuck?*

"Will you listen?"

The plea in her tone does little to calm me down, but once again, I nod.

"All they wanted was to know is if the rumors were true. Because if they were, there would be a significant risk to national security."

What she's not saying is that someone out there fears the current administration and Congress is indebted to me thanks to sizable campaign contributions. And the fear is logical. I donate heavily to ensure legislation permits my business's existence. Too many are desperate to control AI with legislation, and those writing said legislation understand technology about as well as Nana.

"I only took the job because for me, it's personal."

I side eye her, remembering what Daisy said about her career being blown. Someone leaked her identity. I place pressure on the bridge of my nose. She believes the worst possible version of me, the most evil version, which means she didn't use her time with me to get to know me at all. Meanwhile, only someone truly wicked could have played such a perfect role.

"I'm not a bastard. I have a conscience. There's no risk to national security."

Of course, if we do as Russia wants...but that's not her business. Or her employer's.

The irony isn't lost on me. She's been investigating whether I'm a threat to national security while I've been falling for a woman who was never real. At least not with me. Every laugh, every touch, every moment I thought we were connecting—she was working. Gathering intelligence. Playing a role.

And I'm supposed to believe her 'personal' motivation makes this better somehow.

"Did you get the information you need? Are we done?"

CHAPTER
TWENTY-EIGHT

SYDNEY

He strides to the window and stares at the view of the Washington Monument like it has all the answers. I remain seated, acutely aware of the tactical disadvantage.

How do I come back from this? What's my next step?

Arms folded, his back to me, he claims the high ground without even trying. In a low tone that forces me to strain to hear him, he asks, "How much did they pay you to sleep with me?"

I rise slowly, reclaiming some semblance of equal footing. The plush carpet silences my approach as I position myself where he can see my reflection in the glass. There's power in making him look at me, even if it's just my reflection.

"It wasn't like that. I promise."

You did your job. There she is. That's the inner Syd who gets me through the downs—the same voice that talked me through that extraction in Istanbul when everything went sideways and I had to improvise with a paperclip and a tourist map.

We're sluts for hire now? And that's my conscience dressed in Caroline's disdain.

Classic Farm analysis—favoring the ethical implications over the operational success metrics. This is why field agents and analysts rarely date. Different frameworks.

My chest aches. Yet another sign I screwed up because I'm emotional and that wasn't the assignment. In fact, the assignment is to not get emotional. But it happened.

I left the CIA to join KOAN because I believe in the mission. There's a need for an investigative team searching where the government either can't or won't. When powerful people have no accountability, they can't be trusted.

"Should I leave the room and let you pack?"

I lift my head to find he hasn't moved, his back to me, anger wafting off him like steam from a hot spring.

There was never going to be a relationship between us. Get it together and focus on what's important.

Tell him the whole truth. It's your best bet.

"I applied for an intern position within your company. I didn't get the position."

"You had to have lied on your resume."

"I did."

"It's amazing. The arrogance you and your team must possess to believe that you could pass our filters."

The urge to tell him one of our teammates got past his glorious filters is strong, but I won't tank the team. I'm down, but I'm not terrible. Besides, while I believe him, or at least I find it impossible to believe he'd sell state secrets that could lead to deaths, it's not up to me to kill the operation. I'm an operative, trusting leadership.

"Anything else you want to add?" He's itching to kick me out. But I won't leave like this.

"The plan was for us to have a casual meet. Then once again in D.C. A coincidence that couldn't be ignored. And perhaps I could get hired with an in from the CEO, or I might observe something useful. Intelligence gathering is slow and the plans evolve in real time."

He's still giving me his back. Classic avoidance.

Outside, dusk blankets Washington, D.C., transforming the monument into a glowing white sentinel against the darkening sky. The suite's climate control hums softly, keeping the room at precisely 72 degrees—a stark contrast to the emotional temperature between us. The faint scent of his cologne, woody and understated, still lingers in the air between us, a ghost of intimacy now turned hollow. The crystal tumbler he'd been drinking from earlier sits abandoned, amber liquid catching the light from the desk lamp. I can't blame him for turning away.

"When I slept with you, it was because I wanted to. Every single time. I chose to be as real as I could be with you. I loved having sex with you. Probably the best sex of my life. Freeing at a time..." My gaze drops to the floor. He doesn't need to hear how much I needed my time with him. "Everything I told you about me is true."

"Except your employment."

"True. I left the CIA willingly when another job became available."

"You were dealt a raw deal. Pushed out of the field."

How does he know that? It's not publicly available information.

His refusal to turn around and face me shows that he's disgusted by me, and I won't change that, but maybe if I share the ugly reality, that it's not about my career, it's about lives…

"Four of my assets died. The station chief believed my cover was blown. I was reassigned for an indefinite period. When I told you my boss was an asshole, that's true. I don't know that I would consider it a raw deal. While I'm curious about your source, I'll stay on task."

In the window's reflection, I can see his profile. Stern. Unforgiving.

Stay on task.

"My assets weren't the only ones killed. Assets and CIA officers throughout Europe, the Middle East, and Africa were terminated. Most looked accidental. Some were assassinations. Straight out murder. Someone sold a list to our enemies."

"And I'm suspected?" Now he turns around, incredulous.

"ARGUS. Not necessarily you."

He rubs the back of his head. It's a gesture I'm becoming familiar with, one that relieves frustration.

"I didn't take the assignment lightly. But it's important to me that we find the source of the leak. My assets? Our officers? My colleagues? They were good people. With families." I swallow hard, remembering the notification procedures, the carefully worded letters that never actually explained how someone died serving their country. "We've lost more assets and officers in the last six months than in the history of the CIA program. Eighteen people."

My entire career upended because I might have been next on the list. If we don't find the source—a source that no one in the government apparently believes exists—additional names may be added to the memorial wall at Langley.

He drops his head back, looking to the ceiling.

"When I developed ARGUS, it was because I saw a need. Existing surveillance systems and communication databases possess an unwieldy amount of data. I developed ARGUS to allow the good guys to better use the resources available to them. My goals are for good."

"Who are the good guys? In your opinion." Because that's the problem. No one goes out there aiming to be the bad guys. In geopolitics, good and bad hinges on perspective.

"Fair question." He steps across the room and sinks into an armchair. His hands fall to his thighs. "I don't believe we've applied our technology to anyone possessing the data that would reveal CIA operatives."

"But it's possible?"

"It's not a zero-sum possibility." His left thumb raps out a beat and his head tilts. "I'll help you. If we're aiding an entity that is taking out US operatives, I want to know."

"Russia would be an obvious choice."

His gaze roams the room. "Are we being recorded?"

My gaze travels to my bag. "Doesn't your security check?"

Wrinkles form around his eyes as he squints at me

like a judge weighing my veracity. And he's right to question.

"When we learned your security team was on site, we scrapped surveillance plans."

He nods twice, thoughtful.

"An investor in my first company requested that I meet with the Russian embassy today. The investor has no hold over me. Doesn't stand to gain from the meeting."

"Do investors often ask for favors?"

"It's not uncommon. This particular investor invested when no one else would. He earned his money back, but you don't forget the initial investors who give you a chance. You don't want to say no to them, but sometimes you have to." He releases a long sigh. "A few active investors and my partner have been pushing for ARGUS to go public. I've held my ground. Refused. The meeting today felt like something I could give this particular investor."

"And?"

"The embassy contact blackmailed me. And before you ask, no, I don't think the investor put him up to it. His Russian contact probably said something innocuous like they'd appreciate some private time with me if I have it to spare." He leans forward, elbows on his thighs, and looks me directly in the eyes. "Tell me more about KOAN. Perhaps we can work together."

The slither of an opening is like a ray of light in a storm. This is the best possible option—for the team and for the operation. My cracked heart... That's just Mata Hari.

"Are you familiar with the definition of koan?" I ask,

noticing the leather-bound copy of Joseph Campbell's "Hero with a Thousand Faces" on the coffee table. It could be the hotels, but it reminds me of a small personal detail tucked away for this assignment—Rhodes reads mythology and philosophy.

"A paradoxical question without a clear answer, meant to provoke enlightenment." His eyes narrow slightly as he answers, appreciative of the reference. "Fitting for a group that operates in gray areas."

"The answers aren't always obvious," I agree. "Sometimes you have to sit with the contradiction."

For a brief moment, I glimpse something in his expression—a flash of the intellectual beneath the businessman, the thinker behind the tech mogul. And then, there it is...the connection between us. The energy, the charge.

"Don't mistake me." He gestures between the two of us. "There's nothing between us. What I'm proposing is strictly professional. If you'd like to join me as my plus one at the Bastille gala, that's fine. I assume attendance plays into your operation and will give you an opportunity for more intel. But..."

His right eye squints and his head shakes in the negative.

Right. The message couldn't be clearer if he'd written it in skywriting.

"I understand." I swallow down a mix of complicated emotions I'd rather not examine. "Purely professional." I adjust my watch—my father's old Cartier, the only personal item I never leave behind—*recalibrate, reset boundaries*. "The mission parameters have changed, but the objective remains the same."

He studies me, and I maintain eye contact a beat longer than necessary. I'm speaking operational language now, but beneath it runs a current neither of us will acknowledge—that you can't unfeel something just because it's inconvenient. That's not how human chemistry works, no matter how much we pretend otherwise.

His jaw tightens and his head shakes in the negative. Nonverbal emphasis there shall be nothing physical between us. *There is no us. Focus.*

"What did they want? When they blackmailed you?"

"No. First, your company."

"What else do you want to know?"

"Who's funding it?" He sinks into the back of the armchair. "As you can see from my experience, the money source is an important factor."

I open my mouth; struck with the realization he's not going to like my answer. But also, it's information I shouldn't share. "I never asked." It's a half-truth. I never asked what the approved answer is regarding funding.

His lips purse, skeptical.

"I was assured it's well-funded. I didn't join the firm hoping to collect a pension decades from now. I joined because I want to find the leak. It didn't take me long to realize I could do nothing inside the CIA. Not in my new group. This was a chance to chase down the leak."

"Who's the client?"

"What do you mean?"

"Someone hired your company to investigate, right?"

"That's not... We're privately funded." He's looking at me like he's trying to decide if I'm a fool or if I'm lying to him again. "I don't know who initiated the investigation." That's the truth. I consider Hudson. Former special forces. Intelligent. Direct. He shares information on a need-to-know basis, and I... Damn, I'm too used to taking orders. I didn't ask enough questions—of Hudson or Caroline.

"Let me get this straight. An unknown entity invested in a surveillance team to find out who ARGUS is doing deals with and recruited operatives under the guise of a vigilante protector?"

I swallow and give a quick nod, understanding why he's incredulous. If it's not the government wanting this investigation, it could be a competitor.

"I did a background check on you." That's an off-the-wall comment, and I wait, wondering where he's going with it.

"And?"

"You're friends with Caroline Moore."

"That showed up in my background report?"

"Well, you were in the CIA with her."

"Yes." I suppose that intel is obtainable.

"Is she behind this at all?"

"Why would you ask—" His look shuts me up.

"She is one of my close friends. She knows..." I'll leave that thought there. I've probably shared too much as it is. If Caroline chose to conceal her connection to KOAN, it's likely ARGUS would identify links.

"Do you trust her husband?"

"I've never met him." I meet his dark, questioning eyes head on. "Caroline and I met after they separated. They're back together, but I haven't met him yet. If you're asking...I don't have contact with him."

He tugs at his jaw.

"Miles, my partner, has had meetings with staff from

his financial firm." I give him a questioning look. "Finance guys love the idea of AI forecasting markets," he shrugs. "It's a small world. You're sure he's not the one who hired KOAN?"

"Do you see him as a competitor?" I hadn't, but I bought into this project to find a leak.

"In addition to an investment firm, he owns a company that owns satellites. That's a lot of data."

"Then you should approach him for a deal, but... Then again, scratch that. He's third-generation wealth. He's not—"

"How did KOAN find you? I'm assuming you didn't find the job posting on a job board."

I scratch at the side of my face, debating.

"Within the intelligence community, my situation isn't unknown. All things considered, it's not surprising they approached me." It's an honest answer that doesn't out my friend. "Do you need to know anything else?"

He shakes his head, but he's cold. Ruthless is the word that comes to mind.

"What does Russia have on you? What do they want?"

"They want me to buy a database. It's reasonable to expect that once it's purchased, additional demands will be made."

"What do they have on you? Is that why the FBI is interested in you?"

That gets his attention.

"What did the FBI want?"

"I truly don't know. If I were to guess, I'd say he was cultivating an asset, but that's not how the FBI works. Are they investigating you?"

"Not to my knowledge."

"What is Russia holding over your head? You're a single man and never married. It can't be the typical compromising photos. What have you done?"

He closes his eyes and tilts his head back, then exhales loudly.

"No." His voice hardens. "You don't get to know that." He rises from the chair in one fluid motion, suddenly imposing in the space between us. "Are we working together or not?"

The question hangs in the air, an ultimatum disguised as a choice. I recognize the tactic—I've used it myself. Through the window behind him, lightning flashes across the D.C. skyline, illuminating the room in stark white for a split second. In that flash, I see something in his eyes I hadn't expected: not just anger, but a profound wariness. This man has carried his own secrets far longer than I've carried mine.

"Yes," I say finally, making my choice. "We're working together."

He nods once, sharply, like sealing a pact. "Good. Because when it comes to gods and monsters, Sydney," he says, his voice dropping to almost a whisper, "I'm starting to wonder which one I've created."

I have no idea what he means by that, but something in his tone sends a chill down my spine. Whatever Rhodes is hiding, it's big.

CHAPTER
TWENTY-NINE

RHODES

While she mulls over working together, I resume pacing the room, each step measured and controlled—masking the storm raging inside me.

I believed in the protective measures we've taken. I believed our creation wouldn't harm. But we'll see what we find. She's working off rumors.

Sydney.

How did I not see it? Calculated lies.

I'm such a fool.

I need air. Space. The walls of this suite are closing in.

Through the window, I can see the storm has moved beyond the Capitol, lightning flickering harmlessly in the distance. The thunder is a distant rumble. Wind gusts still bend the trees, but the main system has passed—and right now I need the space more than I need shelter.

Without so much as a backward glance, I exit the

suite, blindly heading to Lower Senate Park and its shaded paths. The air is charged but warm, the storm's retreat leaving only restless wind in its wake.

I want to shout. Scream. Break things.

Instead, I claim a park bench and let my head fall back, feeling the wind cool my overheated skin. The phone in my pocket vibrates. The slight buzz grounds me. Comforts, in a way. Work awaits. I can lose myself in work, but to what end?

What did Nana say? *You're going to find someone who gives you a reason to have a life outside of work.*

Huh. Instead of reasons to lose myself in the work. That's what she meant.

Ah, Nana. Come to think of it, I should let her know I landed. It's not something I always do, but I'm usually pretty good about touching base when she knows I'm traveling. And I have no desire to return to the hotel.

She picks up on the third ring.

"Rhodes. Is everything okay?"

"Does something need to be wrong for me to call?"

"No, it's just we're not scheduled and you usually text."

Ah, she's right. But I also rarely find myself sitting on a park bench.

"How'd your Mahjong game go?"

A young woman jogs past, earbuds visible, ponytail swishing. If she had dark hair, she'd resemble Sydney.

"Didn't win."

"That's too bad."

"We don't always win, Rhodes."

The phone pressed to my ear irritates the skin, a

reminder I'm out of my element. I dig in my pocket for earbuds, pop them in and switch the call over.

"Are you by yourself now?"

"I am," I answer, gaze on the branches overhead.

Silence falls between us, and I know she's giving me time to process, time to say what I need to say. She's always been good like that. But I can't talk to her about this.

"What's her name?"

The question has me staring at the phone in my hand with disbelief.

"I wasn't born yesterday."

I snort, and if I wasn't so pissed, I'd probably laugh.

"There is a woman. Or was."

"What happened?"

"She lied."

"Did she have a good reason?"

"Does that matter?" The words come out sharper than intended.

"In my experience, yes."

"But Nana, she's been pretending this whole time. Everything between us—" I stop, unsure how much to reveal. "I trusted her."

"Oh, honey. That sounds painful."

Why did she lie? Because she actually thought I might leak information that would get people killed. And then she slept with me. My free hand, the one not holding the phone, squeezes into a fist.

"Oh, Rhodes." She says my name with a gravity equal to grief.

"What?"

"I promise you; you will find someone who wants you

for you. Not for your money or what you've accomplished."

"Oh. No. That wasn't it."

"Then what was it?"

How do I explain this to Nana?

"There are rumors about me. Or, I guess, about my company."

"I can see how. I have trouble understanding what you do, explaining to my friends, that's… I might be starting those rumors come to think of it."

I scratch my jaw, amused. "Funny," I say, knowing she's making light of the situation. "No, um, she was hired to investigate me."

"Are you in legal trouble?"

"No."

"Good. I know you'd never break the law."

I bend my neck to the side, stretching the muscles. She's always had faith in me.

"But now this girl, this lady friend—"

"Sydney. Her name is Sydney."

"Did she investigate you for personal gain?"

"No," I'm quick to answer. "Not… You know how I've told you my system can decipher large amounts of data and can find relevant information."

"Like finding a needle in a haystack."

"Exactly. Well, my company isn't the only source of needles. But a needle out there hurt some people she cared about, and Syd's trying to find the source of that needle."

"Oh, well, you should help her. If people she cared about were hurt…"

"But she used me to get information."

"Which damaged your pride, your ego. That's painful. Did she hurt you in any other way to get it? Put you in danger?" I pause, thinking of her concern for my safety, her genuine worry.

"No. Actually, no."

"Then help her."

"I've offered." I stormed out, but I did offer.

"Of course you did. My grandson is a good person."

"I try to be."

"You are." I suspect if we were in the same room she'd pat my shoulder.

"And it sounds like this Sydney might be a good person too."

"She lied to me."

"That is unfortunate. But it doesn't sound like she lied to hurt you or for her own personal gain, at least, not in a greedy way."

Silence reclaims the line, and I let it, choosing to side-step Nana's unstated implication that Sara was a greedy one. She never liked my ex.

"You know, the Greek gods typically did not forgive. That didn't work out so well for them."

This time, I do chuckle. "What do you mean by that?"

"Well, they were so focused on punishment and revenge that they created more problems than they solved. Meanwhile, the planet moved on to other belief systems—ones that embraced forgiveness and redemption."

"And I've been acting like Zeus throwing lightning bolts," I admit.

"Just an old lady ruminating. But you're not a god, honey. You're human. And humans get to choose growth over grudges. I know you'll make the right choice. You always do."

Do I? This time, maybe I will.

"I should probably head back. Love you, Nana."

"Love you, too."

CHAPTER
THIRTY

RHODES

I push up from the bench, pop out the earbuds, and start the walk back, Nana's words echoing in my mind. Syd lied to me, yes. But not for greed or malice. She's trying to find whoever got her people killed. If someone had targeted my team, betrayed people under my protection, wouldn't I do anything to find them? The difference is, I'd probably just throw money at the problem. Hire investigators, offer rewards. Sydney? She became the investigation. She put herself in harm's way to get justice for people she couldn't save. That takes courage.

Sure, I can understand the rationale in believing ARGUS is a source of leaks. I can understand why she accepted the assignment. I can even see how everything progressed over the last few days. I can get my head around forgiveness, but there will be no relationship. That's done.

As for working with her...that I can do. I can find the

leak. Finding a leak is no problem. But there's more going on here.

Why did the FBI approach her? She's right. They don't cultivate assets. Did the DOJ authorize an investigation? Did someone lie to Miles so he mistakenly believed it was handled?

The timing of Alex's IPO pressure now seems too convenient. Every week it's another dire funding projection, another investor demanding liquidity. But what if those aren't organic pressures? What if someone's been manufacturing the financial crisis to force my hand? I can't take Alex's word for it.

I'll trace the source, do the research myself. On both points—our financial needs and the investigation. As for the investigation, who else is watching me? Which intelligence agencies are in on this?

The agent may have recognized Sydney, which is why he confronted her, thinking a former CIA officer could be convinced to aid an investigation. Or maybe he has no idea who she is, and the government will approach anyone in my circle. I'll need to update my security team back in San Francisco. I believe they already monitor the staff, but they'll need to take more care. If there's not a surveillance camera over my trash, maybe they'll need to put one over it, just to discover if anyone's digging through garbage. *Absolute insanity.*

Of course, if I do what Russia wants and make a move to buy the Forbes database, the investigations will no longer be clandestine. There are a handful of senators who will make it their mission to stop the acquisition. Political theater. Everyone seeking a payday.

If I'm successful with the acquisition? What does that look like?

The owner of secrets.

ARGUS was designed to analyze data, not collect it. The system processes and analyzes data that is supplied by our clients. The Forbes database would change every-thing—theoretically, it could transform my creation from a tool into a weapon by augmenting clients' data.

Daisy has been clear about the technical integration challenges, but the ethical considerations keep me up at night. The database contains troves of data, including every public FBI and CIA report ever released. What happens when that information interfaces with ARGUS's pattern recognition algorithms? Power beyond imagina-tion—and responsibility I never wanted.

In theory, powerful. In reality, a target by all.

I find myself back at the suite and pause at the door. Inside is a woman who deceived me, yes. But also a woman trying to honor the dead. Prevent others from dying.

I push open the door.

Keeping the company private won't offer the protec-tion I imagined. Not in a world where governments target me.

Hubris.

That one word calls to my subconscious.

Sydney greets me in the foyer, tentative.

"What's going on?" Her voice is soft, her posture tentative. "Where'd you go?"

Those soft brown eyes study me—the same eyes that looked at me with what I foolishly interpreted as desire back in North Carolina. But no, those are dark, calculating eyes. Analyzing my responses, measuring my weaknesses, assessing how to get to know me.

My conscience corrects me. Her expression now seems genuinely concerned, not manufactured.

The actress and the woman—where does one end and the other begin? And why does it still matter to me?

Maybe the actress and the woman aren't separate entities. Maybe they're both Sydney—one who accepted a mission to find justice, and one who found something she wasn't looking for along the way. Just like I did.

"I don't need to know what they have over you," she says, apparently taking a stab in the dark at my thoughts. "I trust you. You're not a bad person. If the leak came from ARGUS, I believe you aren't the guilty party."

She's correct. I'm not a bad person, but will hubris be my downfall?

"You're scaring me. What is it? Why aren't you speaking?"

"Do you study mythology?" She's taken aback by my question.

She blinks and tilts her head, but she reaches for me and her touch warms my skin.

Miles mocked me for my mythology fetish—that's what he called it. The stories remain with us for a reason, contemporary fiction's original tropes. The themes and tales woven through all the modern religions and popular fiction because they tell the tale of our wicked ways.

"I knew nothing about mythology," she says, "until I was assigned to you. I picked up that you have a thing for mythology and read a basic primer."

She studied me.

And she won't be the only one. Life as a target.

I move to the minibar, the crystal tumbler heavy in my hand as I pour three fingers of scotch. The liquid burns a familiar path down my throat—Macallan 25, the same brand my first investor drank when we closed our initial funding round. I've come so far from that one-room office with salvaged furniture and borrowed servers. The suite's plush carpet, the panoramic views of Washington's monuments, the $8,000 suit hanging in the closet—all of it evidence of my success. And now, potential evidence of my downfall.

"What about mythology?" Her gentle probe conveys concern.

Perhaps concern is warranted. I feel lightheaded and ungrounded.

She intensifies her pressure on my arm, seeking an answer.

"Mythology is littered with tales of those whose hubris brings about their end." I turn to face the monument visible through the hotel window—Washington's own temple to power. "The ancients understood something we've forgotten. Creation without wisdom leads to destruction."

"Pride?" Her voice carries a note of confusion, but her eyes remain focused, analytical, as she works the problem.

"Pride is too simple a word. The Greeks called it hubris—the arrogance that makes men believe they can challenge the gods. The presumption that we can create without consequence." I press my palm against the cool glass. "Every Silicon Valley founder believes they're Prometheus bringing fire to humanity. None of us consider that Prometheus was chained to a rock with an eagle eating his liver for eternity as punishment."

She's expecting me to tell her what crime I've committed. And I'm sure with the right congressional inquisition, I could be locked away for years. It's easier to break laws than the average person might assume.

But I'm not looking at my past. I'm looking to my future.

"Icarus? Arachne?"

Her questions prove she indeed read the primer. Icarus ignored the warnings and flew too close to the sun. Arachne believed her skills were her own and not the gods. Both paid dearly.

"And Achilles," I add.

"The Achilles heel?"

"That's not the portion of the story that's relevant. Achilles was the most powerful warrior. His war prize was taken from him, and feeling dishonored, he refused to fight. His refusal led to the downfall of the Trojans."

"Huh, I always thought it had to do with his Achilles heel being the one weak point."

"I simplified the Iliad's version of the story."

"Are you seeing yourself as Achilles?"

I'm not a warrior, but I've created a weapon.

I brush her hair aside before I can stop myself. The strands are damp, her skin soft. And she's looking at me like I've lost my mind, though whether it's for the touch or the mythology analogy, I can't tell.

"For the Greeks and Romans, pride was one of the worst sins a man could commit." I inhale deeply to shake the fog clouding my thoughts.

"Does this have to do with what the Russians have over you?"

She's inches from me and asking if a business deal that violated a sanction is throwing me into a spiral. It's not. I don't treasure years of court cases or having my reputation spun through the shitter, but no, I'm spiraling because it's much worse than that. By creating ARGUS, I am Niobe, bound to suffer the wrath of the gods for declaring my child the most capable and powerful.

ARGUS was meant to be my legacy. Now it could be my undoing. If I refuse Russia, they expose the Saudi Arabia deal and trigger investigations that could strip me of my company. If I comply, I become complicit in something far worse than sanctions violations. The intelligence community, Sydney's former colleagues included—public servants—remain targets. And if I take the company public as Miles wants, I lose control entirely. Three paths, all leading to destruction.

"Rhodes?"

I caress her cheek, and something shifts inside me. The white-hot fury that drove me from this room hours ago has cooled to something more manageable—still painful, but no longer consuming. Maybe it was Nana's gentle wisdom about forgiveness, or maybe it's the growing realization that I've betrayed myself far more than Sydney ever betrayed me. The anger is still there, but it's directed where it belongs now: at the impossible situation, not at the woman who tried to navigate it. Syd's a symptom of a much greater affliction. A warning of what's coming.

"Are you Athena?"

"The goddess of war? In what way?"

"Well, you are a warrior, right? You worked for one of the world's intelligence agencies. You went rogue to hunt down whoever betrayed your people." I take a step closer, close enough to feel the heat radiating from her skin. "And now, what? Where do I fit in? Are you here to assist me or to turn me into Medusa?"

She doesn't answer immediately, but I see the calculation behind her eyes—weighing truth against lies, mission against emotion.

"I'm not Athena," she finally says, her voice barely above a whisper. "I'm just Sydney."

But that's the tragedy of the myths. The mortals never recognize the gods walking among them until it's too late. And I've already looked too long into her eyes to turn back now.

CHAPTER
THIRTY-ONE

SYDNEY

I touch his wrist, tentatively, hoping for connection.

With a slight shake of his head, he withdraws, choosing a lone chair to sit.

He closes his eyes and, with a frustrated sigh, rests his head on the back of the chair.

"The leak—what exactly made you think it came from ARGUS?"

I understand his question. Leaks in the intelligence world have been occurring since before the world wars. There are any number of options.

"We were careful," I say, remembering the meetings, the plan. "Nothing was in writing. There was no list."

"Did you not pay these assets?"

"We did," I acknowledge. "But never the same way. Not all assets wish for financial compensation." I chew at the corner of my lip, debating sharing more, but at this point, I've nothing to lose. "Our caseload expanded.

Consequence of department cuts. Same old thing. I'd been in Paris for about a year. Working at the embassy."

"Didn't that automatically make you likely CIA?"

"Maybe. My cover was that I was the girlfriend of a wealthy American pursuing his PhD at the Sorbonne."

"Did you date him? For real?"

I refrain from rolling my eyes. "No. I'm fairly certain he was—"

"Gay," Rhodes interrupts, and from his tone, I can tell he doesn't believe me.

"I was going to say asexual. I never saw him with anyone. I didn't get to know him well. He also, obviously, worked for the CIA."

"Right. And how did you lure your assets?"

"Any number of ways. Yoga class. Portuguese lessons. Dog park."

"Hiking?"

He hates me. As he should. "I once bumped into someone at the Louvre. That didn't lead anywhere. There are more misses than hits."

"Do the misses often involve sex?"

This time I'm the one closing my eyes, pulling on reserves deep within to remain calm. When my eyelids rise, I sit in silence until he returns my gaze. "I've never slept with a target. Although, in the spirit of honesty, during training, I told myself I would if necessary. There's no reason to be precious about sex."

His chest rises with an inhale. "Right." His lips scrunch. "The end justifies the means. And sex is just sex."

I open my mouth to argue but he dismisses me with a condescending expression that I possibly deserve.

"Let's stay on topic. How is ARGUS connected?"

"I used different processes with each of my assets. Different contact points. Methods. One was a gardener for a high-ranking Russian diplomat. A driver for the same."

"In Paris?"

"Yes. Another was a hairdresser for a different representative's spouse."

"Doesn't seem particularly valuable."

"Intelligence is valuable when pieced together. My most valuable asset was a secretary. When she committed suicide, I obviously suspected she'd been discovered. They watch lower ranking employees with a hawk's eye. But then the others…one by one."

"They didn't know each other?"

"Absolutely not. But it came to our attention that the surveillance feed within the city was uploaded to ARGUS. As is spending data and banking deposits. Online behavior. With the right queries, we were told ARGUS could reliably pinpoint—"

"Contacts within the embassy. You believe someone ran a query and derived a list of suspects?"

"That's what we believe, yes. Not just my assets, mind you. But, when my last asset died in suspicious circumstances—"

"Another suicide?"

"No. Car wreck."

"They pulled you?"

"If someone had a list of my assets, they would know…" I shrug. It's obvious. I wasn't allowed to return to my apartment as it was deemed too dangerous. Met my CIA handler in the park and was instructed to get in a limousine that whisked me away to the airport. Everything in my apartment arrived two weeks later neatly packed by professional shippers.

"If you're right, then ARGUS is being used by clients to comb through surveillance data to answer specific questions. Why assume I'm involved?"

"The assumption wasn't specifically you. The desire is to learn more about how ARGUS works. You're one of the creators. The lead."

"I work with the Pentagon. Closely. The DoD. If the CIA has these questions, why not come to me?"

"Perhaps they did. As I understand it, a congressional hearing was—"

"Hold a hearing and you might as well be making announcements to the world."

"Well, that's why there's a covert investigation. The world won't find out what's going on at ARGUS."

"The Pentagon, our biggest client, doesn't believe us?"

"Maybe your contacts believe you, but maybe their contacts don't." I pinch the bridge of my nose. If we'd fielded employees, it would've been better. Me getting close to Rhodes... "Is it possible that someone within ARGUS is doing queries and selling the data?"

"No." He's too quick to answer. "We have precautions in place."

"If you hadn't pulled strings to close down the congressional investigation, we probably wouldn't be here." My goal isn't to gaslight him, but it is the truth. The FBI floated opening an investigation to the DOJ— also shut down. Red flags.

He folds his hands, elbows on his knees, resembling the thinker. "I understand now. Thank you."

The formality, the coldness. It's all what I deserve but I at least need to try for him to understand. I sink to the floor, hands on his knees.

"My intention was never to hurt you."

I'm kneeling before him, sitting on my ankles. The posture feels foreign—vulnerable in a way I've never allowed myself to be with a target. The subservience is not lost on me. I don't kneel. I don't apologize. And I also complete the mission at all costs.

But this isn't about a mission anymore.

I stare at my hands, remembering them on his body last night. Remembering them on my service weapon in Paris. The same hands that caressed him set tracking devices, picked locks, even coerced innocent civilians into helping us, only for them to lose their lives. Working for KOAN, I've crossed professional lines and violated principles. But more importantly, I've been dishonest with someone who, against all protocols and predictions, I've come to care about and it's not a textbook phenomenon.

"If you discovered I was breaking the law, would you have turned me in?" His eyes hold mine, searching for truth—or perhaps a comfortable lie.

I consider deflecting but opt for honesty. "If you were breaking the law, yes." I pause, weighing my next words. "But laws and ethics aren't always aligned. The CIA taught me that some laws exist to protect power, not people."

His eyebrow raises slightly.

"When I say no one is above the law, I mean it. But I also know that not all laws deserve equal reverence." I think of classified operations I've taken part in—technically legal but morally questionable. "I'd want to know why you broke it. The motivation matters to me."

"Does it?" His voice is soft but intentional. "Or is that something you tell yourself to sleep at night?"

The question hits closer to home than he could know. How many nights have I lain awake justifying actions taken "for the greater good"?

"Fair question," I admit. "I guess we all draw our lines somewhere."

He nods, seemingly satisfied with my imperfect answer. "Fair enough."

"I've gotten to know you over these last few days and I don't believe you're unconscionable. If anything, I believe you're burdened with your responsibility. That's why your partner urged you to vacation, isn't it? It's been getting to you."

He extends a hand. "Don't sit on the floor."

I lay my hand on his, and the warmth of his skin penetrates deep within. As I rise, it feels like he might urge me onto his lap, but he doesn't. I stand before him, uncertain.

But uncertainty isn't warranted. That's just wishful thinking.

"We'll work together? My team with ARGUS. We want the same thing, right?"

His lips purse, and after a slight squeeze, he releases my hand. My heart pinches at the loss.

"My word is good. I'll work with you," he says. "And you're right."

"About?"

"The pressure." His phone sits silent on the side

table. For once, the world isn't demanding his immediate attention. "I haven't taken a vacation in years." His voice carries a weight I hadn't noticed before.

"Not since you launched ARGUS?" He blinks the slightest confirmation. The admission seems to cost him something.

"Rhodes." I step closer, drawn by the vulnerability he's trying so hard to hide. "You don't have to carry all of this alone."

His eyes meet mine, searching, then drift past me to the window overlooking the city. "Do you understand what I built, Sydney? Really understand it?" His voice drops to barely above a whisper. "ARGUS doesn't just connect databases—it sees patterns humans miss. It can trace a digital breadcrumb from a coffee purchase to a safe house. From a phone ping to an identity. From surveillance footage to..." He swallows hard. "To dead operatives."

The full weight of his words settles between us.

"Every query that runs through my system has the potential to be weaponized. Every client I trust could be the next one to sell a kill list." His hand rises to rub the back of his neck—that familiar gesture of frustration, but now I see it's something deeper. Fear. "I created the most sophisticated surveillance tool on the planet, and I'm only now realizing I can't control who uses it or how."

"Rhodes—"

"Everyone who gets close to this world—to me—ends up compromised. Your assets. Your safety. Even this conversation puts you at risk." His eyes return to mine, and I see the terrible understanding there. "Because if someone can identify CIA operatives through ARGUS, they can identify anyone. Including the people I..." He stops himself.

"Including the people you what?"

"Care about." The admission seems to cost him everything. "If the wrong hands get access to what I've built, no one is safe. Not my employees, not my clients, not..." His fingers barely graze my cheek. "Not you."

"I knew the risks when I took the assignment." I'm close enough now to see the exhaustion etched in the lines around his eyes. "But I didn't know I'd care about the man behind the technology." Something shifts in his expression—surprise, maybe hope. His hand rises tentatively, fingers barely grazing my cheek.

"Sydney..." The touch is electric, tentative, as if he's testing whether I'll pull away. I lean into his palm instead, the position awkward, with him sitting and me standing. "The attraction is real," I whisper, echoing my earlier words. "Everything else was the job. But this—" I place my hand over his, "—this was never part of the plan."

He stands then, and for a moment we're pressed close together, the weight of confessions and tentative trust settling between us. Then his phone rings, the shrill tone breaking the spell. He steps to the side table and swipes. "Daisy?"

He quickly moves to his backpack and pulls out a laptop, flips it open, and sets it on the coffee table before the sofa.

"Describe the unusual activity."

On the screen, a message window flashes and I read the words "containment protocols" followed by what appears to be a sequence of alphanumeric codes. A red indicator blinks in the corner—whatever this is, it's classified as critical.

He shifts the computer with practiced efficiency, the movement seemingly natural, but it's a calculated angle adjustment—it's the same technique I use when viewing classified materials in public spaces.

The glimpse was brief, but enough to recognize a data visualization map with multiple blinking nodes—Washington, D.C., New York, and what looked like Moscow. Before I can process more, the screen is firmly out of my view.

I back away quietly, the professional in me cataloging details while the woman in me respects his privacy. His voice drops an octave as he speaks to Daisy, the same tone military commanders use during crisis situations.

I move to the window, wrapping my arms around my middle. Night has fallen and the street below is a blur of red brake lights and white headlights. There are no stars, but it could just be D.C.'s light pollution, and not a sign of clouds. One benefit of living outside the metro area is that on clear nights, the stars shine.

Through the window, the Washington Monument stands illuminated against the night sky, a stark white obelisk piercing the darkness. The air conditioning cycles on with a soft hum, raising goosebumps along my bare arms. The suite smells of Rhodes' subtle cologne and the faint metallic tang of city rain. From somewhere down the hall, muffled laughter and the ping of an elevator remind me that outside this bubble of tension and revelation, normal life continues. For everyone else, this is just another Friday night in D.C.

How will the team react to working with Rhodes?

There shouldn't be an issue. Hudson should see this as a win. And if anyone can help me identify who used ARGUS to pinpoint assets, it'll be Rhodes, at least if ARGUS is as powerful as reported.

A shadow crosses the window frame, and I flinch as Rhodes crowds me.

"You OK?"

I press my palm to my sternum. "I'm fine," I say, shaking my head at myself. "I didn't even realize you ended your call. Is everything OK?"

He tips my chin up as his other arm loops behind me. "I think so."

His nose scrunches, and the hint of vulnerability tells me he's not talking about ARGUS.

"You said the attraction was real?"

"Is," I correct. "The attraction is very real."

Warm breath caresses my cheek. His heady, freshly showered scent and heat envelop me. Beneath my palm, my heart struggles to break free.

"Before, you planned on saying goodbye this weekend. You expected I would never learn the truth."

"You don't want a relationship." My words sound as defensive as they are.

The space between us charges with unspoken possibilities. Part of me—the professional—sees this as a tactical opportunity. Physical intimacy often breaks down psychological barriers, creating bonds that transcend professional boundaries. But as his fingers trace my collarbone, tactical thoughts slip. The heat blooming across my skin has nothing to do with operation parameters and everything to do with the way he looks at me.

He studies my face in the dim light filtering through

the window, as if memorizing details he might not get to see again. His thumb traces my cheekbone with the gentleness of someone handling something precious and fragile.

"I've been alone for a long time," he says quietly. "By choice. It was easier." His hand stills against my face. "But these last few days... I forgot what it felt like to want someone to stay."

The admission costs him something. I can see it in the way his jaw tightens, the vulnerability he's unused to showing.

"I'm here now," I say, though we both know how tenuous that is. "Whatever tomorrow brings, I'm here now."

Something shifts in his expression—decision replacing hesitation. His forehead touches mine, and we breathe the same air for a long moment.

"Sydney..." My name on his lips sounds different than it did earlier. Less guarded. More real.

"I know," I whisper, understanding what he can't say. That this matters. That we've crossed a line neither of us planned to cross. That everything is different now. When he finally kisses me, it's with the desperate tenderness of someone who's found something they didn't know they were looking for—and isn't sure they'll be allowed to keep it.

He seizes me with unexpected urgency, and I understand that we're both seeking the same thing—a moment where the complications fall away, where we're simply two people who've found something unexpected in each other.

The backs of his fingers skim slowly, oh so slowly,

along my neck. Goosebumps rise along my arms. His hot breath warms my ear. He nips at my lobe, and my knees weaken.

I pull back, seeking those dark eyes, but his lips brush over mine, and my eyelids flicker closed, lost in the sensation of a slow, tortured kiss.

He breaks the contact but holds me close, and it feels like he has no intention of letting me go.

"Are we—"

His nose rubs against mine, halting my question.

"The attraction's real." He presses me against his hard erection, confirming the physical reality. "Let's agree on that one point. Take it day by day."

That's actually exactly what I had planned. Yet none of those plans included the way my body responds to his touch, the way my objectivity dissolves when his lips meet mine.

My feet leave the air as he lifts me with unexpected strength, spinning us away from the window's exposure and through the suite into the bedroom. The movement is swift, decisive—perhaps even desperate.

He sets me on the mattress and we both undress, gaze locked on each other as our clothes rapidly come off, our intention clear. I notice how his eyes track my movements with the same intensity he shows when working—he misses nothing. He's fully present, wholly focused.

An operative should always be aware of exits, weapons, vulnerabilities—but as his clothes fall away revealing the lean musculature beneath, my focus narrows to just him. The birthmark on his ribs—shaped like Australia, a physical feature noted in my initial dossier on him—now not a data point but an intimate secret I've been privileged to discover.

Hard kisses rain down over my shoulder, along my chest. A bolt of hot, sharp pleasure shoots through me. My palm glides along rippling muscle, smooth and toned. A brief suckling kiss on my exposed nipples makes my entire body twitch. In the next instant, a rustling wrapper mixes with our breaths. A condom. Of course. We'd obviously return to condoms.

I glimpse the ceiling as the burn of his cock fills me. The muscles between my legs instantly squeeze around him, and he thrusts, the movement so quick and powerful the bed shifts.

Our union is slow and fast all at once. Controlling and surrendering. Fucking and making love. As our bodies blend, it feels like my heart has been ripped from the protection of my ribs and pummeled.

Our movements are animalistic, depraved, desperate. I watch his eyes close. Muscles tight. Corded. We're connected, yet we're not. He lifts my thigh, changing the angle. Insistent on my pleasure. And he apparently knows my body well enough that he succeeds.

Ecstasy rockets up and down my spine as he shudders over me, pulsing deep within. I cling to him, legs wrapped around him, and his head collapses next to mine.

The intensity shakes me to my core.

With a loud groan, he pushes off, pulling out of me and rolling onto his back. He rests his forearm on his forehead, chest still heaving, his deep breaths slowing. I roll onto my side, observing.

Does sex mean he's forgiven me? The weight between us doesn't feel like forgiveness.

What are we doing?

It's got to be what he's thinking, too. The red glow from his laptop screen catches my peripheral vision. The crisis that interrupted us is still there, waiting.

I study the tension in his jaw, the way his breathing hasn't quite settled. This isn't just post-coital vulnerability—he's still carrying whatever weight that phone call brought. "That call earlier," I say softly, my hand finding his chest. "You looked... Worried doesn't cover it. Should I be concerned?" His body tenses beneath my palm, and I feel the shift immediately.

"It's handled." But the way his heart rate spikes tells me otherwise.

"Rhodes, if there's a threat—to you, to ARGUS—I need to know. We're supposed to be working together now. What are containment protocols?" The words tumble out before I can stop them, curiosity overriding post-coital etiquette. My gut clenches.

It's probably the worst thing I could say after what we just experienced, on tentative emotional ground, but we also just agreed to take it day by day and what the hell else was I going to ask? "How was it for you?" seems absurdly inadequate after the intensity we just shared. "Have you forgiven me" is irrational. What's wrong? That's what I need to know.

"Security measures." His eyes close and he swallows, the movement of his throat betraying more concern than his carefully neutral tone. "Just protective protocols. Nothing you need to worry about," he adds, the deliberate vagueness telling me everything and nothing.

Then he pushes off the bed, strides across the room, and shuts the bathroom door behind him. The quiet click of the lock echoes in the silence.

Lying naked, I stare at the ceiling, listening to the water run. We're hot and cold. Day by day, he said. But in my experience, with the passing of enough days, connections always shatter.

After he showers, I take my turn. Before the fogged mirrors, I take my time, not eager to return to the unease. This, right here, is exactly why I don't do relationships. Friction always arises. It's an unproductive waste of emotions and time. Admittedly, this time I'm to blame for the friction, but does it really matter who's to blame? It's still there, it's still uncomfortable.

"Are you fucking kidding me?"

Rhodes' yell thunders through the door, and I freeze, toothbrush forgotten. I strain, stepping to the door, but don't hear anything else.

Did he call someone?

I'm not gaining anything by standing in the bathroom, so I quietly open the door, towel wrapped around me, hair dripping.

"Since when do you listen to NPC's?" He growls each word, head bent, back to me.

Dressed in pajama pants and nothing else, his back muscles remind me of a Roman sculpture signifying the strength of man against his burdens.

"No!" he shouts. "That's final."

He ends the call, and it's unclear who hung up on who, but my money's on Rhodes ending the discussion on his terms.

He lifts the phone, stretches his arm, and I tense,

expecting him to throw the phone, but he sees me, and his arm lowers. He scowls, pissed. Angrier than I've ever seen him, which given what he learned today about me, says something.

"You heard that?" he asks.

"Just the end."

"Miles and I don't always see eye to eye."

"Is he... Did he sell the information to the highest bidder?"

"What? No. I didn't... I told you, we have precautions in place. That was about an ongoing disagreement."

I wait, quietly, uncertain I believe him. Calling his partner to ask about the possibility of someone selling queries, selling secrets, right after our discussion feels logical.

"He wants us to go public. It's not going to happen."

"What's an NPC?"

He grimaces, exhales, and moves to plug his phone into a charger.

"Nonplayer Character."

"What?" ARGUS has nothing to do with the gaming industry.

"It's Miles' terminology. People without real decision-making power. Look, I know how it sounds—"

"Ah," I say, seeing a different side of Rhodes. "So the peons? Is that relegated to anyone within your corporate structure or does it apply to anyone without a B portfolio descriptor?" There was a time when a millionaire wielded power, but thanks to inflation, power now falls to those with limitless wealth, the billionaire class.

He smashes two pillows and pulls back the comforter, sliding into the bed.

"It's not like that."

Hmm. No, I'd say it's exactly like that. And if others within his company have the same elitist attitude, is it such a stretch that they'd find ways to further monetize the power of ARGUS?

"Don't look at me like that," he says, closing his eyes and rubbing his forehead. "It's Miles' word. Not mine."

"Yet you used it."

"To communicate with him. To make a point. He was putting way too much weight in what..." He stops, clearly realizing that he was about to confirm he's no different than his partner, and sees the value of some people to be less. With a gruff exhale, he looks to the ceiling and says, "I wish we could just go back to the watering hole. Swing from a vine. Skinny dip." He directs his gaze at me, but there's an unseeing quality to his expression. "I loved that day."

"We can't go back. It wouldn't be the same."

"I know," he groans, annoyance etched in his scowl.

But does he really get it?

"We can't go back," I say, feeling the need to make this clear, "Because now I know there are snakes."

CHAPTER
THIRTY-TWO

SYDNEY

The suite feels different in daylight—less intimate, more exposed. Morning light slants through the partially drawn curtains, illuminating the luxury that suddenly feels excessive. The Washington monument gleams in the distance, a reminder that in Washington, power and secrets are the true currency. Even the air feels different —the faint scent of the hotel body wash lingers on the sheets, mingling with the subtle note of room service coffee that someone has arranged on the credenza by the window. And beside the room temperature coffee, there's a handwritten note.

Went for a long run. Back after lunch.

. . .

A long run. I trained for a marathon in the past and recognize the terminology. Maybe he's currently training, or maybe he has a favorite twenty-mile course in D.C. Or the more likely scenario, he needs air and distance.

A lot happened between us yesterday, between me coming clean, our agreement to take it casually, and whatever that was last night. The sex was intense—almost desperate—like we were both trying to exorcise something. In my experience, that kind of intensity signifies the spectacular end of something that never had a chance.

My training emphasized compartmentalization—keep the mission separate from personal feelings. But the line between Sydney-the-operative and Sydney-the-woman has never felt so blurred. My hand unconsciously touches the spot on my neck where Rhodes' lips had been hours earlier, and I force it back down to my side. Focus. The operation parameters changed. That's all.

After a shower and slipping on leggings, a sports bra, tee, and running shoes, I head down to the lobby for fresh coffee. On the way down, I shoot a text to Quinn.

ME

Team still here?

I need to update everyone. The surveillance gig is up, or at least, my part is. I wonder how we'll adjust.

Just Jake. Noah on a new project.

On a whim, I grab an extra paper cup, fill it with coffee, and head up to the team's room on the seventh floor.

I rap on Jake's door and a gruff, muffled voice asks, "Who is it?"

"Sydney. Brought you coffee."

The door swings open, revealing Jake in his disheveled glory, bare-chested with low-slung pajama bottoms, his sandy blonde hair in massive disarray, twisting in all different directions, and his facial growth now a full, unruly beard.

"Did you go on a rager last night?" I step past him, passing him the black coffee. "Put on a shirt, dude."

He sniffs the coffee, then drinks. "Thanks."

There are two queen-size beds in his room. It's a standard hotel room and noticeably different from the suite.

After tugging on a T-shirt he lifted from the floor, he pulls on the drapes, allowing the sunlight to flow freely into the room. I take a seat on the end of the unwrinkled bed.

"When did Noah leave?"

"Late last night."

"And you went out?" Quinn filled me in on the video game playing Jake Ryder. He's got a military background and looking at him now, I have to wonder if he parties like the stereotypical guy on leave.

"No." He rubs a hand vigorously over his face. "Couldn't sleep. Didn't knock out until about four." He lifts the coffee in a gesture of gratitude. "Thanks for this." He sips it and eyes me. "How's it going?"

"I came clean." I barely know Jake, but there's something about his bedraggled state that makes him approachable. "He's going to work with us."

He stares me down for a moment, his sleepy eyes assessing, then, assessment apparently over, he says, "Good deal."

"That's it?"

"Syd, I'm a Navy guy." He says it without bravado, the way someone might mention they used to work in accounting. "My role in this dance is protection. You need me to take someone out, that I can do too." His gaze flicks briefly to the window, assessing risks. A habit I recognize from operators who've spent too much time in war zones.

"You're one of the goons trained to get inside people's heads," he continues, a hint of respect in his otherwise neutral tone. "You folks see things differently. If you say he's trustworthy, after what I hear you've been through, then I'll trust you."

"Wow. Thanks."

He lifts a shoulder like it's nothing. "Hey, it's not like I'm leading a squadron into enemy territory based on your gut. There's little to lose here. And we're still fleshing out this team."

"What do you mean by that?"

"It's a new outfit. Owners are pretty hands off from what I can tell, but yet they pop in and ask questions."

"Is it bothering Hudson?" He's former military, too. I

could see how not conforming to rank procedure would bug the guys. Transitioning out of a highly structured organization is notoriously challenging.

"Not sure."

"Do you know the owners? Who they are?" I'm aware Caroline Moore and her husband are the investors, but his terminology has me wondering what he's been told.

"Undisclosed. Explained to me as private investors."

I swirl the coffee in my cup. If I were him, I'd want to know who's paying my salary, but he doesn't seem overly bothered. I suppose lots of companies have investors, or owners as he chose to describe it, who work behind the scenes.

"Hudson's good people," Jake says, and it's clear, to him, that's what's most important.

"I agree." At least, that's my preliminary read on my new boss.

If KOAN doesn't work out, I really will be unemployed, but that's not something I worried much about when I agreed to come on. If the team doesn't pan out, I'll find something else. After I uncover the leak.

"Should I call Hudson?" He squints one eye, and I think that's his way of asking for more information. "To give him the update."

I could tell Quinn, but she's our tech guru. Her response will likely be about as useful as Jake's.

"Go ahead." He scratches his head and stands with a grunt. "I'll hop in the shower. Give you privacy."

I could also go up to the suite, but this is better. Down here, there's no chance Rhodes will walk in and things will get awkward. If I were to shut up, he'd assume I'm keeping secrets.

The bathroom door clicks closed. Hudson doesn't answer, so I look up Caroline's name, then press to call her. She answers on the third ring.

"This is Caroline."

"Hey, it's Sydney."

"Everything okay?"

"Yeah."

"You sound down."

A deep melody mixes with the running shower. I'm pretty sure Jake's butchering a Jimmy Buffett song.

"I wouldn't say down, I'd say–"

"This has to do with the guy."

"Why do you say that?"

"Call it a hunch."

"Can I ask you… Dorian…does he ever…" I can't ask if her husband sees himself as better than everyone else without sounding bitchy. "Does he view those… Does he see the world as a stratified class system?"

Dorian not only has more money than Rhodes, but he was born into his wealth. His uncle was president. He's basically American royalty.

"He wouldn't say that…"

"But he does."

"He's not the best at getting to know the people who work for him." The way she says the words slowly, like she's stringing the sentence together cautiously, is almost humorous. "What's going on? Is MacMillan rude to wait staff?"

A long time ago, Caroline and I, along with a couple of other friends, wrote up a red flag list for dating. Rude to the server was at the top of the list. Logical for our group. We'd all been waitresses at some point during school.

"No." He just categorizes an entire section of the population as NPC's. "But you love Dorian, right? I mean, obviously you do. Not only did you marry him, but after you separated, you got back together with him. So even though he—"

"Dorian's not perfect. I love him despite his imperfections, although, I'll admit, sometimes it can be challenging. But, I mean, you know, you don't get to be in Dorian… or MacMillan's place…without some ego attached. That's what you're talking about, right? He's got a massive ego?"

"No, not really." I wouldn't say his ego is huge, but then again, I'm still getting to know him. There's the rub. "I guess I want to know that I can trust him."

"Ah. You've seen a red flag, which is unnerving. My advice is to take things slow. Get to know him and get to know how you are with him. Those are two different things and I would argue they are equally important."

"I didn't actually call you for advice."

"Of course you did. We've been friends for years. You reach out when you need a sounding board."

Huh. I don't particularly care for what that says about me. "How are you doing?"

I look down at the phone in my hand and the minute counter.

"I'm good. Look, my advice comes from a place of experience. As you know during all those months and years I turned to you when I was down, it's not easy to be in a relationship with a powerful man. We almost got divorced. You've spent less than a week with this guy–"

"Caroline," I snap. "I need to know if I can trust him for a project. That's it. Back in the mountains, he was one person. Now, I'm beginning to see other sides, that's all."

"Of course you are. He was on vacation. He's exiting vacation mode. It'll take time to see all of his various sides."

"True."

"What does your gut say?"

"That he's a good guy."

"But?"

"No but. He's a good guy but he might be open to…"

"Making mistakes? You mean like, he might be human?"

I roll my eyes, not that she can see.

"No one's all bad, and no one is all good. Be careful. Eyes wide open."

"I came clean. He knows I'm working with KOAN. He wants to work with us."

I hesitate. Waiting. Will she be angry?

"He wants to work with us?"

"Yes."

"We're investigating ARGUS."

"If they're the source of the leaks, it's not him."

"All right. Play it out. Have you updated Hudson?"

"Have a call into him."

"We'll regroup at the beginning of the week."

"Are you angry?"

"Angry? No. I trust you. Don't share we have an in on the West Coast."

"I won't."

"And I know you trust him, but remember, eyes wide open, you understand?"

"Always."

"You need me, you call. Hear?"

"Always do." She's one of my closest friends. "And everything's good with you?"

"It is, but I've got to run. Dorian's shouting about something."

"You're not in the office?"

"No. We headed to Maine to get a break from the heat for the weekend." Her voice goes lower, like she placed the phone against her chest. "In a minute!"

"Go," I tell her. "Speak later."

"Speak soon," she says, and the call ends.

I try Hudson again, and this time, he answers.

"Parker. All okay?"

"Yes. I have an update."

"Go ahead."

I pause, glancing at the drapes, knowing that in the CIA what I'm about to say would mean dismissal. "I came clean to Rhodes. We can trust him. He's going to work with us to determine if anyone within ARGUS is selling intel."

"Are you emotionally involved?"

My fingers curl, but there's no point in taking offense. The question echoes our academy instructor's warnings about "agents and emotional compromise."

"Yes." I pause because stating my case too quickly undermines my cause. "However, I'm eyes wide open. I also learned important information. The Russian meeting wasn't a business meeting. Not exactly. They're black-mailing him. They want him to buy the Forbes Intelligence database—obviously to use for their purposes. He hasn't agreed to anything."

"This database—did he mention what it contains?"

"No specifics, but it's valuable enough that the Russians are risking diplomatic exposure to acquire it."

"And you said he's willing to work with us?"

"Yes. If there's—"

"Let me get back to you."

The call ends and I look at the phone in my hand. That was odd.

I pull up a secure search window on my phone and type "Forbes Intelligence database." Nothing relevant appears—either it's highly classified or deliberately obscured.

A feeling of failure overwhelms me. I'm not one who fails, and yet I failed this operation.

I should go for a run. Take a cue from Rhodes.

I step past the bathroom and shout so Jake can hear over the shower, "I'm heading out."

I toss the empty paper cup into a small bin and exit Jake's hotel room. As I head down the hall, following the arrows to the elevator bank, I hear someone knocking on a door. The sound grows louder as I progress down the hall, and I slow when I hear a too-familiar voice.

I peer around the corner, instinctively pressing against the wall to minimize my profile. The hallway carpeting muffles my footsteps as I edge closer.

David Crawford stands in the doorway of room 714, his broad back to me, one hand gripping the doorframe. His posture radiates tension—shoulders rigid, neck muscles visibly taut. He's speaking in hushed tones, but his clipped gestures suggest urgency or frustration.

The door opens wider and adrenaline surges. My

periphery darkens, and I home in on the man in the doorway.

It's the FBI agent from the bar yesterday; the one who tried to plant a tracker on me. His expression is deferential but firm as he responds to whatever the senator is demanding.

I lift my phone, frame the shot carefully, and capture the exchange—Crawford's distinctive salt and pepper hair from behind, and the full face of his companion. The agent's eyes shift suddenly, scanning the hallway, and I withdraw around the corner, pulse quickening.

How do they know each other? Crawford is a member of the Senate Intelligence Committee. Is Crawford staying in this hotel, or is this a dedicated meeting spot?

If it had been a female agent, I'd assume David was cheating on his wife again. But I'm certain he's not gay. Bi? The conversation seemed heated.

I shoot the image off to Quinn.

ME

> FBI agent from the bar yesterday. Can you verify facial recognition with his badge?

I'm down in the lobby when a text comes through.

QUINN

> Zero facial recognition matches. No known bureau personnel.

. . .

Huh. Stolen badge credentials. What do you know?

Rhodes is under Russian pressure to acquire a database. A senator with intelligence clearance is meeting with someone using falsified FBI credentials. The same fake agent attempted to approach me after I was seen with Rhodes.

Could it all be connected?

If so, it has the hallmarks of a multi-pronged intelligence operation—the Russians applying direct pressure while simultaneously using domestic assets to monitor or influence the target. Classic pincer technique. But there's something off about the pattern. If Crawford is compromised by Russia, why would the fake agent approach me so brazenly in the hotel bar? That's not how Russian intelligence typically operates.

Unless this isn't a Russian operation at all. Unless there's a third player I haven't identified yet.

I check my watch. The formal event is in less than ten hours—a perfect opportunity for multiple intelligence services to converge around high-value targets. It would be helpful to identify the relevant players before the event.

Instead of hitting the pavement, I head back to Jake's room. He opens the door on my first knock.

"We're staying," he greets me, freshly showered and awake. "Hudson called. He wants to know who's behind the blackmail."

"That's pretty obvious," I say, stepping inside, but not before doing a visual sweep along the hallway to ensure we're alone. "The ops changing."

"Tend to do that," Jake says with a low-key shrug.

I pull out my phone and share the photo I snapped of a US senator and a man pretending to be an FBI agent. Jake's expression changes instantly—the casual demeanor replaced by the focused intensity I've seen in operators in high-risk scenarios.

"This complicates things," he says quietly, zooming in on the fake agent's face. "I know this guy."

"From where?"

Jake's eyes meet mine, his expression grim. "Not from the bureau, that's for damn sure." He reaches for his secure phone. "We need to contact Hudson. Now."

CHAPTER
THIRTY-THREE

Sweat drips down my brow as I push through mile fourteen, my lungs burning with each breath. I've been running since dawn, punishing my body in a futile attempt to clear my head. Last night's revelations, Sydney's confession, our subsequent intimacy—it's all a tangled mess I can't seem to unravel at any pace under seven minutes per mile.

I check my watch, not for the time, but for the temperature. It's going to be a hot day, and while the trees in Rock Creek Park provide momentary shade, the humidity clings to my skin like a warning. A familiar figure comes into view on the trail ahead—short dark hair, laptop open on her lap, face more serious than I've ever seen. Daisy. I always say she's like a little sister, but really she's my most trusted lieutenant. I tried to get her to come on as a partner, but she refused, claiming she didn't like to stay at one company for too long. Meanwhile, she's still with us, although admittedly, she insists on remote work and hasn't stepped foot inside the office in two years. She's the last person I expected to travel to D.C., but here she is.

I don't slow until I'm right on top of her, and she squeals.

"Jesus F Christ, Rhodes! Mother. Trucker. Gross. You dripped your sweat on me. Ew!"

Her outburst has me both chuckling and scanning the trail to see if anyone's worried I'm mauling an innocent woman. But, at the moment, we're alone on this section of the trail.

"Why are you so smelly?" she continues. "Did you do something maniacal? Like sprint the Watergate steps?"

"No. But that is on my list." My never-ending to-do list.

"Don't. It's over-hyped." She slaps the laptop shut.

"What has you worked up?"

"Nothing."

I'm calling bullshit. Daisy Jonas doesn't do "nothing" moods. She's my paradox—the most brilliant coder I've ever met who refuses to conform to stereotypes. While other techies dress in hoodies and spout AI ethics platitudes at conferences, Daisy climbs mountains (literally—she summited Mount Kilimanjaro last year), practices competitive archery, and can dismantle any tech bro's argument with devastating precision and zero jargon.

She's the only executive at ARGUS who calls me on my bullshit directly to my face. The only one who saw what ARGUS could become before I did. And the only person besides my grandmother who gets away with digging into my personal life. If she's in a mood, there's a reason, and it's not nothing.

I've run too many miles to sit without risking a muscle cramp, so I pace around the bench, letting my muscles cool and the stream of sweat slow.

"You got any water?"

She peers up at me, scowling. "You didn't pack?"

"Should've grabbed the Platypus, but I didn't." This morning when I left the hotel, I wasn't thinking about anything other than not waking Sydney as I bolted.

"What's in your pack?"

I am hauling a small backpack, but it's not a Platypus designed to hold water.

"No water."

Daisy opens her backpack and passes a half-empty bottle of water. It'll work.

"You going to tell me what's up? Did Miles do something?" He definitely pissed me off last night. She doesn't really have any interaction with Alex, although if she did, he'd definitely be pissing her off. Alex and Miles have been pushing the same financial agenda, and Daisy's in my corner on this one.

She shakes her head and pushes her lower lip out in her signature I'm-not-pleased-with-what-you're-saying expression. "Nothing work related."

"Are you dating someone?" It's conceivable she's here in the D.C. area for personal reasons.

"Is that shock on your beet-red face? You think you're the only one who can get laid?"

"I didn't mean it like—are you?"

"No. It's a personal thing." Her gaze drops and she picks at her jeans. "Someone close to me passed away."

"Daisy." I hold out my hands in a what-the-fuck gesture. "Why didn't you say something? Why were you working last night?"

"It's nothing."

"Daisy." It's clearly not nothing; she can't even look at me. "Is the funeral here?"

"No." Her lips purse, eyes still cast downward, and she shakes her head slightly. "He lived in LA. I missed the funeral."

Her shoulders rise and anyone can tell she doesn't want to talk about it, which means she's seriously hurting.

"At any rate," she announces like she's concluded that segment of our conversation, "I'm here because I'm doing a little investigating. If you get a call asking for a reference, I need you to say I'm fab."

"Wait. What? I'm not letting you quit."

She places her palms on each side of her face and stretches her fingers out like her head is going to explode. "Rhodes," she says, gritting her teeth, "I need you to do this."

"Alright. You're going to have to back this one up."

"Fine. Sixty-second version." She finally looks me in the eye and I half expect her to flip me off.

"Go."

"There's a man who basically raised me."

I nod while pacing. This isn't new. Daisy doesn't always see eye to eye with her mother. She has a much younger sister and began working for us remotely when she moved home years ago to help take care of her. I thought things were better. Her sister's in college. Daisy left LA. Lives in Chicago, at least, she did the last time I asked.

"He died." She swallows and looks to the side, lips pursed, and she swipes under one eye. "Unexpectedly. Seems like he wasn't taking care of himself, and I hadn't been home in ages, so I had no idea. I know you're going to say it's not my fault and I get that; I'm working through that. I can't change..." she breaks off and mutters "sixty seconds" to herself. "He was swindled. Lost his entire savings. He was a vet. Vietnam. Living off Social Security basically but he had enough that he said he'd never be a liability on anyone. Anyway, I looked into this company. They target retirees and vets. It's shady as fuck. They're hiring a coder, looking to build a system I'm sure so they can swindle more people online."

"Wait. You're going to work for these crooks so you can, what? Catch them?"

"It's shady. They have to be breaking the law somehow. And they're connected. Maybe even funded by rich-as-fuck big wigs. I'm still working through it. "

"The fund went under?" I ask, trying to follow what's happened.

"Failed."

"And they're hiring?"

"Suspicious, right?"

"Why do you have to do it? Why not... I'll call someone at the SEC. The FBI."

"No. I've looked into this guy. He's connected up the wazoo. The DOJ or the DA or whoever needs to authorize will never sign off. I'm gonna bring the receipts so they have no choice but to open an investigation."

"Daisy..."

"Rhodes." She peers up at me through stubborn, glassy eyes. "I need to do this. Reed could've come to me for money. He didn't. And he probably didn't because his stupid pride wouldn't let him. I couldn't set everything straight, and he..." She inhales. "I can't change what happened, but I'm going to make those bloodsuckers pay. Going after retirees. Vets?"

"But..." I pause, hoping she doesn't take too much offense at the truth. "You're not an investigator."

"No. But I'm going to be using our system to find out everything I can on this fuckwad swindler. It's not the whole company. Sterling Financial has too many employees. Once I get inside, I'll find out each person who's involved and whistleblow like a smoke detector with a dying battery. No one shall ignore me."

I hold up my hands, showing I'm not fighting her on this. It's not really how we planned on using ARGUS, as a matter of fact I'm pretty sure we agreed in our initial ethical discussion meetings to never use it for personal purposes, but even if I told her no, she'd do it anyway. And I suppose her goal is for the greater good.

"And you're in D.C. because the company is in D.C.?" Daisy and I were scheduled to have a secure video call this morning. She texted earlier, said she was in D.C. and suggested we meet in person, and at four a.m. when I couldn't sleep, I planned my long run and suggested we meet on the trail.

She pulls her knees up to her chest and lifts her sunglasses to her forehead. "It's nearby. In Virginia. And I wanted to speak to you in person."

I stop pacing and take her in.

The cicadas are already starting their summer drone, a

backdrop to our conversation that feels both soothing and grating. A helicopter—likely Marine One based on the direction—flies overhead toward the White House. In this city, even the air space is a reminder of power dynamics.

"You're not fucking quitting."

"Fine. But if I get that job, I'm taking it."

"If that happens, we'll call it personal leave. A paid personal leave because you're not really leaving."

She should've joined as a partner but changing the company structure now would be almost impossible so I refrain from saying anything along those lines.

"Whatever." There's an eyeroll, a shift in demeanor, and just like that, she's on to the next subject. I make a mental note to look into this company she wants to infiltrate. "That's not why I wanted to speak in person. I've been digging into your love interest."

And she wants to tell me in person. *This isn't good.*

My stomach plunges, a physical reaction more honest than anything I've allowed myself to feel since leaving the hotel room this morning. Hours of running, and I'm right back where I started—trapped between attraction and suspicion. You can't have a relationship without trust, which is why we're not in a relationship. My psyche needs to clue in.

"Sydney?"

I don't know why I have to say her name. Or why I need confirmation. Perhaps a part of me still hopes there's some explanation that doesn't make me a fool twice over—once for not seeing her initial deception, and again for allowing myself to hope for something genuine between us afterward. The mythology metaphors from last night echo mockingly in my head: Icarus falling after flying too close to the sun. Except in this case, the sun might be a carefully constructed illusion.

"Yep. Your missus."

"Don't call her that." A jogger comes around the bend and I make eye contact, nod, pull my foot up to my ass to stretch my quad, and once the jogger is out of earshot and past us, say, "Just spit it out Daze."

"I got her CIA file."

"How?" I put a hand up, gesturing for her to not speak. "I don't want to know."

"No, you don't. I didn't use ARGUS. Not for this. Her file includes redacted information about an operation in Moscow that went wrong."

"I thought she was based in France when she was pulled back."

"All I'm saying is she's got ties to Russia, even if it was a short-term op."

This news isn't particularly surprising. The assets she was cultivating in France worked for the Russian embassy.

"You needed to say that to me in person?"

"And ARGUS is being attacked by a sophisticated bot network." She delivers this bombshell with the same tone she might use to comment on the weather.

I freeze mid-stretch. "I'm hearing about this just now? About an attack on our primary system?"

"I've got it under control." She waves dismissively. "You were on vacation."

"A vacation you and Miles practically forced me to take," I snap, dropping my voice as a pair of older walkers pass by. "Define 'sophisticated bot network.' Are we talking standard DDoS or something more targeted?"

Daisy's expression shifts subtly—the slight tightening around her eyes that I've learned means the situation is worse than she's letting on. "They're probing for vulnerabilities in our encryption protocols. Not trying to take us down—trying to get in. Whoever designed it knows our architecture intimately."

Jesus fucking Christ. Someone with inside knowledge of ARGUS is targeting us, and meanwhile I've been hiking and sleeping with a woman who admitted to investigating me.

"Daisy." I close my mouth and focus on breathing through my nose to rein in the growing anger. When Miles convinced me to take a vacation, I agreed under the condition I would be apprised of any major issues.

"Don't get like that. I've got it under control. And you knew I was investigating. Remember our call last night? Containment protocols? I kept you updated as I researched. And now I have an answer."

I motion for her to get to her fucking point.

"My first suspicion was Russia. Especially after, you know, the ambassador yesterday."

"Is that why you're telling me Sydney may have worked in Moscow?"

"I traced the attack to servers owned by Zenith—Dorian Moore's company." Daisy's fingers tap a rapid pattern on her laptop lid—her tell when she's connecting dots mentally. "And like I mentioned to you, Sydney and Dorian's wife, Caroline Moore, have history."

"What's the connection to Russia?" She's treading on frayed nerves.

"There might not be any direct connection," she says, looking at me like I'm a simpleton, yet she's the one sitting on the bench like a child with her arms wrapped around her legs. "But Zenith has several contracts with Roscosmos—the Russian space agency. They share certain orbital lanes."

She doesn't need to spell it out. Sharing orbital lanes means sharing data collection opportunities.

"You're saying this could be corporate espionage, not state-sponsored?"

"Except we both know the line between corporations and state isn't exactly clear anymore, especially in tech," she says with a shit-ton of smug pride. "Russia wants access to the Forbes database. Moore may want ARGUS. Sydney works for Moore's wife and has a history with Russian operations. You need to know that she could be running a double operation—serving both corporate and state interests. KOAN's ownership is seriously vague. Like we're talking so covered it's deep shade."

"Double operation? I told you I'm not sure I can trust Sydney."

"Right." She lowers her sunglasses back onto the bridge of her nose and waits. "I'm backing you up."

"And Sydney could be working for KOAN and Russia." Repeating it back to her sounds as repulsive as when she said it.

"Lots of possibilities," she says as casually as if we're standing in front of the deli counter in San Francisco.

"I'll admit that I don't trust this group she's working for. But Sydney's not working for Russia. Not knowingly at least. She's hunting for someone who would leak a list of assets. She thinks someone within our company might have done it."

I take off my backpack and the flow of air over my drenched shirt immediately cools my skin.

"Word of advice," Daisy quips, nose crinkled.

"Yes?" I unzip my bag, searching for my phone.

"Shower before you try anything with the missus."

I shoot her a glare that should warn her to back off this. Besides, it's not like she's my missus if I can't trust her.

"She played you."

She didn't play me is right there, on the tip of my tongue, aching to come out, but I bite it back because the denial would be a lie.

"Now you need to play her."

I crush the plastic bottle in my grip.

"We need to figure out what angle KOAN is working."

I let out a frustrated groan, my only acknowledgement that Daisy is right.

Out of a stream of messages, there's one from an unknown number that stops me cold.

UNKNOWN NUMBER
Icarus

My heart rate spikes. No one knows about my private comparison to Icarus except…

What the hell? Would Syd tell someone? Was someone listening?

"Oh, and I thought you should look at this." Daisy pulls out her phone and flips it to show satellite imagery of the Russian embassy—imagery available in ARGUS's classified feeds.

I scan the time stamp and see it's yesterday. The resolution is sharp enough to identify faces, though I don't recognize the pedestrians. "What am I supposed to see here?"

"Wait for it," she says, a hint of anticipation in her voice.

A black Mercedes pulls up outside the embassy. My security team's car. I check the time again. Five p.m. That would've been after my meeting, when I was back at the hotel with Sydney.

The door opens, and a figure emerges—unmistakably my partner, Miles. He walks directly into the embassy without being checked at the gate.

"What the hell?" The words barely escape my throat.

Miles and I don't always see eye to eye, but we've founded two companies together. With ARGUS, we see eye to eye on everything, except nonprofit status. Lately though, it's been two against one. More and more he's been siding with Alex… Hell, I'm on vacation partly because the executive team meetings have become unbearable—Alex presenting spreadsheet after spreadsheet showing what we're "leaving on the table" by staying private, and Miles nodding along like a bobblehead. He wants to keep Alex on, because ultimately, he agrees with Alex about the need to go public. Meanwhile, his going behind my back to Russia would only undermine his IPO argument and solidify my point—an entity as powerful as ARGUS cannot ethically be driven by profit.

Daisy's face is grim. "Exactly. I'm clueless. And don't forget…" She swipes to another image. "Just yesterday…"

The image shows Sydney in the bar, speaking with the man who identified himself as FBI.

"Everyone around you is playing an angle, Rhodes," Daisy mumbles. "Everyone."

The Icarus text flashes on my screen again. Someone knows I'm flying too close to the sun. And they're warning me about the fall.

SYDNEY

Three rapid knocks on the suite door sound. I hit mute on the television, silencing Gordon Ramsey's infinite wisdom.

"Ms. Parker?"

The gruff voice is not one I recognize. Hotel staff wouldn't use my name. I approach the door from the side.

"Yes? Hello?"

"It's Howard Casey. I work with Mr. MacMillan."

Security?

I crack the door open. The man standing before me wears navy dress slacks, a cream-colored golf shirt paired with a sports jacket, and black running shoes. With his short, trimmed buzz cut, he could be mistaken for military.

"I work with Mr. MacMillan," he repeats. "Do you mind if I come in? I need to check the space."

"You're on his security team?" I study him with professional interest. Stance slightly wider than shoulder-width, weight balanced on the balls of his feet, right hand positioned for quick access to what's likely a concealed weapon beneath his jacket. Not Secret Service protocol exactly, but similar. Private sector with government background.

"Yes, ma'am." His eyes perform a quick scan over my shoulder—assessing threats, mapping exits, exactly as he should.

While I haven't met this man yet, he was on the surveillance pics Quinn shared. I recognize his facial structure and the military bearing. I open the door wide and let him enter, curious to see his methods.

"Mr. MacMillan will return soon. I'll do a quick walk through and be out of your hair in no time."

"Not a problem," I say, stepping toward the sofa, but uncertain as to what I should do.

The way he moves through the space is methodical—corners first, then central areas, maintaining sight lines to all entry points. Well-trained. Which means Rhodes takes his security more seriously than he lets on.

"Go ahead and watch your show," he says as he passes through the perimeter, a device in his hand meant to detect any unexplained signals.

And that's why we don't have surveillance in this room.

"Is it okay if I head in?" he gestures with his head toward the bedroom.

"Go ahead."

My phone sits on the coffee table, the screen black. We agreed I would limit contact with the KOAN team while I'm in this room—at least until I've confirmed we're aligned with Rhodes. His disappearance act this morning has me wondering if he's re-thinking, well, everything.

The suite door opens and Rhodes steps in, face bright red, hair wet, and T-shirt soaked.

"Did you go swimming?"

"Looks like it, right?" In three long strides, he's in front of the concession area and opening a bottle of water.

"Is it hot out there?"

He downs about half the bottle, then wipes his mouth with the back of his hand. "Getting there."

As I say, "Howard from your team is here," the man exits the bedroom.

"Mr. MacMillan."

Rhodes clocks Howard with a degree of surprise, but there's no alarm. He recognizes him and knows who he is, but the formality in his posture and greeting tell me he doesn't work often with Howard.

"Roger's downstairs," Rhodes says.

"Right," Howard replies. "It's all clear here. Have a good day, sir."

After the suite door clicks closed, Rhodes crushes the now empty water bottle in his hand and scores a perfect shot into the circular gold bin at the end of the credenza.

"Do you run with security?"

With one hand, he lifts the hem of his soaked shirt up and twists it over his shoulders. Fine golden hairs stand on end, most likely a reaction to the air conditioning. He's lean, and the faint lines of a six-pack dimple his abdomen. Thinking about touching him last night, about how those muscles felt strained and corded above me, gives rise to a visceral reaction.

"Not when I can avoid it."

"Oh?"

"I'm pretty unrecognizable in D.C. But...these guys I hire here...they're pretty cautious."

"You should listen to them. They're experts, right?" His eyes narrow, questioning. "I assume you hire the best."

"Did you get to know Howard?"

"No," I half-laugh. "I'm just assuming—"

There's something about the way his dark eyes penetrate me that has me altering my course, shifting from light to serious.

"You have access to an extremely valuable tool—it might threaten dangerous people. There are those out there who might have ideas on how to force your hand. And snatching you off the street might sound..." I know how it sounds, but it's not at all inconceivable. He doesn't have a wife or children, and that means his body parts might be the leverage a sick individual might choose. Images from training flash and my throat tightens. He needs to be cautious.

"No one's coming after me. There's no need for concern." His tone conveys it's a preposterous notion.

If he knew what I do—about how aggressors can treat a human being, about the techniques I've studied—he'd be concerned. I've seen what happens to high-value targets when they're cavalier about security. The images flash unbidden: the photographs of business executives taken in Moscow, Seoul, Beijing. The ones who thought they were untouchable. Some never made it home.

I meet his gaze head on. "You need to be careful."

My concern is genuine, surprising even me with its intensity. Somewhere along the way during this op, Rhodes himself has become something I want to protect. The professional part of me recognizes this as a classic sign of operational compromise. The woman, or well, the human in me doesn't care.

I step closer, but he stops me with his hand. "Let me shower."

"Want company?"

His gaze roams my body, possibly looking for sweat. "Did you already work out?"

"No," I admit. I intended to work out, but after further conversations with the team, ended up back in the suite so I'd be here when Rhodes returned.

"We can fix that."

This time, when I step closer, he pulls me in, flat against him. When we kiss, once again, it's demanding. Controlling.

And while my body reacts with tingles and goose-bumps, the pungent scent of sweaty male threatens to overwhelm me. I push against his shoulder, breaking the kiss with a laugh. "I think we should head to that shower."

He smirks and slaps my Lycra-covered ass.

"Let's go." He interlaces our fingers, tugging me along. "We've got to be quick. I've got a tuxedo arriving shortly."

"Oh?"

"Yeah, I forgot to pack one."

"You remembered to send me five gowns and forgot your tux?"

"I planned to wear a suit. But we've been invited to a private reception at the Russian embassy before the event tonight. I'll need to show my respect."

My steps slow as adrenaline surges. I need to alert the team. An opportunity to access the Russian embassy... I mean, I'll be watched. I probably can't do much, if anything.

"Maybe you can help me," he says, spinning to face me in the bathroom. He leans against the counter, arms crossed, watching me.

"How?"

"Let's see if we can determine who is pulling the strings?"

"You mean with your blackmail? You know with Russia it's... All instruction leads to the leader."

"Right. But you want to find out who leaked your list, right?"

"I doubt that information is lying around in a file cabinet." But wouldn't it be lovely if it was?

"Inside the embassy, if you were to get a chance to access an office...any office. Any computer..." He tilts his head, assessing.

"What?"

"No," he shakes his head and scratches his jaw. "It's dangerous."

He steps forward to tug at my top, but I step back.

"What? I'll do it." I may sound too eager, but I'm intrigued.

"If you can insert a drive into a computer," he says, voice dropping to barely above a whisper, "it can install a surveillance package that will provide remote access." He reaches for the towels, continuing as if discussing dinner plans. "The drive has a zero-day exploit that bypasses typical security measures. Twenty seconds is all it needs."

His technical knowledge reminds me that beneath the executive exterior is still the genius who dropped out of Harvard's business school.

"And if I get caught?" A legitimate question.

"If you get caught, of course, you'd need to play it off that you were trying to download something." His eyes meet mine, calculating. "The drive is disguised as a compact—looks like makeup. If they find it, the software self-destructs after three incorrect password attempts."

This isn't amateur hour. The level of preparation suggests Rhodes has either done this before or has resources with serious intelligence backgrounds. I'm both impressed and concerned—how much of this was planned before our "honest" conversation yesterday?

He steps into the shower and twists the water to high.

"I can do it."

I push my leggings over my hips and attempt to step out of them quickly while his back is to me, but when he turns, they're at my ankles. As I awkwardly step one leg out at a time, he steps close and fingers the underside of my sports bra.

I peer up at him, and he says, "Up."

Obediently I raise my arms and he fingers the tight clothing over my breasts and up over my arms.

"You've done this before," I can't help but say, and what's more, I'm slightly alarmed at the jealousy I feel. Unlike me, he has been in a long-term relationship.

"Undressed a woman?" A singular eyebrow raises. "Yes."

His heated gaze roams from my breasts down to my remaining undies and ankle socks. He releases an appreciative sigh.

"Maybe I should've taken you on the run with me."

"Twenty miles? Eh...no thank you."

"But you're a runner."

His genuine surprise has me laughing. "If I'm doing twenty, it's with a purpose. Marathon. Trapped behind enemy lines. Some kind of work."

"So I'm not work?"

His question hangs in the air. He is, and he isn't.

Steam bellows in the shower behind him, beckoning. I finger his running shorts and push them down. His sex hardens in my hand.

"You're not work," I say, meaning every word, terrifying as it is. Before this, I've always maintained the line between mission and emotions. I've played roles, created connections, even flirted when necessary—always with a clear boundary in sight.

With Rhodes, the boundary is dissolving. His touch doesn't just arouse me physically, it reaches something deeper, something I've kept protected. As we step under the warm spray, his hands tracing patterns across my skin, I recognize the danger goes beyond the planned op.

For the first time in my career, I'm uncertain which loyalty will win if forced to choose.

***

Later that afternoon, after a woman arrived at the suite to blow out my hair and style it, I finger through the gowns from Neiman Marcus. Rhodes dressed and told me he'd wait for me in the living area. It's the first moment I've had to myself, given he hired someone to do my hair and make-up.

The suite has transformed into a preparation area—makeup cases spread across the bathroom counter, dress bags hanging from every available hook, the scent of hairspray lingering in the air. Through the window, Washington's monuments are bathed in late afternoon sunlight, the kind that photographers call "golden hour."

The air conditioning hums softly, barely audible over the muted sounds of traffic below. In the corner, Rhodes' tuxedo bag lies empty, the ritzy tissue liner scattered carelessly. I run my fingers along the silky fabric of the gowns, each one probably worth months of my salary.

With one more scan for cameras, I pull out my phone and message Quinn.

ME

Going to Russian embassy before gala. Plan to attempt access to a computer drive to install a surveillance program. Leaving hotel at 4:45. Arriving at embassy by 5:15.

QUINN

Could be a setup

She's not wrong. If he's pissed, it would be one helluva way to get back at me. But Rhodes isn't in the intelligence game. He's a coder. A software engineer. In his heart, he's a good person. He wouldn't sabotage me or leave me to rot in a Russian prison. He also has every reason to explore the directives surrounding his blackmail.

ME

It's not a setup

There's a swift knock on the door and it opens. I'm caught, holding my phone, standing in a black strapless bra, matching lace thong, and black thigh highs, all courtesy of Rhode's personal shopper.

Judging from the way he looks at me, the phone in my hand is not top of mind.

"I was going to ask if you wanted my help picking the dress, but I'm tempted to bail on tonight and keep you to myself."

He's absolutely delicious in his tux.

"I was leaning toward the black lace dress. It matches."

He runs the pad of his finger along the slope of my breasts, skimming the lace, and visibly swallows.

"Hot damn," he says. "God you are beautiful." Then his gaze falls to my phone. "Pick a dress. Then I have something to give to you."

He takes a seat in an armchair. I toss the phone unceremoniously on the bed and remove the black dress from the hanger. There's a red dress, which feels like too much, and more than that, too eye-catching. An emerald-green dress with a full-length gown that while beautiful, is really not my color; an off-white dress that feels a little too bridal for my taste; and a navy dress that is truly stunning, but black has been my go-to color for years and tonight I don't want to be second-guessing my outfit choice.

The fitted black lace dress might be challenging to walk in if it weren't for the high slit. The backless design dips to my lower back, and my fingers have just gripped the zipper when Rhodes' warm touch swats my fingers away.

"I've got it," he says. "You are temptation personi-fied." Warm breath cascades along my shoulder as his lips ghost my skin, lighting goose bumps along my arms. "But there's something missing."

I turn, questioning, and he holds up a velvet box.

"For me?"

"For tonight," he says, and flips open the royal blue velvet lid to reveal a stunning diamond bracelet. The stones catch the light, scattering prismatic reflections across the walls of the circular room.

I'm momentarily speechless. It's not just the obvious value—it's the vintage craftsmanship, the kind of piece that has history embedded in every facet.

"There's a tracking device embedded in this diamond here," he says, tapping one of the larger stones. "And an emergency signal can be activated by touching the clasp three times in rapid succession. It sends an alert directly to my security team."

"You've modified jewelry for covert operations before?"

His eyes meet mine, something unreadable in their depths. "First time. But not my first surveillance device."

"You carry this around with you?" I ask, trying to understand why Rhodes would travel with what must be an extraordinarily valuable heirloom.

"No," he says as he loops the stunning piece around my wrist. His fingers linger on my pulse point, and I wonder if he can feel my uncontrolled heartbeat. "It was my mother's. A gift from my father. My grandmother gave it to me when I visited her just before meeting you in the Highlands."

The timing strikes me—he had this before he knew me, before he had any reason to trust or distrust me. Yet now it's on my wrist, equipped with technology to keep me safe. The contradiction is dizzying: a tool of surveillance that's also an unexpected gesture of trust.

"She said it was time I had it," he continues, voice softening. "For when I find someone special." His smile turns wistful. "She says I've been alone too long."

The weight of the bracelet feels suddenly significant in ways that have nothing to do with diamonds or tracking devices.

"When you agreed to the plan for this evening, I had a resource pick it up and outfit it. When you were getting your hair done, they returned it. By the way, I love your hair up." I slowly turn. "I also love it down."

The energy radiating between us intensifies.

He lightly caresses my cheek. "I don't want you getting hurt."

"You do listen to your security detail," I say, attempting lightness despite the gravity I feel.

"So it seems." His eyes hold mine, and for a moment, I see something vulnerable there—a man worried about a woman walking into danger.

The bracelet catches the light as I move my wrist, sending diamond reflections dancing across his face. It's the most beautiful piece of jewelry I've ever seen. It's on loan but knowing it was his mother's touches me in an unexpected way. While it's temporary, it feels deeply personal.

Of course, that might be his intent—to create intimacy, to establish trust. The professional in me notes these possibilities dispassionately. But as his hand gently cups my cheek, I find myself hoping it's genuine. No, not hoping–believing. And that's more terrifying than any threat.

"Ready?" he asks softly.

I nod, though neither of us moves. We stand suspended in this moment, both knowing that when we step out that door, everything changes. Tonight we walk into the lion's den together—Rhodes facing those who would blackmail him, me potentially crossing a line from which there's no return.

The diamonds at my wrist wink in the light—beautiful, valuable, and now, weaponized. Much like the truth between us.

CHAPTER
THIRTY-FIVE

RHODES

The woman before me stuns in black lace that hugs every curve, diamonds glittering at her wrist like captured stars. Beautiful, daring, and trained in deception.

I so much want to trust her. More than that, I want her to be the fun, carefree woman I met on vacation—the one who challenged me on the mountain, who looked at me as just a man. I want to spend time with that woman again, and I want to do it far past the conclusion of this weekend. But, as the Rolling Stones noted, we don't always get what we want.

In less than thirty minutes, we'll be walking into the Russian embassy—a surveillance fortress. Where my refusal to buy a highly desired database will make me an inconvenience to people who don't tolerate inconveniences. Where Sydney will attempt to plant surveillance software that could be interpreted as espionage if discovered.

The stakes have never been higher, and trust has never mattered more.

Yet, who can I trust? My partner Miles showing up at the Russian embassy, when he's not even supposed to be in D.C., feels like a betrayal, regardless of his motives. We've been friends since Stanford, survived the lean years of ramen and shared apartments, built ARGUS from nothing but lines of code and caffeine-fueled ambition. Although, we also fight like brothers and aren't prone to caving during disagreements. Still, why would he show up there?

My best guess is he's looking for leverage to force me to agree to a public offering—he's been pushing for it relentlessly since our last valuation—although I can't be entirely sure that's his end game. The Miles I knew five years ago wouldn't go behind my back like this to make a point. But power and money change people, reshape priorities, erode principles.

The thought makes my stomach turn, but I can't dismiss it. He's my friend, but he's convinced I'm wrong about keeping ARGUS as a private entity, convinced that my "ethical concerns" are holding back the company's true potential. If I confront him, he'll tell me he's saving me from my worst impulses, just as he did when I refused the China contract last year.

What he doesn't understand is that some lines, once crossed, can never be uncrossed. Some technologies, once unleashed, can never be contained.

And what about Sydney?

Here she is, wearing my mother's diamonds. Agreeing to play a role that will help me uncover exactly what's going on. But how to know if I can trust her?

"It's not a setup." Yes, I read the message.

There are those who claim they succeeded in business by developing the ability to read upside down papers across conference room tables. The ability to read phone screens at all angles is my generation's form of upside-down pages.

And ARGUS takes it several steps further. Our neural networks can reconstruct partial text from reflection patterns in glass, predict message content from subtle finger movements on virtual keyboards, even analyze micro expressions to determine if someone is communicating truthfully.

I've created systems that can extract secrets from the smallest digital traces—and yet here I am, reduced to reading over someone's shoulder like a curious teenager. The most sophisticated surveillance technology in the world, and human trust still comes down to these primitive observations. The irony would be amusing if the stakes weren't so high.

Her phone lights up with an incoming message.

Are we working together? Or will she walk away to discuss with her team?

"Can we take a few minutes? Before we leave?"

"Certainly." The muscles in my chest loosen with the word, although I'm not certain what she's planning to do. It's her eyes, the softness in her words. I hope I'm reading her correctly.

She dials a number and sets the phone to speaker, holding the device in her hand in such a way that the light reflects off the diamonds circling her wrist.

"Hello," a man's voice says.

"This is Sydney." Her voice shifts subtly—more

formal, clipped at the edges. Professional Sydney reporting in. "I got the message."

"Where are you?" The man's voice is authoritative, with the measured cadence of someone accustomed to command.

"I'm in the hotel. With Rhodes." Her eyes flick to mine, a silent question in them. "And you're on speaker, Hudson."

A beat of silence—milliseconds long but heavy with the unspoken risk assessment happening across the connection.

"Copy that," Hudson says, though I detect the slightest modulation in his tone. "It's good to update you both."

I position myself closer to Sydney, my shoulder nearly touching hers—a subtle claim to partnership that won't be visible over the phone but sends a message to her. We're in this together, or not at all.

"Quinn identified communications between congressional staffers and known Russian operatives. When I looked at the list of names, I recognized one of them—Benjamin Dristol."

The name means nothing to me, but Sydney pales.

"Chief of staff for Senator Crawford," she explains. "Any communications from Crawford?"

"Not that we've seen but…"

"He could use Dristol for all communications."

"As a member of the Senate Foreign Intelligence Committee, that would be a wise move."

"You know, when we ran into him the other day, Dristol was there, seated at a table. I bet they were having cocktails together. I didn't think anything of it."

"To be fair," I hear myself saying, "He likely has after work sessions with his staff regularly."

"Maybe." There's a faraway look in Syd's eyes, and I can't help but wonder how much of this is because of Crawford, and if she is in fact not over him. The idea doesn't sit well. "Is Quinn on the line?"

"Right here," a feminine voice answers.

I take that to mean Quinn is a woman.

"Did you find any connection with the FBI agent?" I catch Syd's eye in such a way she knows I want more information.

"I confirmed the FBI does not have a current investigation into ARGUS. I also confirmed your FBI contact's real name is Jason Reid. He's not FBI, nor was he ever FBI. He did however work for the CIA from 2007 to 2015."

"Interesting. Before my time. Anything on why he left?" Sydney asks.

"No, but I didn't access his employee file."

"How'd you confirm–"

"Jake's visual recognition and first name assisted and believe it or not, one of my contacts at a foreign intelligence agency had the information."

"Which one?" I ask, curious.

"Classified," Quinn answers, and Syd gives a little shrug.

Fair, I suppose. I mean, this is a private black ops group and nothing is technically classified but protecting her sources is completely understandable.

"By the way, another person on our team, Noah, has been trailing Reid. He observed him meeting with an employee at a private security firm. Westinghouse. Did a search and Crawford has hired them in the past. Didn't make an effort to keep it secret. It's in public records. But rumors are Westinghouse has taken odd jobs from the Russians, too. It's all speculation, but we know for certain Jason Reid pretended to be Ian Gregory with the FBI, he's familiar with Senator Crawford and Crawford's chief of staff, Dristol, and he had a meeting with Westinghouse, a private security firm with rumored connections to Russia."

"So tonight we should watch Crawford in addition to the Russians," Sydney says. "I can't imagine this Jason Reid or Dristol would be at the events, but if they are, we should keep an eye on them too."

"If you're able to access intel from the Russians, it could be highly valuable. We have circumstantial information at best and no comprehension," Hudson says, referring to my plan to install a surveillance virus onto a computer tonight. That's what Sydney's text to her team must've been about.

I have Sydney attempting the install but hearing all of this has me questioning my plan. Perhaps I should be the one attempting to break into a Russian office. They want something from me so it will be easier to sweep under the rug if caught. Only trouble is, I doubt I'll be left alone.

"Understood," Syd says.

"Jake and Noah are in position to provide support outside of the Russian embassy. I'm working on getting a waiter into the event, but Russian security is tight. I don't think it's going to happen. If you need backup, you'll need to get off Russian embassy property. Copy?" Hudson asks.

"I'll bring my security with me," I say.

"That's good. But they won't be allowed into the party with you. Standard protocol."

Hudson's statement makes sense. I haven't given it much thought, but it's true security personnel don't usually mingle at events I attend.

"Are you on the way in a hot minute?" Quinn asks.

Sydney's posture changes subtly—a barely perceptible straightening of her spine. "Yes. I need to go to the ladies, but we'll be out the door in a hot minute." Her voice remains casual, but the repeated phrase isn't subtle.

"Safe travels," Hudson says before the call disconnects, leaving an electric silence in its wake.

I watch her hips sway as she seductively saunters to the restroom, the black lace dress highlighting every curve. But my appreciation is tempered by suspicion. "Hot minute" repeated twice—not a coincidence—an obvious signal to get her alone before our departure for the embassy, and she acknowledged it without hesitation.

The coded phrase should bother me more than it does. But I find myself analyzing not what she said, but how she said it. The slight tension in her shoulders when she had to use operational language. The way her eyes kept finding mine during the call, as if anchoring herself to something real. Miles and I have worked together for years and he chose secrecy and most likely deception. Sydney had minutes to exclude me from this call and chose transparency. She could have taken this conversation in the bathroom, but she put it on speaker. She could have hidden her team's positioning, but she let me hear their operational support. The bracelet she's wearing—my mother's diamonds, signifies my own leap of faith. If I can't trust the woman wearing my mother's diamonds and walking into a Russian embassy for me, then I can't trust anyone. And a man who trusts no one is already defeated.

I coded the tracking device myself, but the real surveillance tech is simpler: I'm watching someone choose to trust me while asking me to trust her in return. Some algorithms can predict human behavior with 94 percent accuracy. But trust isn't about probability—it's about choosing to believe in the 6 percent chance that someone might surprise you.

Tonight, we're entering a digital panopticon where every surveillance trick will be leveraged and likely used against us. If Sydney and I can't establish genuine trust now, we won't succeed.

Trust goes both ways. I stare at the closed bathroom door and make my decision. When she emerges, we'll face tonight together—whatever that means for both of us.

CHAPTER
THIRTY-SIX

SYDNEY

The strain of violins greets us past the gold-roped embassy entrance, strings vibrating with what sounds like Tchaikovsky—a calculated cultural choice. Two security officers disguised as attendants stand in the east corner. Cameras are positioned discreetly in brass light fixtures. The diplomatic security team strikes me as more muscular than diplomatic.

Rhodes expected a private reception but based on the uniformed staff at the entrance and the gold posts with engraved signs in Russian and English, this is a larger event. More people mean more eyes, but also more cover. The crowd may make it easier for me to step away unnoticed.

I maintain a relaxed smile while studying the marble-veined floors, mapping potential exit routes as Rhodes speaks to the young man reviewing the guest list. The man's posture suggests FSB training rather than simple hospitality staff—the Russians don't take chances.

When Quinn signaled I needed to call in privately, I didn't expect to learn Rhodes had slipped out and visited the Russian embassy earlier this afternoon while I was getting my hair done. The revelation sent a cold ripple down my spine.

Why wouldn't he mention his visit? If not to me, why not mention it to the team when we were discussing plans for this evening? Why hide it?

Trust in this business is measured in disclosed information—what someone withholds often reveals more than what they share. Part of me wants to believe there's an innocent explanation, that Rhodes is simply being thorough, protecting me. The other part—the part trained at Langley to see patterns of deception—whispers that I'm being played.

Yet here I am, wearing his mother's diamonds, walking into a Russian embassy on his arm. The professional in me catalogs this as a potentially compromised operation. The woman in me still feels the ghost of his touch. Both sides know ambivalence is not an option.

Rhodes offers his hand with a formality befitting eighteenth century royalty. He's missing the white gloves, but he's a chameleon. Gone is the laid-back man I met on a hike. There's no sign of the intense entrepreneur. No, he's graceful and attentive. An erudite gentleman.

"Ms. Victoria Romanovich," Rhodes says, addressing an elegant brunette in a floor-length sequin gown that catches the light like liquid mercury. His voice carries a warmth that doesn't reach his eyes. "May I have the pleasure of introducing Sydney Parker."

The woman turns, and I instantly recognize the calculating assessment behind her smile. Her gaze flicks over me with practiced casualness, but I catch the momentary pause on my face, my hands, the bracelet. She's comparing me to intel photos, confirming my identity.

"So pleased that both of you could join us this evening." Her smile is cordial and professional, with the polished artifice that only comes from diplomatic training. Her English is flawless but deliberately accented—a tactical choice many intelligence operatives make to seem less threatening.

"Ms. Romanovich works in the Russian embassy as a diplomat," Rhodes explains, his hand at the small of my back, the pressure slightly firmer than necessary. A warning? Reassurance? "I am fortunate to call her friend."

"And what do you do, Ms. Parker?" Her gaze drops deliberately to our joined hands, lingering on the diamond bracelet. "Or excuse me. My mistake." The apology is delivered with the swift precision of a surgeon's scalpel. "You are here as Mr. MacMillan's guest and not as a colleague."

"That's quite right," Rhodes says. "Sydney is my date."

"Lovely. Do you live in the area?"

With that one question, I am certain the Russians have already pulled a background report on me and know that I do, in fact, live in the area.

"I do. Rhodes and I recently met, and he asked me to join him." My smile mirrors Ms. Romanovich's.

Another couple enters and approaches the young man with the invitation list.

"I hope you enjoy yourselves. If you follow the golden

rope out to the courtyard, you'll find drinks and light hors d'oeuvres. I'll be greeting guests, but I hope to see you later."

"Thank you, Victoria."

As we stroll along the carpet lining the stone corridor, Rhodes leans into me, his warm breath caressing my ear. "She's the one who communicated the threat. I debated telling her you're my girlfriend, but even if I had, she'd still see you as CIA. There's little chance she's unaware of your background."

And what part of that does my body react to with warmth and girly emotion? The girlfriend word. Ridiculous. This isn't the time or place.

With our fingers linked, we follow the long corridor, passing two rooms with closed doors on our right, then round the corner to an open archway into an opulent room with three violinists, tables draped in burgundy, and elegantly dressed couples milling about with champagne flutes. The ceiling height is twenty feet, easily, and glass doors open into a courtyard. On the far end, two doors lead out.

I scan the crowd, searching for recognizable faces, stopping when I spot Dristol, Crawford's chief of staff, speaking with a woman I recognize as embassy personnel. She's an assistant to an assistant, if I recall correctly from our intel. Her outfit supports my conclusion, as in lieu of a gown, she's wearing a dark purple business skirt suit.

A man offers us champagne and we accept, but as if by mutual decision, we hold it without partaking.

"Do you know anyone here?"

"Believe it or not, I don't spend my days mingling in

embassies." In a lower voice he adds, "Or memorizing the names and faces of those who do."

Analysts are paid to not only know the players, but those who circle the players, including but not limited to gardeners and nannies. He's not an analyst, he runs a company. Now, the company he runs is an intel gold-mine, some might even call ARGUS a potent weapon, but owning ARGUS only means he has access to data, not that it's populated in his head.

Two couples, both in their fifties or sixties, slowly dance in the decadent setting.

"Would you care to dance?" he asks.

"Certainly." The action will quiet the worry and give us something to do other than hold a glass of liquid we're not drinking.

He sets our glasses down on the tray of a passing waiter, and takes my hand, leading me within a few feet of the violinists. All the violinists are older men, and it's impossible to discern from appearance if they are Russian or American.

We sway to the music, my hand resting on his shoulder, his palm warm against my lower back. In this moment, we appear as any other couple—intimate, connected—but the history of deception makes this simple touch complex.

With the violinists providing acoustic cover from potential listening devices, I lean close, my lips nearly touching his ear. "You came here earlier." The accusation is soft but unmistakable.

Still in his arms, I lean back slightly to study his reaction—the slight dilation of his pupils, the infinitesimal tightening around his eyes.

His dark brown eyes reflect not guilt but amusement, as does the quirk of his lip. He pulls me closer, our bodies moving as one with the music.

"I wanted to ensure your safety. Pre-scan the location. Back-up points." The explanation is logical, reasonable—exactly what I might have done myself. He leans in and brushes his lips across mine, the contact brief but electric. In my ear, he adds, "Don't doubt me, Syd."

The nickname vibrates through me—intimate, personal. I feel caught between my instincts that warn against emotional attachment and the undeniable pull I feel toward him. In this world of shadows and half-truths, his touch feels like the only solid thing I can hold onto. And that alone is terrifying.

"Excuse me, sir." A gentleman in a black traditional tuxedo says. "I was wondering if I might have the next dance."

Both Rhodes and I take in the stranger. If I were to guess, the tall man with gray wisps and wire-rimmed spectacles is German, but he could easily be Russian. There's a notable accent, but it's difficult to decipher origination.

"If you're amenable, Ms. Romanovich would like to meet with you in the library," the man says to Rhodes.

"Are you—"

"I'm fine," I assure Rhodes, cutting him off.

As he departs, presumably knowing the direction of the library, I face the interloper.

"There aren't many dancing," I murmur with a wistful glance at the bar.

"I concur." He smiles. "Might I interest you in a drink?"

"I'm Sydney," I say, this time offering my hand for a professional exchange.

"Archibald," he says, taking my hand in his with a light grip. It's the handshake of the timid.

A waiter with a tray of smoked salmon passes, and Archibald speaks in Russian to the young woman, telling her to refill her tray once it's mostly empty. He doesn't hide his concern for her performance as his gaze trails the woman who apparently reports to him.

"Go on," I urge him. "I'm going to go to the restroom."

"Do you know where it is? Just head straight out and it's the first door on your left."

"Thank you," I say and smile as he heads off to follow the staff member.

In the hall, I pass the restrooms and see a small placard with the word LIBRARY in both Russian and English and an arrow. This building is a working building, so the directions are not surprising.

I pass the double doors that apparently lead into the room. There are no sounds emitting through the thick wooden doors. I press a button on my earpiece, turning it on, enabling me to hear the device transmitting from Rhodes, a small device tucked away in his trouser pocket that we tested back in the hotel suite.

I continue down the corridor as Rhodes' voice enters my earpiece.

"Is this your final decision?" Romanovich's voice comes through with crystal clarity. "Or is this your method of negotiation? This has much benefit to you. As I am sure you are aware, it would be unfortunate if certain secrets became public before the Senate Intelligence Committee's upcoming review of surveillance technologies."

Rustling sounds distort the audio momentarily. Is he deliberately creating interference by fidgeting with the device in his pocket?

"Do you wish for something more substantial than the preservation of your company?" Her tone is now honeyed, seductive even. "We can provide compromising information on those within your government who are...problematic to your interests."

"I own ARGUS." Rhodes sounds confident, unfazed. "Do you believe I can't get information on my own?"

"Not this you cannot." A chair creaks, suggesting she's leaned closer. "Not everything comes from satellites or the internet. We have human sources—deep and long-established. All we ask is that we have a private arrangement. We shall pay you your fee, like any other client. But we understand you need an extra incentive for the additional risk an arrangement with our country poses."

"Am I to take your word that your information is valuable?" Rhodes asks, his tone suggesting polite skepticism rather than outright rejection.

"No." Papers rustle. "We have evidence. The information in this folder shows exactly who within the Senate Intelligence Committee has betrayed your country. Information I believe will be useful to you as you negotiate contracts."

Static crosses the line, and the connection ends.

Voices down the corridor carry, and I rush into an empty room. It's not an office, but rather a waiting room. To the side is a small desk with an old desktop computer.

Based on the wires, it appears to be connected to the internet.

I follow Rhodes' instructions, retrieving the compact-shaped drive from my evening bag. The USB connection slides out with a practiced twist—the design elegant enough to pass as luxury makeup but functional enough to breach security.

The computer is an older model running what appears to be a modified version of Windows—not connected to their primary security network, which makes it both a safer target and potentially less valuable. I insert the drive, power on the system, and wait the excruciating fifteen seconds for it to boot.

The machine awakens to a browser rather than requiring credentials—a careless oversight that works in our favor. The drive automatically executes its payload, a silent infiltration program that I watch deploy through a small progress bar disguised as an advertisement. The process should take twenty seconds maximum to establish the persistent backdoor.

Eighteen... Nineteen...

The door handle turns with a metallic click.

I kill the browser window, drop to the floor, and slide under the desk in one fluid motion—a maneuver I haven't had to execute since training exercises at The Farm, and never in a gown. My heart pounds against my ribs as I curl into the shadows.

Heavy footfalls enter the room—masculine, deliberate. A chair scrapes nearby. Papers shuffle. Then a phone rings elsewhere, and the footsteps retreat. The door closes with a soft thud.

I count to twenty, not ten—a lesson learned from an

operation in Moscow where ten wasn't enough. I check the drive; the installation completed despite the interruption. I remove it, restore the computer to its original state, and slip out into the hallway, my pulse gradually returning to normal.

As I round the bend, Dristol spots me. He's with Romanovich, and based on how close the two are standing, they are in the midst of a private conversation.

"There you are," Rhodes says, capturing me with his arm, pulling me against him. "Have I told you how stunning you look tonight?"

"Yes." I smile, casting a glance Dristol's way.

Rhodes brushes his lips against my temple, then leads me down the corridor, back to the event.

"Dristol and Romanovich are tight. Did you notice?"

"Yes. It doesn't mean their bosses are in on it."

His statement is only plausible for Dristol—in Russian intelligence, someone at Romanovich's level would never operate without authorization from above.

"They could be rogue elements," he says, his hand tightening almost imperceptibly on mine.

In thinking about what I overheard Romanovich offer Rhodes, is it possible someone on the Senate Intelligence Committee sold a list of assets to Russia? Could the leak go that high up? I assume he declined the deal, but I'd love to know what the Russians have on our politicians.

We reach the entrance to the event room, pausing in a quiet alcove momentarily shielded from cameras and observers.

"Were you successful?" he asks, his voice barely above a whisper.

I squeeze his hand in silent confirmation, allowing a

genuine smile to surface. The adrenaline of a successful covert operation courses through me—a familiar high I'd almost forgotten since being relegated to the role of analyst.

The reception has grown more crowded, faces blurring into a kaleidoscope of power players and puppets. We'll be departing soon for the Bastille gala, but the real event has already happened here, behind closed doors and in whispered conversations.

"Did it go well for you?" I tilt my head, remembering how the transmitted conversation cut off at a crucial moment. "With Romanovich?"

"It was something," is all he gives me, his expression carefully neutral. But the tension in his jaw tells me whatever she shared after the connection ended may have changed the game.

As we move back into the crowd, I'm acutely aware of the diamonds at my wrist, transmitting our location to his security team. The irony isn't lost on me—we're both playing roles, both wearing devices that track and record, both on a hunt to reveal truths.

In this hall of mirrors where many watch all, Rhodes MacMillan is the one I'm holding onto.

THIRTY-SEVEN

RHODES

Few homes in D.C. are as spectacular as the French ambassador's residence. I'd understood it was quite the honor to be invited to the ambassador's reception for the Bastille Day Gala, but it didn't mean much to me until amazement lights Sydney's eyes.

The strains of classical music fill the air as we're guided through the home's foyer, passing classical paintings, elegant tapestries, and stunning flower arrangements. I've attended dozens of these events—diplomatic receptions, embassy galas, fundraisers where powerful people gather to see and be seen. The opulence has always felt hollow, necessary but meaningless. But watching Sydney take in each detail with genuine wonder transforms the experience entirely. Every carved molding, every piece of art becomes something worth noticing because she notices it.

It would all mean nothing to me except for Sydney's

wide-eyed wonder. Yes, I am invited to places such as this, and I can give her this life.

The thought arrives with startling clarity, catching me off guard. Where did that come from? I've spent years perfecting the art of keeping women at arm's length, even while suggesting otherwise. Especially while suggesting otherwise. A well-placed comment about "someday" or "when we" has always been my go-to move—just vague enough to be non-committal, just specific enough to keep them interested. It's a practiced technique that's served me well, keeping relationships light and temporary while making women feel like they're part of some greater possibility.

But this thought wasn't calculated. It wasn't a line or a strategy. The image that flashed through my mind was visceral and immediate: Sydney at my side at events like this, not as my guest but as my partner. Someone who would appreciate the beauty without being impressed by the power. Someone who would ground me when the political theater became too much.

Could I be more pompous?

The self-awareness hits like a cold splash of water. Here I am, mentally redesigning this woman's entire life around my wealth and access, as if she's some project to be managed or prize to be won. As if she couldn't achieve any of this on her own, as if her amazement at the ambassador's residence means she's been waiting her whole life for someone like me to elevate her circumstances.

But even as I mock myself, I can't shake the feeling. The rightness of her being here. The way she fits.

Sydney squeezes my forearm. "Look at that staircase."

The elaborately carved staircase is beautiful. "I believe that leads to the private chambers," I say, knowing this only because I glimpsed a small sign and the passage is blocked with a velvet rope.

"I've never seen such a beautiful railing," she says, more to herself than to me.

Here it comes. The autopilot response, honed through years of practice. The casual reference to a shared future that sounds romantic but commits to nothing. I can feel the words forming—smooth, charming, and ultimately hollow.

"Remember it. When we build a home we can have one commissioned."

But as the words leave my mouth, something shifts. This isn't just another line. The image in my mind isn't vague or theoretical—it's specific. Sydney running her hand along a custom-carved railing in a home we designed together. Morning coffee in a kitchen we chose together. The kind of domestic intimacy I've avoided since splitting with my ex. Surprise flashes across her features. "If you like."

The addendum tumbles out, an attempt to backpedal, to restore the casual nature of the comment. But it's too late. I can hear the difference in my own voice, the way the suggestion carried weight instead of practiced lightness.

Her eyes narrow, studying me with an intensity that makes me wonder what she sees. Then she seemingly dismisses whatever conclusion she's reached as we step outside onto the terrace and she takes in the guests.

But I can't dismiss it as easily. Because for the first time in years, when I mentioned building a future with someone, part of me—a part I'm not quite ready to acknowledge—actually meant it.

Senator Crawford sees us and holds up a champagne flute in acknowledgement. A woman, presumably his wife, shifts to see who he is addressing. She's in a royal blue floor-length gown. A sapphire necklace leads enticingly to her decolletage boosted by her strapless dress. As we approach, I notice the dress and jewelry set off matching blue eyes, but there's a coldness there. She has the expression of a taskmaster or a haughty professor.

Crawford stands by her side but the tension between the two of them is hard to miss. Crawford extends his hand.

"Rhodes. It's a beautiful night, is it not?"

He's right, it is. As we stand on the terrace surveying the crowd, the festive aura is impossible to disregard. Golden light spheres and candles glimmer throughout the terrain, including bobbing in the pool for a magical effect.

"It is." My fingers fall over Sydney's where they rest on my forearm. "May I introduce my date? Sydney Parker, this is Senator Crawford. And I'm sorry–" I stop myself, as I realize this might not be his wife, but he picks up where I awkwardly stopped.

"Nice to meet you Sydney. And, this is my wife, Glenda."

Sydney and Glenda exchange cordial smiles. It could be my imagination, but I sense Sydney shifting closer to my side.

"Is this your first time attending?" Glenda asks.

"It is," I admit. "They didn't have it last year, right?"

"Yes, that's correct. They don't throw it every year,

but when they do…” Her gaze takes in the event which could easily command a million dollar price tag. “I believe this one is my all-time favorite.” Her attention falls to Sydney. “You’re quite fortunate this is your first.”

“I’m thrilled to be here,” Syd answers without missing a beat, coming across like she’s never been anywhere near anything so extravagant. And, maybe she hasn’t, but she’s well-traveled and lived abroad. I expect she’s truly impressed, but I also suspect this isn’t her first high-powered affair.

“You look familiar to me,” Glenda says. “Are you sure we haven’t met her?” She directs the question to her side, in the general direction of her husband.

Crawford sips his champagne, contemplative. When he lowers it, he’s decisive. “Were you by chance at the US Embassy in Paris?”

“Yes,” Sydney answers as I accept two champagne flutes from a passing staff member.

“I knew it,” Glenda says. “I never forget a face.”

“Ah, yes. Now I remember your boyfriend…” He pauses, gaze cutting to me. “…at the time. A chef, right?”

“Yes. He’s still in Paris.”

There’s an awkward beat as we all four stand with glasses.

“Ah, there’s Devon,” he says, looking through the crowd. “He looks a little lost. Will you excuse us?”

“Of course,” I say, and we watch as Crawford and his wife approach Dristol. He seems to have arrived on his own, without a date.

“I need to ask you something,” she says, voice low, politely smiling as we traverse the steps away from the terrace to an opening on the pavers by the lawn. "The deal. Shouldn't you take it?"

I pause, realizing what she overheard. "I wouldn't honor it. Therefore, it's probably best not to take it. I'd prefer to not make enemies of those with a proclivity for tossing enemies out windows."

"Yes but is there a way…" She scans the crowd, smiling, and it's at this moment I realize she's purposefully expressing awe at our magical setting, "Think about what you'd learn."

"I can't imagine they'd offer me direct evidence of what you're seeking."

"No, but we'd get valuable leads."

I bend to whisper in her ear, using the movement as an excuse to place my arm on her lower back and draw her near, when a dark shadow steps forward, blocking our view of the event. I follow the tuxedo lines up to a face I recognize, the recognition stirring mixed emotions.

"Miles. I didn't realize you'd be in attendance."

"Didn't I tell you?" He angles his body to align with Syd. "And is this beauty the one who stole your heart on the holiday I forced you to take?"

"The one and only," I say, squeezing her hip lightly. "Sydney Parker, this is my partner, Miles Johnson." He takes her hand in his, and I'm taken in by the contrast between her light and his dark skin.

Within moments he has her laughing. Miles is charming, always has been. That's why he's the business lead and the people person.

As if sensing I have topics I want to address with my partner, Sydney makes an excuse that she needs to visit the restroom before we're seated for dinner. As we both watch her leave, I shift the conversation to business.

"Daisy's going to be taking a leave," I say.

His lower lip juts, thoughtfully, and he swirls his remaining champagne and tosses what's left back in one swallow. "She's your department, not mine." He sets his glass on a passing tray. "Everything okay?"

I could tell him I'm not sure, give him the details, but if Daisy wants to do that, she can. The three of us have spent plenty of time together over the years. "Why were you at the Russian embassy?"

A slow smile spreads and he looks past my shoulders, causing me to do the same, but I don't recognize anyone in the crowd.

"Going right for it, huh?"

"Did you put them up to making the offer? You don't actually want an investigation, but you want to force my hand. You want to trap me, don't you?"

"Rhodes." He says my name under his breath, and it's a mix of a huff and muted anger. "You're holding us back."

"From a public offering?" I ask, seeking clarification I don't need.

"From growth. Look, I get the ethical concerns."

"Do you?"

He glares. "Yes, I do. But if you hold us back, someone else is going to do exactly what we want to do. The only way to guide the growth is to own it."

"We do own it."

"But you're holding it back."

A few heads turn and Miles smiles, nodding, recognizing he spoke loudly enough to garner attention.

"We can talk tomorrow."

"We'll need to," I say. "Don't think I'll easily forget that you went behind my back in an effort to trap me. And if I know you, your end game is to kick me out of the company? Force me to step down."

"It's not what I want, man," he says, tapping my elbow, as if a simple touch will sweep his backstabbing effort under the carpet.

"When you say it's not what you want, is it what Alex wants? All those investor meetings he's been pushing, the constant IPO pressure—has he been building a coalition against me? Are they looking for ways to force me out? Because you know me better than that, Miles. I won't be forced out."

"Let's talk tomorrow. I'll swing by your hotel. This isn't the place to have this discussion." He steps away, effectively ending the conversation.

As Miles departs, Senator Crawford approaches. His wife is nowhere in sight.

"Wanted to ask you," he says, one hand on his chest as if he's pressing down a tie, yet he's wearing a bowtie and cummerbund. "Any chance you have time to meet tomorrow, before you head home?"

"I do."

"Great. I'll shoot you a text in the morning." He smiles, and I'm about to ask him where Glenda is when he smiles at someone nearby, pats my back and steps forward to a man I recognize as one of his fellow senators.

I watch him, wondering what he could want to meet with me about. Is it possible he's going to push the Russian case? Or is he wondering if I took the bait?

Dristol and Romanovich were quite cozy. Is Dristol operating on behalf of his boss?

Miles orchestrating pressure from one side, Crawford requesting a meeting from another. There are too many converging forces for coincidence.

When Sydney returns from the restroom, I fill her in as dinner is announced.

"Interesting," she says. "What do you say we enjoy the evening and debate all the possibilities in the morning?"

It's a wise suggestion. "As you wish, beautiful."

She leans in and I brush my lips across her temple.

"This isn't the place to talk it through," she says, as if an explanation is needed. With a glossy smile, she adds, "And I feel like I'm at Cinderella's ball. Will you be my prince?"

"Yes. But fair warning. If you lose a shoe, I won't hunt for it. I'll just buy another pair."

"He wasn't actually looking for the glass slipper. He was looking for her."

I tap her bracelet.

"Lucky for me, these days life's improved for the princes."

CHAPTER
THIRTY-EIGHT

RHODES

"You ready?"

Sydney stands before me in black Lycra leggings and a loose exercise top that hangs off one shoulder exposing the thin black line of her sports bra. Her glossy hair swings in her high ponytail as she strides across the room to peer out the window.

It's the morning after the gala, and in a perfect world, she and I would be enjoying a leisurely morning with breakfast in bed. But the world is far from perfect, and we've been up since dawn preparing for my meeting with Crawford.

Everyone within KOAN believes the senator is going to reveal he's involved with Russia. I'm skeptical we'll get anything of value. Men like Crawford are experts at the game. If he plans to force my hand, to do an underhanded deal that benefits one of his benefactors, his encouragement will be shrouded and vague. Before he was a senator, he was a lawyer, and as such, he'll always be wary that anything he writes or says may show up in a court of law or be blasted on social media.

"I'm ready. Are you?"

She peers out the window, presumably scanning the street.

"We're in position. Is your earpiece working?"

I tap my ear in the affirmative, and she says, "Confirmed."

She's talking to the team, not me.

"It's go time. Head on out through the lobby and get in your car. Your security team is downstairs waiting," the male voice in my ear says.

My security hasn't reached out to me, but they aren't necessarily supposed to. It's five minutes prior to the time I requested a car.

"I'll be going out the back." Syd blows me a kiss, and I pause, standing in the circular entry, aware others are listening. "You nervous?" she asks, probably misreading my hesitation.

"After last night? No." A blush blooms along her cheeks and my cock twitches at the memory of taking her hard and fast, her palms planted on the hotel window, gown hitched to her waist.

"Alright then," the male voice says in my ear. "It's go time."

With one last glance at Syd, a breath of fresh air against the D.C. backdrop, I head down the hall. In the lobby, I inform Smith, the contracted weekend security detail, that he's not required. He appears happy enough to be dismissed on a Sunday, and I can't blame him. I could bring him with me, but having another person in the room with us won't set up a particularly conducive environment for Crawford.

KOAN will be parked outside in a turquoise van plastered with tourist stickers and environmental protest logos. The vehicle is a masterpiece of covert design: solar panels disguised as roof racks to power the equipment, while the sixties-era curtains hanging in the windows conceal directional microphones and signal boosters. The van will blend perfectly with the traffic arriving for the afternoon's environmental protest, and I have to say I'm impressed they managed to commandeer such a perfect surveillance vehicle in a few short hours on a weekend.

Sydney will listen in the vehicle with the team. The earpiece nestled deep in my ear canal is virtually undetectable—a custom design that operates on frequencies specifically chosen to bypass standard security sweeps. The silver disk in my pocket, disguised as a challenge coin, is a marvel of miniaturization: a full-spectrum transmitter with enough battery to broadcast our conversation for six hours and sensitive enough to capture whispers from across the room.

It's a fascinating piece of tech I'd like to study further, but first, I've got two meetings to get through. First the senator, which isn't a particularly big deal for me, although I'm hopeful we'll gain something valuable from my time, and then I move on to a confrontation with Miles. He and I are most likely in for one of our knock down drag out meetings of the minds. Then when all that's over, I'll talk to Sydney and see if I can't convince her to return to California with me, although I'm smart enough to know her willingness will depend on what we learn.

Senator Crawford lets me into the Hart Senate Office building himself, as it's Sunday.

"Nice party last night," he says in greeting, his tone casual, as if we're just two friends.

"It was. Your wife is lovely." The words flow easily, a professionally cordial response.

I'm not lying, although I wonder how Sydney is reacting in the nearby van, hearing me exchange pleasantries with her former lover. Last night at the gala, I watched her face carefully as Crawford introduced his wife—searching for any crack in her composure, any hint of the history between them. But Sydney was flawless—poised and sincere.

It shouldn't bother me, this ghost of a relationship from before we met. I have no claim to her past. Yet something primitive stirs when I look at Crawford—this man who knew her before, who shared something intimate with her while married to another woman.

Crawford bows his head at the elevator bank and rocks back on his heels. "Thank you for agreeing to meet here. Glenda likes to sleep in after a big night."

"Understandable."

The elevator dings, and the sound amplifies the awkward silence.

"It's quiet here on a Sunday, huh?"

"It is most weekends. That's not to say that people aren't working from home."

Right now, he's calm, making small talk, maybe trying to subtly emphasize that his office does important work.

Last night, after we observed Dristol and Romanovich, Quinn and Daisy aligned efforts and uncovered evidence that points to Dristol selling state secrets to Russia.

Of course, it's not Dristol who asked to meet with me. And it's doubtful he'd do anything without his boss's knowledge, which means Crawford is likely in on it. Possibly using his chief of staff for execution of the sales.

Crawford could've requested this meeting for related reasons, or this could simply be another pitch for expanding into his home state.

"You and Sydney," he says, then sniffs and rubs his nose.

Allergies? Perhaps discomfort.

"You seem happy."

The elevator doors slide open, relieving me of an immediate response.

She's listening, MacMillan. Take advantage.

"We are happy. When I met her, I wasn't in a great place, but she's unexpected. She's reminded me that there's a world outside Silicon Valley."

The swimming hole comes to mind: the memory an elixir. Today, she's dressed like that version of herself, although perhaps slightly more citified. I'd like to bring her back to the mountains, back to nature. I may need to buy that piece of land from my friend's family.

"She's a lovely woman," Crawford says, opening the door into a small conference room. "You're a lucky man."

It's curious he didn't bring me into his office. I scan the sparse room and note a black glass bulb. Does he want our meeting on video?

His choice.

"When I met her before, like you, I wasn't in a great place."

I get the sense he wants to say more, but I'm not about to probe into their shared past. That's not why I'm here.

We stand there, my hands in my trousers, fingering the silver disk to activate it since he's clearly not going to scan for a listening device. Crawford appears slightly dazed in his brown trousers, a multi-colored striped button down, and brown leather braided belt—his version of Sunday casual.

"Anyway," he says, blinking like he's snapping himself out of a dream, "Have a seat. You're probably wondering why I asked to meet with you on a Sunday."

"The question crossed my mind."

I sit, leaning back in the chair.

"I always make time for my valued donors. Especially ones with a product as impressive as ARGUS."

"Thank you," I say, wondering where the hell he's going with this.

"It's my understanding that you're doing some impressive work for the Pentagon. It's so impressive though…" He drums his fingers on the armrest, his expression pensive. "Some of my colleagues have concerns about national security. Some are saying what you have is a weapon. And, I wanted to spend some time, me and you, one on one, getting your perspective on that."

"You're saying that some within congress consider ARGUS to be a security risk?" I speak slowly, processing the unexpected direction of this conversation.

"From what I understand, your system combs through vast amounts of data, even images, from multiple sources and finds connections. Smarter people than me have framed it as the most advanced surveillance tool on the planet."

"If it's used that way, then yes."

"And you vet your employees, right? I know I saw a file on that…"

"Yes. Absolutely. Although, our employees have limited access to query the data. We support, yes, but we aren't the ones using the system. The client is."

He inhales. "Right. You know, what I'm going to say I imagine won't be news to you given you're with Sydney."

He leans closer and I scratch below my ear, hoping the guys out in the van are getting this.

"We've had leaks."

We… "You mean the CIA?"

"And other agencies. Could it be an employee within ARGUS?"

"Absolutely not," I insist, although a seed of doubt took root when Sydney shared her reasons. "We have safeguards in place."

"Would you be open to an official inquiry just to…"

"David, can I be straight with you?"

He leans back, crossing an ankle over his knee. "I expect nothing less."

"When I walked in here, I believed the leaks were coming from the Senate."

Am I going off plan? Yes. But I want to see how he reacts. Also, if he thinks he can back me into a corner with his threat of an inquiry, he's wrong.

He shifts in his seat, putting his feet flat on the floor and pulling out his phone.

"Do you have any evidence?"

I stare at him, watching him read his phone screen,

and wait. I hoped this meeting would provide evidence or at least confirm my theory.

His skin flushes as his thumb swipes the screen.

"I'm going to need to cut this short. Can we continue this talk next week?"

He's out of his seat.

"Is everything okay?"

"A personal matter. It's my wife. I've got to go."

"Just like that? I tell you I believe the Senate is the source of leaks, and you manufacture a crisis and leave?" Is he out of his mind?

He rubs his forehead and purses his lips. "It's not, it's a personal matter."

Steps sound along the corridor and the door opens. Dristol enters. "You got the message?" he asks Crawford in a voice so low he likely intends for me to not hear.

"Yes. I'm on my way now." Crawford glances back at me, the slimmest hint of apology in his expression.

"If you want, I can take this," Dristol says.

"How'd you get here so quick?" Crawford asks the question loud enough it's clear he's not looking to hide anything.

"I've been trying to reach you for the last thirty minutes. Couldn't get you so headed here."

Crawford shakes his head back and forth. "Damn the connection on this floor. Comes and goes."

His comment has me wondering if the team outside has heard anything, but it doesn't matter. He shared nothing of substance.

"Anyway, thanks." Crawford places a hand on Dristol's shoulder and steps to the door, stopping in the doorway. "I don't think there's much for you two to discuss. Rhodes, you want to walk out with me?"

"Oh, I'd like to talk to Rhodes, if you don't mind," Dristol says.

"That's right. You two met last night at the pre-party bash." Crawford's phone vibrates and he checks the screen. "I've gotta go. Rhodes, my assistant will coordinate a time for us to continue next week. Devon, don't keep him too long. It's the weekend."

With that, he's out the door.

"You may want to sit," Dristol says.

Crawford's sudden departure, Dristol's convenient arrival, it's too orchestrated to be a coincidence. They're keeping Crawford's hands clean while Dristol does the dirty work.

I do as he asks and sit. "What can I do for you Devon?"

He claims the seat Crawford vacated. Doesn't say a word.

Down the hall, I hear a heavy door close. Possibly a fire escape door.

A shadow crosses the threshold.

"Well hello Jason Reid," I say for the van's benefit. "If it isn't the fake FBI agent, alias Ian Gregory."

Reid scowls but Dristol grins.

"I told him you had a powerful resource at your fingertips," Dristol says.

I suppose it's good they've assumed I've used ARGUS to verify Reid's credentials. Better that than they suspect I'm working with anyone.

"Here's the deal," Dristol says. "I need you to acquire the Forbes database."

"Are you speaking for Crawford right now?"

"If you care at all for your reputation, you're going to do what they ask. It's in the best interest of the United States of America."

"Is that so?"

"It is. To be clear, I want to be your friend, not your enemy. I'd prefer for ARGUS to remain a private entity, but I hear the conversations in the halls. A growing number want to claim it's a national security risk. Take you over. If you work with us, those voices won't travel far."

Any government taking over ARGUS is an Orwellian nightmare. It's not going to happen.

"Who put you up to this?"

My gaze flicks to Reid, who has closed the office door and stands sentry, arms folded in front of his waist, watching the scene.

"Your partner has expressed consternation at your insufficient willingness to do what's best for the growth of your company."

Miles. The bastard really is working against me. Is this part of building a case to justify forcing me out? Part of his trap or what he ultimately wants and he fears I'll refuse?

I scan the two men closely, wondering if they're recording the meeting in a bid to aid Miles.

The two men share similar menacing countenances.

"Are you here to threaten me?"

"No," Dristol's quick to say.

"Excellent," I say, standing up.

"So you'd rather news hit the wire?" He asks the question slowly, his attention on his trimmed nails.

He's definitely in bed with the Russians. It's the same threat they held over me. These guys are all working together.

But is he working with his boss or independently? We'll need to access the communications to Crawford's phone. It's conceivable they were listening in and stepped in when they realized Crawford was about to work with me to identify the leak. Perhaps they didn't attempt to reach him thirty minutes earlier.

At this moment, that specific truth doesn't matter. They're looking at me like they're holding all the cards, but preparation wins.

"In your role on the Hill, you're familiar with PR strategy, correct? Sometimes the best response is diversion." I open my backpack deliberately slowly, keeping a close eye on both Gregory and Dristol as I extract the iPad we prepared specifically for this meeting. Of course, I planned to share it with Crawford, but here we are.

The device contains isolated evidence Quinn and Daisy compiled—nothing that can be traced back to the source if this goes sideways.

I press play and watch Dristol's skin blanch.

The evidence is damning—Dristol's face is clearly visible in meetings with Romanovich in locations ranging from coffee shops to park benches. Timestamps. Locations. Phone records. The financial transactions and offshore accounts are the most damning pieces of evidence.

"Photographs of meets. Financial transactions. All easily assembled once you know what you're looking for and with access to the right databases." I deliberately leave unsaid the implication: once you know what you're looking for, you might find much more.

Dristol's throat works as he swallows. He rubs his neck, sniffs—stress responses.

"We live in a world of deep fakes."

His defense is weak, perfunctory. I watch his eyes—not focused on the evidence, but darting to the corners of the room. Is he looking for cameras? Exits?

"Deep fakes are increasingly common," I concur. "But these are real. And we have live witnesses. You know, thanks to last night."

He leans back in his seat. He doesn't bother to hit replay.

"There's got to be a way." He breathes in deeply and taps his index finger against the table. "It's best for you if we work together smoothly. This theoretical evidence—it can easily be misunderstood. And for you, think about what's at stake. If the winds pick up on a deal that violates US policy, you could see every government contract disappear. Billions of dollars."

What Dristol doesn't understand—what people like him never understand—is that my refusal isn't negotiating posture. It's the fundamental principle ARGUS was built on. *Do good.* The moment I agree to work with someone like this, I'm no better than the surveillance state opportunists I set out to counter. More practically, once I negotiate with one, it's only a matter of time before my willingness to deal is exploited by others. That's why I'm here now. One questionable deal—one mistake—at a weak moment.

The mythological references from earlier flash through my mind. This is another form of hubris to fear

—not mine, but theirs. The arrogance that makes men believe they can control anything powerful once it's unleashed. They think they can use ARGUS without consequence, just as Icarus thought he could fly anywhere, never falling.

"What exactly do you want?" *Might as well get it on tape.*

Reid steps forward into Dristol's sight line.

Something passes between them. With Reid's face partially hidden by his stance, I can't read the two men, and find myself scanning Reid's waistline, wondering if he's carrying. I've been told FBI agents always carry, but he was never FBI. Quinn said he's former CIA.

He's a slim guy, slightly shorter than me. And Dristol's out-of-shape. I'm not afraid of either of these men, unless there's a gun holster beneath Reid's sports jacket.

In my ear, Syd's voice comes through. "Ask him what's in it for him. How does he monetize it."

"What I don't understand," I begin slowly to capture the men's attention, "What's in it for you? I see how I increase my fortune with the acquisition, but I'm not seeing the payout for you two."

It's a valid question, unless Miles is paying these fuckers. The thought pushes me over the edge into angry. Would he really do that? Hire these twats instead of just having it out with me?

"Let's say we have a vested interest. And it's no concern of yours," Reid answers.

He moves to leave, and in my ear, Syd says, "Save it. Buy an additional meet."

I'm not convinced I need more on this prick. I've got a powerful tool at my fingertips. But, in team spirit, I say,

"Let me sleep on it." It's a phrase I use all the time thanks to Nana, the queen of ruminating.

Dristol stands, pushing his chair back. "You asked what we want?"

I nod.

"Not much. Access. That's all. After you purchase the database, give us unfettered access for one week. That's it."

"And what would I get?"

"We become your ally."

I pointedly look at Reid, questioning why I need a guy with a fake badge as an ally.

"He's connected," Dristol answers my unspoken question. "In a group that theoretically doesn't exist. He uses an alternative identity when it's useful."

I'm not buying it, but I wonder if the team listening in is.

"Sleep on it," Dristol says. "I'll be in touch to coordinate a follow up. And in terms of what we can give you… a shield. No inquiries into the past. If there's a database you want access to, we can make it happen."

For the thousandth time, that's not how ARGUS works.

"We work to quiet the national security drumbeat, interest in legislation and state ownership. Seems to me you get a lot out of working with us."

He thinks he's luring me into a trap. Yet he's the one under surveillance.

"How can you eliminate AI legislation?" I ask, playing along.

"I'm not working alone. I've been playing the D.C. game for decades. Long before Crawford. That's why he hired me. I can be persuasive."

He's not saying it, but I'm betting he means black-mail. Extortion. Which would further explain his interest in ARGUS.

"Query access. That's what you really want."

He smiles his affirmative answer. "After you buy that database."

"You kill the AI bill that just passed the House, and we may have a deal."

Thanks to that arrogant, cocky attitude, I know I've got him.

He grins, becoming all teeth. "I hope to work together," Dristol says, extending his hand.

I take it, forcing a smile. "Same here."

CHAPTER
THIRTY-NINE

SYDNEY

"Sooo..." Jake removes his headset with deliberate slowness, the gesture loaded with skepticism. He spins in his chair to face me directly, the cramped surveillance van suddenly feeling even smaller. "What's your take on lover boy?"

"Come again?" He heard everything I heard.

"Any chance he's playing us? Cause it certainly sounded to me like his tune changed when killing AI legislation got placed on the table."

"He carried the listening device into the room and activated it himself." The evidence of Rhodes' transparency is literally recorded in our system, which makes Jake's insinuations odd.

We didn't have a visual on the room, but we heard and recorded everything.

"We know he did at least one illegal deal. He's not

crispy clean. Who's to say he's not stringing us along now?"

"Me. You're grasping at straws."

Although, I have to admit. He engaged—came across as genuinely intrigued—when, as Jake put it, the AI legislation nugget dropped.

"Do you think Crawford's the one selling state secrets?"

I chew on a pen cap, considering Jake's question. "It's conceivable. But the way Dristol and that Reid guy showed up... My hunch is Dristol's been making money on the side. Crawford probably has no idea."

Crawford's reputation on the Hill, one I learned about too late, is that he has an insatiable thirst for sex, a weakness for women, if you will. But adultery aside, for a politician, he's decent.

"And Reid?"

"Not sure. He doesn't dress like someone who's loaded, although that could be for costume effect. If he's a hired hand, Quinn will find a financial trail. Another possibility...maybe he left the CIA on bad terms, and he's jaded."

When the CIA flipped my career on its head, I certainly didn't hold the warm fuzzies.

"Or they're all in it together and we just watched a charade."

"No. That's not it." I dismiss Jake's notion with a wrinkled nose.

"You sure about that? It's hard to keep your head on straight when you're shagging the daylights out of the—"

"Will you shut the fuck up?" I push up from my chair

with enough force that it slams into the counter behind me. "I'm not wrong about Rhodes. He's playing them at my direction."

Jake's condescension ignites fierce defensiveness. I've spent my entire career being underestimated—first as a woman at Langley, then as the "emotional" operative after the France debacle. Intel from operatives like me informed Jake's military operations. A little respect would be nice.

My certainty isn't just emotional—it's analytical. Rhodes had multiple opportunities to betray us but didn't.

"Right. It's not possible he's playing both sides and concocting a deal for a get out of jail free card." Jake's disbelief is palpable, his expression suggesting I've lost all objectivity.

I thrust a hand at Jake. "Hundred bucks says I'm right, you're wrong. Rhodes is working with us, and Crawford doesn't know what's going on. Dristol and Reid —those are the two we want."

The childish bet is beneath me, but something about Jake brings out my competitive streak.

His country boy grin spreads wide. "You're on, spy girl."

Nerves fire off as I twist the knob to the suite, checking for tampering signs on the door or lock. Nothing. But the sensation of stepping into uncertain territory remains.

Rhodes is a good guy. I know it. We prepped for this

together, and unlike many partnerships I've had in this business, and in life, this one feels balanced—respectful rather than manipulative.

I step past the foyer and Rhodes looks up from a laptop, his expression intense, focused. He's sitting on the sofa, bent over the coffee table, one socked foot peeking out from the side, the picture of concentrated work.

The room smells faintly of coffee and the subtle notes of his cologne—now familiar enough that I associate the hints of cedar with safety and comfort. The dichotomy isn't lost on me.

"That was interesting," I say, tackling the elephant head on, observing his eyes for any micro expressions that might reveal deception. There are none—just the same clear, intelligent gaze that has become increasingly difficult to distrust.

"Before you say anything," Rhodes says, his fingers still moving across the keyboard, "I've got a plan. It's been in the works since ARGUS's early days. A failsafe, already built, for situations just like this. An Override Protocol."

He turns his laptop screen toward me, showing complex encryption schemas and network architecture diagrams that would be incomprehensible to most people. But my tech training helps me recognize the sophisticated firewall systems and mirrored servers. But that's recognition, not comprehension.

"What does it do exactly?" I ask, scanning the snippets visible on the screen.

"At its core, it blocks unauthorized access at a fundamental level—"

"Wait." I lean forward, studying the screen, recognizing the architecture patterns. "These are mirrored servers, aren't they? You're not just blocking access— you're redirecting it."

He nods, manipulating the diagram to expand a section showing nested security protocols. "Exactly. Creating what appears to be a nearly impenetrable barrier between ARGUS's actual systems and any external intrusion, while actually giving them access to something else entirely."

"A digital trap." The elegance of it hits me. "You're not just defending—you're gathering intelligence on who's trying to break in."

"The system was designed from the ground up with the assumption that eventually someone—government, competitors, hackers—would try to force their way in. So why not learn from their attempts?"

"You'll pretend to give Dristol access. He's a midwestern senator's chief of staff. You realize a ton of those men talk a big game. All smoke, no substance. There's a good chance he can't deliver what he promised."

"True," he says, "But we didn't get much in that meeting. But with this, we will." His eyes light up with animated intensity—the look of a brilliant mind solving an intricate puzzle. "Let's give Dristol what he wants, but on our terms. I'll design a global view dashboard—visually impressive, loaded with just enough real data to seem legitimate. I'll show it to him and insist on guarantees. Make it seem real. We'll see who he brings in. Who he gives it to. What he does with the data. I'll give him the motherlode. A window that appears to have access to every single one of our clients."

He pulls up another screen showing a sophisticated interface mockup—graphs, maps, data visualization tools that would convince most intelligence analysts they're seeing the real thing.

"I'll mirror interfaces, make it look real. You said KOAN is looking to monitor US corruption among those who wouldn't otherwise be investigated. With this, we can see everything. Find out who's flying right—"

"And who's crooked."

What he's suggesting could cause massive intelligence chaos. If someone accessing the mirrored, false data, leaked it...it could send all sorts of false signals around the world with untold consequences on geopolitics. Intelligence is the ultimate butterfly. A flapping of a wing in Malaysia can be felt in the Baltics within twenty-four hours.

But if there's corruption at the highest levels, a trap like this is an ingenious way to expose it.

"Obviously, I can't do it unless you're on board. You and your team heard it all. Your call. You don't want me to do it, I go back and tell him I slept on it and the answer is no."

As much as I want to give the green light, it's not my call to make. For all practical purposes, I'm a hired gun.

"Let me call Hudson." I call but get voicemail. "It's Sydney. Need to run something by you. Please call me back."

Rhodes looks up from the laptop, fingers resting on the keys. "This is ready, but I won't press go until you green light."

"You've still got the silver disk and ear comm?"

In answer to my question, he points at a metal box with a lid.

"What's your take on Dristol and Reid? Do you think they were listening in before they arrived?"

"Clearly." His attention returns to his laptop. "You don't have access to anything at Langley anymore, do you?"

"No. They've got a thorough lockout procedure. Why? What do you need?"

"Curious about Reid."

My phone buzzes and I flip it over. It's Jake. I swipe to answer.

"I'll accept Venmo," I answer, referencing our wager.

He barks out a laugh, but it fades quickly. "Smart ass. That's not why I'm calling. Rhodes' security pulled up outside the hotel. Headed inside hot and heavy."

"Thanks for the heads up."

"Yep. I'm headed inside. Leaving the van. If something's up, shout."

I end the call, and Rhodes asks, "What's up?"

Three hard knocks in rapid succession pound the door, then two more with increased force. Not the polite tap of hotel staff or the measured knock of expected visitors.

Rhodes and I exchange a glance. Without exchanging words, we position ourselves strategically—Rhodes angled toward the connecting door to the bedroom, me with clear sightlines to both the main door and the windows.

The knocking comes again, more insistent—someone who knows we're inside and isn't taking no for an answer. From the force and rhythm, whoever it is isn't just impatient. They're furious.

Rhodes' outsourced security? Or someone else entirely?

RHODES

"Who is it?" Sydney asks, standing to the side of the door as if expecting bullets to fly through the wood.

This is insanity. We're losing a grip on reality.

I step past her and sling the door open.

Mile's fist comes within inches of my chest before his reaction time catches up to the reality of the open door.

"What the hell, man?" My business partner and friend pushes past me, charging into the room.

Behind him are two men, both fit and intimidating, in navy golf shirts, khakis, and matching sports jackets that do little to hide the bulge of their holstered weapons.

My gut instinct is to shut the door on them, but they're probably outsourced security on ARGUS payroll.

"Let them in," Miles barks.

"Security? Why?" I stand in the doorway, hand on the knob, Sydney at my side, peering at the men.

"It's fucking needed, given the shit you've been pulling. Don't leave them out in the hall."

I look to Sydney, questioning, and she gives a brief nod.

I'm not sure why I'm questioning letting these men enter the hotel suite. Miles is pissed, but he's not a violent guy. He can't stand guns. He refuses to play violent video games.

Right now, he's annoyed I won't cave. I maintain controlling interest, and therefore the company can't go public without my approval.

Before closing the door, I peer down the hall, half-expecting Alex to be waiting in the wings.

Satisfied that he's nowhere to be found, I take in my old friend, too worked up to stand still, pacing between the circular sitting area and the adjacent room with a long dining table, a portion of the suite Sydney and I have yet to use. Daisy swears that Miles aims to mimic Ryan Reynolds in all things fashion, and in his tapered dark jeans, brown wingtips, subdued tee, and flexy light suede jacket, I'd say he nailed the look today, even if the suede jacket has no place in July in D.C. The black square dark-rimmed glasses create a funky, cool vibe, all designed to hide the inner geek. Before I left on vacation, he'd been growing out his thick black hair, debating attempting gravity-defying dreadlocks, but he must've lost patience, as his hair is shorn down almost to the scalp.

"Still holing up with your vacation find, I see," he says, speaking in the general direction of Sydney, but avoiding her direct gaze. "She's lovely, but can we clear the room? I'm happy for you and all, but we need to talk."

He's in max asshole mode.

One of the suited security men places his hand on the door knob as if he's going to open it for Sydney to leave.

"Sydney, you remember Miles Johnson, my partner and a backstabber. Oh, and she stays." Miles needs to calm the fuck down. He's jittery, agitated. "Did you stop taking your Adderall?"

"Fuck you." His anger is visceral. "Do you have any idea how much you're fucking up right now?"

Miles and I go way back, but I've never seen him like this. He's so worked up, so in his head. How the hell am I going to get through to him?

"Did Alex put you up to this? Is he behind this? Has he gotten in your head?"

"Alex? What the hell is wrong with you? I'm not here for Alex. Or the IPO. You think I can't tell when you mirror a site? You think I don't know what you're planning on doing? What the hell, MacMillan? You think I'm going to let you throw everything we've worked so hard for away?"

"What exactly do you think we've been working for?"

I'm standing in the center of the round room, a hallmark of Suite 7, the crystal chandelier directly overhead, and I swear, I feel like Zeus, waiting for one of the misguided gods to explain to me exactly how he's fucked up.

Miles glowers. He's Apollo, ready to battle.

"You brought up Alex. Well, he's right. This is our chance for generational wealth. Alex is right! Do you get that? Building on campuses that bear our names. MacMillan Avenue. Johnson Business School. This is a stepping stone to imprint businesses across the world.

What exactly is your plan? Huh? 'Catch' the bad guys?" Using his fingers for air quotes, he looks like a buffoon. "Don't you get it? The government is playing nice right now. We play along, give them what they want, and we'll move forward with a public offering, and we grow. We get what we want; they get what they want. We don't play along, they declare we're a risk to national security, and they take over. We become a government-run utility. If we're lucky, we don't end up in jail. You need to wake the fuck up! This is not your call!"

"Have they threatened you?"

"Jesus fucking Christ, MacMillan! Are you listening to me?"

Syd sits on the sofa, head bowed, but she's sure as fuck listening. Probably recording.

"Why did you visit the Russian embassy yesterday?" He stops pacing as realization registers.

My eyes are now open, but I'm still trying to understand what I'm seeing.

"It's not always an us versus them scenario," Miles says, voice hushed, defensive. Zero trace of denial.

"You've struck deals with multiple governments," I say, barking out a half-chuckle that tastes bitter in my throat. All this time I suspected Alex was the problem, the one pushing the financial agenda. But it was Miles all along. The realization crashes over me in waves—not just the betrayal, but the magnitude of it. This isn't a disagreement about company direction; this is Miles systematically undermining everything we built together. Miles. Not Alex.

Nearly twenty years of friendship, of sharing apartments with paper-thin walls during our startup days after dropping out of business school and pissing off our parents, of celebrating breakthroughs at three a.m. with cheap beer, of standing beside him at his father's funeral. All of it sacrificed for what? Control? Profit? Fear?

"You tried to trap me. Put them up to blackmailing me." My voice sounds foreign to my own ears—too controlled, too calm for the hurricane of emotions beneath. "That's the backstabbing knife I was referring to, by the way. Was that meant to force my hand? To back me into a corner?"

That's the piece I've been trying to figure out. It could so easily backfire. He wants us to go public. A public scandal, a congressional investigation, would tank a public offering.

"You want to force me out of the company. Right? Did you go to Dristol to help with that endeavor, or is that just a side hustle? Have you been greasing the wheels, selling information to jackasses like Dristol, for what? Extra money? Why? You don't need more money. Why do this?"

The mythology metaphors from my conversation with Sydney flash through my mind. Miles isn't playing the role of Apollo, god of light and truth. He's Icarus, flying too close to the sun of power and wealth, not realizing his wings are melting. He's the one who will fall.

He deflates, releasing a sigh that carries the weight of decisions he can't unmake.

"You're not going to cave, are you?" The anger in his voice can't quite mask the resignation. "Too fucking pompous for your own good."

I want to rage at him, to demand explanations, to remind him of what we stood for.

Do good!

Or at the very least, do no fucking harm.

But beneath my anger is something worse: grief for a friendship I now realize is lost, perhaps long before this moment. Miles Johnson is not the man I befriended. When did he change? How did I not see it?

Miles sinks onto a sofa and leans over, forehead in his palms.

This version of Miles…this moment…it's surreal.

"What have you done?"

Sydney now stands in the doorway with a calculated stillness. I haven't been watching her directly, but I'm peripherally aware of her subtle movements—positioning herself where she can better monitor the security guys, the almost imperceptible touch to confirm her phone is still securely tucked into the side of her leggings.

Miles hasn't looked directly at her since his initial dismissal. He's underestimating her—seeing only the woman I met hiking, unaware she's an operative who planted surveillance software in a Russian embassy. His security team, however, keeps repositioning slightly to keep her in their sightlines. They, at least, recognize a professional when they see one.

Her eyes catch mine for a split-second—a silent communication that conveys both caution and readiness.

"Miles, when we built ARGUS, we agreed. The only way to ensure an ethical company is to remain a nonprofit—to never let growth or profit become our sun. Never. I caved on the nonprofit front. That wasn't enough, was it? What're you doing now? All those executive team meetings where you and Alex tag-teamed me about profits—was that all theater? Were you already selling us out?" Instead of a surveillance device at the Russian embassy, I should've asked Daisy to monitor Miles' communications. *Fuck me.* The rumors about ARGUS deciphering state secrets and selling them are true...because of Miles. "Did Alex put you up to this?"

"You are one arrogant son of a bitch," he growls. "Alex is an employee. I'm your partner." He pounds his chest with his finger, proud. "Your co-founder. But fuck it all if I don't do it all! I'm the one who brings in our funding. I'm the one who gets us contracts. You sit back and futz around writing code and doing fuck all!" He's back to pacing. "It doesn't even matter. I don't need to waste my time or energy. This little trap you've built. It's pissed off some powerful people. Dristol? Reid? You don't think those NPCs are reporting to someone?"

"Of course I do." Hence the override protocol. No one would've caught on. No one. As a matter of fact, how did Miles? He must've looked to see what Daisy was accessing, maybe what we were both accessing.

"What's done is done. You chose poorly, friend." He sighs dramatically, as if he's starring in a Tony-worthy play. "You're going to need to go with these guys." He looks to Sydney. "Your lady friend too."

"Go where?"

He throws his hands up in the air, and mutters, "Arrogant prick. I thought I could send you off on vacation, get you away from it a bit, but fuck you and your need to make every decision and keep everything under your control. What's best for the company never matters. It's all about what you want. How you see things. And you've got this naive fucking view."

He's still pacing, going off in some madcap soliloquy,

while one suit steps forward, closer to me, tracking Sydney the entire time.

"What's the plan?" My gaze lifts to the chandelier above. "Where exactly do you want us to go, Miles?" If his goal is to go public, he won't want a scandal. The founder dying a suspicious death won't serve his purposes. "I'm too young for anyone to buy a heart attack."

Suicide, I suppose, might be something they could pull off. Car accident. Plane crash.

"They're not looking to kill you," Miles says, resigned. "At least if you wake the fuck up, they won't. That's what they've told me," he says, lips pursed, his expression one of disappointment and hopelessness. "They're going to talk to you. Help you see reason. And..." His head cocks sideways in the direction of Sydney. "She's going to help them with that."

Motherfucker. "Torture? You're willing to work with a group who wants to use torture to get their way?"

"If not her, it'll be Daisy."

Jesus. If anyone out there is listening to this, I hope they just dispatched a security detail to Daisy.

"You know, I knew you were a greedy bastard, but this is a new low. Daisy is your friend too."

"What the fuck do you not see? I don't have a choice. And neither do you."

"We always have a choice," I say, although, as I play through the options, I'm not sure we do. One thing I do know is that he should've brought more than two men with guns if he was planning on forcing us to willingly walk through a hotel and quietly get into an awaiting car.

He pulls out his phone, reading the screen.

"Daisy's here in D.C., right?"

Miles' question carries a deliberate casualness that immediately sends warning signals through my veins. Daisy—brilliant, loyal, irreplaceable Daisy—who stood against going public, who tracked the bot network attacking ARGUS. Who knows every back door and security protocol in our systems. Who is going through her own shit right now and doesn't need to be used as a negotiable token.

"Did you do something to her?" The question comes out dangerously quiet, my control hanging by threads.

His lips twist into something that's not quite a smile. If I'm reading him correctly, he actually looks apologetic, which terrifies me more than anger would. Miles isn't one for remorse. *What has he done?*

"She's fine. For now." He taps his phone screen, turning it to show me a location pin. "She's with colleagues who are very interested in discussing technical specifications. They're particularly curious about the fail-safe mechanisms she designed."

Daisy didn't just help me build the system, she engineered critical security measures that even I don't fully understand. In the wrong hands, that knowledge could compromise everything.

"Go on," he says, the command soft but unmistakable. "These guys aren't patient."

Daisy is how they're getting me out of the hotel without making a scene.

"If you have Daisy already, Sydney isn't needed."

"Change your mind, Rhodes. It doesn't have to be like this." Miles won't meet my gaze, which makes his plea so half-hearted I ache to shove my fist into his clean-shaven jaw.

I look to Sydney for direction. How do we work this so she stays behind? I don't want her used as a negotiating device. All kinds of horrific movie images come to mind. I shouldn't have sent my security home. I thought after a fight with Miles, I'd have a few hours to convince Sydney to join me on a flight back to the West Coast. No security needed. This is insanity.

What about Syd's team? Are they still listening?

Syd's gaze meets mine, steadfast and calm.

"I need to go to Daisy," I say, stating what's obvious to me but may not be to Syd. I can't let someone who works for me get caught up in this craziness. "If they leave you out of this," I look from Sydney to Miles, "I'll go without a fight."

Sydney flattens her palms against her thighs. "Let you go alone? No. Besides, if they leave me here, I'll call the authorities."

Jesus fucking Christ Syd, why did you have to say that?

Miles snaps his head up, finally looking directly at her. Recognition dawns—she's a risk and can no longer be dismissed as a random.

"You guys just keep fucking up."

The irony of his statement isn't lost on me. In his worldview, standing for principles is the mistake. Growth and expansion are the goals. Refusing to compromise is the failure. How did we land on such divergent paths?

"You're both going to go and you aren't going to fight us because it's the best option. When you get to your destination, you're going to listen. With an open mind."

As we move toward the door, Sydney slightly ahead, a

notification flashes on my phone. The Override Protocol indicator shows 87 percent completion—approximately twelve minutes remaining before the system fully deploys. The digital genie is escaping its bottle. All we need is for the right person to stumble upon it and make a wish. But will anyone stumble on it? Because it certainly sounds like Miles here has warned his partners.

One of the security men opens the door, gesturing us through with practiced professionalism. As we step into the hallway, Sydney's hand brushes mine—a momentary contact that communicates more than words could. A silent promise. Whatever comes next, we face it together.

CHAPTER
FORTY-ONE

SYDNEY

The parade of black SUVs slices through the rainy streets like a funeral procession—which it might become if I don't find a way out of this. In any other city, three identical vehicles might draw attention, but in D.C., black SUVs are as common as coffee shops. Even the protesters huddled under dripping umbrellas, their "Protect Our National Parks" and "Save the Sequoias" signs wilting in the rain, barely glance our way.

I clock the men in the front seat as we glide down Massachusetts Avenue—past embassies that offer diplomatic sanctuary to those in danger, past the Naval Observatory where the vice president's residence is heavily guarded, past landmarks that represent the democracy these men are actively undermining. With each passing minute, we move through populated areas toward Rock Creek Park.

The man beside Rhodes hasn't spoken since we left

the hotel, but his hand hasn't moved from his jacket pocket either. I can feel the weight of his attention on me —not as a person, but as leverage.

My fingers itch to send a message on the phone, but between the man beside me and the one in the front passenger seat, all that would happen is they'd become cognizant of my phone and possibly toss it out the window.

When they arrived at the hotel room as a pair, I thought they were there as intimidation, not as force. I didn't foresee them using an abducted person's welfare as leverage. Once outside the hotel, with the three SUVs, it became clear their plans extend beyond intimidation.

Our KOAN team is new, untested. I hope they're all over this. I hope they heard us.

Rhodes absentmindedly toys with my wrist. It's ironic. Last night I wore his bracelet for protection. I considered stalling in the hotel, asking if it was safe to leave the bracelet in the hotel room and making a show of putting it on because I didn't trust the staff to leave it behind, but after brief consideration, I nixed the idea. It wouldn't come across as believable and might rouse suspicion that we're working with someone, especially if one of the men studied the bracelet and identified the tracker.

The fact they believe I'm a random woman he met, a nobody, is probably the only reason my phone is still with me—the outline in the pocket on my leggings is clear. Still, the men have eyed me warily at times. My quiet submission and desire to join Rhodes might have thrown them off from any suspicions they harbored that I have training, that I might be more capable than the average woman on the street. If the Russians know my background, which is conceivable, then they haven't tipped these guys off.

The SUV appears to be standard with minimal internal modifications, making it predictable if we need to attempt escape. The rear-view mirror is angled to keep us in view.

The rain works in their favor—limiting visibility, providing acoustic cover, and reducing civilian presence.

The plan, in theory, if Miles' outbursts are accurate, is to threaten Daisy, and possibly me, to force Rhodes' hand. The problem with the theory is that I can't see them trusting Rhodes. With ARGUS at his disposal, he's most likely a dangerous risk to the men behind this operation. If they view Daisy as loyal to Rhodes, she's a risk. She also possesses knowledge that could hurt them. Then there's me. Even if they believe I'm a random woman, Rhodes' vacation fling, I've heard them and have seen their faces. I'm a loose end too.

I count nine hired men in the entourage, taking us to an unknown destination. Are they all mercenaries? All willing to participate in murder? Or will the detail splinter after we're delivered to a secure site? Even if they're being paid a mint, nine people are a lot to trust with cold-blooded murder.

As we leave the city behind, I become more convinced the game plan changed this afternoon. When Rhodes refused to work with Dristol, alarms went off. Which means this isn't well thought out. This is damage control. I'd bet money on it. They left Miles behind at the hotel, which means he's not a part of the solution. Or he's not getting his hands dirty.

Rhodes threads his fingers through mine. The music in the car, an unnerving cheerful Beach Boys album, lends a surreal quality to the moment. The convoy slows as we turn into what appears to be an abandoned warehouse complex near the Anacostia River. Through the rain-streaked window, I catch glimpses of rusted shipping containers and overgrown chain-link fencing. The perfect place to make people disappear.

"End of the line," the man beside Rhodes announces, his hand finally emerging from his jacket pocket to reveal a compact pistol.

As we come to a stop, my phone vibrates with what appears to be a spam text about extended car warranties. But I recognize the code buried in the message—Quinn's signal that KOAN is close. I'd been hoping they were tracking my location through the cell towers.

Rhodes catches my eye, and I give the slightest nod. We're not alone.

The doors open simultaneously across all three SUVs. It's game time. Watching the men interact, they know each other. All American. Likely former military or police.

As we're hustled toward the warehouse, I note potential escape routes and defensive positions, useful if we get a chance to break away. Skylights in the building's roof could provide alternate entry points.

Three armed men stand to the side, one with a cigarette. Two men from our caravan lead, the others follow us through a rusted, metal door. A heavy chain dangles. Before we arrived, the door may have been secured.

Inside the warehouse, industrial lights flicker, revealing a woman with short dark hair zip-tied to a metal chair in the center of the space. Her laptop is open on a nearby table, and even from this distance, I can see the ARGUS portal open on the screen. She's alive, conscious, and absolutely furious.

The warehouse stretches roughly a hundred feet in each direction, with the captive positioned dead center under a bank of industrial lights. Shipping containers create a maze along the left wall, while the right side opens to loading docks with roll-up doors. A mezzanine level wraps around three walls, accessible by metal stairs at each corner. Perfect sniper positions.

"The prodigal tech genius arrives." Dristol emerges from behind a shipping container to our left, flanked by Reid and two more men I don't recognize. Reid positions himself between us and the main entrance while the other two spread wide, creating a semicircle that puts us in a kill box. Rhodes and I instinctively move closer together, our backs to a concrete support pillar. From this position, I can see three potential escape routes: the loading docks to our right, a service door near the mezzanine stairs, and what looks like an emergency exit behind the container maze.

"Let the women go," Rhodes says, his voice deadly calm. "Your issue is with me."

"Actually, our issue is with what's in your head. And the information you can access. Ms. Jonas too." Dristol gestures toward the bound woman. "But since you've been so uncooperative, I'm questioning if we can realistically expect a change in heart."

Reid steps forward with what looks like a high-end tablet. "We've been told we can convince you to work with us, but I'm not sold. And this one here, she's feisty."

He pulls out a combat knife, testing the edge with his thumb.

Daisy's eyes widen, but she keeps her mouth shut. A thin line of blood appears where the zip-ties have cut into her wrists from her struggles. "We've got no leverage over her," Reid continues, moving closer to Daisy. "But we do over you. I don't doubt we can convince you to take the actions we desire today. But I worry about tomorrow."

Daisy glares at Dristol. "Go to hell."

It would be lovely if Daisy played it slightly friendlier, as her actions underscore his points. But I don't blame her. I'd be reacting the same way if I was in her place.

"Miles wants me to step away from the company. Is that what you want? If I step away, agree to leave, Daisy comes with me; we no longer have database access, we're no longer a threat, right?"

Dristol laughs, a sound devoid of humor. "Oh, Rhodes. You don't get it. Miles hoped you would cooperate. He had ideas. From my perspective, today's events aren't about getting you to cooperate. You've shown you can't be trusted. Our goal today is to get what we need and then eliminate risks. Witnesses. Your girlfriend here heard everything in the hotel. I'm not sure the extent of what you've shared with Daisy, but I'm certain you shared too much. And you?" He gestures in my general direction. "If we hadn't intervened, you planned to show Crawford your evidence. Am I right?"

Reid taps his earpiece. "Alpha team has dispersed to patrol the perimeter. Bravo team on standby. Are we doing this all here?"

Reid poses the question to Dristol, who is clearly in command. He steps to the laptop and presses a button.

"Fifty-one percent now," Reid announces, gaze directed at Daisy's laptop screen. "At this rate, we'll have everything in about twelve minutes. Not your little trap. The real thing. Right Daisy?" If she could shoot fire from her eyes, he'd be crispy. "After that, well..." Reid shrugs. "We'll have what we need. We can safely exit."

The implication hangs in the air like a death sentence.

I discreetly angle my phone, aiming to ensure the GPS signal stays strong. Every second we're here, KOAN is getting closer.

The movement draws Reid's attention. "You dumbasses didn't take her phone? Get it from her. We'll need to drive it back to DC. Did you check him? This can't be the last location their phones ping." He runs his hands through his hair, scanning the warehouse. He doesn't look pleased.

An armed man steps up behind me, hand out for my phone. Another man approaches Rhodes, presumably to check him for a device.

The lights go out all at once.

Dim light filters through the yellowed skylights above.

The two men closest to us pause, lifting their holstered guns. They step back, keeping us in clear line of sight while scanning the warehouse.

Hurried footsteps mix with Reid's profanity.

Emergency lighting kicks in three seconds later, bathing everything in an eerie red glow.

"Contact left!" one of the mercenaries near the containers shouts, but his voice is cut short by the distinctive sound of a suppressed rifle from the upper level. The mercenary who'd been reaching for my phone drops immediately, his sidearm clattering across the concrete floor.

The warehouse erupts into chaos. Muzzle flashes strobe from the mezzanine. Two mercenaries by the loading docks return fire while Reid and another gunman take cover behind Daisy's chair—using her as a human shield. I grab Rhodes' hand and we dive behind the shipping pallets to our right. Cover. We're unarmed. Gaining cover is priority. From here, we have a clear line to the laptop table, about thirty feet of open ground.

"Stay low," Rhodes whispers, then pulls out what I now realize isn't just a phone—it's a tactical communicator. "ARGUS, emergency protocol seven-seven-alpha."

"Rhodes, what are you—"

"Activating kill switch for all external access," he says into the device. "Authorization: Icarus-One-One-Seven."

Here we are in the middle of a firefight, and he's in command, cutting off access to ARGUS remotely, mitigating risk should they succeed in eliminating us.

He crawls to the edge of our cover and retrieves the pistol from the downed mercenary, checking the magazine with practiced efficiency before returning to position.

A figure drops from the rafters directly above Dristol. It's Jake, moving like a shadow despite his bulk. He lands behind the container where Dristol took cover, cutting off his retreat to the main entrance.

"Sydney!" Rhodes shouts over the gunfire from our position behind the pallets. "The table—Daisy! The laptop!"

Lives first. Mission second. Equipment last. Daisy's hunched in the chair, positioned dangerously in the open.

I sprint across the open space in a diagonal line toward Daisy's position, using shipping containers for cover against the mezzanine shooters. Rhodes covers my advance with a pistol he grabbed from the first downed mercenary, positioning himself at the corner of our pallet barricade. Apparently, there's more to the tech genius than meets the eye.

One armed mercenary, crouching near a cabinet, swings his weapon toward me. I see the muzzle tracking my movement and realize my current path puts Daisy directly in his line of fire behind me. I dive left toward a concrete support pillar instead, forcing him to reposition and giving Rhodes a clear shot. Two rounds center mass, and the threat drops.

"Nice shooting," I gasp, sliding behind the table where Daisy sits zip-tied to a metal chair.

"High school rifle team," he says grimly. "Some skills you don't lose."

Daisy's eyes are wide but alert—no signs of head trauma or shock. Good. Her wrists are secured behind the chair with heavy-duty zip ties, ankles bound to the chair legs.

"You okay?" I shout, scrambling to pull a tactical knife from the waist of a downed mercenary.

"Peachy," she says, eyeing my stolen knife. "Hands first. Circulation's going."

I work the knife blade under the zip tie around her wrists, angling it away from her skin. The plastic is thick —industrial grade—but the blade is sharp. It takes precious seconds of sawing before the tie snaps.

Daisy immediately brings her hands forward, flexing her fingers as I move to her ankles.

"Laptop," she says urgently. "Reid was trying to—"

"Can you run?" I cut her off, slicing through the ankle restraints.

She flexes her ankles, wincing as blood flow returns. "Not gracefully, but yes."

Gunfire erupts closer to our position. I grab Daisy's arm, guiding her. "Stay low. We're moving to that stack of containers—straight from here."

I snatch the laptop from the table with my free hand–now that Daisy's mobile, we can multitask. "Stay low. On three. One, two…"

We break cover together, Daisy's legs functional as we sprint toward better concealment.

The shooting stops.

I scan Daisy, head to toe, identifying minor abrasions but nothing serious, and hand the laptop to her. She flips it open and taps away.

Sirens approach in the distance, the sound filling the void of artillery.

The lights flicker on, and Hudson, decked out in tactical gear, enters, announcing, "All clear."

We all slowly come out from cover. My ears ring in the silence now that the artillery has stopped.

Jake has Reid in custody, zip-tied and none too gently deposited against a shipping container. Two of the mercenaries are down permanently, three more are wounded and disarmed, and the rest apparently decided flight was the better part of valor or were taken out outside the warehouse.

"How did you find us?" Rhodes asks Jake.

"We've been watching since those guys went up to the suite, watched you get in the SUV." Jake grins and taps his earpiece. "Quinn's been tracking Sydney's phone GPS since you left the hotel, but even if they tossed her phone, we wouldn't have lost you. The further out you went, the further we fell back, but we were there. Waited for you to stop, then moved in. Cell tower triangulation and a little patience. Disarmed four outside the building, two on the property perimeter. Whoever these guys hired are weak on tactical training," Jake says. "Syd, they had no idea you were anyone other than a girlfriend, that's clear as day."

"That's right. Girlfriend. Introductions, Rhodes?" Daisy's smiling, despite her split lip. Her wrists are red, and she's rubbing the sore skin, but other than that, she's remarkably calm and put together given what she's just been through.

"Oh, she posed as his girlfriend," Jake says, clearly thinking he's clearing up a misunderstanding.

"Is that right, Rhodes?" Daisy asks, cupping one of her wrists against her middle, eyes taking in the warehouse, but despite it all, still in full possession of her sense of humor.

Hudson, my boss, pointedly looks my way.

"It's complicated," I mutter.

"No," Rhodes says, surprising me by slipping his arm around my waist. "It's not complicated at all." He looks down at me with an expression I can't quite read. "You work for a private intelligence firm. You were investigating me. Now you're... Well, now you're with me."

"Roady boy," Daisy says, shaking her head. "Did we bet on this? No, dang." She snaps her fingers. "That bet was with Miles and it's looking like he's not going to be in a position to pay me."

"I'm pretty sure I won a bet on this. I'll share the winnings," Jake says, grinning at Daisy.

Before anyone else can comment, Quinn's voice crackles through someone's comm: "FBI inbound, five minutes. Local PD in route. Ambulance in bound."

Reid—still unconscious from Jake's chokehold—starts to stir.

Rhodes bends over Dristol. Awake, but despondent. Possibly in shock.

I don't see any injuries, but Rhodes checks him and places two fingers against his neck.

"Tell your friends," he says quietly, "that ARGUS is not for sale." Dristol groans and Rhodes bends closer. "How did it work? You got intel, sold it to the highest bidder? Is that all this is? And you somehow wrangled Miles into working with you?"

Dristol lowers his eyelids and curls into a ball, as if by closing his eyes he can make reality go away.

Hudson addresses one of the KOAN team I'm not familiar with, saying, "You stay here, watch over. We're going to head outside and greet the first responders. Send them in."

Outside, the rain has reduced to a drizzle, and the afternoon sun peeks through the clouds, descending below the tree line, filtering streams of gold between the leaves.

As we watch the emergency vehicles speed along the gravel road in our direction, Jake asks Daisy in a gentle voice, "You okay?" I don't know him well, but given his gruff persona and untamed beard, gentle is unexpected.

"Better now," she says, smiling almost shyly up at him. "Thanks for saving the day."

Hudson steps forward. "We've got a location on Miles Johnson. Authorities are going to bring him in. He's in on this. You agree?" His question is directed at Rhodes.

"There's no doubt," Rhodes answers, tugging me against his side.

"I've got contacts within the FBI. You're going to need to meet with them, but it should be brief. There won't be an official mention of KOAN." He looks pointedly between Rhodes and me. "We'll say we're your security on all official documentation."

"Let me get this straight. Technically, KOAN doesn't exist?"

"For now," Hudson says, "That's preferred."

"Not a problem for me." Rhodes says to Hudson, then asks me, "Are you going to want to ask questions? Seems to me these guys are likely the source of your leak?"

"I'd like to confirm that," I admit. "If I were to guess, when they get Dristol into interrogation, he's gonna sing like a canary."

"The out-of-shape schmuck balled up like a little boy on the floor in there?" Jake snorts. "He's totally breaking."

The sirens grow louder, making conversation difficult, and within seconds, we're surrounded by first responders. Jake never leaves Daisy's side, and I briefly wonder if Hudson instructed him to stick by her, to ensure he heard everything she shared.

It's interesting to me that KOAN isn't supposed to exist. It's something I'll need to ask about later. As I'm leaning against one of the SUV's while Rhodes answers questions, my phone rings. It's Caroline.

I hesitate to answer, but the sirens have been silenced, leaving only emergency lights flashing, and I don't want her to worry.

"Hey," I answer. Rhodes shoots me a questioning look, and I mouth the word "Friend." He resumes answering the FBI agent's questions. If I'm not mistaken, he's also been joined by someone flashing an NSA badge.

"All good?" she asks.

"All good. You'll get a full report. But I'm almost certain we found the leak."

"ARGUS," she says, and I think I detect concern.

"Multiple parties," I answer. "Rhodes' partner's involved."

"He didn't know?"

"No. Blindsided."

"So you're still with Mr. Wonderful?"

I meet his gaze and he winks.

"Yeah. Your advice was solid."

"Good. I'm happy for you. Tomorrow, let's talk. If he really wants to work with us, I have ideas."

We talk for a while longer, about nothing really, and given everything going on around me, I only half listen, but I don't rush her off the phone, as it's soothing to hear the voice of a friend.

When we're finally allowed to drive away, leaving the mess for the FBI to sort, I allow myself to relax. The operation is over. The leak exposed. A larger conspiracy will likely unravel. The bad guys are captured or dead.

And as for Rhodes and I, we're not ending today headed to different states.

"So," he says quietly, "we never talked about your resume." It's true. I sent it to him but I didn't think he'd had time to look it over—and Quinn doctored it anyway. "I have some ideas. An offer, if you will."

I look at him—this brilliant, kind, surprisingly deadly man. "An offer?"

"For a partnership. Real partnership. ARGUS, KOAN, whatever it takes to keep doing what we just did."

"Which is?"

"Rooting out the bad guys. Doing good."

In the distance, floodlights bathe the Lincoln Memorial's classical columns in light, a stark reminder of the fragile democracy we just helped protect. It's been one hell of a weekend.

"I like the idea," I tell him, squeezing his hand. What he's proposing needs to be discussed with Caroline, and I need to learn more about this organization I've joined that prefers to not be mentioned in debriefings.

"I was hoping you'd say that," he says. "I think we're going to make a hell of a team."

As the SUV meanders through the streets, weaving through traffic to return to our hotel, I can't help but hope.

When we pull up at the hotel, several government-issued sedans and SUVs are parked along the street, out of the way of the hotel's valet. A man approaches and Rhodes lowers the window.

Jake, Daisy, and Hudson are in the vehicle behind us, so I'm not concerned. Noah, who is sitting in the passenger seat up front, positions himself to observe and react if needed.

"Mr. MacMillan?" The man says.

"Yes, that's me."

"I'm Special Agent Rozwell. I know you've had a long day, sir, but we have Miles Johnson in custody. We were wondering if you might be willing to join us for the initial questioning. At this point in time, we have yet to press charges, and we won't be able to hold him for long unless we do."

He looks at me. "You up for more?"

Before I can answer, Noah says, "Hudson wants us to head back for a debrief. Out of D.C."

If he wants us to stay low, getting out of D.C. is probably a good bet.

Rhodes squeezes my hand. "You go. I might be in for a long night anyway."

CHAPTER
FORTY-TWO

SYDNEY

When we pull up to the rental in the Highlands, our headlights sweep across two steel-gray Tahoes with North Carolina tags parked in the gravel drive. The vehicles look oddly official against the rustic cabin backdrop —a reminder that we haven't fully escaped the events in D.C.

"Who's here?" I ask Jake, tension creeping back into my shoulders. After everything that's happened, unexpected visitors trigger wariness even in this peaceful setting.

"I've been with you in D.C. Know as much as you."

It's about ten o'clock at night, and the mountains embrace us with their particular symphony—crickets at peak chorus, the distant rush of the creek we crossed on our way in, the whisper of wind through pine needles. A full moon hangs low and heavy over the ridge, bathing the clearing in silver light that transforms the ordinary house into something almost magical. After the harsh fluorescent lights of government buildings and hotel rooms, the natural illumination feels like a homecoming of sorts.

As Jake turns off the ignition and we step out, the cool mountain air fills my lungs—clean, restorative, untainted by city pollution or political machinations. For a moment, I pause to look up at the stars, impossibly bright and numerous here where light pollution can't reach them. They remind me of the diamonds on my wrist—Rhodes insisted I put the bracelet back on before I left D.C. I agreed, because him knowing he can track me is one less thing for him to worry about as he confronts his business partner.

Jake presses a code into the keypad on the rental and twists the knob.

"Howdy," he says in greeting. I step inside behind him, as he adds, "Those are some grim faces."

Sitting at the kitchen table, all three facing the foyer, are Hudson, Noah, and Quinn.

"Hi," I say. "Have you guys been back long?"

We split up at the private landing strip. Some might call it an airport, but that name feels like an undeserved embellishment. Jake had to go to the restroom, and I called to check in on Rhodes, but didn't reach him. The others jumped in Hudson's car and came straight back here.

Hudson insisted he wanted all of us out of D.C. It feels like overkill to me, but he is the boss.

"Not too long," Hudson says.

"You guys get some updates?" Jake asks.

Quinn's gaze falls to her hands. Noah scratches his

neck. Something is wrong. Is it Rhodes? Did something happen?

"No updates yet. That's out of our hands and will require security clearance. But…"

"What is it? You're making me nervous."

"In the morning, we'll do a postmortem. Review the good and the bad," Hudson says, repeating what we already knew.

"Alright. So? Why are y'all sitting here like someone died?" Jake asks.

"We got word about the leak," Hudson answers, his voice gentler than usual. The hardened former military officer rarely shows this side, which tells me how serious this is. "Dristol. As expected, he's a goldmine. Singing like a canary."

"And?" I lean forward, every nerve ending suddenly alert. This is the question that's haunted me since France —the betrayal that cost lives I was responsible for. "Was it Dristol? Or someone else?"

"It's classified," Hudson says, exchanging glances with Quinn. "Dristol's guilty. But he didn't act alone. Someone based in D.C. High clearance. Out of the public eye. They were selling asset names to the highest bidder. Dristol learned how much he was making and decided to create a similar business." His jaw tightens. "But the individual has been detained. The FBI wanted me to assure you personally the leaks have stopped."

My eyes burn unexpectedly. Maybe they were burning before I walked in the door—it's been a long day, and the cabin pressure in the small plane we flew here played havoc with my sinuses. But this burn is different. It's the release of a weight I've carried for months, but the vindication comes too late for those we lost.

Quinn reaches across the table, her fingers briefly touching mine. "Your assets in France," she says quietly. "They didn't die because you made a mistake. It was always the leak."

Noah nods solemnly. "System failure, not operator error."

It's the absolution I never sought out loud but desperately needed to hear. We're trained not to dwell on losses, to compartmentalize and move forward. But the responsibility for human lives isn't something you shrug off, no matter how much training you have.

"I didn't cultivate those assets lightly," I say, my voice steadier than I feel. "I took on responsibility for their livelihoods. Their safety."

"We know," Hudson says. "That's why you're good at this."

The simple validation hits harder than any medal or commendation could. These people understand the weight of what we do, the cost of failure measured in human lives rather than spreadsheet numbers.

"There's no way you can tell me?" I ask, needing to know who betrayed us.

Hudson shakes his head. "That's above my clearance level. All I can tell you is they're in custody and the breach has been sealed."

I take in the three of them, coffee mugs filled with what I'm guessing is tea, or maybe whiskey, knowing these guys. "Is that what the long faces are for?"

"Partly," Hudson admits. "The other part is that this changes things for you."

"How so?"

"You have options now," Quinn says carefully. "Your record's been cleared. The France operation has been officially reclassified as compromised by the leak, not operator error. More than that, it doesn't appear your name was included in the sold data."

"Which means?" Though I think I know where this is heading.

"Which means," Hudson continues, "you could go back to Langley next if you wanted. Full reinstatement, probably a promotion given what happened to you. Likely not in France. A different territory, I'd assume."

The possibility hangs in the air between us. Six months ago, it would have been everything I wanted. Now, after working with this team, after what we accomplished in D.C. ...

"I'm good," I say finally. "You know, the way you were looking at me, I didn't know if something happened to Rhodes, or if you were about to fire my ass."

Jake barks out a laugh. "Spy girl, I told you, all's good."

"Forgive me, southern gent," I say back to him, echoing what I heard Daisy call him earlier today, "if I didn't take your word as gospel."

"We'll go over it all in the morning, but your job's safe if you want it," Hudson says. "You did good work. Real good work. Now grab a mug, pick your poison, and join us. Noah's been pushing for a card game."

"A game?"

Quinn grimaces. "Yeah, that's what I said."

After a lengthy debate about rules and stakes, we sit around the table playing quarters until nearly midnight, the tension from the day gradually melting away. There's something therapeutic about the mundane ritual—friends around a table, talking and laughing, no life-or-death decisions required.

With a yawn, I stretch and say, "Alright guys. I'm calling it. So, which room in this place are you giving me?"

"That's right," Jake says. "Spy girl has yet to spend a night in this here humble abode."

I roll my eyes and look at Quinn. "Is there still an extra room downstairs?"

There's a knock on the front door and all of us look at each other like we're uncertain we heard correctly.

Jake stretches his jaw and gets up, moving toward the front door.

Hudson calls out, "Wait a minute, Jake."

We've all had a bit too much to drink, but Hudson has the presence of mind to locate a firearm.

Given everything that's happened, it's not the worst idea, but it's hard to believe anyone would come after us down here. That's the reason this location was chosen. It's off the beaten path and where we won't be observed.

"Look who can't stay away," Jake bellows, his voice carrying the warmth reserved for people he's decided are worthy of trust.

The firearm disappears from Hudson's hand as footsteps sound in the entryway. My heart seems to stutter, then race, responding to a possibility my conscious mind hasn't fully processed yet.

Rhodes strides in, silhouetted against the porch light. He looks exhausted—shadows beneath his eyes, his normally perfect posture slightly curved with fatigue

—but to me, he's never looked better. Real. Present. Here.

Our eyes lock across the room, and everything else fades to background noise—the team's murmurs, the clink of glasses, Jake's knowing chuckle. In that electric moment of connection, something shifts inside me, a certainty crystallizing where doubt once lived.

I'd told myself I'd see him again, that what we built in those intense days wouldn't simply evaporate when I left D.C. I'd even half-convinced myself it was true. But watching him cross the room toward me now, having followed me to this remote mountain outpost after such an exhausting day, erases every lingering question.

We're real. Not an operation, not a temporary alliance, not a vacation fling. Something enduring that neither government pressure nor professional obligation could sever.

"I thought you'd be stuck in D.C. for weeks," I say, my voice betraying more emotion than I'd intended as I rise to meet him halfway.

"Oh, I'll need to return. But I'm not their employee. Tomorrow's gonna be a shit storm. Nothing I can't deal with remotely though. For now, it's better I'm on the East Coast to deal with it," he says, shrugging like it's no big deal he ended his day and flew down here.

"Have you got a bag?"

He twists, showing me a backpack slung over his shoulder.

"Your stuff's in that?"

"Doesn't take much."

"Alright, you two," Quinn says, getting up and pushing her chair under the kitchen table. "Extra rooms downstairs. Take a left at the end of the hall. I'm calling it a night."

One by one, my team files downstairs.

Jake calls out, one foot on the stairs, "There's thin walls in this joint. Just saying."

"Jake!" Quinn yells from downstairs.

My cheeks heat in embarrassment, although it's unnecessary. These guys aren't judging, at least, not really.

"You ready to go to bed? You need anything? Water?"

"Nah. I'm toast. Ready to call it a night."

I go back to the entry where I left my bag, and Rhodes takes it from me, telling me to lead the way.

We walk through the downstairs hallway, navigating the unfamiliar space together. Behind closed doors, evidence of the team's nighttime routines filters through—lights casting thin golden lines beneath doorways, floorboards creaking under unseen footsteps, water pipes humming as faucets run. The house smells of fresh laundry, coffee lingering from earlier, and a faint woodsy scent through an open window somewhere.

"It feels like camp, doesn't it?" I ask Rhodes as I close our door, suddenly aware of how small the room is—a queen bed taking up most of the space, a simple dresser, and a reading lamp casting warm amber light across plain white walls. The bedspread is faded blue plaid, worn soft from washing--not the plush comforter we shared days ago, but something with character, with history.

Practical, unpretentious, worlds away from the luxury hotel suite in D.C.

"It's fine for tonight," he says, dropping his backpack on the bed. The mattress sinks slightly under its weight.

He unzips the bag and pulls out a toothbrush and toothpaste, domestic items that somehow feel intimate.

The overhead light casts shadows across his face, highlighting the fatigue around his eyes, the tension he's carried through a day of inquiries and betrayals. When he runs a hand through his hair, I notice it trembles slightly —a small tell from a man who maintains such careful control.

"When everything was wrapping back in D.C., all I cared about was finding you." The confession hangs in the air between us, unadorned by qualifications or explanations. Just raw truth.

I understand what he's saying, but it's a lot because I feel the same. I'd been trying to ignore it, but sitting with the team, I'd felt a yearning, wondering how things were going for him and when I'd see him again. Instead of saying all that though, I say, "Well, you heard what he said about thin walls," and half-smile, so he sees I'm teasing.

Rhodes doesn't take the tease, though. "It's not about sex, Syd. In fact, this room could have stone walls and I'm too wiped to do anything but hold you tonight. But I want to hold you. So, here I am."

I'm struck silent. We stare at each other, my heart thundering from fear, the kind of fear one feels before taking a leap from a plane. It's something you want to do, but the self-protection part of you is screaming, "Are you out of your mind?".

I study Rhodes. When he commits, he's all in. I've never been all in before, but I want to take the leap. I want to try.

There's an attached bathroom, and he steps inside,

flipping the light on. We move about like a regular couple, quietly getting ready for bed.

When we climb in, me in a T-shirt and him in boxers, I roll into his side, my head on his shoulder. The lights are out and the house is quiet.

"Are you okay?" I ask softly, feeling his muscles tense beneath me. The slow, steady thud of his heart vibrates against my ear—slightly elevated, belying the calm he projects. "With Miles? That had to have been hard."

His chest expands with a deep breath that seems to draw from somewhere beyond his physical body—the kind of breath people take before diving into cold water or delivering difficult news.

"It'll take me a lot more than a few days to process," he admits, his voice vibrating through his chest into my ear. "Twenty years of friendship. College. Two companies. We built ARGUS from nothing—sleeping on office floors, living on ramen, working until we couldn't see straight." The memories color his voice with a warmth that makes the betrayal all the more stark.

"I knew we were growing apart. Knew he saw a different future for the company. But I never imagined..." He trails off, searching for words. "I think what gets me the most is that he was okay with the idea of Daisy, a mutual friend, undergoing physical torture to get his way. There's a line there that I didn't think he could cross."

"Well, he wasn't going to be the one administering it," I point out, trying to offer some perspective.

"True." His arm tightens around me slightly. "Nevertheless, he set it in motion, knowing exactly what it meant." His voice drops lower. "He was willing to let them take you, too. That's something I can't reconcile with the person I thought I knew. I misjudged him."

The simple truth in his words touches me deeply.

"That's...either he's changed fundamentally, or I never saw him for who he really was." The vulnerability in his admission feels like a rare gift. "That's what I'll be processing for a long time. If I missed something that significant in someone I trusted completely, what else might I be missing?"

I lift my head to look at him directly. "Sometimes people surprise us—for better or worse. It doesn't mean your judgment is flawed. It means people are complex, and pressure reveals their true priorities."

His eyes search mine, finding something there that softens his expression. "Including us?"

"Especially us," I confirm. "Neither of us expected this when we met on that mountain trail."

"True."

"You can't hold yourself accountable for someone else's weakness."

"Weakness? You think that's what it was?"

"Well, morally weak, right?"

"Hmm. Maybe. Earlier today, I saw it as hubris. The belief that he knew best, that he could force the direction forward." He lets out a long sigh.

"What happens now?" I ask, tracing idle patterns on his chest, feeling his heartbeat against my palm.

"Tomorrow I plan to hire a protective detail for Daisy."

"What?"

"She's investigating a shady firm. You'd think after today she'd let me hire private investigators but she won't listen. I'm not sure I can trust the outfit I used to hire a protection detail in D.C., so I'll ask Hudson."

"It's not exactly what KOAN does, but I'm sure he'll help you out. Or he'll know resources. But, what about everything else? Does today impact ARGUS?"

He's quiet for a moment, gathering thoughts. "Well, there's going to be a congressional investigation. Multiple ones, probably. The Senate Intelligence Committee is already drafting subpoenas." His voice remains steady, but I can feel the tension beneath. "I might need to shut ARGUS down entirely."

I shift up onto my elbow, searching his face in the dim light. "Do you think it will come to that?"

"Maybe." His eyes meet mine, resolute despite the exhaustion. "What I know for certain is that I won't let any government commandeer it—not after what we've seen. Our government already proved it doesn't deserve that level of trust. There are too many cracks in the system, too many opportunities for someone with selfish motives to take advantage."

His hand finds mine, fingers interlacing. "If I continue operating ARGUS, it will be with an independent over-sight committee. People I trust, with diverse backgrounds —ethics experts, civil liberties advocates, technical specialists. No single entity should control that kind of power."

The conviction in his voice reminds me why I came to trust him in the first place. This isn't about profit or power—it's about responsibility.

"You should talk to Hudson," I suggest, an idea form-ing. "Our mission aligns with your ethics—using tech-nology to hold powerful people accountable when traditional systems fail. ARGUS could help root out corruption rather than enabling it."

His expression shifts, interest kindling. "A partnership rather than government oversight."

"Exactly. The technology isn't inherently problematic—it's how it's used. In the right hands, with the right guardrails…"

"It could do what I originally designed it for—making the world more transparent, not less." A genuine smile touches his lips. "I'd need to meet with Hudson, understand KOAN's structure better."

"Caroline's open to it," I say.

"Caroline Moore? Dorian Moore? He's the one behind KOAN?"

"No. It's all Caroline. It's her baby. I don't know why she's so secretive about it. I'll need to ask. But I like the idea of KOAN and ARGUS working together." I hesitate, then add, "And I could help navigate. I understand both worlds now."

The possibility hangs between us—not just a personal future, but a professional one where our separate skills might create something better than either could achieve alone.

"We'd be like Prometheus and Athena," he says softly.

"How so?"

"Bringing fire and wisdom to humanity." His fingers, the ones that have been brushing up and down my arm in comforting strokes, slow. "Do you really find mythology interesting? Or was that part of the cover?"

"I find it interesting because you do," I admit, honesty feeling easier in the darkness. "The same way you might find intelligence operations interesting because of me."

"Got it." His fingers trace lazy patterns along my arm. "Meeting halfway."

"While I find mythology and philosophy interesting, I wouldn't choose to read Campbell's *Hero with a Thousand Faces* on vacation if left to my own devices." I smile against his chest, remembering my studious preparation.

His chest rumbles with quiet laughter. "Did you actually read that by the pool or something?"

"Yes. And I strategically positioned it in my lap in the hotel lobby, hoping you'd notice." The confession feels lighter now, almost amusing in retrospect.

"I never noticed the book," he admits. "All I saw was this outdoorsy, stubborn, determined woman who struck me as quite different from anyone I'd ever met. Someone who challenged me from the first moment—on the trail, in conversation. Someone who reminded me that with the right person, life can be pretty fucking great."

"I'm still all of those things," I remind him, suddenly needing him to understand that my cover wasn't entirely fabrication. "At least, I hope."

His hand finds mine in the darkness, our fingers interlacing with the easy familiarity of much older lovers. "That's what makes this real," he says quietly. "The parts that remain true despite everything." He presses his lips to my hair, and his chest rises and falls through a deep inhale and exhale. "Was there anything else? That wasn't true?"

I consider. "I tried to keep my story as close to the truth as possible."

"You didn't know what ARGUS could uncover."

"Right, but it's also just smart practice." I circle his

nipple with my nail, thoughtful. "I told you my parents live in Alaska."

"Yeah?"

"They don't."

"Where—"

"When I first started, I'd say that. No one looks for anyone in Alaska. When you asked, I suppose I preferred the lie to the truth."

"Where are they?"

"My father died five years ago. Coast Guard. In line of duty. Boarded a vessel." I close my eyes, remembering my mother's tear-stricken voice, telling me on the phone, as I was on a different continent. "My mother died about a year later. Heart attack. In retrospect, she'd had symptoms but I thought she was suffering from depression. Side effects from meds to help her sleep. That wasn't the case."

His hold on me tightens.

"Anyway, I don't tell anyone that. Ever." The moment's heavy, too heavy, so I lighten it with, "And everything else...about me...true."

"Syd, I'm falling for you, you know that, right? This? Us? I'm all in."

"Same." Yes, I should say more, but I can't right now. I'm exhausted and too emotional, but I'm so grateful he's here with me now, that he followed me down here so we could hold each other tonight.

Outside, the night has deepened, the mountain silence broken only by distant owl calls and the soft whisper of wind through pine needles.

"One thing's certain," Rhodes murmurs, his voice carrying the edge of sleep, "I'm looking forward to discovering everything about you." His lips brush my forehead. "No more covers. Just us."

When I lift my head to look at him, something shifts in his eyes—a tenderness mixed with desire that sends warmth spreading through me. This time, when our lips meet, it's different. No urgency, no desperation. Just us, finally free of every pretense. We move together slowly, making love with quiet intensity, coming together with nothing between us, like we have all the time in the world. Because we do.

As his breathing deepens into sleep, I remain awake a moment longer, watching moonlight filter through the window blinds, casting silver patterns across unfamiliar walls. The world of Washington—with its political machinations and competing ambitions—feels blissfully far away.

Tomorrow will bring debriefs and decisions, congressional investigations and career choices. But tonight, in this quiet room far from the world's demands, we've found something neither of us expected when this began.

Not a mission. Not a project. Something real.

Something worth building a future around.

EPILOGUE

ONE YEAR LATER

RHODES

The moving truck blocks half our narrow mountain road, but I can't stop grinning. The air carries that particular crispness that makes the Highlands special—clean mountain air mingled with the scent of pine and distant wood smoke.

Below us, the valley stretches out in a patchwork of forests and small clearings, the town barely visible through morning mist. This view—this exact vista—is what made both of us stop and look at each other wordlessly during the property tour.

The movers call to each other as they navigate a sectional sofa through the front door, their voices carrying in the mountain air. It's a symphony of new beginnings—cardboard boxes being cut open, furniture being arranged, a house transforming into our home.

About two months after meeting Sydney on a hiking trail, I made an offer on this spec home when it was in the initial stages of construction. The fact it was unfinished allowed me to ensure the house was wired to meet our needs for working from home. It's in the mountains, not too far from the KOAN offices off Church Street.

Over the last year, we've spent time all over. Sydney went back with me to San Francisco for a couple of months while I worked to handle the fallout from Miles and relocate ARGUS. We've spent time in D.C. on and off as needed for various business projects. When we're in D.C., we stay at Sydney's Maryland condo, which she owns. We've stayed there enough that her once spartan condo feels like a home now, and there are photos of us rock climbing in Colorado, swimming in the Pacific, and dining at a Napa vineyard. For our six-month anniversary, I surprised her with a trip to Paris, took a private tour of the catacombs as she's fascinated by the history, and she introduced me to several friends she'd made from her time in France. For our nine-month anniversary, we went to Rio de Janeiro and visited the Amazon.

I've never taken more vacations in my life, which, given the transformative changes at ARGUS, is incredible. The congressional hearings last year were brutal, but they ultimately vindicated our position. The new ARGUS operates with an independent oversight board that includes both domestic and international experts in ethics, technology, and civil liberties—a structure Caroline Moore helped design based on KOAN's model.

We've shifted our focus entirely away from government surveillance contracts toward tools that increase transparency in public institutions. The partnership with KOAN has been revolutionary—their intelligence expertise combined with our pattern-recognition technology has already exposed three major corruption networks that traditional investigations missed.

Daisy now leads her own division focused specifically on counter-surveillance tools for journalists and human rights workers in authoritarian regimes—turning the technology that almost destroyed us into a shield for those most vulnerable to surveillance abuse. The gleeful way she explains her work to potential clients reminds me why I started ARGUS in the first place.

The irony isn't lost on me: a year ago, I was contemplating shutting ARGUS down entirely. Now it's doing more important work than ever, but with greater balance that allows me to prioritize what truly matters.

Working with the KOAN team has been an unexpected gift—these people who once surveilled me have become extended family. Jake, Sydney, and I go rock climbing regularly when I'm on the East Coast. Jake's southern drawl and straightforward perspective, a refreshing change from Silicon Valley's tech bubble. Quinn's technical brilliance rivals Daisy's, though their styles couldn't be more different; watching them debate encryption protocols is like witnessing an intense chess match.

Hudson maintains his professional distance, but I caught him smiling when Sydney and I announced our house plans during a team dinner. Even Caroline, initially skeptical of my intentions with both her friend and her organization, has become a trusted ally in navigating the complex world where technology meets intelligence work.

What began as an awkward partnership of necessity has evolved into something none of us expected. Last week, when the KOAN team helped us pack up some personal items from Sydney's condo, there was a moment—everyone laughing as Jake attempted to bubble wrap Sydney's collection of unusual rocks from our travels—when I realized how completely our worlds had merged. The surveillance expert and the tech founder, surrounded by people who bridge the gap between those identities.

Nana loves Sydney. She pulled me aside on our first visit and whispered in my ear that this one was the real thing. I couldn't agree more.

I doubt Sydney remembers, but today is our one-year anniversary. The builder tried to shift our move-in date, and I about lost it on him. Sydney didn't get why it mattered what day we moved in, but it does to me.

We've basically been living together, shifting from temporary rentals, hotels and condos, but we're moving into a home that is ours on our anniversary. Sydney picked the countertops and cabinets, and I selected the entertainment system and adjusted the floor plan so we both have offices with stellar mountain views. We picked everything down to the paint colors together.

As we planned this home, the world around us continued to evolve. Senator Crawford is up for re-election next year and faces stiff competition. While he wasn't directly involved, polls show his constituents question the accuracy of the investigation findings. It doesn't help that his wife left him for another man, and rumors abound about his indiscretions.

Miles awaits his trial. He hired lawyers who have been using every delay tactic in the book. Perhaps out of guilt, perhaps because he needed the money to fund legal costs, he sold me his shares in ARGUS. I've distanced myself from his trial. I don't know the extent of the evidence the prosecution has against him, and I don't want to know. He's called me a few times, but I haven't taken his calls. I don't owe him anything.

Alex stayed and helped me through those initial first months after Miles' arrest, but he accepted a role as CFO at a company with plans to go public, and I couldn't be happier for him.

In my hand, I hold a key ring with keys to every lock on the property. We don't actually need keys. The house is equipped with every security feature, including a retina scanner for front door entry. But there's always a chance we could have a blackout and the backup generator might not work, so we also have keys. Plus, I like the symbolism.

It's funny. I spent seven years in a relationship and never felt ready for marriage. But I'm ready now. With every fiber of my being, I'm ready.

But I'm not sure Syd is. She's younger, and I absolutely get it.

I debated proposing today—our one-year anniversary —but held off. Before me, her relationships never lasted a year. It's something that shouldn't matter, but it's been in the back of her mind. She mentioned it when I casually mentioned we'd made it nine months. I've made comments about us getting married, of course. And she's responded with jokes. Her go to. She'll say things like, "Are you sure about that, Rhodes?" or "Let's break my record first." Well, now we've broken her record.

I already have the ring. Actually, I have two. My mom's ring and another ring I saw that I thought looked like Sydney. The golden topaz in the center is associated with Apollo, and the diamonds around it and the band, if one believes the Romans, are gifts from the gods and can be used as protection in battle. My mother's is a classic set solitaire, elegant and also perfect for Syd.

Sydney appears in the doorway, her raven locks up in a high ponytail, shorts that are short enough I'm sure the movers are appreciative, and a cotton tank that flatters her svelte shoulders and curves.

"There you are. Do you want to come look where they put the sofa? I know you were specific about the distance from the television. It looks fine to me but...while we have them here..." Her gaze drops to my hand. "Why do you have keys? I thought that was the point of the retinal scan."

"Well, yes, but still, just in case—"

"If the world as we know it ceases, we'll have keys." She's mocking me. She does that.

I step up to her and place the keys in her palm.

"These are the keys to everything. To this house, to my place in Colorado, to the ARGUS office, to my grandmother's home in Charlotte, to everything." I wiggle the one bulky key to the car, which we don't need because our phones unlock my car. "The Rivian. Everything. Right here."

"Well...thank you. You have a copy of the key to my condo in D.C. You should add it. That way, we'll have all the keys in one place, and we can put them in the junk drawer in the kitchen."

"We have a junk drawer already?"

"Everyone has a junk drawer, Rhodes. Everyone."

"I see."

She steps away but then stops, eyeing me.

"What's up? Is everything okay?"

"Do you know what today is?"

"Move in day?"

"It's our anniversary."

Her golden-brown eyes widen with awareness. "That's why it was so important we move in today." She points at the key ring in my hand. "And the keys. Look at you, so romantic."

"Well, a year ago today a woman pretended she was injured, just to get to know me. That's pretty romantic, too, don't you think?" She grins, but I grow serious. "I want lots and lots of anniversaries with you, Syd."

She loops her arms around my shoulders, clasping her hands behind my neck.

Two movers exit the house headed to the truck, but we disregard them.

"I want the same, Rhodes. This year has been everything to me. I want countless anniversaries with you."

"Yeah?"

"Yeah."

She kisses me and the world falls away. She's always been able to do that. Carry me away to a mental space where it's only the two of us and I'm my old self, free of the weight of the world.

"Marry me," I say, the words emerging so naturally they surprise even me—light on my tongue, barely audible above the distant sounds of furniture being arranged and the mountain breeze rustling through nearby pines.

Time seems to pause as Sydney's eyes widen, those remarkable golden-brown irises catching the morning light. For a heartbeat, I see a flicker of wariness.

"Are you sure, Rhodes?" Her voice carries that blend of teasing and vulnerability that I've come to recognize as uniquely hers. But beneath the question is a deeper one—are you sure about me, with all my complexities, my history, my inherent distrust of permanence?

The weight of the two rings sitting in the glove compartment of my car—one classic and elegant, one uniquely designed for her—suddenly feels insignificant compared to the weight of this moment.

"I've never been more certain of anything in my life," I tell her, my voice steadier than my racing heart.

Something shifts in her expression—the last wall coming down. Her smile breaks across her face like the sunrise across the mountains we both love, transforming her features with a joy I've seen glimpses of but rarely this complete, this unguarded.

"Then yes," she says, and then louder, as if testing how the commitment feels in the mountain air. "Yes!"

I lift her off her feet, spinning her in a circle as her laughter—that open, full-throated sound I've spent a year working to earn—echoes against the mountainside. The movers pause their work, watching us with knowing smiles, as Sydney wraps her arms tighter around my neck.

When I set her down, she presses her forehead against mine, both of us breathless from spinning and laughter. "You know what Nana would say about this?" I murmur.

"That her mythology stories finally taught you something?"

"That the greatest hubris isn't flying too close to the sun," I say, brushing a strand of hair from her face. "It's believing you can build a life worth living without love."

Her smile softens. "And what do you say?"

I look around at our half-unpacked home, the mountains stretching endlessly before us, this woman who saw through all my carefully constructed walls to something worth saving. "I say the ancients were wrong about one thing—sometimes the gods reward those brave enough to reach for what they need most."

Her commitment is absolutely everything. But this—our quiet defiance of the tragic endings that fill mythology stories—this is everything else.

BONUS EPILOGUE

SYDNEY

Buying for a man who has everything has its challenges, especially when said man employs a house manager tasked with anticipating his needs. Caroline questioned if I really wanted to do this after she saw the property report. Due to gradient inclines, associated risks of landslides, and the proximity to state-owned land, most of it can't be developed, which is why the land has been used for pasture for ages. But when I ran into the owner while hiking one day last fall and struck up a conversation, I mentioned that if he ever decided to sell, to please call me before putting it on the market.

My skin tingles with anticipation...literally, tingles. I'm not sure how many more times in our lives I'll be able to surprise him, so I want this to be perfect.

Quinn's helped me. She and Hudson mostly work from the Highlands, and to avoid detection, I've been going to the office, leaving my phone—which I know

Rhodes tracks from time to time when he's curious about where I am—and heading out with a Garmin Hudson insisted I take if hiking alone, as he says it's common sense to take a communication device when heading out on a trail.

My husband comes out of the house, backpack slung over one arm, phone held out below his chin, dictating a message to someone somewhere. I take a minute to take him in. He's in hiking boots with bunched thick socks that complement his strong calves. His shorts cover his muscular quads and thighs. The t-shirt he's wearing beneath his faded flannel fits snugly over the muscular landscape I know intimately. The flannel, thrown on likely as an afterthought given it's unbuttoned, catches the wind. He stops, squints at his screen, presses what I assume is the send button, and lowers his shades.

His thick dark hair has grown long enough that it catches in the mountain breeze, and he's growing his beard out again—oscillating between meticulously trimmed and the kind of scruff that makes him look like he belongs on these mountains. The contrast between the polished tech mogul and this rugged version of my husband never fails to stir something primal in me. Whether clean-shaven in a boardroom or windswept on a trail, he remains one of the most compelling men I've ever encountered.

"Gorgeous day." He joins me at the back of my Scout and throws his backpack in. "After our hike, we should head over to the apple orchard."

"We can do that." His hand rests on my hip and he brushes his lips against my temple. "Ready? Want me to drive?"

"Nah, I'll drive. That way you can catch up on your email."

Rhodes got in last night from a conference on the West Coast where he was a speaker. He's turned his attention to efforts for environmentally-friendly data centers that recycle water to minimize environmental impact and water use.

Twenty minutes later, we're parked at the Glen Falls trailhead. The familiar scent of pine and earth fills my lungs as we shoulder our packs. Rhodes is already studying the trail map posted on the wooden kiosk, but I know where we're going isn't marked on any map.

"Want to take the usual route?" I ask, trying to keep my voice casual.

"Actually," he says, adjusting his pack straps, "I was thinking we could explore a bit. Maybe head off-trail like we did that first time."

Perfect. He's making this easier than I thought.

"Lead the way," I tell him, and his eyes light up with that boyish excitement I love.

We follow the main trail for about a mile before Rhodes veers off onto the narrower, less maintained path that leads toward the swimming hole. The sounds of other hikers fade away, replaced by the gentle gurgle of the stream and the rustle of leaves overhead. Fall has painted the mountains in brilliant oranges and reds, but the canopy is still thick enough to dapple the trail with shifting patterns of light and shadow.

"Remember the first time we came this way?" Rhodes asks, glancing back at me. "You were so worried about trespassing."

"I was being responsible," I protest, but I'm smiling. "Besides, look how that worked out."

His laugh echoes through the trees. "Best trespassing of my life."

As we near the clearing, I can hear the familiar hollow plunks of water hitting rock, and my heartbeat races. Not from the hike, but from what's about to happen.

"You know," I say, trying to sound nonchalant, "I have something to tell you."

"Oh yeah?" He's focused on ducking under a low branch.

"That land we're about to walk onto? The pasture that connects to the swimming hole?"

"The private property that technically makes us trespassers?" He grins over his shoulder.

"It's not private anymore. Well, it is, but..." I take a deep breath. "I bought it. Closed last week while you were away."

Rhodes stops so suddenly I almost walk into his back. He turns around slowly, his expression cycling through confusion, surprise, and something that might be awe.

"You bought it?"

"All of it. The swimming hole, the pasture, even the little cabin that's falling down near the road. It's ours now. Well, yours. It's your anniversary gift. I had trouble coming up with something you didn't own that you would want."

For a moment, he just stares at me. Then his face breaks into that unguarded smile that still makes my knees weak.

"Sydney Parker MacMillan," he says, and hearing my

married name in that tone sends warmth spreading through my chest, "you are full of surprises."

"Do you like it?"

Instead of answering, he drops his pack right there on the trail and pulls me into his arms, kissing me with an intensity that makes the forest spin around us. When we break apart, he's grinning like a kid on Christmas morning.

"Like it? Syd, this is..." He shakes his head. "This place changed everything for me. For us."

"That's why I wanted it to be ours. Really ours."

We emerge into the clearing, and it's exactly as it's always been—the natural quarry with its crystal-clear water, boulders perfect for jumping, and the echo of water against stone walls. But now it looks different somehow, knowing it belongs to us.

"The water's going to be cold," Rhodes warns, but he's already shrugging out of his flannel.

"The air is likely colder than the water," I counter, "but the nice thing is the snakes are probably becoming less active."

"Want to test that theory?"

I'm already kicking off my boots, not out of eagerness to test my snake theory but because I anticipated skinny dipping—it's part of the gift, after all. "Race you in."

Just like that first day, clothes are abandoned without ceremony. Rhodes beats me to the edge, but only because I get tangled up in my sports bra. He stands poised on the familiar boulder, and for a moment he looks exactly like he did two years ago—stoked to be with someone willing to take a leap.

"Together?" he asks, extending his hand.

I take it, and he counts, "One, two…"

My cheek muscles burn from the wide grin. "Three!"

The water is shocking and perfect, stealing my breath. We're both laughing as we surface. Rhodes pulls me against him in the water, both of us treading water and grinning like idiots.

"I can't believe you bought our place," he says, water droplets clinging to his dark lashes.

"Our place," I repeat, loving how that sounds. "No more worrying about trespassing. No more wondering if we'll be able to come back."

"We can come here whenever we want."

"Maybe we can put out snake traps," I say, scanning the shoreline. I've done a little research and learned that if there are any snakes around, our feet stomping and the splash in the water likely scared them off, so I'm more or less joking.

"I'll keep you safe."

"I know you will," I say, and I love that he'll do everything he can to take care of me, but of course, that goes both ways.

His gaze lifts to the canopy overhead. "You want to build out here?"

I knew he'd go there. My man loves architecture. "We just built a house," I remind him. "And it's closer to town."

I love this land, but I really have no desire to live forty-five minutes from town.

"Hmm," he shrugs, and I lean in and nip his earlobe, sucking off a water droplet.

"Sadly, it's not buildable. We wouldn't get the permits."

"Gradient?" he asks.

"Among other things," I answer. "But we can go camping out here. Maybe make it an anniversary tradition?"

"Anniversary," he says slowly with a grin, then kisses me again, softer this time. When we break apart, he's looking at me with that expression that still makes me feel like the most beautiful woman in the world.

"I love you, Mrs. MacMillan."

"I love you too."

We float there for a while, holding each other in the clear water, surrounded by the quiet beauty of our own little piece of paradise. The fall sun filters through the trees, warming our faces even as the water keeps us cool.

"You know what this means, don't you?" Rhodes asks eventually.

"What?"

"We're going to have to install that rope swing I keep talking about."

I laugh, remembering his stories about swinging into the water as a teenager. "Only if you promise not to break your neck showing off."

"I make no such promises."

Later, we spread our clothes on the warm rocks and lie naked in the sun, on a blanket I packed stretched across sun-warmed stone. Rhodes traces lazy patterns on my back while I rest my chin on my folded arms, watching water striders dance across the surface of our swimming hole.

"Best gift ever," he murmurs against my shoulder.

"Better than the new climbing wall in the garage?"

"Way better." He presses a kiss to the back of my neck. "Though I do love that climbing wall."

"I know you do. I hear you in there at five in the morning."

"I'm quiet."

"You grunt. A lot."

He nips at my shoulder, making me squirm. "I do not grunt."

"You absolutely grunt. It's very caveman-like."

"Maybe that's because you make me feel very caveman-like."

I turn in his arms, loving the feel of his skin against mine, warm from the sun and smooth from the water. "Is that so?"

"Mmm." His hands skim down my sides. "Especially when you pull off surprises like this."

"I'm glad you like it."

"I love it. I love you. I love that you bought the place where I fell in love with you."

"Where we fell in love with each other," I correct.

"True." He shifts so he's looking down at me, propped up on one elbow. "Though I think I was a goner the second you jumped off that rock."

"You were not."

"I was. You were so..." He searches for the word. "Fearless. Beautiful. Completely yourself."

"I was terrified I was going to hit the bottom. Feared it would be a slimy, muddy mess."

"But you jumped anyway."

"Sometimes the best things happen when you jump."

"Is that your philosophy now?"

I think about everything that's led us here—the

mission that brought us together, the lies that became truth, the careful distance that became love so deep it sometimes takes my breath away.

"With you? Always."

The sun has shifted, and without the warmth, the chill in the air is more noticeable. Rhodes reaches for his flannel and drapes it over both of us.

"We should probably head back soon," he says, but makes no move to get up.

"Probably."

Neither of us moves. This place, our place, holds us like it did that first day. But now instead of the uncertain tension of new attraction, there's the deep contentment of coming home.

"Thank you," Rhodes says quietly. "For this. For knowing exactly what would matter to me."

"We're partners," I tell him, the word carrying all the weight of what we've built together. "In everything."

"In everything," he agrees.

And then the chill in the air is forgotten with his kiss. We make love slowly, out in the open, cushioned by the blankets I packed. When he shudders above me, my legs wrapped around his waist, holding him close, his dark eyes meet mine. "I swear, I think that gets better every time."

I smile, knowing he says that often, but loving how true it feels.

Later, as we're getting dressed, Rhodes suddenly stops with one sock halfway on.

"What is it?" I ask.

"I just realized something."

"What?"

"We own a swimming hole."

"We do."

"That's possibly the coolest thing anyone's ever said."

I burst out laughing. "You own a tech company worth billions of dollars."

"Yeah, but that's just business. This?" He gestures at the clear water, the surrounding trees, the boulder where we first jumped together. "This is ours. This is our origin story."

As we pack up to leave, I look back at the swimming hole one more time. The late afternoon light glimmers over the water, and I can almost see us as we were that first day—uncertain, attracted, teetering on the edge of something that would change everything.

Now we're standing on solid ground, sure of each other and the life we're building together. But this place, our place, will always be here to remind us of how we started. Sure, there was deception and distrust, but we worked through it. No matter what comes, we'll work through it.

"Ready?" Rhodes asks, shouldering his pack.

I take his outstretched hand. "Ready."

As we walk back through the forest toward the trail-head, Rhodes suddenly stops and pulls me close.

"What now?" I ask, teasing.

"I'm just thinking about all the times we'll come back here. All the anniversaries, all the summers, maybe someday with…"

"With what?"

"Kids," he says softly. "Little ones learning to jump off that rock."

The image makes my heart skip. "Getting ahead of yourself there, MacMillan."

"Maybe. But when you know, you know."

"And you know?"

"I know I want everything with you, Syd. Every anniversary, every season, every adventure."

"Even the scary ones?"

"Especially the scary ones."

I stand on my toes to kiss him, tasting the promise of all those tomorrows.

"Then let's go home," I say. "The day's not over. I've got more planned."

"Have you now?"

"You know me...something wicked." I grin, wiggling my eyebrows while tugging on his hand.

He slaps my ass and I squeal as he pulls me back against his chest. "You're a temptress, Mrs. MacMillan."

As we emerge from the forest, the sun is setting behind the mountains, painting the sky in shades of pink and gold. Rhodes helps me into the Scout, but before closing my door, he leans in.

"Best surprise ever," he says again.

"Just wait until you see what I have in store for you."

His eyes widen. "There's more? You were serious?"

"There's always more with us, isn't there?"

"God, I hope so."

As we drive home through the mountains, past the apple orchard we never made it to, with the windows down and the cool autumn air flowing through the car, I think about how far we've come from that first uncertain hike. Back then, everything was a question mark. Now, everything is true.

The land papers are tucked safely in my desk drawer at home, but the real gift isn't the deed or the swimming hole or even this perfect day. The real gift is having someone who understands that some places are sacred, that some moments are worth preserving, that some love stories deserve their own piece of the world to call home.

Rhodes reaches over and takes my hand as we wind through the mountain curves, and I think about all the anniversaries still to come, all the times we'll drive this same road back to our swimming hole, our story, our beginning.

Our love story started with a lie. But here, we shed the pretenses. Out there in the real world, those pretenses still exist—the walls, the machinations, the world's wicked ways. But when we're together, the shadows subside, giving way to light.

Read Jake and Daisy's story in Only The Devil…

I've survived combat zones and classified missions.

But watching her walk into danger? That might kill me.

The assignment seemed straightforward: pose as a dutiful boyfriend while she infiltrates a finance mogul's operation. Keep her safe. Keep my distance. Get the evidence and get out.

Simple, until the mogul hired me as his personal security.

Now I have a front-row seat to his empire of greed—and his predatory interest in the brilliant woman I'm supposed to be pretending to love. Every day I watch him dangle millions in front of her like bait, testing her limits, pushing her boundaries.

The problem? My feelings for Daisy stopped being pretend early on. It didn't take me long to fall hard for the stubborn woman on a mission.

She thinks she can handle Sterling's world. She thinks she can resist the temptation of life-changing money. But I don't trust wealth and power. And when bodies start dropping and cryptocurrency millions vanish overnight, I realize we're not just hunting a white-collar criminal.

We're trapped in his web.

Daisy's got secrets she won't share and a past that makes her desperate enough to risk everything for justice. Sterling's got enough money to buy loyalty, silence, and alibis. And me? I've got a heart condition that ended my military career and feelings for a woman who might be playing a deeper game than either of us signed up for.

In a world where everyone has their price, I've found the one thing I won't sell: her safety.

Even if it costs me everything.

AFTERWORD

In the shadows of glass towers, ancient sins wear digital masks.

The characters in The Sinful State series grapple with humanity's oldest failings—the seven deadly sins that have driven our stories since civilization began. **Only the Wicked** opens this exploration with pride, or as the Greeks understood it, *hubris*—the fatal arrogance that makes mortals believe they can challenge the gods themselves.

Rhodes MacMillan embodies our era's Prometheus. He has stolen fire from the heavens in the form of ARGUS, a surveillance system so powerful it can see all, know all, judge all. Like every Silicon Valley founder, he believes he's bringing light to humanity. What he hasn't considered is that Prometheus spent eternity chained to a rock, an eagle devouring his liver, as payment for his gift to mankind.

The ancients understood something we've forgotten: **creation without consequence is illusion**. Every myth warns us—Icarus flying toward the sun, Arachne weaving in competition with the gods, Niobe boasting that her children surpassed Athena's. All paid for their hubris with destruction.

Yet here's the paradox that haunts our modern age: Can one succeed in today's world *without* hubris? The very ambition required to build empires, to create technologies that reshape civilization, to believe your vision can change the world—isn't this the same pride that the ancients warned would bring divine retribution?

Rhodes asks himself the question that should terrify every creator in our age of artificial intelligence, surveillance capitalism, and digital omniscience: "By creating ARGUS, am I Niobe, bound to suffer the wrath of the gods?"

One wonders what Shakespeare would make of our modern Prometheuses, coding their way toward both salvation and damnation.

Welcome to a world where ancient sins cast shadows, where the price of playing god has never been higher, and where love might be the only force powerful enough to humble even the most prideful among us.

GRATITUDE

Only the Wicked marks several firsts for me: my first fully mapped series, first dual released audio production, and first translation project.

PJ Fiala once told me she has her covers done before she starts writing. I can't wrap my head around that level of planning, but Patti, thank you for the inspiration to think ahead.

Regina Wamba, I've wanted to work with you for years, and I'm thrilled the stars finally aligned. This style is different for me—I'm nervous but excited. We should both thank Adrienne Giordano for her wisdom and for giving me the courage to stretch. Thanks, Coach!

Jenn Prokop, your feedback on the raw manuscript was *chef's kiss*. Karen Cimms, your careful attention to every edit means so much—thank you!

To my beta readers: Thank you for the early feedback. Stephanie, I hope you read the bonus epilogue—that's for you!

To ARC readers: you're the absolute best. Your feedback and reviews give this book a fighting chance of reaching new readers.

And to my readers—with so many options out there, thank you for choosing to spend your time with my stories.

ALSO BY ISABEL JOLIE

Sinful State Series

Only the Wicked (Rhodes and Sydney)

Only the Devil - Releasing December 4, 2025

Only the Lovely - Releasing February 26, 2026

Arrow Tactical Security Series

Better to See You (Wolf and Alexandria)

Sure of One (Jack and Ava)

Cloak of Red (Sophia and Fisher)

Stolen Beauty (Knox and Sage)

Savage Beauty (Max and Sloane)

Sinful Beauty (Tristan and Lucia)

Gilded Saint (Sam and Willow)

Scarlet Angel (Nick and Scarlet)

Blind Prophet (Dorian and Caroline)

The Twisted Vines Series

Crushed (Erik and Vivi)

Breathe (Kairi and David)

Savor (Trevor and Stella)

Haven Island Series

Rogue Wave (Tate and Luna)

Adrift (Gabe and Poppy)

First Light (Logan and Cali)

The West Side Series

Blurred Lines (Jackson and Anna)

Trust Me (Sam Duke and Olivia)

Finding Delilah (Delilah and Mason)

Forgetting Him (Jason and Maggie)

Chasing Frost (Chase and Sadie)

Misplaced Mistletoe (Ashton aka Dr. Bobby and Nora)

Standalone Romances

How to Survive a Holiday Fling (Oliver Duke and Kate)

Always Sunny (Ian Duke and Sandra)

The Romantics (Harrison and Zuri)

ABOUT THE AUTHOR

Isabel Jolie writes the kind of romance that keeps you up late into the night. Her steamy contemporary novels feature tough, unforgettable heroes and the strong women who challenge them, all wrapped up in edge-of-your-seat suspense and those sizzling happily-ever-afters we all crave.

With over twenty-five novels published since 2020, Isabel's stories have found their way into readers' hands (and hearts) everywhere. When she's not crafting her next swoon-worthy hero, you'll find her lakeside in North Carolina with wine and a good book—because even romance writers need their book boyfriends.

Her characters always face impossible choices, but they never forget the most important rule: love wins. Every. Single. Time.

Sign-up for Izzy's newsletter to keep up-to-date on new releases, promotions and giveaways. (**Pro-tip** - She offers a free book on her home page…just scroll down after arriving at her site.)

Shop and save on ebooks and signed paperbacks direct from Isabel at www.isabeljoliebooks.com

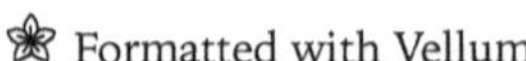 Formatted with Vellum